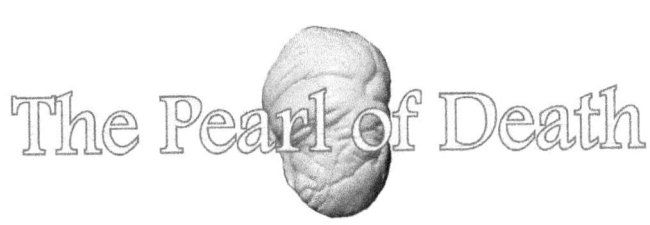

The Pearl of Death

Terry Wright

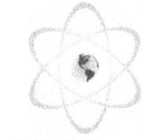

2014, TWB Press
www.twbpress.com

The Pearl of Death
Copyright © 2011 by Terry Wright

Though based on a true story, this is a work of fiction. Names, characters, places, and events are either a product of the author's imagination or changed or enhanced from history or legend for dramatic effect. Any resemblance to any actual person, living or dead, is not entirely coincidental, as those resemblances are a matter of public record derived from history books, news stories, published personal accounts, and Chinese legend.

Cover Art by Terry Wright

ISBN 978-1-936991-72-3

Prologue

Guangdong Province, China, 1745

Captain Chen Wei jumped to the wooden dock alongside his 500-foot *Zheng He* treasure ship, *Tek Song*, and faced the thunder of hooves rising beyond the dark harbor village of Guangzhou. Though the sky blazed with stars, dawn would soon break. Delays had plagued him all night, cargo manifest mix-ups and worm-rot in the mid-deck hold. He fought for internal peace, to be one with the Tao, the Way, but even that couldn't cage the trepidation rising in his soul.

In the distance, unseen horses snorted and pounded earth. A faint glow of torch fire appeared on the horizon, silhouetting thatched roofs and stone chimneys. As his heart drummed with dread, a northern Manchurian wind fluttered the skirt of his robe and tugged at the unbraided locks of his black hair. The smell of guano and brine filled his nostrils. For the past twenty years he'd worked for East China Shipping. This was the part he feared most, Imperial interference.

"Zhu lai," a lookout shouted down from the crow's nest. "The master comes."

A hundred horsemen appeared, funneling from the village streets to the shoreline road, moving toward the dock, their torches an approaching wave of fire.

"Get aboard, everyone," Chen told his crewmen working on the dock.

They ran up the gangplanks and watched from *Tek Song's* polished banister. In all, he had four hundred men behind him, all merchant sailors working at various positions on the old ocean-going junk. They weren't afraid of the gathering forces, but no one wanted to fight them either. Besides, their arrival had been forewarned when an envoy delivered a message from the Palace:

"Hold sails for the Emperor's guard arriving at dawn with Imperial cargo."

Chen ground his molars. He didn't want any Imperial cargo on his ship. Whether it was slaves, diplomats, or Qing Dynasty gold, it always meant trouble from insurrection or pirates. However, as the Tao would have it, Chen had no choice but to comply. He straightened his shoulders, struggled to remain calm.

Kicking up dust, the horses stopped, whinnied, and pranced as they lined both sides of the road leading to the cargo-laden dock. Ox horns trumpeted from the formation.

By torchlight, eight horses approached between the ranks, their riders wearing the long robes of the Emperor's guard, purple and gold and embroidered with dragons among clouds. Behind them, torch fire illuminated a flat wagon drawn by two horses draped in red silk. On the wagon sat a large crate emblazoned with the Emperor's seal of crossed swords.

Chen felt a sting in his throat as the assembly ground to a halt before him. "What have you brought for the *Tek Song*?"

"A shipment from Emperor Qianlong," the officer of the guard proclaimed.

"Our holds are filled." Chen knew the mid-deck hold was unusable due to worm-rot of the hull.

"He commands you to make room for this cargo to Bacolod. I have the official order." The officer extended a rolled parchment with his gloved hand.

Taking the document, Chen didn't break the wax seal to read it but stepped between the sweating horses to the wagon. The tall and narrow crate, long as the wagon and twice as high, was made of solid oak and tied down with horsehair ropes, slick with pig fat lard. Water dripped from the wagon, water that had sloshed from the crate during the wagon ride. "What is this strange cargo?"

The officer stroked his Fu Manchu. "It's a pearl."

"One pearl?" Chen frowned. "The crate is a mite oversized for such small cargo."

"Not just any pearl..." He cleared his throat. "The Pearl of Lao-Tzu."

The Pearl of Death

Chen's breath hitched. "Our sacred Taoist pearl?"

The officer nodded. "Qianlong has sold it to a Spanish governor in the Philippines."

A dread like no other seized Chen's solid frame. Twenty-three-hundred years ago, Lao-Tzu, the *Old Sage*, had cultured the pearl from a small amulet he'd carved of *The Three Friends'* faces: himself, Confucius, and Buddha. He then placed it in an oyster to begin the pearling process. Each generation of followers transplanted the cultured pearl into larger clams until finally it resided in a giant clam.

He glanced at the water-filled crate and now knew the magnitude of what was inside. The pearl was meant to be a talisman of peace, longevity, and profound wisdom for all Taoists, but only if it were held in this high regard and never exchanged for money or power—or else men be damned. Backing away from the wagon and its cursed cargo, Chen trembled. "Take it back to the temple."

"Read the order," the officer spat.

Looking up at him, Chen felt a cold sweat break out on his brow. "Qianlong has made a grave error. He's transmuted the pearl of peace into a pearl of suffering...a pearl of death."

The guardsmen laughed, their teeth glowing yellow in the flickering torchlight. "Tao superstition," one man said. "Confucianism," another added. The Buddhists were not sympathetic to Chen's belief in the Tao.

"I don't want it on my ship."

Whinnying, the officer's spurred horse lunged forward. "Then I will order your death and the ship seized." He waved his torch.

A hundred horsemen drew their swords.

With a high-pitched whistle, *Tek Song's* lookout called the crew to arms. Two hundred fierce men rushed to the gunwale, all brandishing knives and axes, swords and clubs.

Standing alone at the gangplank, Chen's heart lurched, but he forced himself to remain calm, the Taoist teachings he believed now curbing his urge to fight.

Be still like a mountain and let the great river flow around you.

It was better to do nothing than risk the lives of his men.

"We will comply with the Emperor's order."

"Your decision is a wise one, captain." The guardsmen sheathed their swords.

Crewmen scrambled down to the dock and rigged two poles to the crate. It took twenty men on each pole to lift the giant clam and its water-filled container from the wagon and work it up the gangplank to the worm-rotted mid-deck hold, the only space available for this additional cargo.

His men slung the heavy crate from the rigging and lowered it into the hold. Rats skittered away as the load hit bottom with a solid thud.

"Tie it down fast, men," Chen ordered. "I want no accidents. The worm-rotted hull will not sustain the force of shifting cargo."

Rope ladders went over the edge. Men scrambled down to the crate. By the time the chore was completed, the sun had broken the horizon. Long shadows from *Tek Song's* nine masts leaned west, the direction the guardsmen had retreated, their mission accomplished.

Chen looked down into the hold at the crate and the dozen ropes dripping pig fat that secured it to floor anchors. Through slats in the lid, he saw the yawning giant clam submerged in saltwater, its cockles richly adorned with red coral and white sea anemones. Its gaping mantle shimmered a golden brown with iridescent blue and green spots along the edges. Clear spots on the mantle served as windows for sunlight to enter and nourish the algae that grew inside. It was a beautiful harbinger of doom.

Leaning forward, he wondered if the windows would reveal the huge pearl. It was worth a fortune to anyone who'd ignore Lao-Tzu's curse. Emperor Qianlong didn't understand the true danger of selling the Taoists' treasure.

Palms pressed together, Chen bowed and backed away from the hold, praying for the pearl's mercy.

Passengers began arriving. The *Sugar Run* they called it, to the Philippine cane fields and a better life, or so they believed. Chen knew the hardships they would encounter, the slave labor they'd endure, but it was his responsibility to get them there safely, pearl or no pearl.

Sixteen hundred men, women, and children formed lines

and shuffled up the gangplanks. Hunched and sun-ripened workers quickly took stowage wherever they could find room, both above and below the cluttered deck. They wore the conical straw hats and tattered robes of the peasant class. Straw rugs for bedding, woven baskets for their belongings, oil lamps for cooking and heat were all they brought with them. And their dreams of a better life.

When all were aboard, "Hoist the sails," Chen ordered his crew.

Two hundred deckhands took to the lines and cranks, heaving and grunting. Slowly, the north wind breathed life into the square bamboo and silk mainsails as they climbed the ninety-foot masts. Mooring ropes were cast off. With a groan, the *Tek Song* inched its two thousand ton wooden hull from the dock. Two rudder men wearing baggy black pants and white sleeveless shirts grabbed the thirty-six foot tiller and steered the junk into the harbor.

On shore, the crowd cheered. Children danced in circles. Rockets sizzled into the sky and popped.

Chen took his usual position on the prow, hands on his hips, and inhaled the sea breeze. Waves lapped the hull as *Tek Song* cut through choppy water. Screeching seagulls sawed the air, dove and soared as if racing the tall ship toward the open South China Sea. At full sail, the *Tek Song* rode low in the water, creaking under the weight of her cargo: thousands of porcelain plates and bowls, tons of tea and silk, and two thousand passengers and crew.

Plus one giant clam and its pearl.

However, there were also stowaways aboard the *Tek Song*, much smaller in size but greater in number. With an insatiable hunger, rats converged on the pig fat dripping from the ropes that held the clam's crate firmly in place. Once the drip pools had been consumed, they took to the ropes, licking and biting and gnawing to get every succulent drop.

***

Twenty-eight days into the voyage, Chen finished his morning meal of noodles and pork and strode the polished deck. The rising sun blazed across a dazzling red sky and gave him cause for alarm. A squall line of angry clouds towered to the south and west. At four knots, the *Tek Song* cut through the narrow strait between Mindoro and the Calamains: gateway to the Philippines. It was an impossibly slow speed to outflank the approaching typhoon.

"The fathoms are dropping, captain," the rudder man said, warning of shallow water.

"Ready the ship for the storm," Chen ordered. "Pass the word. Get everyone below deck. And secure the hatches over the cargo holds."

As his crewmen sprang to their duties, Chen stood again on *Tek Song's* prow, the motions of the sea now lifting the bow and crashing it back down. The spray of seawater hit him with a chill and tasted bitter.

Wind howling, the red sky faded to black, and the sea swells began digging deeper and piling higher. Crewmen lowered the mainsails and raised a single steerage sail. Twenty men manned the tiller to help control the eight-ton rudder and keep the ship from going sideways to the mountainous walls of water.

The *Tek Song* pitched and rolled as angry waves charged the hull and tossed the ship about in the swirling and foamy sea. Chen held on to the mast rope, spit seawater, and worried over the storm. It was the worst he'd ever seen.

Below, in the mid-deck hold, the giant clam's heavy crate lurched back and forth on rat-gnawed ropes that frayed under the strain. The relentless rolling and pitching tossed the crate to and fro, each time breaking more ropes until none were left.

Violently, the ship rocked to port. The sliding crate crashed into the worm-rotted wooden hull. Splinters flew, seams split, and seawater sprayed in. The badly damaged crate slid across the hold to starboard, shedding oak slats and spilling saltwater. Just as the giant clam closed up to protect itself from the disturbance, the crate hit the starboard hull and broke apart. The sliding two hundred fifty pound clamshell shot back to port, and like a battering ram, it struck the weakened hull and burst through to the sea.

Roiling currents stirred up by the storm tossed the giant clam about as if it were driftwood. Tumbling through the shallows without control or direction, the clam was at the mercy of the waves and undertows. It bounced off the sandy bottom, pirouetted in the swirling currents, and rolled along with the waves that rushed toward a nearby shore. But the extra ballast that the huge pearl added to the clam's weight caused it to break free of a wave as it crested over a reef.

Down, down, down the giant clam tumbled until it crashed into the coral bed and lodged upright on the bottom. Sensing stillness, the clamshell opened and siphoned in a relieving gulp of fresh seawater.

Topside, Chen only felt the violent pitch and roll of the ship and the sting of rain on his face. The wind had blown the *Tek Song* far off course, somewhere down the coast of Palawan. Now, each minute that passed blew them farther out into the Sulu Sea. It wasn't until the rudder men complained of a problem that he feared they were in trouble.

"She keeps going to port," one man yelled, his face streaming water. "We're pushing hard to starboard, but she won't come about."

Chen feared either the rudder was damaged or his ship was taking on water. "You there." He pointed to the nearest crewman. "Check below."

"Yes, sir."

Chen took hold of the tiller. It required all his strength to handle his share of the load. Icy rain beat him without mercy.

Shortly, the crewman returned, stooped against the gale. "There's a hole in the mid-deck hold, captain." Fear filled his eyes. "The men are trying to patch the hull with boards and braces...but they are not succeeding. The worm-rotted hull keeps breaking away. Many men have already drowned."

"Did we hit the reef?"

"The Emperor's crate broke loose." The drenched man staggered on the heaving deck. "The giant clam busted through the hull."

It was the way of the Tao. The pearl was gone, and Chen was left to save his ship or die trying.

The *Tek Song* listed heavily to port, exposing the deck to pounding waves. Deck hatches broke apart and seawater spilled into his ship. Panicked passengers streamed on deck, crying and clutching each other. Waves crashed over them, sweeping many into the sea. A shifting crate struck a woman and smashed her against the aft mast. It creaked and snapped and toppled over, crushing the people below. Sea spray choked the air.

"We will drown," someone cried out, clinging to the slanted deck. People stumbled and fell overboard. Their belongings swirled by in a flood of debris.

Chen felt the sting of rain and guilt. He shouldn't have allowed the pearl onboard. He should've fought for what he believed. Now, his belief in the Tao had put everyone's lives in peril. But what was the purpose? Was it the Tao's way of stopping Lao-Tzu's curse? It was the only good answer Chen could think of, and in a way, it gave him great relief. The pearl of death would be at the bottom of the sea where it could do the world no more harm.

"Be at peace with your fate," Chen shouted. "The Tao is eternal." He clung to the tiller as if it were a lifeline, the water and wind beating him senseless.

"It's the pearl we blame," someone growled.

A mountainous wave plowed into the *Tek Song* and tore Chen and his men from the tiller, instantly washing them into the sea. Swallowing water, Chen felt numb with cold and fear as his body sank. *Though the body dies, the Tao will never pass away.*

For two hours, the Sulu Sea held the *Tek Song* in its outstretched arms. Tons of water flooded the porcelain, the tea, and the silk. Two thousand souls cried out as the sea pulled them under, along with their dreams of a better life.

The Pearl of Death

Chapter One

Palawan, Philippines, May 7, 1934

Barefoot, Etem Matito strode past stands of coconut palms on his way down to the beach. He wore his favorite diving shorts, long to his knees, and carried his black rubber flippers, snorkel and swim goggles. Standing at the breaking surf, he studied the roiling sea that reflected a glare from the burning sun. Beyond the bay, the water rose up with an angry heave, crashed over the reef, and broke into waves that tumbled into the windswept bay. Conditions were bad for pearl diving.

He swallowed his trepidation over the hard work he would face in the coming hours.

Down shore, six 30-foot skiffs leaned in the sand, wide V-hulls with single masts and dual outriggers. A dozen oars protruded vertically from the gunnels, six on each side, like the bristles on a caterpillar.

Two of Etem's fellow pearlers, Maricar and Ning-ning, stood beside one of the boats. Wearing colorful sleeveless shirts and long shorts, they loaded ropes and string bags for the morning's dive.

"Hey, Etem," Maricar called.

Ning-ning lugged a heavy coil of rope. "Why have you arrived early?"

"I promised Timoteo a swim."

"He is not here." Maricar helped Ning-ning lift the rope into the skiff.

Etem glanced toward the palm trees, looking for his eight-year-old son. "He dawdles with his little brother."

Maricar squinted toward the reef, his black hair whipping wildly in the wind. "We will have to row hard to clear the bay."

A child's squeal announced Etem's youngest son chasing Timoteo across the sand.

"Come on." Etem had to shout over the wind. "I must dive soon. Tito. Go back to your mother. Where is she?"

"I'm coming." Liawayway ran out from the palm trees to the smaller boy and picked him up from the sand. Her white headscarf glowed in the sunshine. The long dress she wore fluttered in the wind and revealed glimpses of her olive-skinned ankles. "Timoteo wants to go with you."

"The reef is too dangerous."

"I'm not afraid." Timoteo ran to his father. "The shallows are boring."

"Better to be bored than dead, my son."

"Your lunch will be ready at noon," Liawayway said.

"I'll see you then." Etem looped an arm around Timoteo's shoulders and watched his wife and Tito walk up the beach and disappear into the palm grove. He'd dive thirty times before lunch and thirty more in the afternoon. He would be done before evening prayers.

Timoteo wriggled out from under Etem's arm. "I want to dive the reef."

"You're too little."

"When will I be big enough?"

"When you are twelve."

"Can I go with you, at least?" His pitched voice carried the exuberance of foolish youth. "I'll help row. I won't get in the way. I promise."

Time was running short for their swim, and Etem noticed Timoteo had not come prepared. "Where are your goggles and flippers? Have you left them in the kitchen again?"

Timoteo's face drooped. "Oh, darn."

"You play with your brother and forget what you are doing."

"I'll get them. I'll run."

A group of men slogged down the beach. Etem grabbed his son's thin arm. "Look. The other divers are coming. It's too late for us to swim."

Timoteo slumped, hung his head, whimpered.

Etem glanced to the windy sea, a moment of compassion

seizing him. If his son would stay in the boat, perhaps it would be all right for him to come along.

"Run tell your mother you'll be going with me...but only to ride in the boat."

His eyes shot up with surprise. "Thanks, Dad."

"Hurry."

Running backwards, "What about school?"

"It's only until noon. Tell her."

"Okay."

Etem watched the whites of Timoteo's feet sling sand, elbows pumping as the boy raced up the beach with news of his good fortune.

"Don't make us late."

More pearlers arrived. Etem parked his swim goggles on his forehead and tossed his flippers into the boat.

"Etem," Ning-ning said, watching Timoteo run up the beach. "Allah has blessed you."

"Yet he tests me every day." Etem leaned his weight on an outrigger strut. He and nine men pushed the skiff into the breaking surf.

Ning-ning jumped aboard. "You have a beautiful family. Your boys are strong." He grabbed Etem's wrist and pulled him into the boat. "But I fear Timoteo is too young to dive the reef."

"He is impatient like I was when my father made me stay in the shallows."

"I remember. I went with you many times...because of what happened to my father."

Sitting on the plank seat, Etem recalled the day Ning-ning's father got his leg caught in a giant clam. He was forced to cut himself loose at the knee.

Etem glanced at the knife he carried in a cloth sheath tied to his waist, the sharp blade he used to wrench mollusks from the reef, clams and oysters, and thanked Allah he'd never had to make a decision so dreadful: life for limb.

"Timoteo will stay in the boat," Etem assured his fellow divers. "He can help with the ropes and string bags."

"I will let the boy row with my oar." Maricar chuckled.

Trim divers held their oars and looked to the palm grove, impatience burning in their eyes. The other boats had already launched and set off for the reef.

"Here he comes." Maricar pointed. "Get ready to go."

Ning-ning pointed too. "Look what he carries with him."

Timoteo hugged goggles and flippers to his ribs as he ran.

"He must think he's going to dive the reef."

"I already told him he'll stay in the boat."

"Seems he did not hear you."

Etem helped his panting son climb aboard. "Hold on to the seat. I must help row to the reef."

Two men floated the boat and jumped in. Oars hit the water. The boat headed into the wind.

The men fell into a rhythm. They had bent to this work countless times. The bay was dotted with pearling skiffs from many villages, all laboring against the wind, the men singing the song of the pearlers as they rowed:

"In the sea." *Stroke.* "In the sea." *Stroke.*

"A pearl." *Stroke.* "Waits for me." *Stroke.*

"In the sea." *Stroke.*

Before long, the skiff bobbed in wind-driven swells above the reef. Etem broke a hard sweat rowing and couldn't wait to get into the water. He slung a string bag around his neck and stabbed his feet into his flippers. Goggles in place over his eyes, he turned to Timoteo. "Watch the men and learn what they do. You may help when asked but don't get in the way."

From his place on the plank seat, Timoteo looked up at his father with a wan smile. "I'll be bigger someday."

Etem smiled and tousled the boy's hair. "Yes, you will."

Working in teams of two, one diver and one rope puller, the men threw rock-weighted ropes overboard. Because it was difficult for a diver to swim to the surface with a string bag full of mollusks, a strong puller was essential. Maricar was Etem's puller.

Etem bit down on the snorkel's mouthpiece, tasted the bitter tang of rubber, and flipped himself overboard, the contact with the water refreshing. After taking a deep breath, he dove, grabbed his designated rope, and hand-over-hand followed it toward the bottom.

The snorkel made gurgling sounds as it filled with water. Pressure in his ears built. By putting his tongue tip in the mouthpiece he kept water out of his mouth.

Other divers followed their ropes down. The boat hull bobbed in the swells five fathoms above.

Feeling strong and alert, Etem went to work scouring the reef, knife in hand, prying mollusks from their footing and placing them in the string bag.

One, two, four, seven, twelve clams...

Colorful fish darted about the coral and through the swaying kelp, almost near enough to touch but always out of reach. Etem never felt alone underwater.

Pumping his legs, he outflanked one of the divers working a stubborn shell loose and found a bed of gaping oysters around a red coral array.

Fifteen, eighteen, twenty clams...

He didn't know which, if any, of the oysters and clams contained pearls. This would be discovered later under the watchful eye of the tribe's Panglima as the shells were pried open. The Mohammedan chief was an ex-pearl-diver determined to capitalize on America's presence on the islands. He'd brought in the newly invented rubber snorkel gear to maximize his Dyak divers' productivity. For his investment, he kept half the proceeds. The rest he would split equally among the pearlers.

Twenty-five, twenty-eight, thirty clams...

Etem's lungs heated. The full string bag became difficult to tow. He looked up to the skiff bobbing in the swells and decided to return.

He tugged twice on his rock-weighted rope and held on. The rope tightened and pulled him up. He anticipated a welcome gulp of fresh air.

Breaching the waves, he blew the snorkel clear of water and inhaled. Timoteo greeted him, leaning over the gunwale with his hands outstretched for the string bag. Etem felt a surge of pride for his son's enthusiasm.

Other divers surfaced and handed up their full string bags. Driven by the wind and choppy sea, the skiff drifted down the reef into an area he didn't recognize. No other boats were near.

"Are you having fun, Dad?"

Timoteo's goggles rested on his forehead.

"You stay in the boat, you hear?" Etem managed between

gasps.

"I just want to help."

"You are not diving."

"I know. I know."

"Don't make me tell you again."

As the boat drifted farther into unfamiliar territory, the string bags were emptied and returned to the divers. The weighted ropes were thrown overboard. Etem dove, hoping his son wouldn't do anything stupid.

Back on the bottom, he wished he could relocate the oyster bed he'd found earlier, but trying to find it would waste precious time due to the boat's strong drift. He went directly to work searching the new area.

Undulating kelp and sea grass thrashed in the current. Swimming above the fray, he scanned the bottom for oyster beds and spotted the yawn of a giant clam, nearly obscured by the kelp and coral outcrops.

Taklobo was a common inhabitant of these waters, but he'd never seen one so large. Or with shells so black. And the mantle looked all splotchy and gray.

Ugly.

And old.

Diving closer, he judged the shells were four or five feet across. Layer upon layer of coral encrusting the jagged cockles meant this clam had been here for a long time. Embedded in the coral. Hiding in the kelp. Safe from human eyes.

Until now.

A *taklobo* this size might hold many pearls, perhaps black pearls, the rarest of all. And perhaps it held nothing. Raising the clam to the surface would take extensive excavation. If he returned to the skiff for help, it would drift, and he would have difficulty locating this clam again, if ever.

To discover the clam's riches, he would have to do it himself, right now, though common sense told him to leave the *taklobo* alone. Its riches were well guarded. Still, what if..?

He decided to work fast, cut into the open clam to see what was inside. The heat in his lungs became a burn. With the knife in his right hand, he cut the clam's mantle. It resisted the blade, tough as sandal leather. Black liquid belched from the wound.

Leaning closer, he fanned the fetid water but couldn't see inside.

His lungs begged for air.

He cut the opening larger, careful not to touch the muscle inside, which would trigger the shells' instinctive reaction to close. But the *taklobo* was slow. He was young and fast.

Still, he would not act the fool for this clam.

As a safety precaution, he braced the knife lengthwise between the shell cockles and dared another look inside the gaping wound.

Sunshine revealed the luster of pearls, bedded deep between muscle and shell. The sparkle and sheen made his heart race with excitement. Pearls, more than a handful. Maybe two. He'd found riches beyond belief. A windfall for his village. He would be the hero of his tribe.

All he had to do was reach in and claim the prize.

Lungs on fire, he stuck his left arm into the clam, between the jagged cockles, past the razor-sharp guardian corals, up to his armpit before he was able to wrap his fingers around the pearls.

But something didn't feel right. He hadn't grabbed a handful of pearls...just one pearl.

A solid lumpy mass the size of a giant conch shell.

Unlike any pearl ever found.

He was rich.

The clamshell quaked, jarring Etem back to his senses. He gripped the knife in his right hand, made sure it was squarely aligned to brace the shells should they close.

Air leaked from his lungs and burbled up the snorkel.

Time was running out.

He tugged on the pearl. It held fast.

The clam refused to let go of its treasure.

Etem gripped the pearl with determined fingers and pulled harder. The prize came free, felt heavy and awkward. He bobbled it, caught it, bumped the muscle, felt a surge of dread.

With a jolt, the clamshells snapped shut on his arm. Coral cut into his flesh, sending wisps of blood swirling through the water around him.

Allah, help me!

He dropped the pearl. Writhing to free himself, the more he

pulled, the more searing pain shot up his arm to the back of his eyeballs. The crushing force on his biceps seemed enough to break bone.

He remembered Ning-ning's father, how he'd cut off his leg to escape a giant clam. Etem's knife, still in his right hand, had slipped when the shells closed, as if the clam had spit it out.

How could he have let this happen?

Terror rose in his chest. He looked at the shiny blade in his hand and embraced the terrible decision he had made.

Allah, be merciful.

He placed the sharp edge on his left shoulder, hesitated to cut off his arm for fear of the pain, of living without an arm, without a hand. How would he dive again? How would he support his wife and two sons?

One more time he would try to free his arm. He would do it for them.

He pulled. Twisted. Strained. The pain was unbearable, but he couldn't get loose. The *taklobo* would make him pay dearly for touching that pearl.

He gritted his teeth and plunged the knife into his shoulder. An involuntary guttural scream emptied his starved lungs. Stinging seawater spilled in.

The Pearl of Death

Chapter Two

One-by-one, divers surfaced alongside the skiff, bobbing in the heavy swells. Timoteo waited for his father. The concerned slant to Maricar's brow told him something was wrong. His stomach felt wormy. "Why hasn't my dad tugged on the rope?"

Maricar held the rope with both hands, waiting as a fisherman would wait for a bite. "He has been down longer than normal." Uncertainty clouded his eyes.

The wind moved the skiff sideways. One weighted rope wasn't enough to stop the drift.

Ning-ning surfaced. Maricar shouted to him, "Etem is missing. Have you seen him?"

Timoteo didn't wait for the answer. Dread overcame his father's warning to stay in the boat. He pulled the goggles over his eyes and jammed his feet into his flippers.

"Sit down," Maricar shouted.

Timoteo jumped overboard. His thin body tensed from the water but quickly acclimated as he dogpaddled with his masked face in the water. His eyes scanned the coral bed far below. It was the deepest water he'd ever seen. Fish swam everywhere he looked. He suddenly felt small. Fear overshadowed the beauty. Nowhere could he see his dad.

"Get back here," Maricar yelled at him from the boat as it drifted farther away.

Swimming against the wind, Timoteo found it hard to make progress. He inhaled and dove. The going became easier, but after a few strokes he had to resurface for air.

He inhaled and dove again.

His father had to be near. He pumped his knees. His flippers pushed him through the water as easily as swimming in the shallows. But this time he was alone, without his father.

If only he could call out, *Dad! Dad where are you?*

Another trip to the surface, another breath, another dive.

A red cloud undulated below him. He didn't understand what it was. With wild strokes, he swam deeper, deeper than he had ever swam before. His ears ached.

Dad. You were right. I'm too young to dive the reef.

Two more strokes. His small lungs hurt for air. He traced the red cloud to its origin, a man splayed out on the coral.

Dad!

Etem's legs waved in the current like sea grass. His arm was caught in a giant clam. A monster had his dad in its wavy jaws. Would it eat him before his eyes?

Dad! Blood leaked from a long cut in his shoulder.

The pain in Timoteo's ears was more than he could stand.

Pumping hard, he raced for the surface, letting out his air on the long way up. It seemed an impossible distance to swim, but he dared not give in to his demanding lungs. His dad needed him.

Breaking the surface, Timoteo gasped. Through the water-blur of his goggles, he made out the shape of the skiff, the oars slapping water at a frantic pace toward him.

"I found him." He swallowed water. "He's bleeding...a monster...it's going to eat him..." He gulped air and dove again but only to see that his dad was still there, an awful sight, pale, still, lifeless.

Timoteo fought tears. Why couldn't he have found him swimming from clam-to-clam, the string bag full, having only lost track of time? Not like this, limp amidst the waving kelp.

Come up, Dad! Please come up.

Timoteo surfaced for air. The boat arrived.

"I can't swim deep enough."

"Get in the boat." Ning-ning tossed an anchor from the bow. Divers jumped overboard. Ning-ning dove in after them.

"Take my hand." Maricar leaned to the water, hand outstretched for Timoteo.

He kicked, treaded water, looked side-to-side, unsure of what to do. Helplessness felt heavy on his chest. The waves tossed him up and dropped him down. He wanted to help save his dad, but he was too small.

"The men will get him."

Taking Maricar's strong hand, Timoteo burst into tears. It was the eight-year-old boy in him wailing, not the pearl diver he wished to be. Like his dad.

His dead dad.

No.

He could still be alive.

Hauled into the boat like a hooked fish, Timoteo tore off his goggles, kicked off his flippers, and dropped to a seat in the pitching hull. "My dad! My dad!"

"We'll get him, boy. Be quiet."

Ning-ning surfaced. "We need machetes and rope."

Maricar leaned over the gunwale. "What happened?"

"A *taklobo* got him."

"Allah have mercy."

"He tried to cut off his arm."

Through tear-soaked eyes, Timoteo looked at his own thin arm. How easily a knife could cut through it. But his father's arms were big and strong.

"Can you free him?" Maricar shouted.

A wave heaved the skiff upward.

"The clam won't let go. We must bring it up with Etem."

"That will take too long."

Timoteo's chest felt cold. Hopelessness filled him. Desolation. Loneliness. How would life be without a dad?

It was the end of the world.

Chapter Three

In the shifting skiff, Maricar fought to maintain his balance. He retrieved machetes from under a plank-seat and stuffed them into a string bag. His eyes clouded with tears, tears for his best friend. Tears for the young family who would lose a father.

"Timoteo." Maricar clambered over a bench seat, dragging the heavy bag of machetes. "Help me with the string bag."

The boy sat trembling on the seat, fists clenched between his knobby knees, bawling.

Maricar couldn't blame him. He tossed the string bag overboard and watched it go down toward the divers.

"Enough crying, boy." He dragged a massive coil of rope to the gunwale. "Help me."

"He was too far down." Timoteo sobbed.

Maricar tied one end of the rope to the mast. "It's not your fault."

"The rope," Ning-ning shouted up, bobbing in the froth.

Maricar could hardly stand in the heaving boat much less lift the heavy rope over the gunwale. "Come on, boy."

"My dad was right. I'm too little."

"I can't do this alone. They need this rope to get your father."

That spurred Timoteo off his seat. With his help, Maricar was able to heft the coil out of the boat and into the sea.

Ning-ning grabbed the rope and disappeared beneath the waves.

Maricar sat by the mast where he could hold on better. "You need to be strong, Timoteo. For your mother and Tito."

"My dad is going to be all right."

Though Timoteo's resolve sounded convincing, Maricar

hesitated to agree. Etem had already been down more than ten minutes.

***

Below the rough water, Ning-ning guided the uncoiling rope to the bottom. His fellow divers worked to break the reef's hold on the giant clam. With machetes, they hacked into the kelp and chipped away at the coral growth around the shell, which remained closed tight on Etem's arm.

He looked eerie with his blue lips agape and his terror-filled eyes wide open. Ning-ning couldn't bear to look at him.

Allah give me strength.

The *taklobo*, cloaked in black and gray and encrusted with coral, appeared demonic, the way its cockles shaped a ghastly smile around Etem's arm.

Hate stabbed Ning-ning's heart. He swam down to the string bag, grabbed a machete. He'd break the shell into scrap. Drive the blade through the devil muscle inside.

He'd kill it. Make it let go of Etem.

He swung the machete, but the water sucked power from the blade and dampened the blow.

With those wavy-cockled lips, the monster appeared to be laughing at him. He shoved the machete between the shells and tried to pry the clamshell open, but the muscle inside had the strength of ten men and would not budge.

Anger burned a hole in his stomach. He joined the other men, started chipping and digging at the coral until his empty lungs forced him to go up for air.

Below, the excavation clouded the bottom with a storm of coral debris. Lifeless Etem stared up at him. This was no rescue mission. It was a body retrieval.

After taking turns and many trips to the surface, Ning-ning and the divers freed the giant clam and tied the rope around the closed shells.

Two men, fresh from the surface, supported Etem's body and nodded to Ning-ning. They were ready. He gathered slack from the rope and gave it two tugs.

***

The signal, two tugs.

Maricar pulled on the rope until the slack lay at his feet.

He pulled. The clam didn't budge.

A wave hurled the skiff upward. The rope nearly yanked him overboard. He let go until the boat slid down a swell then grabbing the slack, he whipped it around the mast, propped his feet against a plank seat and hung on.

The skiff surged up the swell again.

Burning in his hands, the rope got heavier. Waves rushed over the bow and spilled into the boat. Water swirled at his feet. He couldn't hold on much longer.

"Don't you dare let go," Timoteo said behind him, now pulling on the rope. Maricar wished for Ning-ning's strength backing him, but Ning-ning was still in the water. The boy's help would have to do.

The skiff shot down a steep swell.

Maricar pulled in more slack. "Hold on, boy."

Up the boat surged. This time, instead of taking on water again, the hull crested a wave.

"We did it," Maricar shouted. "The clam is coming up."

"Pull." Timoteo strained on the rope. "Pull up my dad."

At least the boy had stopped crying, his sorrow replaced with determination, but it would take more than determination to get the clam and Etem into the boat.

Bubbles broke the surface. Divers appeared, tossed machetes into the skiff and climbed into the bucking hull, exhausted, but helped Maricar with the rope.

"Pull."

Progress was slow. He took advantage of the heaving sea, told his men to hold tight on the up-swell and gather slack on the down-swell. Several men leaned over the opposite gunwale to counterbalance the heavy clam being raised. If not for the outriggers, the skiff would have capsized.

Timoteo sat on the rear bench, breathing hard, his tear-swollen face blank with shock.

Ning-ning surfaced for air and dove again.

Two more swells. The rope tangle grew in the bottom of the boat until the clamshell thudded against the hull.

Maricar dared a look over the edge. Etem bobbed in the

water next to the giant clam. His mouth and eyes were wide open, his face white as beach sand. A gash in his arm revealed bone.

Something inside Maricar broke, the sense of his own mortality taking hold. How fragile life was. How cruel.

Two divers supported Etem's body. Ning-ning treaded water beside them. "We need more ropes."

"More ropes," Maricar ordered the men who were trying to catch their breath. They untied rock-weights and discarded them overboard. Four diving ropes were tied around the clamshell.

With more ropes and more men pulling, he managed to haul the clamshell aboard and lay it carefully in the bottom of the wide hull, on its side with Etem splayed out alongside.

Timoteo fell on his father's chest, tears, saltwater and blood mixing a brew of unbelievable human anguish. "Make it let go," the boy cried, pulling frantically on his dad's trapped arm. "Let go of my dad."

The divers gathered around, holding on to each other for support in the tossing boat.

Maricar had seen drowned divers before and knew this meant the end for Etem. "Allah, be kind to his soul."

He pulled off his shirt and draped it over Etem's face. They had been like brothers. To see him die this way welled up hot anger inside Maricar's chest.

"Devil clam." He kicked the shell.

Timoteo looked up with desperate eyes. "Make it let him go."

"We can't." He took hold of Timoteo's arm and hoisted him up. "The clam won't let go until it is dead."

"Then kill it."

"Go sit down."

"Kill it now."

Ning-ning guided Timoteo to a seat. "That's no way for you to talk."

"It killed my dad. I want it to die."

Maricar shuddered. The clam would be dead soon enough, but no acts of revenge could sooth Timoteo's young heart. He had seen firsthand the dangers of the reef, the dangers of pearl diving, and the death of his father.

"Pull anchor," Maricar told his men. "And unfurl the sail. We must take Etem to Dr. Bogtong so he will see how his death occurred."

Hugging Timoteo, Ning-ning looked up. "Who will tell his wife?"

The question pained Maricar. He looked down at the dead body of his friend who had been so foolish to put his arm inside a giant clam.

"What in Allah's name were you thinking?"

Chapter Four

Sitting on her prized Coca-Cola beach towel, Liawayway ran her fingers through the sun-baked sand and watched Tito dig a trench with his toy shovel and bucket. The wind slapped her headscarf. Etem would return soon. She planned to greet him, mostly to witness Timoteo's proud smile and be the first to hear of his new adventure on the reef.

"Don't go in the water," she said to Tito. His shallow trench snaked very near to the breaking surf. He had not yet learned to swim as well as his brother.

"Ah, Mamma."

"Dig this way now, and I will help you."

"I don't need any help." He crawled up to the place where his trench began. His brown body glowed in the sunshine.

These boys of hers, how did they become so stubborn? Etem let them be their own little men, but he hadn't taught them restraint and self-preservation. If they had their way, they would both be diving for pearls today.

Squealing voices drew her attention to a clutch of girls splashing in the nearby surf. Gulls fluttered above them, hanging in the wind and snatching breadcrumbs a girl tossed in the air.

Touching her stomach, Liawayway fleetingly wished for a girl someday, a girl she could teach to cook and sew, a girl who would not follow her father into the sea.

Down the beach, a boy flew a kite. Cupping her hand above her brow to shield the sun, she watched the kite dip and soar in the wind.

"Look, Tito. Look at the kite."

A group of bronzed, muscular men appeared from the palm trees, running flat-out toward the beach, pointing and shouting.

"Bapór." A boat. *"Bapór."*

She looked to the bay. A lone skiff approached under full sail. And the men were rowing. What was the hurry? And where were the others?

As the skiff neared, the diagonal marking on the sail became visible.

Etem's boat. Was there an accident? Timoteo was on that boat. Her heart lunged.

The boat pitched bow-up and crashed down through the rolling surf. Ning-ning and Maricar were rowing with the others. Behind them, Timoteo lurched back and forth on his seat. Relief swept over her.

Her son was safe.

But where was Etem?

The boat came aground in the shallows. Men from the beach ran to the boat. She couldn't make out their chatter over the wind and the snapping sail.

Still, Etem was nowhere she could see.

The rowers jumped out, and along with the men who'd met them, they beached the boat.

Still she couldn't find Etem's tan, lean frame or the familiar curly mop of his hair.

The men gathered around the boat and looked inside.

Dread stabbed her chest. She got up from the beach towel. The wind peeled it off the sand and hurled it away. Stooping, she picked up Tito and started running toward the boat. Her bare feet sunk in the sand, slowing her progress. She recognized Maricar getting out of the boat.

"Maricar. Where is Etem?"

The men turned. Their faces were wrenched in terror.

Maricar stepped forward, held out the palm of his hand. "Liawayway, stop."

She kept slogging toward him with Tito bouncing in the crook of her arm. "What is going on?"

"Don't come any closer."

The back of her neck prickled. "Where is he?"

"You don't want to see him like this."

A hot blade of fear pierced her heart. "What happened?"

"Mamma," Timoteo cried out from the boat.

Ning-ning snatched him up and jumped to the sand.

"Liawayway, stay back. Please."

"Etem."

Ning-ning set Timoteo on his feet and joined Maricar who was running toward her.

The hot blade twisted in her chest. "Etem!"

Both men grabbed her arms, stopped her forward momentum. She tried to break free. The tears on Timoteo's face stopped her struggle. "Timoteo. What happened to your father?"

"It's my fault. I'm sorry, Mamma."

"What did you do?"

Maricar jumped in. "He did nothing."

The men forced her to turn away from the boat.

"Let go of me."

She scuffled with them, kicking sand.

Tito wailed in her arms.

She was no match for the pearl divers' strength. They forced her up the beach toward the palm trees. Timoteo dogged behind. "I couldn't swim deep enough, Mamma."

"He was very brave." Ning-ning kept moving her along.

"You must tell me." Tears burned her eyes. "Please."

"First we will get the doctor."

"How bad is he hurt?"

"We think he is dead," Maricar managed. "Bogtong will know for sure."

"D-dead?" She choked on the word. "Etem is dead?"

Her eyes met Ning-ning's for an instant, then he cast his gaze to the sand. "It was an accident."

Her knees buckled.

The men stopped her from falling, kept moving her up the beach, dragging her feet in the sand.

"Allah," she cried. "Why have you forsaken us?"

Chapter Five

The Dyak tribe's village sat at the mouth of Boligay Creek, a panorama of tropical rainforest, waterfalls, clapboard shacks and thatched huts. Prominent citizens lived in wood and brick homes, like Dr. Bogtong's residence, which also served as the village clinic. Because business was slow, he'd removed his thin glasses and prepared an early lunch: a baloney and sole sandwich, which he set on a palm leaf on the table. He opened a Coca-Cola and was about to put the bottle to his lips, anticipating with every nerve of his body the tingling, bubbly refreshment, when the yelling of men on the beach stopped him.

A fight? Maybe he should intervene. No. He would let them settle things on their own.

His second attempt at taking a drink was interrupted as well. This time by a woman's scream. He cringed.

"Mother of Allah." He moved to the front room and looked out the window. A single pearling skiff sat tilted in the sand, just out of the roiling surf's reach. Men surrounded the hull, looking in. Even from this distance up the hill he could see their grave expressions. Perhaps someone had been injured. He should investigate, but then again, he was about to have lunch. He looked at the fizzing bottle, the delicious curve to the thick glass that fit so nicely in his hand, and headed back to the kitchen. If he was needed, someone would call on him.

He chugged on the bottle until it was half empty.

"Ah." He burped. *Americans are the greatest inventors.*

He'd eaten half his sandwich when pounding on his door interrupted his lunch.

"Yeah, yeah."

But first, he guzzled down the remaining refreshment.

More pounding.

"Dr. Bogtong," a desperate voice called out. "You in there?"

"I'm coming." He put on his glasses. "I'm coming."

At the door stood two young men he knew well, Maricar and Ning-ning. Their faces looked frightful. "What is it that brings you to bother my lunch?"

Maricar was breathless. "It's Etem."

Bogtong pushed open the screen door. "Etem?"

"He's dead."

The Coke gurgled in Bogtong's stomach. "You know this for sure?"

"He drowned."

Dread smacked Bogtong in the chest. The loss of a diver, a husband, a father of two boys, this was a tragedy for the entire tribe. "Liawayway? Does she know?"

"Yes," Maricar said. "She was on the beach waiting for him."

"And the boys?"

"Timoteo was on the boat," Ning-ning said. "He tried to save him but witnessed the death."

"The boy jumped in the water," Maricar added. "I couldn't stop him."

Such an event could affect Timoteo for a long time. Bogtong wished for another Coke, but there would be no time for such stimulating luxury. Besides, he would have to share. Better for him to tend to the investigation, as all deaths on the island had to be fully documented. "Where is he?"

"In the boat."

Bogtong's chest pumped with urgency as he followed the men down to the beach. The sooner he got this over with, the sooner he could get back to his sandwich. Wind whipped at his white smock and baggy white pants. Sand leaked into his loafers. The rolling surf thundered to shore.

What were these men thinking, pearl diving under such miserable conditions? It's a wonder they all hadn't drowned.

By the time he reached the beached skiff, his throat burned and made snorting sounds like a boar. He looked into the hull at Etem's body, the shirt over his head, and his undersea murderer, the blackest, ugliest *taklobo* he'd ever seen. His dry throat tightened. The wind and sea swells had nothing to do with this drowning.

"Why did this happen?"

"We don't know," Ning-ning said.

The other divers backed away as if not wanting any part of the interrogation.

"This *taklobo* is big. It is sessile. Can't swim around, can't chase him, yet Etem is caught and killed? How is this possible?"

Maricar shrugged. "It was an accident."

"Accident? He accidentally put his arm in a clam?" That was beyond ridiculous.

Ning-ning chimed in. "He knew better than to disturb a *taklobo*."

"But he did. Against all common sense. How am I going to explain such a senseless death to the Panglima?"

"The chief?" Maricar's round white eyeballs filled with panic. "Does he have to know?"

"We tried to save Etem," Ning-ning said.

"I have no choice but to tell him." Bogtong climbed into the boat to get a closer look. After adjusting his glasses, he lifted the shirt, flinched at the blank stare in Etem's eyes. Allah's mercy was not always merciful, but more often brutal. He placed a finger on Etem's neck. The skin felt cold. No pulse. He dropped the shirt. The clam had trapped the entire left arm. A cut ran diagonally across the shoulder. Bogtong looked up at Ning-ning. "You tried to cut him free?"

"He did that to himself."

Gave Bogtong the chills just thinking about cutting off his own arm. Back to his examination, from this angle, a gash in the clam's mantle became visible. Etem had cut into the clam. It had closed in self-defense. Normally this would not have been life threatening, as giant clams rarely snapped shut suddenly or even closed tight enough to trap an arm. It was the cut in the mantle that allowed the shells to close like bear trap jaws.

Looking up at the men who looked on with forlorn eyes, Bogtong hoped they would learn from this sad lesson.

"Etem has caused his own death." Bogtong stood. "My question is, and I'm sure the Panglima will want to know, why wasn't anyone diving with him? This death might have been prevented."

Ning-ning spoke up. "There were five of us in the water."

"I was in the boat," Maricar said in his own defense.

"The wind pushed us into a new area," Ning-ning said. "There was thick sea grass and kelp. We couldn't always see each other."

"No excuse. The buddy system—"

"We are sorry."

"If there is an inquiry, safety violations could bring stiff fines and shame on the village. The Panglima will not be happy. You could be banished from the tribe."

"I was in the boat," Maricar repeated.

Ning-ning gripped the gunwale, his face grooved with panic. "You are the chief's friend. You can show this to him." He gestured to the clam and Etem lying at Bogtong's feet. "Tell him what happened. He will see that we are not to blame."

"The Panglima must report the death to Manila. Even our friendship cannot change that." Bogtong sighed. "You boys are in a lot of trouble."

Chapter Six

The Panglima lived among the palms, a two hour hard paddle up Boligay Creek to the bamboo dock. Bogtong left Ning-ning and the men in the skiff to stay with Etem's body and made his way up the path toward the house, a two story Foursquare with white pillars and shuttered windows. Goats and chickens roamed the front yard. He hoped the chief would have a Coca-Cola for a weary traveler.

Stalking up the wide steps and crossing the porch to the door, he inhaled the scent of fried fish. He remembered the half-eaten sandwich and wished he hadn't left it in his kitchen. Maybe he would invite himself to stay for dinner.

He knocked on the door.

A servant answered, a skinny man who parted his hair down the middle. He wore white shorts and spoke Tagalog. "*Magandang gabi*, Dr. Bogtong." Good evening.

"I must see the Panglima."

"*Tuloy.*" Come in.

Bogtong stepped inside, waited in the foyer for the Panglima to formally bid him welcome. The servant trod across a Navajo rug, a prized acquisition from America, and slipped into the next room.

On the walls around Bogtong hung Southwestern paintings, cowboys and Indians from a land far away. A testament to the Panglima's fondness of American history and art, he considered the Philippines America's new Wild West.

The servant returned. "He will see you now."

Bogtong followed him to the reception room. The Panglima sat cross-legged on a palm rug. His ten-year-old son, Pula, sat next to him. The tribe's future leader mimicked his father's pose.

~32~

The Pearl of Death

"Enter, my friend." The old man sat barefoot. He wore baggy blue jean overalls, a green flannel shirt and a red bandana on his head. Gray locks poked out in coils over his earflaps, and a cluster of wild hairs prickled his chin. His heavy brows and high cheekbones gave him a fierce look that exuded authority that dared not be questioned. "May I offer you anything?"

"A Coca-Cola would be fine." His mouth watered.

The Panglima nodded to the servant who then quickly left the room.

Bogtong removed his loafers, as was the formal custom when greeting the Panglima, and sat cross-legged in front of him. After bowing heads to each other and grasping wrists, "My chief, I am sorry to come to you this way, but I have bad news."

As Bogtong explained the reason for his visit, Pula lit a cigar for the Panglima and offered one to Bogtong, who waved him off, so Pula lit it for himself.

"The divers fear they will be blamed."

"Etem has a family." The Panglima blew smoke in the air.

"A wife and two boys."

"Who will take care of them now that they have no provider?"

Pula blew smoke in the air.

"I don't know." Bogtong coughed. "The tribe will have to pitch in—"

"I cannot afford charity."

"I will ask for volunteers."

The Panglima's heavy brows sank, hooding his eyes. "You will choose one diver to take responsibility for the family or I will banish them all."

"Begging the Panglima's forgiveness..." Bogtong breathed smoke as harsh as the decree. "Would you not show mercy if your own son was on that dive?"

"I would." He reached over and scrubbed knuckles on the boy's head.

Pula ducked and blew cigar smoke into his father's face. "I wasn't there, Poppie." He laughed a little boy laugh, which contrasted sharply with the fat cigar squeezed between his small fingers.

"See, doctor." The Panglima shifted his dark gaze back to

Bogtong. "He wasn't there. Your point is senseless."

"Our single men, you know they support their elders. None can afford the additional expense of Etem's family. It would take the entire tribe to help out."

"I have spoken."

Bogtong bowed. The Panglima's word was law in the tribe, even if it meant the financial ruin of one young man. "As you wish."

"Good." Cigar smoke streamed from the chief's nostrils. "I will see the body now."

Bogtong escorted him to the creek and the skiff tied to the dock.

On seeing the body, the Panglima threw down his cigar and turned his back to the skiff. "A life so young. Wasted. Reminds me of my pearling days, when I worked for the largest pearl fishing fleet on the Sulu Sea, seen too many divers die this way. I hoped Allah would spare me the sight of another."

"They were looking for pearls inside giant clams?"

"Where none usually exist, or of poor quality. Riches, bah, a deadly myth, as you can see. Etem was fooled." The Panglima looked over his shoulder at the stoic men in the skiff. "Kill the clam and remove Etem, but leave me the shell. I will keep it on my porch in his memory."

Bogtong raised his arms to rally the men. "You heard the chief."

They lifted the giant clam from the skiff, along with Etem's body, and four men propped the shell upright. Two supported Etem, and two others ran their long spears through the mantle and into the defenseless muscle.

The clam trembled and chattered.

Bogtong felt the sting of each spear thrust, again and again as the men jabbed the clam. He could imagine it screaming in agony and begging for mercy. Then, as if taking one final gasp, the shells shuddered and opened, releasing Etem's arm.

The body fell away, and the men carried Etem to the skiff, free at last from the grip of his murderer.

The other men hauled the heavy clam up the hill, following Bogtong to the Panglima's porch. "Leave it here and wait for me at the boat."

The Pearl of Death

Inside, the servant presented Bogtong a bottle of Coke.

He chugged heartily while the Panglima wrote the affidavit explaining Etem's death, then with a rare smile, presented a copy to Bogtong for the official medical record. "I will accept a canoe-load of conch shells for my service."

"A small price to pay for this matter to be closed." He finished the last swallow of Coke and savored the rush of energy coursing through his body.

The servant handed Bogtong his loafers, took the empty bottle and bowed, backing away.

On the porch, the Panglima examined the *taklobo* lying on its side, black goo oozing from the puncture wounds and seeping into the porch boards. "A fine specimen. The oldest I've ever seen, maybe three hundred years. The shells alone are worth nine hundred American dollars."

"We are glad it is now in your trusted and noble hands." Bogtong pocketed the Panglima's affidavit of death. "Thank you."

The old man's expression turned woeful. "Three days of mourning Etem's death will commence immediately. On the fourth day your men must return with the conch shells."

"Of course." Bogtong looked at the sun about to set behind nearby Maruyog Mountain. "We should be off to the village if we're to make it back before dark. Goodnight, my good friend. You are as wise as you are venerable." He stepped down from the porch.

"Bogtong," the Panglima called after him.

He stopped and turned back. "Yes, my chief?"

"By the fourth day you will give me the name of the man who will see to the family's needs. Understood?"

Bogtong bowed. A pit grew in his stomach. Which young man would he saddle with that burden?

Chapter Seven

In the waning glow of dusk, Bogtong scrunched himself low in the skiff as it slipped through the chop toward the Dyak village. The wind had subsided, and the rhythmic slapping of the men's oars caused him to yawn. The decree that he was to decide the future of Etem's family felt as welcome as a sea urchin in his underwear. That was the price he would pay for bringing the matter to the Panglima.

"Bogtong." Ning-ning roused him from his thoughts.

"Huh? What? What is it?"

"Look."

A strange array of lights flickered among the palm trees lining the beach.

"A camp."

Bogtong sat upright. The familiar gnaw for a Coca-Cola rush bit him. His eyes focused on the village night fires, only a hundred yards beyond the strange camp. The Panglima had not mentioned any visitors to the area.

"They are close to our village." Ning-ning picked up a machete. "We will drive them off."

That's all Bogtong needed to cap off his day, a spear and blade battle. "If they meant us any harm, they would not have made their presence so noticeable."

The skiff carved a path toward the beach. Nearing the strange lights, Bogtong scrutinized the glow of gas lanterns strung on ropes between the trees and slope-roofed tents anchored to the ground.

Ning-ning jabbed his paddle in the air. "Tax collectors."

Bogtong licked dry lips. It was too early in the season for a proper assessment of the tribe's income. "See who it is," he whispered. "And be quiet about it."

The Pearl of Death

The boat slid onto shore. Ning-ning and two others jumped out and slinked off.

Five men lifted Etem. Bogtong led the way up the beach to his house and turned on a light. The men laid Etem on the clinic room's examination table.

Shaking, Bogtong damped his sweating forehead with a towel. His tongue hurt. He spread the towel over Etem's body. Only his head and feet were left visible.

Ning-ning returned with his spies. "Americans."

Bogtong tried to swallow. "Soldiers?"

"Civilians." He held up two fingers. "Sitting at a small table. Drinking liquor."

Bogtong wished for a drink of his own. Preferably Coke.

"We outnumber them. So nothing to worry about."

"I recognized one American. The geologist. Wilbur Cobb."

"Ah, yes." Bogtong remembered a motorboat stuck on a sandbar. "The Iwahig River. Two years ago."

"Now he is here. He brought surveyors. I saw the equipment."

Sweat broke out on Bogtong's neck. The American was a good man, paid for his rescue with blankets and pans. It was the company he worked for that would bring trouble to the island. He felt faint. Weak in the knees.

"Are you all right?" Ning-ning asked.

"Fine. I'll be fine. Just give me a minute."

Bogtong rushed to the kitchen pantry, grabbed a Coke. His hands shook with excitement, anticipation, need.

He pried off the cap and guzzled the bottle dry. The warm fizz burned his throat and threatened to push back up his nose.

Divine.

Plopping the bottle on the table, he belched, sat in the chair, elbows on his knees and fists clenched, waiting for the potion to work magic on his body.

The bellow of a buffalo horn rose above the din, the long-drawling tone of the Dyak tribe's death call, the beginning of three days of mourning.

Anguished faces soon filled his doorways and windows, all straining to get a glimpse of Etem's body. The entire village had converged to wail the tribe's dirge and howl in mournful prayer.

Bogtong covered his ears. His heart pounded as if it would explode, and his brain buzzed with dizziness from a sugar rush pulsing through his body. He wanted to enjoy the sensation, but all the wailing interfered with his high.

Stop! Stop! Stop!

But they would not stop, not for three days, because if they did, the devils of the sea would keep Etem's soul forever.

Chapter Eight

The jungle night held the day's heat in its sweltering fist. Wilbur Cobb wiped sweat from his brow and sat at the camp table. Another shot of scotch slipped down his throat. He wheezed. Day one in Palawan. Four to go.

By the glow of the kerosene lantern, the mosquito net draped from the pipe-frame cabana shined like daylight. In the darkness beyond, the surf slipped in and out, soft as a lover's whisper. The yawn of his tent flaps beckoned sleep.

He slammed the empty glass on the table. The lantern and scotch bottle jumped. "One more," he told Bambi, the expedition medic sitting across from him.

"I think you have had enough."

"They don't pay you to think."

Bambi poured another splash into the glass. "The others have hit the sack. Tomorrow will be an early rise."

He and his geological team had five days to survey an ancient burial site south of the Dyak village. By order of the Panglima, the area would be off limits to any digging or core sample drilling. Wilbur's employer, Benguet Consolidated Mining Company, believed in pacifying tribal leaders, as the islands were rich in gold and nickel and chromites. Give the heathens their sacred land with one hand, and with the other, steal their wealth out from under their bare feet.

Wilbur didn't make the rules.

He downed the scotch. Huffed away the burn. Scotch tasted meaner in the jungle than in the clip joints of San Francisco. He stood and parted the mosquito netting. "Wake me at dawn."

"Good night, Mister Cobb."

Wilbur walked to his tent, pushed past the flaps and zipped

the door shut. The canvas smelled of mildew. It must've been 100 degrees. He kicked off his boots, sat on the squeaky cot and peeled off his shirt. He'd sleep naked if it weren't for those damn mosquitoes.

Bed net in place, he settled into the cot, head on the pillow. The hard lump of his stashed Colt .38 pressed against his ear. Security in this hard land was good to have close by.

He took a deep breath. A gentle spin swam in his head, the warm sensation of serenity, the numbing kiss of alcohol, sweet relaxation...

The bellow of a buffalo horn sounded through the trees, a long and mournful tone, loud enough to wake the entire island. Wilbur's tranquility shattered like a broken vase. Damn natives. What were they up to now? He pitched over on his side.

A scream.

Wilbur's spinning head snapped to full alert.

A chorus of wails rose from the nearby village, like the natives had reason to shriek at the top of their lungs. It wasn't an attack on his camp. They'd have snuck in silently and slit everyone's throats with bore-tooth daggers. No. This was an emergency of some kind. A disaster unfolding. A story worth getting out of bed to investigate.

Adrenaline had a way of killing a good alcohol buzz. He scrambled to his feet and jammed on his boots, grabbed his shirt...and the Colt.

Bambi and the others had already gathered outside his tent. They carried rifles and pistols at the ready.

"What's all the ruckus?"

"A death dirge, Mister Cobb." Bambi would know, being native to Palawan. "It is the custom when a tribe member dies. To cry and chant prayers. You should all go back to sleep."

The wailing intensified, like fire driven by high winds.

"With that racket?" one of his men said, a surveyor dressed in sleeveless underwear and jungle fatigues.

"Will they attack?" This came from the company genius with thick glasses and too many Tarzan novels under his belt.

"Let me think." The scotch turned hot in Wilbur's stomach. The Dyaks were peaceful. Usually. And because of his past encounters with them, he felt comfortable camping this close to their village. "I'm going in to find out what happened."

"You don't go unasked." Bambi sounded stern. "A white stranger would find a spear in his heart."

"Someone will remember me." He handed his Colt to Bambi.

"Don't stake your life on it."

Nothing ventured, nothing gained. Whatever drove these natives to tears was a story he wanted to know. He lifted the lantern from the table. "You guys guard the camp."

***

Wilbur wasn't a stocky man. He had a soft face and a smooth frame, but he was fit enough to tackle anything the jungle had to throw at him, including this network of paths that cut through the trees from the beach to the village. He took the first right turn he encountered. Fifty yards separated him from the screaming Dyaks. He hoped they weren't in the mood to kill a white intruder.

Lantern held low to keep the glare from his eyes, he moved uphill through soft sand and over worn roots. The wailing got louder with every step. And Bambi's voice resounded in his head, the warning about getting a spear in his heart. Goose bumps pricked his neck.

Other paths merged with his. Twenty yards from the village, he met up with Dyaks: men, women and children, their small brown bodies aglow in the lantern light, all wailing and chanting as they skittered past him. He felt eerily invisible as he followed them into the village. Everyone gravitated to one house. They milled around. Hugged each other. Cried. Some fell to their knees while praising *Allah, Allah, Allah*, so intently they seemed unaware of his presence, or they didn't care.

Wilbur pressed through the weeping throng to the screen door and peered in. "Hello? Anybody here?" By the light of a single ceiling bulb, a table was visible. The soles of two feet forming a V. Toes-up. A towel-covered body. "What's going on in there?"

A native stepped to the door. Short. Squatty. He wore all white. Thin glasses perched low on his broad nose. The face looked familiar.

"Bogtong, that you?"

"Mister Cobb." He flung open the screen door. "Come in. Come in."

"I don't mean to disturb you." Wilbur set down the lantern and stepped into the house. Two young natives sat against the wall, both wearing only shorts and looking up at him with white-ringed eyeballs. "Your people awoke our camp." The body on the table drew his eyes. "What happened?"

"Etem has been killed."

Wilbur leaned toward the table and gazed into the contorted face of death. A young man. No tattoos to indicate he was anyone special. "Why all the fuss over him?"

Bogtong sighed. "He left a wife and family, two boys."

A broken family was nothing new on these islands. The jungle was an unforgiving place. If the heat, or the snakes, or rival tribes didn't kill these natives, the mosquitoes did. Then there was the ocean, riptides and sharks...

"What killed him?"

"*Taklobo*." Bogtong spat out the word as if it were poisonous.

Wilbur blinked. Unusual way to die. But spectacular. A story he wanted to know more about. "I would like to see a clam big enough to kill a man."

Bogtong frowned. "Not for three days. The tribe will be mourning." Then his brows arched. "However, on the fourth day, I might let you come with us to the Panglima's residence to see the clam for yourself."

"You might?" Dyaks never did anything for nothing.

Bogtong grinned expectantly.

"What is your price?"

"Coca-Cola, in one of those new six-packs I have heard advertised on the radio."

Wilbur had brought several cases of the soft drink to the island, but he also brought other supplies that would be more beneficial to the tribe than soda pop. "How about a box of atabrine. It's a new malaria drug."

Bogtong shook his head. "Coke."

"We have cases of rations with beans and crackers and chocolate."

"You dare to insult me, Mister Cobb?"

The two natives on the floor sprang to their feet and flanked Bogtong. Both brandished six-inch bore-tooth blades and bared gnarly teeth. They didn't stand much taller than five feet, sinewy bodies with small paunches, but they owned the reputation of being fearless in a fight. Ask Magellan.

Wilbur's pulse shot up. He gritted his molars and wished he had brought his Colt. Even then, there would be a good chance he wouldn't make it out of the village alive.

Too many natives, not enough bullets.

He inhaled, stood his ground. Showing fear would only incite the little thugs to draw blood. A show of humility might defuse the situation.

"I am sorry to offend you, doctor." Wilbur bowed his head.

Bogtong held a level gaze for a heartbeat then broke out a smile. "Maricar. Ning-ning." He waved the natives back. "Where are your manners?"

Wilbur exhaled. "I'm only trying to help."

"Then make it two six-packs, Mister Cobb."

He looked at the natives' fierce eyes and wiry hair. They poked their knives at him as if intent on enforcing the doctor's demands.

"Two six-packs it is." Wilbur backpedaled to the door, not willing to turn his back on the natives and bet his life that Bogtong had a tight rein on them. "I'll return in four days to see this killer clam of yours."

***

In a shack set off from a narrow dirt path, the wailing sounds of the villagers leaked in through the cracks. Liawayway sat on the clapboard floor cross-legged and wept into her hands. Her body shook. Etem was dead, and so was her heart, only it had not yet stopped beating.

Neighbors had left food wrapped in palm leaves by the open door. The smells of fish and rice and snake stew wafted in. An uncapped bottle of Coke sat on the floor in front of her. But she could not drink it. She could not eat. She could only cry.

Being the wife of a pearl diver, she knew the risks but never thought harm would come to her husband. That happened to other families. Not hers. Hers was a devoted family, devoted to each other, devoted to Allah, and true to the Qur'an. She covered her hair with a hijab and masked the curves of her body with long straight dresses. She got down on her knees and prayed five times a day to affirm herself with the graces of Allah. And for what? This? *Kirot Ang Aking Puso.* A pain in her heart that bled like an open wound.

Allah's betrayal cut deep to the tender flesh of her children. Tito was too young to understand. He'd gone to sleep on his blanket in the corner, calling for his father to tuck him in, but Timoteo had witnessed the death. The boy had rocked back and forth and cried and cried and mumbled that it was his fault. He was too small to save his father. How would this guilt eat at his soul? And for how long? Why did Allah burden a child with so much grief?

Timoteo had finally gone to sleep next to Tito, but only after she'd told him everything would be all right, a lie she didn't believe herself. A widowed mother of two in the jungle without income, how would they survive?

What would she do—?

A knock.

She looked up. Bogtong stood outside the doorway. What did he want? Couldn't he see she was in misery?

"May I come in?"

"Leave me alone."

He stepped inside anyway, sat on the floor, eyeing the Coke bottle. "I'm sorry about Etem. Will you visit him at the clinic?"

She couldn't bear to see him yet. Wiping tears from her eyes, a pang of annoyance gripped her. "Why do you not mourn with the others?"

"Praises to Allah are wailing inside my head, but I am worried about you."

Everyone was worried about her, for now, while the pain was ripe and Etem's memory was clear. How long would it be before they forgot and abandoned her? Abandoned her as Allah had abandoned her.

"Why did God do it, Bogtong?" Liawayway couldn't hold back that tight feeling of hate in her stomach, the squeeze of anger gripping her heart. "God is not great. He is a beast."

"The clam was not at fault." Bogtong reached out, ran an index finger along the sweating curve of the Coke bottle. "A beautiful thing of nature." His voice sounded whisper soft, filled with love as he stared at the bottle. "A docile creature...unless it is attacked by a knife-wielding diver."

"What was Etem thinking?" She sobbed.

"His desire to find pearls must have been very powerful."

Bogtong grasped the bottle, lifted it from the floor, gentle as a bird taking flight, his eyes filled with a powerful desire of his own. "Do you mind?"

The doctor was a leach. Still, she had no place enjoying something that Etem could not. "It is yours."

He chugged from the bottle, licked his lips. "The Panglima told me it was the oldest *taklobo* he'd ever seen. Etem may have thought it held a fortune in pearls."

"Did it?"

"Giant clams are not good pearl producers." He guzzled more Coke. "Most are of poor quality."

"So he died for nothing?"

"It was Allah's will."

Bitterness boiled in her stomach, hot as octopus soup. "You expect me to take solace in Allah's will?" She jumped to her feet. "He willed us to be without Etem?" She shouted down at Bogtong. "God wanted Etem to die? He used the clam to do his killing. It is Allah who is the murderer."

"Be careful of your words, Liawayway. Once you let them go, you cannot bring them back."

"I will scream Allah's name in vain if I wish. God damn. God damn. God damn." The words were out, and she didn't care. Still more formed in her head, like dry wood tossed on a raging fire. "And I'll never again soil my knees in his grace. I will not pray to a murderer."

And words would not be the end of her assault on Allah, her rebellion against God, her blasphemy.

She tore off the headscarf. Her hair tumbled to her shoulders in curls. A chill shuddered up her backbone. She felt naked in front of Bogtong...but somehow suddenly free.

He looked up at her in wide-eyed shock. "Cover yourself,

woman."

"Get out of my house."

***

Bogtong awoke in his kitchen, seated in a chair at the table, his arms folded under his forehead. He had fallen asleep to the mournful cries and chants of his tribe, the same dirge that greeted him this morning. And a vision played in his mind.

Liawayway.

He could still see her face, the anger lines gouged under her dark eyes as she bared her head to him. He'd never seen her hair before, long, curly and privileged only to her husband. A need had stirred inside him, to take her for himself, as shocking a desire as the sight of her blasphemy that was etched into his brain. The devil's work...

An empty Coke bottle on the table came into focus. A familiar anticipation warmed his stomach. Liawayway's head of sumptuous hair was quickly forgotten in favor of a more urgent need.

He rose from the chair, and on morning-stiff legs moved to the pantry and his dwindling supply of Coca-Cola. He should have demanded more from Wilbur Cobb. A truckload more.

With open bottle in hand, he felt empowered and swallowed heartily. The bubbly burn raced down his throat. He would soon feel whole again.

Outside, smoke drifted through the trees from night fires burned down low in the village center. The dim light of dawn revealed mourners gathered together on their knees, praying to Allah, praying for Etem's soul.

In the next room, the body lay on the examination table. Maricar and Ning-ning sat on the floor, backs to the wall, heads slumped together in sleep. One of these young men would have to take responsibility for Etem's family. It would ruin the future of the one chosen. Bogtong dreaded the decision he had to make.

He finished the Coke. Burped. His body swelled with renewed energy. He set the bottle on the table next to Etem's ear and kicked Ning-ning's foot. "Get up."

"What?" He opened his eyes, blinked, and then scrambled to his feet. "What is it?"

Maricar slumped over until his head touched the floor.

Bogtong kicked him too. "And you."

A moan. Maricar pushed himself upright and looked out sleep-heavy eyelids. "What time is it?"

"You have to bury Etem."

"Me?"

"A hole must be dug."

Ning-ning stood at Etem's side, touched his towel-covered arm. "I will do it."

"You both will do it." Bogtong held open the screen door. "There are shovels in the sand out back."

After pulling Maricar to his feet, Ning-ning herded him out the door. Bogtong followed.

He climbed the hill a ways up from the house, looking for a suitable place for the grave. From the base of a tall coconut tree, he looked out over the bay. The Sulu Sea beyond the reef had calmed during the night, as if a thorn had been removed from its heel.

Ning-ning joined him, breathless, shovel in hand. "It is beautiful up here."

Below, Maricar started trudging up the hill, shovel propped on his shoulder like a rifle.

"This will be Etem's final resting place." Bogtong turned to face Ning-ning. "But there is another matter we must put to rest."

"We?"

Bogtong's throat tightened as if his voice box would snuff the words he had to say. "You are fond of Etem's wife?"

"Liawayway? Of course, but—"

"And Timoteo?"

"He's a lot like me when I was his age. What does—?"

"And Tito?"

"He's a little brat, but yes, I'm fond of him too."

Bogtong took a breath. Maricar was already halfway up the hill. There was little time left for this discussion. "Why don't you have a family?"

"I'm saving up for one."

"You think you will be a good provider?"

He leaned on the shovel. "What's this got to do with

~47~

Etem's family?"

"The Panglima has tasked me to assign responsibility for their support. One diver to save all the others from banishment."

"I gladly accept." Ning-ning didn't even blink.

"It would strap you financially."

"So?"

"It will change your plans for a family of your own. At least until the boys are grown or Liawayway remarries."

"Etem's not even buried yet, Bogtong, and you already talk of her having a new husband—"

"I have not chosen you." There. It was said.

Ning-ning tilted his head. "Not me?"

"I hope you understand."

Maricar made it up the hill. "Understand what?" He was breathing hard after the long climb.

"I have chosen the one who will support Etem's family."

Maricar slapped Ning-ning's shoulder. "You couldn't have picked a better man."

"Better yes." Bogtong turned to Maricar. "But I've picked one who is more in need of the responsibility."

Maricar leveled a serious look on Bogtong. "Who?"

"You."

Panic flashed in Maricar's eyes. "Hey. I loved Etem as much as anyone, but I don't want to support his family."

"I have decided. Half of your income will go to Liawayway."

"No. I will not agree to this robbery."

"Then all nine of you on that pearling skiff will be banished from the tribe. As well as Liawayway and the boys. The Panglima has decreed this."

Maricar threw down the shovel. "Why me? I was in the boat."

"You lose your temper because you don't take responsibility for Etem's death with the others. The tribe isn't all about you. It's about us. We are responsible for each other. Perhaps you will learn this and become a better man. My decision is final. Start digging so we can have a nice funeral for Etem."

It was time to go back to the house for another Coca-Cola.

Chapter Nine

On the fourth day after the funeral, a lone canoe rode low in the water of Boligay Creek. Wilbur Cobb sat on the stern plank and swatted mosquitoes, which thrived in the breezeless jungle heat. Any one of the little buggers could carry Malaria.

Half naked, Maricar and Ning-ning worked up a sweat, paddling the boatload of conch shells upstream. The knife-wielding enforcers in Bogtong's service were now armed with long spears edged up against the canoe hull within easy reach.

Riding the bow plank and dressed in white, Bogtong wore a ratty straw hat and drank from one of his newly acquired bottles of Coke.

Wilbur sat up to his bootlaces in conch shells. The creek smelled oily and dead. Insect wings buzzed all around, and the cackle and caw of tropical birds in the trees made the muggy air seem alive and vibrant. He savored every sound and every smell and every tug of every stroke of every oar.

Bambi and the others had stayed back at base camp to finish the surveying project for Benguet by morning. This foray into the jungle was an opportunity Wilbur couldn't pass up, not for all the ore samples on Palawan. Few white men ever got the chance to meet a Panglima in person. Fewer still would ever see a man-killer clam.

This was the adventure Wilbur came to the Philippines to find. He planned to write a book someday, go on tour and lecture about his travels. City-folk would pay a dime, or maybe a quarter, to hear his stories of faraway places, natives, and the attack of a giant clam.

He smacked a mosquito feeding on his arm.

From somewhere beyond the next bend, the beating of

gongs and drums and women's voices chanting and singing rippled across the water.

Bogtong straightened. Cocked his head.

The paddlers stopped paddling, picked up their long spears.

Anxiety stung Wilbur's chest. "Bogtong, what is it?"

"A Mohammedan celebration. They praise Allah for the gift."

Wilbur kicked the conch shells. "These?"

"No. *Nakar*. Pearl. They sing of a pearl."

Had they gone wacky? "What pearl?"

Bogtong shrugged, signaled the natives to paddle on.

The canoe rounded the bend. A bamboo dock appeared on the left bank. Nearby, flat-nosed women wearing headscarves and long dresses waded in the shallows, beating laundry on rocks and singing with joyful voices. At the canoe's approach, they quickly turned their eyes away, as religious tradition dictated them to avoid eye contact in the presence of strangers.

Children had no such restrictions. Naked as the days were hot, they jumped in the water and splashed and waved and swam toward the canoe, shouting and giggling.

The canoe slipped up to the dock. Jumping out with their spears, Maricar and Ning-Ning tied the bow and stern. Children swarmed all around, chatting and bouncing up and down.

As Bogtong got out, he tipped the canoe.

Wilbur clutched the hull rim, thankful he wasn't pitched into the water.

"Mister Cobb, stay where you are."

"That wasn't the deal, Bogtong." He stood to step out of the canoe. "I'm going with you."

"Maricar," Bogtong shouted. "See that he stays put."

The natives crossed long spears in front of him, blocking his way onto the dock. Those fierce eyes again dared him to disobey.

If he had his .38, they'd be treating him with a little more respect. "What are you trying to pull, Bogtong?"

"Let me get an eye on the situation. I'll tell you when it is safe to approach the Panglima."

"Don't be long." Wilbur plopped down on the plank. The Panglima must have one hell of a bad temper.

Bogtong's white form trudged up the path. The natives stood guard, spears at the ready while naked children crowded in, begging with outstretched hands.

Wilbur checked his pockets for candy or gum but he had nothing to give them.

Except...all these conch shells.

He started handing them out. Kids squealed with delight, and more came running. Maricar and Ning-ning glanced at each other and shrugged, seemingly at a loss as to whether they should intervene. Bogtong wasn't around to tell them what to do.

The canoe emptied quickly.

By then, Bogtong came running back down the path. He was breathless when he reached the canoe. "Mister Cobb. It is magnificent."

"What?"

Gasping, "I have seen it with my own eyes." He bumped aside the native guards. "Come. The Panglima will see you now."

Wilbur's curiosity spiked. He climbed out of the canoe.

Bogtong's eyes scanned the empty hull. Excitement drained from his face, now replaced with puzzlement. "The conch shells are gone."

Wilbur pointed to the children, some on the shore filling their shells with sand, others knee deep in the creek, scooping up water with their new prized possessions. How such a simple gift brought so much joy.

"Oh." Excitement returned to Bogtong's eyes. "That's okay. The Panglima has something much better now." He tugged Wilbur's arm. "You must see this pearl."

"Pearl?"

"After three days on the porch..." he gasped, "the *taklobo* began to stink, so the Panglima sent his servants out to gut and clean the shells. They found inside a giant pearl." Bogtong made motions with his hands like he was plying a melon.

He had to be exaggerating.

"Etem must've seen it, reached in to take it..."

Wilbur got the picture. The diver risked his life for a pearl and lost. Must be one hell of a pearl. "Let's go."

Bogtong took point. Maricar and Ning-ning followed

behind.

At the Panglima's house, preparations for a celebratory meal were already underway, bamboo chairs and place settings at an outside picnic table. Red and white-checkered tablecloth, smoldering brick charcoal pit, the place looked a lot like a backyard barbeque back home. Even the black Plymouth parked in the driveway fit into the American scene nicely.

However, a clutch of natives carrying long spears looked out of place. They wore feathered skirts and beaded necklaces and began to dance to the bang of gongs and pounding drums. Maricar and Ning-ning jumped in, pitching their spears high and low while twirling and stomping their bare feet in the dirt.

"Spear dance," Bogtong said into Wilbur's ear. "Watch and enjoy. Then we will have tea."

"Tea?"

"Afterwards, we will eat. Accept the Panglima's generosity with grace and humility, in Allah's name. Say nothing of the giant clam you came to see until I give you a signal." He tipped his straw hat. "Hospitality before business. You don't want to offend the Panglima." Bogtong made a slicing motion across his throat.

Wilbur swallowed. His adventure was getting more adventurous. And dangerous.

He followed Bogtong toward the table. Looking over the seated natives, Wilbur tried to figure out which one was the famous and feared Panglima. Six men sat facing the spear dancers. They wore colorful bandana head-wraps and long-sleeved flannel shirts with the buttons buttoned clear up to the collars. Two natives stood watch behind them, Winchester long rifles strapped across their backs, bandoleers crisscrossing their bare chests and holstered pistols at their hips, like some kind of jungle Brunos.

"Sit there." Bogtong pointed to a chair at the end of the table. "Reserved for special guests. But do not acknowledge the Panglima. Do not look at him."

"Which one is he?"

"He's wearing the red bandana. Mind your plate and the entertainment."

The gongs and drums took on an ominous beat, like

Wilbur's heart. What had he gotten himself into?

He sat in the appointed chair. Bogtong took a seat to Wilbur's left, his back to the dancers.

Wilbur chanced a glance at the man wearing the red bandana. He sat with his back straight and proud, an old man in native years, maybe forty with a scruffy chin beard and deep-set dark eyes. On his right sat a boy, maybe ten years old, baby-faced with a handsome nose.

Bogtong leaned to Wilbur and whispered. "That is the Panglima's son, Pula."

Fearing to press his luck, Wilbur blinked and diverted his eyes back to the spear dancers.

Two shirtless scrawny natives wearing open Western vests and brown shorts walked around pouring tea into everyone's cups. The servants differentiated themselves from the other natives by the way they combed their ratty hair, parted down the middle.

Spear dance over, the gongs and drums fell silent. A native with a Brownie camera flitted about taking pictures of the festivity-goers.

The Panglima stood. "*Maligayang pagdating*, Mister Cobb." Welcome.

Expecting a meal before getting down to business, a pang of uncertainty hit Wilbur. He shifted his eyes from the Panglima to Bogtong, who tipped his straw hat.

Wilbur hoped to keep his ignorance of native customs from showing. He stood to address his host. "Sir—"

The crowd murmured.

The armed natives stepped forward, hands on their pistols.

The Panglima glared at him from under harsh brows.

Wilbur swallowed his fear. "Panglima..." He bowed his head. "I'm sorry for the loss of your diver, Etem."

The Panglima's eyes softened. He waved off his bad boys. "Bogtong tells me you wish to see a clam that killed a man."

"I'd like to tell the story to the world."

"You are a writer?"

"Yes. Travel and historical." Sounded better than a geologist who worked for a company that would rape the land beneath their feet.

The Panglima signaled one of the servant natives. He made a whooping call toward the house. Another servant came out carrying what looked like a large white rock. It must've been heavy because he carried it with both hands, and as he set it on the table in front of Wilbur, it landed with a solid clunk.

He could hardly believe his eyes.

The Panglima swelled up like a Palawan peacock. "I present to you the Pearl of Allah."

The lumpy gem glowed with a bright, pearly sheen. It had to be the largest pearl ever found, maybe ten inches long and eighteen inches around and looked like a deformed brain, but as he examined it more closely, he could see the likeness of a crooked-eyed face and a turban-wrapped head.

"The Pearl of Allah?"

The Brownie clicked a picture.

Wilbur touched the pearlescent surface, felt suddenly faint. Weak-kneed. He reseated himself and stared at a pearl so grand that it could have come from the pages of the greatest adventure novel ever written. What would people back in the states pay to see such a wonder? A dollar?

Two servants approached lugging the giant clamshell. The possibilities just kept getting better. The killer clam and the world's largest pearl together had to be worth five dollars a person. Surely, any man who possessed such splendor would be rich. He'd be famous.

Wilbur's pulse raced with excitement. "I would like to buy this pearl." He looked up at the Panglima standing there beaming with pride.

"It is not for sale."

"Name your price."

The Panglima returned to his seat. All eyes riveted on him. "It would be sacrilege for me to part with this pearl formed by God in the image of Mohammed, Allah's great profit, and earned by the sacrifice of Etem's blood. I defy the richest men in the world to show me a similar pearl. The satisfaction of owning such a treasure is worth more than money."

That wasn't what Wilbur wanted to hear. He started to his feet again when Bogtong grabbed Wilbur's arm. "Let it go."

The servants hustled the pearl and clamshells away.

Gongs and drums started up again.

Disappointment at seeing his vision of fortune and fame slip away, Wilbur had to admire the Panglima's religious resolve. These natives would hoard one of the world's greatest treasures, and there was nothing he could do about it.

A scream pierced the air.

Wilbur flinched, looked to the path where a thin native boy wearing only shorts stood by a bicycle tipped on its side at his feet. Tears streamed down his face. "Give it back to the sea."

Again the drums and gongs fell silent.

Bogtong leaned into Wilbur. "That is Timoteo."

"It killed my father," the boy shouted.

What was a kid doing this far back in the jungle? "How could he ride a bike from the village?"

"There is a road through the trees. A very short distance compared to the winding creek."

Breathless from running, a woman rushed up behind Timoteo.

The natives gasped.

Curly hair hung to her shoulders. She wore a skirt high enough to reveal her calves and a blouse low enough to reveal her cleavage. The natives stared at her in stunned disbelief.

She bent to the boy and lifted him from the dirt. "I am so sorry for the interruption."

She grabbed up the bike and fled with the kicking boy.

"Give it back to the sea," the boy shouted.

Only then did Wilbur realize his mouth hung open. His heart beat hard, and his curiosity piqued for this Palawan princess.

"That, my American friend, was Liawayway," Bogtong whispered. "Etem's widow."

Wilbur blinked. He'd never seen a native woman so beautiful. "What's her story?"

"She's spoken for."

"So soon? Her husband just died."

"The young pearler Maricar is her new keeper."

"That knife happy punk—"

"The Panglima has ordered this."

"I'd like to talk to her."

"There is not enough time to arrange it. You are leaving tomorrow. You can meet her when you return."

"That could be never."

"Then you are out of luck."

Disappointment weighed heavy on his chest, but only for a moment. The servant with the Brownie was rounding up everyone for photographs with Wilbur.

Finding his Palawan princess would have to wait.

Chapter Ten

Wanping, China, July 7, 1937

Beyond the walls of the Wanping fortress, along the fertile banks of the Yongding River not far from Beijing, small farms checkered the countryside. As most farmers in China were tenants of the land, Moy Yong and his wife, Moy Lei, tilled the soil and planted yams and barley. They eked out a living for their family: one teenage daughter, Moy Rea, and their ten-year-old son, Moy Linshin. On this hot July night while sitting at the dinner table, Linshin's stomach boiled with gas pains. He stared into his plate of noodles and fish and hoped he wouldn't soil his shorts. He would ask to go to the outhouse to relieve himself, but it was improper to leave the table before bàba Yong had finished his meal.

"Linshin, you are not eating." Māma Lei reached for the bowl of noodles. "Yong, your son has not labored hard enough today." She spooned more noodles onto her plate. "He has not worked up an appetite."

Bàba Yong continued eating without looking up.

Hurry, my father. Linshin had worked plenty hard weeding the field, but he shouldn't have dug up a yam root for a midday snack. The stomachache he'd gotten from the theft quickly became a punishment more than he could bear.

Rea held out her hand for the bowl. "I will have his."

Māma Lei obliged her. "At least the food won't go to waste."

The boom of canon fire echoed from a distance. Linshin squeezed his butt cheeks.

Bàba Yong stopped eating. "Damn Japanese."

Linshin cringed. *Don't talk, bàba. Eat.*

"Why must they practice their war maneuvers at night?" Yong waved his spoon. "They know it puts everyone on edge."

Māma Lei glanced to the window where distant flashes lit the darkness. "The guns are closer tonight. The explosions are louder."

The only explosion Linshin worried over was the blast about to take place in his chair.

"There was no announcement," Māma Lei said. "The Japanese agreed to warn us before maneuvers."

"We should have beaten them back in Manchuria." The anger in Bàba Yong's voice echoed the feelings of most Chinese. "Now they think they own everything." He was active in the resistance and supported the National Revolutionary Army. "What is next? Beijing?"

"Eat your supper, Yong."

Linshin agreed with Māma Lei.

"What's done is done." She spooned fish.

Bàba Yong began eating again.

Thank you. Thank you. Thank you, my father. Iron fists squeezed Linshin's insides. How could he hold on until bàba's plate was empty?

"You too, Linshin." Māma Lei's eyes seemed blind to his distress. "Eat."

A loud explosion rattled the house.

Linshin almost dumped his bowels.

Bàba Yong dropped his spoon. "Go look, Rea." He pointed to the window. "See what is happening."

Rea dashed from her chair and looked out. "The Luguoqiao Bridge."

Distant gunfire rattled.

"They are fighting."

Māma Lei rushed to Rea's side and peered out the glass. "Trucks are coming."

Bàba pushed back his chair and stood. "Get away from the window." He took two steps to the cabinet and removed a pistol.

Linshin saw his chance to escape. "Bàba." He bowed and ran for the door.

"Where are you going?"

"I'll be right back." Linshin burst into the night, the

horizon ablaze. Wanping fortress was burning. Fire silhouetted the stone outhouse twenty steps away.

"Come back here," Māma Lei cried.

Every muscle in Linshin's body begged for release.

Ten steps.

His stomach felt on fire.

Five.

Trucks roared down the road, headlights bouncing, coming toward the farm.

He made the outhouse. Pants down. His butt found the porcelain-rimmed hole in the floor. A wave of diarrhea shot out.

Sweet relief.

The stone outhouse had no door but faced away from the farmhouse. Dark woods of Acer bushes and bamboo stretched in front of him. Sounds came from behind him: truck engines roaring in, dirt crunching, brakes squawking, voices shouting gibberish.

A second wave of diarrhea chilled him. He wished for the burning grip on his stomach to end.

Gunfire popped.

His father's voice shouted, "How dare you—"

A gunshot. A woman screamed.

Was it Māma Lei or Rea? What was happening? Vomit climbed Linshin's throat. Diarrhea spewed again.

Men laughed.

He clenched his fists. Swallowed hard. One breath. Two breaths. Push. He had to finish. He had to get back to the house.

Breaking glass. Breaking dishes.

Rae's shrill voice filled the night. "Leave māma alone. Don't touch her."

Linshin couldn't breathe.

Men's voices. Demanding. Laughing.

He pulled up his shorts and jumped from the outhouse.

Trucks rumbled down the road. Some towed canons on wheels, backwards. Tanks clattered by, turrets sweeping back and forth. This time Linshin's guts ached for a different reason.

Fear.

Keeping low, he stumbled toward the house. A truck idled in front, big claw-like tires, a canvas top cover, and a big red dot on the cab door, visible in the light cast from the house as a soldier stepped outside, zipping his pants.

Truck headlights revealed other soldiers standing around smoking.

Sobs drew Linshin's attention to the broken dining room window. Heart racing, he slinked to the sill and peered over.

Bàba Yong lay sprawled in a heap on the floor, his head concealed by a toppled chair. On the dinner table, naked Māma Lei kicked her feet under the weight of a soldier lying on top of her, his pants to his knees, his butt muscles flexing with sharp jabbing thrusts.

Horror gripped Linshin. Never before had he seen such an act. Man on woman. Flesh on flesh. Brutal. Defiling. He wanted to kill the soldier, but with what? These small hands? Powerless hands. If only he had a gun.

Tears of helplessness burned his eyes.

Rea cried out.

He cranked his head to see in the kitchen. Rea sat in a chair, her bare knees facing him, a soldier straddling her, his crotch in her face, pumping his hips. She gagged with each plunge. At the foot of her chair, bàba's severed head stared up at the atrocity being committed on his daughter.

A wave of numbing horror seized Linshin. What could he do to save her?

The soldier on the table climbed off Māma Lei. Blood leaked from her slack mouth. Her eyes stared out blankly. Another soldier climbed on top of her, started humping her like a dog.

No, māma, please no.

Rea made choking sounds. The soldier grabbed her hair and slammed her face into this crotch.

Something inside Linshin snapped, perhaps the fine line that separated human from animal. Hot anger replaced the gaseous pains in his stomach. All sense of time and place blurred into a scream like no scream he'd ever screamed.

The soldier jumped off Rea, whirled around, devil eyes seeking the screamer.

Rea shouted, "Run, Linshin, run."

The soldier on top of Māma Lei rolled off and grabbed for

the gun belt hanging around his knees.

Linshin ducked below the sill, his eyes so filled with tears he could hardly see the soldiers running toward him from the truck.

Gunshots exploded from inside the house. Bullets shredded the windowsill.

"Run, Linshin, run."

An inner strength possessed him, powered by fear and hate, he ran for the woods.

Gunfire popped.

Keeping to the shadows, he veered side to side through the planted yams, sobbing and gasping, his legs agile and quick as a deer. Bullets zinged past him and spit dirt at his feet. His once loose bowels were now wrapped tight as bamboo shoots.

He made it to the trees, crashing through brambles and tripping over roots.

Soldiers raced after him, shouting and shooting.

Linshin knew these woods. He stayed right, ran past the old weeping Ficus tree and around the bend to a thicket of Acers in the woods behind the outhouse.

Breathing deep and slow, he knelt out of sight and watched the soldiers return from the trees and gather around their leader. He pointed toward the woods and barked orders. Soldiers scattered, running toward the outhouse with flashlight beams sweeping the trees.

Other soldiers dragged Rea from the house and lifted her into the back of a truck. Her kicking and screaming provoked the soldiers to laughter. Where were they taking her? He wanted to shout, "Rea," run to her, rescue her from the soldiers, but if he did, they'd kill him like they killed his father. Cut off his head...

Dogs barked.

Panic shivered up his back.

Silhouettes in the headlights revealed dogs sniffing the ground, tails up, moving with the soldiers toward the outhouse.

Toward his sanctuary in the woods.

He could hide from the soldiers but not the dogs. They'd sniff him out, for sure.

There was nothing he could do but run.

Chapter Eleven

Itching. His arms. His back. Itching. Like his skin crawled with ants. Biting ants. Linshin popped open his eyes.

An old man looked down at him, conical straw hat tilted on his head. An odd slant on his thin mouth. A gray, pointy chin beard hung to his chest. He wore heavy robes of purple and yellow and leaned on a twisted walking stick. "I thought you were dead, boy."

Lying in prickly weeds alongside a road, Linshin realized his mouth tasted like dirt. How did he get here? What..? He remembered his bàba. Dead. His māma. Dying. His sister. Screaming. Loaded into a truck like looted merchandise. His family. Gone. He wished it was a horrible dream. He tested his voice. "Did you see the soldiers?"

"The Japanese passed through last night. I hid in a barn."

"I have to go home." Linshin struggled to his feet.

"Easy, boy." The old man steadied him. "What is your hurry?"

He looked the old man over. "Do you have a gun?"

"Oh my. No gun. What would you do with a gun?"

"Kill Japanese soldiers."

"A high aim for one so small."

"They took my sister. I've got to find her. Have you seen her?"

"No, no sister."

Dizzy with images of last night's horrors, Linshin scanned the area, the trees, the path he'd taken from the farm, the ditch where he'd hidden and where he'd fallen asleep.

"I'm going back."

He set out, retracing his steps, only this time without all the cutbacks he'd taken to throw off the dogs.

The Pearl of Death

"Wait up." The old man moved swiftly for his age. "It is unwise to go back. Go forward. Always forward."

Linshin led the old man to the woods by the outhouse and knelt behind the Acers where he'd knelt the night before. The truck was gone. A curtain flapped from the gaping broken window that had revealed horrors no boy should ever witness.

The Japanese were gone.

Nerves a-jitter with dread, he moved toward the house where two heads were skewered on spikes planted in the ground on each side of the open front door as if left to stand guard. The faces were bruised and bloodied but recognizable, the faces of his bàba and Māma Lei, their drooping eyes wrenched in agony.

Flies buzzed in and out of their open mouths.

Linshin's stomach knotted. His knees buckled, and he retched in the dirt with hacking heaves of vomit between gasps of air, his mind a smear of confusion and loathing and guilt. If only he wasn't ten. If only he was strong. If only...if only... He looked up at the old man. "See what they did?" Linshin croaked out. "They killed them."

The old man's face whitened with shock. His eyes were dead holes. "Stories I have heard, Japanese cutting off heads and spiking them this way. Lined the streets of Shanghai, thousands in a row."

Fists clenching dirt, Linshin fought for his next strangled breath. "Why?"

The old man set a trembling hand on Linshin's back. "Hell has come to China."

"Māma. Māma Lei." Tears gushed from Linshin's eyes. Ran down his face. Mixed with the dust and vomit and the stink of death wafting through the air. "Bàba."

"Get hold of yourself, boy."

"What am I to do?"

The old man grabbed Linshin's arm with surprising strength and pulled him to his feet. "Come with me and find stillness."

"You are a stranger."

"My name is Share Lew Shī, the wandering priest of Wong Lung Kwan."

Linshin had heard of the school for Taoist priests high in

the mountains. "You are a master?"

"And a good teacher, I have been told." Share Lew tapped his walking stick on the ground. "We go now. There is nothing left for you here." He turned toward the woods.

"But my sister. I must find her."

Share Lew stopped but didn't turn around. "You will never see her again."

"You cannot know that."

He spoke to his feet. "The Japanese have taken her with other young women...to comfort the soldiers."

"Comfort?"

"Rape. Surely you are old enough to know what that means."

Moy Linshin had seen Japanese comfort with his own eyes.

"The soldiers will kill her when they have had their fill. You cannot stop what will happen. It is the Way of the Tao."

Linshin imagined Rea's head on a spike, too. "The Tao is cruel."

"The Tao is eternal."

A knot of despair gripped him. He glanced up at his bàba and māma to ask them what he should do but quickly diverted his eyes away, unable to look at their frightful faces for even a second.

He never felt so alone, so lost, so sick to his stomach disgusted and afraid, but perhaps the Tao had brought Master Lew into his life for a reason.

Chapter Twelve

A torturous mountain path stretched before Moy Linshin, winding upward through a forest of green pines and Chinese redbuds. The apricot fragrance of Osmanthus flowers should have had a soothing effect, but nothing could ease the pain in his heart for the loss of his family.

He took each treacherous step with care. More than once his feet had slipped on the loose stones, which caused him to fall and rip his only pair of pants. Ahead of him, Share Lew Shī trudged uphill with barely a labored breath. They had traveled many days to reach this mountain, and still their final destination seemed unreachable.

"How much farther?"

The master kept climbing.

"What will we do when we get there?"

Nothing.

"Will I learn about the Tao? What is the Tao?"

Share Lew stopped climbing and stroked his gray chinbeard. "The Tao is interconnected with all things in the universe, an inseparable organic unity that maintains its own harmony and balance."

"I don't like it already."

He resumed his climb. "The way of the Tao is not always the easy way."

Linshin grunted. *No easier than this hike up Mount Luofu.* He slipped and skinned his knee where the pants were torn. Master Lew kept moving upward. He didn't look back. If Linshin didn't rise on his own, the old priest would leave him to die on this path. If that too was the way of the Tao, then what was the purpose of this journey?

On his feet again, he hurried to catch up, but his young

body was no match for the Taoist master who forged ahead like a mountain goat. He'd claimed to be one hundred and two years old and credited his longevity and good health to the spring-fed well of Wong Lung Kwan.

Moy Linshin licked his dry lips. Right about now he could use a healthy drink of that water.

Around the next twist in the path, Linshin caught up with Master Lew, only because he'd stopped walking. He stood before a towering granite archway over the path. Carved in the rock, two dragons faced each other, both reared up on their hind legs. They appeared to be reaching up for or tussling over a strangely shaped object suspended in midair between them.

Linshin stared up at the mammoth gateway and fought to get his wind. "What is it?"

"The Pearl of Lao-Tzu." Master Lew's voice was a whisper.

The object wasn't round and smooth but ugly-oval and lumpy. "That doesn't look like a pearl."

"Things don't always appear as they should."

Beyond the stone gateway, white walls and overhanging roofs of the monastery buildings rose up the mountainside on terraces of stone, lavishly garnished with plum, peach, and Yulan magnolia trees, many blooming pink, purple, and yellow. Glorious waterfalls spilled into ponds where red and white lotuses competed for the beauty. Never had he seen such wonder.

Share Lew planted his walking stick. "Welcome to Wong Lung Kwan."

Linshin felt small.

Share Lew leaned on his stick. "Twenty-five hundred years ago, Lao-Tzu left this mountain, disgusted with the greed and corruption of men." Reenacting the event, Share Lew moved under the archway. "Before Lao-Tzu passed here, the gatekeeper asked him to leave behind his wisdom, write it down so that men should know it forever. Lao-Tzu dismounted his yak..." Share Lew mimicked the action. "...and wrote eighty-one verses of the Way and the Law." He made scribbling motions on the palm of his hand. "Then the old sage rode off toward the valley, never to return."

Linshin followed the master down the path. "What

happened to him?"

"No one knows."

They came upon a pavilion sheltering the statue of a man with crossed arms. He wore long robes and a twisted hair bonnet.

Linshin shrunk back. "Is it Lao-Tzu?"

"Wei T'o." Lew bowed before the statue. "God of the teachings and protector of the books."

Linshin cowered in the shadow of Wei T'o.

Master Lew raised his walking stick to the monastery beyond. "There are many schools here, thirty-six halls, nine temples, and six palaces. This is where you will stay with the other students and monks."

Linshin could hardly breathe. A life far different from the farm. How would he ever fit in?

"You will learn medicine and science, art and music, mathematics and history, not only history of the world but of Taoism, as well, and the teachings of Lao-Tzu and the martial arts, both Shaolin and Wudang Kungfu."

Making a fist, "I will be a master, too." Linshin threw a couple of fast air punches. "Like you."

"Easy, my young apprentice. There is more to fighting than fighting." Master Lew put the walking stick to the ground. "Follow me for your first lesson."

Terry Wright

Chapter Thirteen

Palawan, PI, April 1939

Wilbur Cobb gazed out the windscreen of the Fokker Trimotor and watched the rocky coves and sandy beaches of Palawan slide beneath the groaning airplane. It had been five years since his last expedition to this island, since he'd seen the Mohammedan chief's sacred pearl, since he'd lived the adventure that played in his mind daily. Now he was back to lay claim to the natives' land in the name of Benguet Consolidated Mining Company.

Beyond the left wing, clear to the horizon, the Sulu Sea sparkled under a blazing tropical sun. Submerged reefs and coral atolls held untold treasures. Off to his right, rugged mountains jutted skyward, smothered under a carpet of tropical rainforests. A vast ecological frontier.

"What do ya think of them Japanese?" the pilot shouted over the roaring engines. "First Manchuria, now China. You heard what they done in Nanking? Won't be long before them bastards decide to take over the Philippines."

"Attack an American colony?" Wilbur shouted back. "They wouldn't dare."

"They think their emperor is a god. Nothin' they won't do for him."

Looking out the window, Wilbur recalled how the United States had purchased the islands from Spain, after the Spanish-American War—for a whopping twenty million dollars. Besides being a mecca for timber, the Philippines had become second in world gold production, after California, and held the world's largest deposits of iron ore. It was easy to understand why the Japanese would want to pinch these resources for their war effort, but the United States was here, stealing them first.

The plane took a jolt of rough air. Wilbur's stomach lurched, the noise and vibrations a perpetual assault on his body.

He looked back through the open cockpit bulkhead to the men strapped to webbed seats in the cabin. They wore fatigues, army combat boots, and bushman hats, the preferred team uniform, except the medic. Bambi. He wore a tie, a swirl of rainbow colors.

"You guys all right?" Wilbur shouted.

"When we gonna get there, Mom?"

"I gotta take a pee," Bambi chimed in.

"Smartasses."

The pilot chuckled. "We should be landing in Puerto Princesa..." he checked his instruments, "...in about ten minutes. Are you sure you brought the right equipment?"

"We could use a better plane."

Benguet had the best equipment and the best geologists, geophysicists, and mapmakers in the world. Ten of them were sitting behind him. They had enough equipment and supplies to last three months in the jungle—including plenty of ammunition to defend themselves against wild beasts and anti-American rebels. And if those dangers weren't enough threat to his mission, there were the mosquitoes. Bambi brought along plenty of atabrine to treat the malaria that kept most outsiders away from Palawan. However, in spite of his best efforts, Wilbur worried that some of his team might not make it back to Manila alive.

As the fifteen-year-old wooden airplane beat his nerves to a pulp, he wondered about the adventures that lay ahead. Seemed nothing could surpass his last visit to Palawan. After the Panglima's celebration, he'd left the island in the same manner in which he'd arrived. Quietly.

He had taken with him to Manila a fabulous story of a man-killer clam, an unbelievable pearl, and a beautiful Palawan princess. One day he would tell it to the world. Someday he'd return to San Francisco, tuck two dames under his arms, and book speaking engagements in all the big cities, coast to coast.

Until then, this was the life of a rock-hunting adventurer. Sweltering jungles. Sweaty men. And daydreams. He hadn't seen a white woman in ten years.

"Ever been to Palawan?" the pilot shouted.

"Third time."

"The French-bred women here are the most beautiful in the Philippines."

No argument there. Liawayway. Hard to forget that name, sort of rolled off the tongue. *Liawayway.* He wondered whatever happened to her.

The pilot leered. "You like them, yes?"

"Rule number one. Never get involved with the natives."

Shuddering, the plane banked right and flew low over the water. The right wing engine started banging as if it were about to come unglued. Blue smoke spewed from the exhaust.

Every muscle in Wilbur's body stiffened. "What the hell?"

"Damn thing." The pilot grunted as he pumped the fuel primer on the floorboard. "They told me it was fixed."

The engine coughed and sputtered. Flames shot out the pipes. The plane bobbed in the air like a wounded duck.

Swallowing hard, Wilbur looked down at the water and held his breath. Thirty-two, he was too young to die.

With a pop, the engine caught its noisy rhythm again. The pilot leveled the plane and cast Wilbur an uneasy grin. "See. No problem."

Wilbur breathed again. Another hair-raising tale for his adventure tour.

The pilot pointed out the windscreen. "There it is...Puerto Princesa."

Wilbur stretched his neck to see over the nose cowling and through the center engine's whirling propeller. Ahead lay a clutch of thatch-roofed shacks built on stilts and jammed against the shore, so close together they looked shipwrecked.

Dozens of rickety boats floated in brown, greasy water.

On shore, the pointed roofs of Spanish-style buildings with arched windows rose above dense foliage interspersed with dozens of Nepa huts scattered about like tossed dice.

The roaring plane overflew the clutter and on to the bay where rowboats and US battleships shared the waterway. The semblance of a city took shape. Dilapidated flat-board buildings with glinting tin roofs lined a main street clogged with open-air buggies and canopy trucks.

Wilbur smiled. Another adventure begins.

Weaving drunkenly over a dirt runway, the plane slammed down with a bone-jarring bang. The tail wheel hit the ground, and the brakes squealed.

"You ought'a get that fixed too," Wilbur shouted.

The plane careened off the runway and turned around. Wilbur's eyes burned from oily smoke that leaked into the cabin. The cackle of idling radial engines hurt his ears.

"See...we made it just fine." The pilot pointed the nose toward a corrugated steel building. He had to lean his head out the window to see where he was going. "They are waiting for you already."

The seat rattled. Wilbur clenched his jaw and wished for the beating to end. By the time the plane stopped and the engines shut off, he was ready to jump out and kiss the ground.

Six trucks pulled up. The men went to work unloading equipment from the cargo hold and piling it into the truck beds. A map was spread out on a hood. "We'll take this cut here," one man said and pointed his lit pipe toward the nearby mountain. "The bend in this river will make for a good base camp." He looked up. "Where is the fuel truck?"

Wilbur swatted a mosquito on his neck, the first of thousands to die in this manner. The hot and muggy air was abuzz with the little bastards.

"Bambi." He hated shouting the medic's nickname. "Put the medical supplies in the panel van over there. See if there's room left for the seismometer." Walking through the throng of moving men and supplies, Wilbur batted at the rising dust and wished for a scotch.

Horn honking, a Desoto truck approached, blue with a green canvas roof. He counted the vehicles he had on site. Six. Yes. They were all here. So who was this?

The truck stopped. A man jumped out, a local, Wilbur knew, by his short Filipino stature. He wore sweat-stained white clothes, a silly straw hat, and black loafers, an oddly familiar native with thin glasses that rode low on the bridge of his nose.

Niggling worry rose in Wilbur's gut. He stopped and watched the man approach the pilot standing under the wing.

"Where can I find Mister Cobb? Do you know him?"

Wilbur groaned. Bogtong.

The pilot pointed at Wilbur and grinned.

"Thanks a lot," Wilbur mumbled. What the hell was it this time?

As Bogtong approached at a brisk gait, he waved. "Mister Cobb. Wilbur Cobb?"

"What are you doing here?"

The native doctor smelled of sweat and dust. "Thank Allah I have found you." He removed his hat and held it waist high with both hands. "Would you have a Coca-Cola? I am very thirsty." He drew a soiled sleeve across his sweating brow.

"We have water."

"A Coke would be better."

"And I'd rather have a shot of scotch." A case of it was buried among these supplies somewhere. "Bambi," Wilbur called out. "Water for our friend."

Bambi delivered a canteen. "I hear you're a doctor."

"University of Manila, thank you." Bogtong guzzled the water, much of it leaking down his chin and the front of his shirt.

"I'm going to be a doctor someday too."

Bogtong handed Bambi the canteen. "Good for you."

Wilbur exchanged glances with Bambi. "Are you guys done yakking?"

"Sorry, bwana."

"Enough with the bwana crap." *Whap!* Wilbur killed another mosquito.

The plane was nearly unloaded. It was time to get going before they ran out of daylight. "I'm busy, Bogtong. What is it you want?"

"Yes, of course." Bogtong smacked his lips. "You have brought with you the drug atabrine?"

"Of course."

"I need it."

It was hot and dusty, and Wilbur's patience was about to crack. "What for?"

Bogtong's eyes narrowed. "Over the last five years, half our tribe has died from malaria. It is like a plague on our Dyak village. Death is everywhere...since the Panglima acquired the

Pearl of Allah. And now his son has fallen ill."

Wilbur remembered the boy, Pula.

"A very severe case. Quinine is ineffective."

Tough break. "I can't give you our atabrine."

"Then Pula will die."

Dying children were a fact of life on these islands. However, the son of a Panglima wasn't just any child. The future of an entire tribe could hinge on his survival.

Wilbur felt torn. He had his team to worry about. Three months in the jungle. He would need the atabrine for his men. Or himself. But his Dyak friends and the Panglima were in dire need right now. Helping them could win Wilbur many favors. Still, he had an expedition to run, a timetable to keep. The natives would have to fend for themselves. He tipped his bushman hat to Bogtong. "I've got to get back to work." Wilbur walked toward the plane.

The doctor dogged along. "The Panglima begs you."

Wilbur pictured the proud chief on bended knees, how humiliating and humbling that must feel. Leader of the Dyaks. Father of a dying boy. Begging for help. He was a big enough man to do that, but Wilbur wasn't his salvation.

"You must help him," Bogtong said.

Wilbur grabbed the doctor's arm and yanked him to a stop. "Why me? Why does he beg me? The Navy is stationed here. Their ships are in the harbor, and what about the local hospital, the clinics? Why not them?"

"I have tried. There is no atabrine on the island. Only quinine. The Navy won't talk to me. My order to Manila for the drug will take too long. Pula will die before supplies reach the village. You are the Panglima's only hope."

Wilbur kicked dirt. Digging out that case of scotch sounded pretty good right now.

"Trouble, boss?"

Wilbur looked at the concerned faces of his men gathering around.

"What else is new?"

"Our chief's son is dying." Bogtong appealed to the men. "I'm asking Mister Cobb to help."

"He wants our atabrine." Surely his men would understand.

The men looked at each other, said nothing.

"Come with me to the village, Mr. Cobb." Bogtong clasped his hands together, begging style. "See the dire need for yourself."

Bambi jumped in. "Public relations work, boss. It's only a small delay."

Of course the Filipino medic would side with the Filipino doctor. His men nodding in agreement surprised him, though.

"You guys are okay with this?"

"It's a boy's life," one of them piped up.

Another followed with, "Let him have my atabrine."

"Mine, too."

Wilbur didn't like the way the men looked at him expectantly. If he didn't go, the boy would die, and somehow it would be Wilbur's fault. So he'd better go. Maybe he'd get another look at the Panglima's pearl. And the Palawan princess. Liawayway. Might be worth the trip after all.

Wilbur put a solid arm around Bambi's shoulders and glanced at his men. "All right. We'll meet you guys at the river bend base camp."

Bambi scrunched his face. "We?"

"You just volunteered to go with us."

"Me?"

"You're the medic. Get the atabrine."

"Yes, bwana."

"And while you're at it, find my case of scotch."

Bogtong put on his hat. "I will drive."

Chapter Fourteen

The mudslinging ride south took more than four hours, including a rest stop in Aborlan and evening prayers in Narra. Wilbur guessed Bogtong had a Coke problem. He couldn't pass a vendor without buying one or two. The floorboards were littered with rattling bottles.

As night fell, the sweeping beacon from Light House Tower on Brooke's Point shined through the trees. Wilbur looked at Bambi snoozing in the back, his tie askew, his olive limbs smeared with greasy insect repellant that shined in the moonlight. Next to him sat a brown box marked *Atabrine*. One box. It was all the team could spare. Wilbur hoped it would be enough.

The Desoto rumbled down into the Dyak village. Wilbur's stomach grumbled. "We should find a place to eat."

"There is a shucking feast tonight, in the village center, for the pearl divers of Boligay. Big pots of boiled clam, fish, oysters, corn and potatoes...lots to drink and—"

"Stop it." Wilbur's appetite was excited enough.

Bambi stirred, stretched. "Count me in."

"We must see the Panglima first." Bogtong steered onto a road lined with huts and shacks aglow under yellow street lamps. Sun-bronzed children darted through the headlight beams and squealed. A growling dog chased the truck, snapping at the tires. Smoke from wood fires drifted across the road.

The two-story house came into view, all the windows brightly lit. Bogtong turned into the drive and parked next to a black Plymouth.

"I will go first." Bogtong got out. "Wait here."

Wilbur watched him charge up the porch steps. Boligay Creek gurgled in the background. He remembered walking up the hill to this house five years ago, his chest filled with expectation and excitement. Now it felt heavy with worry.

The door creaked open throwing light across the driveway. A hunched servant appeared. Bogtong spoke to him in Tagalog. *"Magandang gabi."* Good evening.

"Tuloy. Please, come in."

"Where is the Panglima?"

"He is with Pula."

Bogtong waved Wilbur to come on.

He got out of the truck and took the brown box from the back. Another moment of nostalgia struck him as he spotted the picnic table and barbeque pit set about in shadow. Memories swam in his head. The spear dancers. The pearl. The Palawan princess. He inhaled a steeling breath and joined Bogtong at the front doors.

Bambi arrived with the doctor's black bag.

Stepping inside the house, Wilbur removed his bushman hat and felt as if he'd entered the Wild West. A Navajo rug lay on the hardwood floor, and on the walls hung paintings of cowboys and Indians. The sweet smell of rawhide filled the air.

Feeling off-kilter from culture shock, Wilbur followed Bogtong and the servants upstairs to a small bedroom. Inside, an oscillating fan whirred from a corner table. A woman wearing a sweat-stained dress and headscarf sat on a low bed, sobbing. The Panglima sat next to her, hunched over and praying, "Allah, please do not forsake me."

The bitter odor of bile stunk the air.

On the bed lay the teenager, Pula, unrecognizable from the boy Wilbur remembered, a strapping ten-year-old sitting next to his father at the celebration. Now a white towel lay on his forehead. Sweat shined on his thin and shaking body, only clad in wet underwear. Sunken eyes looked up from a ghastly greenish yellow face.

"Mister Cobb." He breathed. "Help. Help me. I am dying."

Handing Bogtong the box of atabrine, Wilbur felt pity worm in his chest. He'd seen a lot of sick natives, poverty, and human hardship during his travels. It made him feel helpless. And angry. These people prayed to Allah, and Allah dished out misery in return.

The Pearl of Death

Lifting Pula's wrist, the heat of fever gave Wilbur a chill. A weak pulse gave him cause for despair. "My God."

The Panglima looked up with desperate eyes. "Can you save my son?"

Having experience with the disease on jungle expeditions all over the world, Wilbur knew Malaria was a tricky killer. There were four kinds of fever and several stages of development. The mosquito injected parasites that matured in the liver, entered the bloodstream, and invaded the red blood platelets where the little bastards multiplied until the cells burst, producing cold sweats and high fever. Untreated, he knew anemia would set in. Enlarged spleen, kidney failure, and heart congestion would finally do the killing. He guessed Pula's temperature at 104. Already his lips were cracked and bleeding.

This was the sickest kid Wilbur had ever seen. The grieving father needed to know the truth.

Leaving Bogtong to watch over Pula, Wilbur took the Panglima out to the hallway. The words would be hard for the chief to hear, but Wilbur had to say them. "We may be too late."

"Do something." The Panglima gripped Wilbur's arm with such force, that if not for the pleading in his eyes, the gesture could have been mistaken for a demand, or even a threat.

Wilbur didn't want to watch the chief cry. The situation was dire but not hopeless. Pula wasn't dead yet. "All right. I'll treat your son, but you must promise me you won't interfere. No medicine men. No chanting. No jungle remedies. It's my way. A free hand. You got that?"

"Yes, anything. Please." Hope blossomed on his jungle-battered face. His eyes sparkled with tears. "Save my son. Allah will reward you with his good graces."

No thanks. Wilbur had seen enough of Allah's good graces.

He walked back into the room. Bogtong opened the box of atabrine. Bambi prepared a hypodermic. With the boy this sick, he'd need injections, as atabrine taken by mouth would be immediately regurgitated.

Wilbur knew he was about to cross a dangerous threshold. If Pula should die, even if Wilbur had only touched him with his fingertips, the Panglima would blame him for the death. The Mohammedan natives would string him up and gut him, for sure.

With a knot of fear strangling his stomach, Wilbur gave Bambi the nod to go ahead. The medic swallowed, took a deep breath and gave Pula the first shot.

Wilbur exhaled. "The drug will make him vomit. Bogtong, do you have any anti-emetics?"

"Jamia root."

"No hydrochloride?"

Bogtong shook his head.

"Pepto-Bismol?"

"This is not San Francisco, but we are not without our remedies."

"All right." Scratch *jungle remedies* from the list of taboos. "Get the Jamia."

Bogtong rushed out.

Wilbur turned to the woman sitting on the bed. "I need you to go downstairs."

"He's our only son." She sobbed and gripped Pula's hand. "I cannot leave him."

"Bring fresh towels. It's the best help you can give him."

Rising, "Allah be with you, my son," she whispered and released his hand. Her stern eyes landed on Wilbur. "Do not let him die, Mister Cobb."

"I won't."

She backed out of the room.

Wilbur shared a look of dread with Bambi. "Now we wait."

***

In the village center, Wilbur followed Bogtong through the small crowd that had gathered. The evening feast would go on without the Panglima. He'd remained behind with Bambi to watch over his son. Hopefully not to watch him die.

Steaming black kettles boiled over the fires. Plates of clam and fish and fruit were passed around. The air seemed alive with flavors of the South Pacific. Wilbur's stomach hurt with anticipation.

A Coke in one hand and a heaping plate in the other, he made his way to a table Bogtong had selected, a table where a Palawan woman sat staring into space. Her frizzy hair needed brushing, and she wore a brown sweater with frayed sleeves.

The Pearl of Death

"Liawayway." Bogtong sat down next to her. "Wilbur Cobb will be joining us."

He almost dropped his fork. This was the woman his memory had framed so beautifully? She looked beaten and worn and used up. What the hell happened to her? "Ma'am." He removed his hat.

She didn't look at him, just stared, her brown eyes heavy with sorrow.

He didn't know what to say, sat across from her and dug into his meal. Bambi would need a breather soon. And he should get some of this food while it's hot.

Bogtong asked Liawayway, "Where are the boys?"

She didn't answer.

Wilbur looked up from his plate. "Timoteo, right?"

Her eyes darted to him, sharp as any blade. "You know my son?"

"I saw him five years ago."

"A lifetime ago." The words leaked from her like a punctured tire.

"Wilbur has come to save Pula," Bogtong told her.

Disdain shadowed her already distraught face. "So you are the hero I have heard about."

"He is a geologist," Bogtong said. "Where are your manners?"

"How lucky for Pula." Tears welled in her eyes. "A great American hero has come to save the Panglima's son. But who will save my sons?"

Wilbur heaped his spoon with boiled clam, wanting no part of this conversation.

Bogtong leaned close to her. "What is the matter with you?"

"It's Timoteo," she whispered. "He is in jail again."

"Stealing food from the market?" Bogtong looked at Wilbur, speaking and chewing at the same time. "The boy is thirteen. Fearless. Since his father died."

"It is not that," she hissed. "It is the pearl."

"The Pearl of Allah." Bogtong waved his spoon. "You must remember it, Mister Cobb."

"Of course." How could he forget the largest pearl in the

world?

"Timoteo blames the pearl for his father's death."

Liawayway slapped the table. "You talk to this stranger as if my problems are his business. He does not care about my son."

She was right. Wilbur cut a potato. Her son sounded like a juvenile delinquent.

"The boy watched his father die," Bogtong went on. "That can explain a lot about his behavior, not to mention the reason he blames the pearl for everything that has gone wrong around here."

"Maybe he is right." Liawayway swept a finger across the tribal gathering. "Look around. This square used to be filled with villagers. Now half of us are dead. Some of us are still dying. All since the pearl has come to Palawan."

"Malaria is not the pearl's fault."

"The pearl is destroying my son."

"Now, now." Bogtong put a hand over Liawayway's.

She jerked back, brows furrowed. "Do not treat me like a child."

"I assure you, Timoteo will grow out of his anger."

"How can you say that? He is getting worse."

Wilbur wished he could eat in peace. "Do you two always fight like this?"

"Stay out of it, mister big shot American." Liawayway's narrow eyes pierced him like a dart.

Wilbur went back to his meal, thankful Timoteo wasn't *his* problem.

"Etem is dead because of this pearl." Liawayway's voice brimmed with frustration. "Every chance Timoteo gets he tries another way to break into the chief's vault to steal it. To throw it back into the sea. To..." She stopped.

Wilbur looked up.

Her eyes let loose a flood of tears. "Today he was caught with dynamite."

"Allah, have mercy." Bogtong slapped a hand on his forehead. "Where did he find dynamite?"

"He is driving me crazy. The pearl is cursed, and the curse will grow, perhaps to destroy the world."

The word curse snagged Wilbur's curiosity. "What curse?"

"Nonsense." Bogtong chugged Coke. "Curses have no scientific merit."

Wilbur didn't believe in curses either, but a curse would make for a good story.

"People everywhere are suffering and dying." Liawayway clenched her jaw. "Look at Japan invading China, Germany invading Poland—"

"You listen to the radio too much." Bogtong wagged his spoon at her. "It is scaring you."

"Because of the pearl, the world is coming to an end."

"You give this pearl too much power."

She scowled. "No more power than Coca-Cola has over you."

He shrugged. "I like it."

"It is bad to like something that much." Liawayway folded her arms. "Coke is bad. The pearl is bad. You should listen to Timoteo."

"He is just a boy."

Wilbur had enough of their argument. He wished he were in the middle of the jungle with his team, sipping scotch around a campfire, slapping mosquitoes, and telling tales of San Francisco. "I'm going to check on our patient." As he stood and walked off, he heard Bogtong scold Liawayway.

"See what you did? Chased him away. He's a nice man."

"Shut up," she snapped.

"He is an American man."

"I hate Americans."

Chapter Fifteen

On the fifth day of Pula's treatments, dawn came to the Dyak village in a fury. Wind-driven rain soaked the jungle and pelted the truck's canvas roof. Lying crooked across the seat, Wilbur felt the steering wheel dig into his side. His head hurt from the scotch he'd drunk while sitting up with Pula half the night. Now it was Bogtong's shift to watch over him.

The chatter of monkeys in the trees and the loud, persistent *angk* of Palawan peacocks made sleep impossible.

Wilbur sat up, straightened his hat. Through the rain-streaked windshield, the Panglima's porch lights still glowed. Dark second-story windows looked down on him like the weeping eyes of an old man.

Bambi slept in the back. He had rolled up his sleeves and loosened his tie. Last night he'd given Pula two injections of atabrine. The supply was down to one vile. Another twenty-four hours worth. If Pula wasn't cured by then, he'd be dead, the Panglima would blame Wilbur, and his adventure would come to a screaming and painful end.

The house door sprang open. The Panglima bounded out, arms splayed to the heavens as he ran into the rain and fell to his knees on the lawn.

Wilbur flinched. "Bambi. Get up."

The medic grumped and turned over, rubbed sleep from his eyes. "What is it?"

"Look."

The Panglima bowed low in Muslim prayer, crying and wailing. His flannel shirt and coveralls became quickly drenched.

"Pula must be dead," Bambi choked out.

Wilbur's heart rate sputtered like a dying engine. "Son of a bitch."

Servants rushed to the door, each vying for position to get a view of their chief.

Wilbur grabbed the door handle, the burn of fright searing through his veins. He'd make a break for Boligay Creek, follow it downstream to the ocean, take his chances with the crocs and snakes. Anything was better than facing the Panglima now.

Bogtong appeared behind the servants. Wilbur piled out of the cab and into the rain. He owed Bogtong a goodbye wave, or at the very least a so-long-buddy look before fleeing for his life, but the expression on the doctor's face didn't fit the panic that should have been racing through his mind. He was smiling. What the hell?

The Panglima sang praises to Allah.

Bambi jumped down from the truck bed, landing behind Wilbur. "That's odd."

"Wilbur Cobb," Bogtong called out. "Pula's fever broke."

A hesitant wave of relief rolled over Wilbur. Pula wasn't out of danger yet. The fever had reduced him to skin and bones. He was helplessly weak. He could relapse and die at any time.

The Panglima rose from the lawn. Rain and tears ran down his face as he turned to Wilbur. "You, my friend." He lumbered forward. "You have saved my son." Bear hug. He smelled like a wet dog. "Thank you, thank you, thank you."

Water dripped from Wilbur's hat brim. "You're welcome. Now we can go back to our team."

"I beg of you to stay until he makes a full recovery."

"Bogtong can take care of him now." Wilbur turned to Bambi. "Come on, let's find a ride to Puerto Princesa."

A rough hand grabbed Wilbur's arm and spun him around. He found himself speared with the Panglima's fierce-eyed glare. "I insist."

Wilbur swallowed. *I still might not get out of here alive.*

Chapter Sixteen

Down the road from the Panglima's house, horses, tricycle cabs, and canopy trucks surrounded Tiki-T's diner. Wilbur parked the Desoto and shut off the engine. After three weeks of eating fish and python stew as a guest of the Dyak's tribal leader, he yearned for greasy American food.

"I don't know." Bambi looked out the windshield. "It might be a rough bunch in there."

"No problem." Wilbur tucked the .38 in his waistband and climbed out of the truck.

Inside, he found standing room only. Tagalog chatter intermingled with Spanish, English, and the clanking of dishes and silverware. The words *Japanese* and *Germans* jumped out from the conversations. War loomed. Everybody knew it. Everybody talked about it. Nobody wanted to get involved.

Tiki-T's smelled like any diner in any-town USA: bacon frying, coffee perking, and rank cigarette smoke drifting in the humid air. Wilbur squeezed between two Navy boys at the counter and got the waitress's attention, a cute little oriental dame. "Two coffees, black."

"In a minute, GI."

Did all Americans look like GIs to her? "Thanks." He flipped two dimes on the countertop.

The radio, broadcasting in English from the airfield at Puerto Princesa, announced the news of Pula's full recovery from malaria, thanks to the efforts of Wilbur Cobb, an American geologist on special assignment to Palawan.

"Hey, everybody." Bambi pointed to Wilbur and grinned. "This is him. Wilbur Cobb."

Applause clattered around the diner.

"It was nothing. Please. Enough." Wilbur's cheeks heated

with embarrassment. "Bambi did all the work." He clenched the medic's shoulder in a you-should-keep-your-mouth-shut hard grip.

Pula's recovery was nothing short of a miracle. Wilbur had instructed servants to carry the weak and crippled boy down to the creek for daily water therapy. At first, the grueling routine exhausted Pula, but slowly he began to regain his strength. Within two weeks he could walk with the aid of a stick, and he soon looked forward to his daily swims.

With his teenage-boy-appetite restored, he started filling in his skeletal frame and began to look more like his previous strapping self. He was even able to go fishing with Bogtong.

Wilbur had not only saved the boy, he'd developed a friendship with the Panglima's family that he hoped would last a lifetime.

The radio announcer: "Everyone is invited to a feast tonight in the village center to honor Wilbur Cobb."

"Mister Cobb," a native called out from a corner booth. He wore a white sleeveless shirt. His sinewy biceps displayed tattoos of clamshells with gaping cockled jaws. "I saw you with Liawayway."

Wilbur hadn't seen his haggard Palawan princess since that first night at the clam-shucking feast. But he'd thought about her often. Wondered about her. Wondered why he was wondering—

"You like her, yes?"

Catcalls reverberated through the diner. Everyone was looking at Wilbur and laughing.

He thought about walking out, but he didn't want to be disrespectful. After all, the Dyaks were only interested in the well-being of one of their own.

"She has fallen from Allah's grace," someone shouted.

Another chimed in, "You should marry her, take her to America."

Now it sounded as if they were trying to get rid of her.

His jaw tightened. He wanted to tell them to mind their own business but settled for, "No thanks, boys. She hates Americans."

The tribe was not going to get rid of her that easily.

Besides, now that Pula was better, it was time to go back to the team. He still had a job to do on Palawan. When that was finished, he'd fly back to his headquarters in Manila, and maybe back to San Francisco. Someday.

When the great adventure was over.

"You should see her again," the native in the corner booth shouted. "Give her another chance. After all, she is an infidel now. She bares her head like a Western whore."

Laughter spilled through the diner like a black coffee stain.

Angry adrenaline shot into Wilbur's bloodstream. He stalked to the corner booth, fully intent on telling the pill to keep his pie hole shut, but the native jumped to his feet and brandished a six-inch blade.

Now the diner fell silent.

Wilbur's neck hairs prickled. He recognized the crumb from five years ago. Maricar. And the Dyak sitting with him looked familiar too. Ning-ning.

Wilbur fought to breathe easy. The hard lump of his .38 tucked in his waistband, within quick reach, gave him a degree of confidence. "What's your problem, boy?"

"You think Liawayway is not good enough for you."

"Put the knife away."

"You Americans are all alike. We are just a bunch of stinkin' natives to you Yankee Doodles. Jungle bunnies and Flips. The whore deserves better than you."

That did it. Wilbur reached for the gun. "Listen here, you sawed off little piece of shit."

Bambi jumped in front of Wilbur. "Easy, boss."

"Get out of my way." The gun was almost drawn.

Bambi grabbed Wilbur's arm, spoke low and firm. "Let me find out what's got him steamed, then you can shoot him."

Wilbur ground his molars. Yeah. What the hell was this guy's beef anyway? "All right." He relaxed his grip on the gun butt but kept his hand close.

Bambi spoke Tagalog to Maricar. The two shouted back and forth. The only words Wilbur recognized were *Liawayway* and *Bogtong*. Bambi's voice quieted.

Maricar sheathed the knife.

Bambi stepped back.

Maricar sat down.

The diner racket started up again.

Bambi pointed across the room. "Look, boss. A booth is empty." Seemed a customer hadn't stuck around for the fight. Bambi prodded Wilbur toward the booth.

He sat down, his adrenaline burn slow to cool.

"Are you loony?" Bambi whispered. "Good thing nobody saw you had a gun. MPs would have been here in a heartbeat."

"You should'a let me plug him."

"What's gotten into you?"

"He had no business talking about her like that."

"Liawayway?"

Wilbur's last memory of her wasn't endearing, but her first impression lingered. He'd rather remember her the way she looked five years ago: long flowing black hair, low cut top, a true Palawan princess. "She's not a whore."

"Why, boss." Bambi leered. "I believe you're smitten."

"Shut up."

The waitress brought coffee. "You boys all right?"

Wilbur looked the oriental woman up and down. Nice, but lacking Liawayway's bronzed islander appeal. "Sorry about the commotion."

"Maricar is an asshole." She smacked her lips. "What'll it be?"

"Ham and eggs with your greasiest hash browns."

"We only got one kind of greasy hash browns, mister."

Bambi jumped in, "You got shit-on-a-shingle?"

"You want a side of bacon with that?"

"Sure."

She sauntered off.

Bambi's eyes followed the waitress's legs until they went behind the counter. "Sassy broad." He sipped coffee.

"So what's Maricar's problem?"

"He's been supporting Liawayway and her boys since Etem was killed." Another slurp of coffee. "If he could get someone to marry her, he'd be off the hook."

"That's no reason to pull a knife on me."

"He doesn't like you, boss."

Their first meeting in Bogtong's clinic crossed Wilbur's mind. "It's not the first time he's threatened me."

"He calls you Bogtong's little puppy dog."

"Good thing I don't understand Tagalog." He'd have shot Maricar for saying that, for sure.

"The problem is Liawayway's son," Bambi went on. "Timoteo is one screwed up kid. He hates the Panglima's pearl. The pearl of death, he calls it. Blames all his problems, his bad grades, all the tribe's problems, the malaria epidemic, everything on the pearl."

Wilbur looked into the coffee mug, imagined how the boy must've felt seeing his father die. "It's understandable."

"He wants the pearl thrown back into the sea. The Panglima won't give it up, not for anything."

"He wouldn't sell it to me, even when I asked him to name his price."

"Maricar likes Liawayway. He would have her for his own if she let him, but he is fed up with Timoteo."

"I'm glad he's not my problem."

"And there's another thing..."

The waitress brought breakfast, set plates on the table and rushed off.

Wilbur wasn't interested in anything else Maricar had to say. "Just eat. We're going back to camp."

Bambi picked up his fork, looked at the pile of goo on his plate. "Not until after the feast tonight."

"Bogtong can drive us this afternoon." Wilbur forked the slab of ham.

"You can't save Pula then insult the Panglima by ignoring his celebration in your honor."

A feast in the village center, Wilbur remembered the last one, the last time he saw Liawayway: frazzled, hurt, angry, the last thing he'd heard her say: *I hate Americans.* Why risk a repeat performance? "The Panglima will understand."

"He could make life miserable for you."

"I saved his son, for godsake."

"*We* saved his son, boss, and I will not disrespect him. You are going to the feast."

"Liawayway might be there."

"That's the other thing Maricar told me. She likes you."

Yeah, right. "She hates Americans."

"Maricar is jealous of you. That's why he pulled the knife." Wilbur set down his fork. He'd lost his appetite. And that wasn't the fault of Timoteo's pearl.

***

Brass gongs reverberated. The feast got under way. Natives jammed the village center, many coming from outlying tribes to rejoice in Pula's recovery. Wilbur couldn't wait for the celebration to end so he could leave the Dyaks without insulting their Panglima.

"Look." Bambi nudged Wilbur's arm. "Over there. Liawayway."

Following Bambi's nod, Wilbur's gaze fell on an hourglass shape standing at a food table. She wore a colorful wraparound dress, white with blues and greens that draped loosely over her breasts. White flowers adorned sleek black hair that spilled over bare, bronzed shoulders. She looked more like the Palawan princess he remembered. The sight caused a stir in a part of him that hadn't stirred since San Francisco. He bit his tongue.

Two shirtless boys stood with her, one a foot taller and lighter skinned, the other short and thin boned. Wilbur assumed they were her sons, one of them the notorious Timoteo.

Bogtong approached, Coke bottle in hand. "Please come meet Liawayway's boys." He sweated like a junkie on a bender. "She promised to behave. She likes you. Really."

"So I've heard." Wilbur fought the temptation to get near her. Someone might get the wrong impression, like what happened at Tiki-Ti's. And he didn't want a romantic rumor to follow him back to Puerto Princesa. His team would rib him to no end for getting involved with a native woman. "No thanks."

Bogtong persisted. "Allah beseeches you."

"Go ahead, boss," Bambi said.

Wilbur sneered. "You're not helping."

"What can it hurt?" Bogtong threw in. "Meet the boys you are curious about."

"I'm not curious."

Bambi grinned. "Liawayway is dressed for romance tonight."

Wilbur huffed. She looked tempting enough, but he'd

rather just look, not touch. Then again, what jungle adventure would be complete without romance? Ask Tarzan. "All right, but only for a minute. I'm hungry."

"Follow me." Bogtong headed toward Liawayway.

With anxiety building a fire in his chest, Wilbur tagged behind him through the jubilant crowd. He passed steaming pots of potatoes and vegetables, and fire pits with rotating skewers of pork and poultry. Sweet aromas floated in the air. The night tingled with festive song and the heart-thrumming vibrations of brass gongs and native drums.

He caught glimpses of Liawayway through gaps in the throng, plate in hand, dishing up food for her boys. His heart beat faster with each step he took toward her.

A tall glass of scotch would go down good about now.

As the distance between them narrowed to nothing, she stopped spooning food and looked up. He expected poison-dart eyes to drop him dead in the dirt. Instead, she smiled a smile that lit up the night like a burst of fireworks. The flames of anxiety in his chest flared into a firestorm of desire.

"Look who I found," Bogtong announced.

"Mister Cobb." She almost whispered his name.

Fanning the flames, he removed his bushman hat. "Ma'am." His heart beat as hard as the pounding gongs. "It's nice to see you again." He tipped his head to the boys. "And these are your sons?"

They scooted closer to her, looking up at him in awe.

"They hoped to meet the American hero."

"I don't know about the hero part."

The tall boy stepped forward and extended his hand in earnest. "I'm Timoteo."

Wilber shook the boy's hand, surprised by his strong grip. "I've heard about you, young man."

"I'm thirteen years old."

The smaller boy followed his brother's lead. "I'm Tito." White teeth sparkled from a broad smile. "I'm ten."

"Yes, and I've heard of you, too. I'm sorry about your father."

The boys stared at him, eyes startled and suddenly guarded.

Bogtong kicked Wilbur's boot.

"Okay." *I shouldn't have mentioned their father.*

"It was five years ago." Liawayway tightened her upper lip as if fighting back tears. "Best forgotten now."

Really? She would forget Etem now, so suddenly, after five years of mourning? She'd spurned Maricar and every other suitor. She'd denounced Allah and Islam. Became an object of ridicule in her tribe. Now it's best forgotten? Sounded as if someone had coached her on what to say. Wilbur cast a suspicious glance at matchmaker Bogtong.

Chugging Coke, he appeared oblivious to any conspiracy.

"Mister Cobb." Tito's voice sang with excitement. "You saved Pula?"

"Yes. He's fine now."

"The Chief will reward you," Timoteo put in. "He'll give you anything you want."

"Then my ticket to San Francisco is in the bag."

"You are leaving?" Liawayway's gaze dropped.

It moved him to think she'd be sad to see him go, until he remembered she hated Americans. Maybe it was just wishful thinking on his part. That she cared. Still, he didn't fraternize with the natives.

Bogtong winked at Liawayway.

Wilbur caught the gesture. The good doctor had told her to be nice to him, probably a ploy to get him to take up with the widow and her kids. "Are you trying to chisel me, Bogtong?"

"She is a good woman."

"I'm sure she is—"

Maricar stepped up beside Bogtong, stopping Wilbur in mid sentence. The native crossed his arms and glared at the American who had stolen his woman's affections. Or the way he saw it. If he thought his presence would intimidate Wilbur, he was wrong.

"I'm leaving tomorrow. My team is waiting for me. Two months in the jungle and I'm going back to Manila and my next assignment for Benguet. Maybe New Zealand."

Liawayway's dark brows rose. "And San Francisco? When will you go there?"

"Who knows?" He didn't see a stateside assignment in the near future. That wasn't entirely a bad thing. He didn't want to fall back on bad habits. He had fond memories of the City by the Bay, and Beth and Jane and Suzie, and the wild nightlife of big-band clubs and fast roulette wheels, ring-a-ding-ding parties and drunken brawls.

He'd been on a collision course with his headstone.

So he gave up the glitz in exchange for adventure in the roughest parts of the world. The scotch and memories were all he had left of the good old days.

"Then maybe you will come back to see us someday."

"Yes, of course." Wilbur speared Maricar a sideways glance. There was no reason to return to this village, but Maricar didn't need to know that. Let him sweat.

Easing his attention back to Liawayway, Wilbur let his gaze slide up and down her body, let his mind etch her image into his memory, a memory he would take with him wherever he should go.

Maricar could have his woman back, wouldn't even have to thank him.

The gongs fell silent, stilling the crowd. A black Plymouth pulled up to the village center. Car doors swung open. The Panglima's wife got out first, her face shadowed by a black headscarf and veil.

Pula emerged next, smiling and waving to the expectant crowd. He wore a white shirt with the sleeves rolled up past his elbows, baggy black trousers, and nothing on his feet. Thick bandoleers loaded with brass bullets crisscrossed his chest. The six-shooter holstered to his belt seemed gigantic compared to the boy's slight hips.

The Panglima climbed out, dressed in brown coveralls, a blue flannel shirt, and the ever-present red bandana tied around his head. He raised his hands to the tribe. "Praise Allah."

The villagers cheered.

A servant completed the entourage, thin and dressed in a baggy gray suit, his hair parted down the middle. He carried a heaping tray covered with a green scarf.

Together, they moved into the village center. The gong drummers went at it again, pounding away with a rhythm that made chills skitter up Wilbur's neck.

The Panglima offered him a seat at the head of the table,

the highest position of honor at the feast. Pula sat on his father's left and directed his mother to sit with him.

Bogtong and Bambi sat on Wilbur's right. Liawayway took the chair nearest Wilbur on the left and set down the food plates for her boys. They scrambled into their chairs and eagerly dug into the meal.

The Panglima took his seat. Everyone was talking at once.

"When will you come back to see us?" Liawayway passed Wilbur a bowl of potatoes.

He stabbed a potato and put it on his plate. "I thought you hated Americans."

"I only said that—"

"It's all right." He switched his attention to Timoteo. "How's the chicken?"

"Good." Timoteo passed him the platter.

"Thanks."

Liawayway scrunched up her brows. "You're a strange man, Mister Cobb, hard on the outside, soft in the center." She touched her heart.

He forked a plump chicken breast. What did she know about—

A gunshot cracked through the air.

Wilbur flinched, spotted Pula with his pistol drawn and pointed up, gun-smoke wafting from the barrel.

What the hell was the kid doing?

Pula showed everyone a wily grin and holstered the gun. "My father will speak now."

The Panglima stood and raised his arms. "Allah has smiled upon us today."

"Praise Allah," the Dyaks chanted.

Wilbur exhaled. Crazy natives ever hear of tapping a glass with a spoon to quiet their dinner guests?

"Mister Cobb," the Panglima began. "It is time for you to leave our village."

Wilbur set down his fork and nodded.

"Before you came, my son was mortally ill. I have seen so many of my people die of malaria, I was terrified. Quinine did not help him. I did not know what to do. So I held the Pearl of Allah in my hands and prayed for God's help. In my prayers, I vowed that no matter how much I valued His pearl, I would willingly give it to anyone who could save my son. Then, as if testing my sincerity, Allah sent you. Though I wondered how a Christian could do this great deed, I let you treat Pula. And you have saved him. As a token of my true gratitude, I offer you your reward. Here, my friend, claim this."

As if on cue, the suited servant approached with the pearl held in both hands and set it on the table in front of Wilbur.

"The Pearl of Allah," the Panglima proclaimed.

Wilbur's throat tightened. He couldn't have heard him correctly. Looking first at Liawayway, and then to Timoteo's wide-eyed face, he knew he couldn't take the tribe's sacred heirloom.

"I cannot accept this."

Bogtong kicked Wilbur's foot. The stern look on the doctor's face said, *don't argue with the Panglima.* To turn down this gift would be an immeasurable insult. Still...

Wilbur looked up to the Panglima. "You don't owe me anything. You're my friend. The friendship of your family and tribe is compensation enough."

Eyes glistening, the Panglima crossed his arms over his chest. "This pearl was paid for with the blood of a young man. Now you have earned it by saving the life of my only son. Who could be more deserving?"

A murmur went through the village center.

Wilbur couldn't refute that. He wouldn't. This was his pearl, now and forever. Opening his hands, he set both palms on the lumpy surface, half expecting it to be hot as a camp stove. Instead, it felt cold and hard.

A tremble inside his chest grew. An ache bore deep in his bones. His stomach felt queasy. Chills sliced through him like blades of cold steel. Fingers tingling, he feared the pearl was affecting him in some physical way, but the geologist in him fought the notion of any mystical energy flowing into his hands. His reaction was strictly psychological, perhaps a subconscious fear of the Almighty, an awe of the unknown, or the guilt of receiving such a splendid and unexpected gift.

"I thank you from the bottom of my heart." Wilbur bowed to the Panglima.

The Pearl of Death

"Allah be with you."

The natives cheered their Panglima's generosity. They seemed overjoyed at being rid of the pearl.

Except Timoteo. He glared at Wilbur with venomous eyes. "Give it back to the sea," the boy hissed. "Or you too will be cursed by the pearl of death."

Wilbur swallowed. How quickly he had turned from hero to villain in the boy's eyes. Liawayway and Tito stared at Timoteo with a not-this-again look on their faces. They'd been through this with him before.

Timoteo jumped up. "Get rid of it before it is too late."

Wilbur couldn't fathom the value of his pearl, as ugly as it was, yet unique. He would never throw it back into the sea. Cursed or not.

Besides, the pearl of death was destined to become the greatest adventure story ever told. He was going to make a fortune with this treasure.

Chapter Seventeen

During the two-month expedition that followed the great feast, Wilbur kept his pearl in a box carved from Philippine Rosewood. If it wasn't bundled in his bedding, it was packed in his duffle bag. Tonight, at base camp on the river bend, he set the box on the folding table, as he did every night, to contemplate how the pearl could change his life. In the glow of lantern light, he poured scotch from the last bottle, one glass for himself and another for Bambi sitting with him. Jungle heat and muggy air felt like a hot, wet towel against his skin. This was their last night on Palawan.

Mosquitoes buzzed the air. Monkeys chattered and a root hog snorted from somewhere in the bush. Tart wood smoke drifted across the camp. Most of his team had bedded down for the night, some reading in their tents, some already snoring. Tomorrow they'd be drinking in a Manila bar and sleeping on pressed white sheets in their company apartments.

Bambi sipped his scotch. "Are you going to sell your pearl? Have it appraised?"

How could the Pearl of Allah be compared to dollars and cents? Still, it was a good suggestion. "I know a guy in California." Wilbur leaned back in the folding chair. "Beverly Hills."

"When we get back to headquarters, take a leave of absence. Go see him."

"I think I will." Wilbur rested the glass on his belly and stared at the box. "And one day I'll take the pearl on tour and show it off to the world." He savored another belt of scotch. "Tell the greatest adventure story ever told."

"You might be famous like Dr. Livingstone."

Wilbur was thinking more along the lines of Howard

Carter. He'd discovered the tomb of Tutankhamen. Some said it was cursed, too, like this pearl. Another gulp of scotch went down, his gaze still on the box. "Do you think the pearl is cursed?"

Bambi examined his glass. "Timoteo is just a boy. Everything bad that's happened is easily explained."

"I understand why he wants the pearl returned to the sea. If I were superstitious, I might agree."

Bambi leaned forward. "You say you are not?"

"What?"

"Superstitious."

"Of course not."

"Then why haven't you taken the pearl from the box? Not once since you owned it. You just stare at the box."

He downed the scotch. "I don't want it scratched." It wasn't superstition or curses that bothered him, but the feeling he got when he held the pearl, that disturbing, lightheaded chill. Made him realize how small he was in the world, how insignificant compared to the power of nature and God.

It was best to keep the pearl in the box.

***

The next morning, as the sun rose over the Sulu Sea, Wilbur and his team drove their mud-spattered truck convoy into Puerto Princesa and onto the dirt airfield. In front of the steal corrugated building sat the Fokker Trimotor. Sunshine gleamed off its three radial engines. The boxy wooden fuselage sweated morning dew. Wilbur wished he hadn't drunk so much last night. His head hurt from scotch. Even in tip-top condition, he dreaded the hammering flight back to Manila.

As the trucks squealed to a stop, the pilot appeared from the building. Stray dogs ran up to him, begging, and he shooed them away. "Hola." He buttoned his flight jacket. "You boys are right on time."

Wilbur stumbled out of the cab, squinted at the bright sky, and wished he were taking a boat to Manila. "Let's get a move-on, men. Bambi, get my duffle bag."

"Sure thing, bwana."

If he ever heard the word bwana again, he'd slit his throat

with a bore-tooth dagger.

As the men started unloading the trucks and loading the plane, the pilot ambled up to Wilbur. "Sure is a nice morning to fly." He scanned the blue sky. "But like I was telling the lady, we got a full load."

"What lady?" Pain jabbed Wilbur's right temple. He glanced around. A Desoto was parked alongside the building, blue with a green canvas top. It looked like Bogtong's truck. The lady in question must have been Liawayway. "What the hell is she doing here?"

"They want a ride to Manila."

"They?"

"She has two sons, good boys, you know."

Christ! Another matchmaker. "Not you, too."

"I tried changing her mind about leaving Palawan. The Japanese got everybody jumpy."

"Japanese?"

"Rumor is they're planning to attack the Philippines. You haven't heard?"

"I've been in the jungle for two months." Wilbur's head pounded.

"General MacArthur is building up Luzon's defenses. The Americans are recruiting heavily for the Philippine Army."

Bambi tossed Wilbur's duffle bag into the plane's cargo hold like it was a sack of laundry.

"Damn it, Bambi! Be careful with that."

"Sorry, boss."

"Wilbur Cobb." Liawayway's stern voice came from behind him.

The muscles between his shoulder blades stiffened. God, he didn't want to tell her she had to stay.

"Mister American hero."

He turned to admonish her for bothering him, but her tear-swollen eyes stopped him. Tangled hair spilled onto an oversized Army jacket draped on her shoulders. The summer dress she wore looked slept-in wrinkled.

"I can't help you."

"You saved Pula. For this you received a great gift. But it is not heroic to do something good for payment. It is heroic to do something good for nothing in return. So here is your chance to be a real hero. Take us with you."

"I can't."

"But the Japanese are coming."

Wilbur pointed to the pilot. "Did you tell her that?"

"It's all over the radio," he spat. "The Philippines is ripe for Japanese expansionism. They raped and murdered their way across Manchuria and China. If they come here, these natives don't stand a chance."

"Take us to Manila." Liawayway's eyes bled desperation. "Save us from the Japanese."

"It's just a rumor." It had to be just a rumor. The Japanese wouldn't dare...

Liawayway tightened the jacket collar around her neck. "In Manila, there are many American soldiers. My sons will be safe there." She cast her eyes toward the steel building.

Wilbur followed her gaze. Tito and Timoteo stood by the door, knobby-kneed, their hair mussed, a couple of poster boys for Save the Children Foundation. A moment of compassion seized him, but there were countless needy kids in the Philippines. Why were these two so important? And Liawayway, her predicament wasn't any different than the other natives on this island. Should he haul them all to Manila?

And would they really be safer there? Sure, the more forces, the more protection, but it was those very forces the Japanese would attack with the most ferocity.

"Please." Liawayway touched his arm. "Take us."

The tone of her voice was a chisel chipping away at his stone-hard resolve. She was beautiful, yet fragile. Gutsy strong, but vulnerable. What harm would it be to take her and the boys to Manila? But... "There's no room on the plane."

"A-hum," the pilot poked in. "I could come back for them."

"Benguet isn't paying you to transport locals. You'll be fired."

"Not if I was transporting their lead geologist."

"Have you been drinking?"

"Stay here with her. I'll tell your boss you were delayed and that I must return for you. Then I'll bring you all back to

Manila."

"Stay behind?" Oh no. He'd finished the last of his scotch. Tonight he would sleep on clean sheets. "I can't—"

"Please." Liawayway squeezed his arm. "You have the pearl. It will bring you great wealth, but we have nothing though my husband found it. My son watched him die for it. Do this for us. You owe that much."

"Owe?" Wilbur swallowed. How did his gift become a debt? He glanced at the boys. Sure, they'd lost a lot. Taking them to Manila was something he could do for them. They might be safer. Might not. Maybe they could start a new life. Maybe not. But to give them the opportunity, all he had to do was say yes.

He asked the pilot, "When will you be back?"

"Two days." He pointed toward town. "There are restaurants in Puerto Princesa...and a hotel. Perhaps you can take your new family on a picnic to the falls." He grinned.

Wilbur wanted to slug him. These natives weren't his new family. They were a temporary setback: two days without scotch, two nights without clean sheets. This hero business was no better than stepping in water buffalo dung.

"Bambi. Get my duffle bag off the plane."

Liawayway squealed. Her boys ran to her, hugged her waist. "Thank you, Wilbur Cobb."

He huffed. "Thank Allah." *Some hero.*

Bambi set Wilbur's bag at his feet. "Have fun, boss."

"I'll see you in Manila."

Bambi climbed aboard. The other team members followed him, ten of the best men in the business. He would miss their welcome-home party at headquarters. Already he missed his scotch.

The pilot waved. The door closed. One at a time, three engines caught with a rumble and a belch of smoke. Wilbur stood next to Liawayway and her sons as a cloud of dust rolled into the air. The plane began to move, engines rattling and sputtering with an uneven rhythm.

Birds took flight. Stray dogs lit out with their tails tucked between their legs.

The roaring plane tore down the runway and lifted off.

The Pearl of Death

Liawayway waved goodbye. Tito and Timoteo waved too.

Wilbur crossed his arms and watched the plane climb over the bay. He wished he was going home with them.

Blue smoke spewed from the right engine. The wing dipped. Wilbur squinted, worried at first, then remembered that had happened before. The pilot would fix it.

Fire flared from the right wing.

That was something different. But the pilot would fix it.

Black smoke smeared a dirty streak across the blue sky.

"What's the matter with it?" Liawayway squeaked out.

Wilbur tried to make sense of what he was seeing. The wing was full of gas. The plane was made of wood. Gas, wood, and fire—

An explosion tore off the right wing. The plane rolled, and loping on the left wing, it flipped into a dead-stick spin. The severed wing plummeted straight down, wagging a black tail of smoke in its wake.

Wilbur couldn't breathe. He stared, frozen in horrified disbelief at the crippled plane spinning toward the bay. Down, down, down. Bambi. The pilot. His team. Their terror. Who was screaming? Who was praying?

The plane struck the water and disintegrated in a red and yellow ball of fire.

Liawayway screamed.

"Son of a bitch." Bile climbed up to the back of his throat. His legs failed him. He fell to his knees, fists clenched. "No, God, no."

Clutching Tito, Liawayway dropped to her knees with Wilbur. "I'm so sorry," she sobbed.

"They're all dead." Wilbur threw his arms around her, embraced her, his body jerking with uncontrollable sobs.

"The pearl did it," Timoteo shouted, standing there, eyes streaming tears. "The pearl of death."

"No, no." Wilbur reached up, grabbed the boy's arm. "The plane, it broke, the engine, it was bad."

Timoteo yanked his arm free. "You should have thrown it back in the sea."

"It's not the pearl's fault."

"It is the curse."

"The pearl wasn't even on the plane. Look." Wilbur released Liawayway, opened his duffle bag, and hands shaking, found the box and pulled it out. "It's here."

"But it *was* on the plane."

Wilbur opened the box, removed the heavy pearl and showed it to the boy. "It's just a pearl. There's no curse—"

That light-headed feeling hit him again. Dumbstruck at the sensation, he gazed into the pearl's pure lustrous white surface. His heart felt as if it were swelling in his chest, threatening to sieve through his ribcage. Was it the hand of Allah tearing the soul from his body? Was it the shock of losing his team or the reality of his own brush with death?

One thing was certain. If not for the pearl, Liawayway wouldn't have come here to plead her case. If not for the pearl, he would have been on that plane. If not for the pearl, he too would be dead.

He looked out to the bay. Fire leaped and rolled on the water. Small boats arrived at the crash scene, bobbing in the waves, a wall of smoke towering above them. He imagined torn bodies and burned flesh sinking in the bay. Squeezing his eyes shut, he bent over and cried.

Liawayway rubbed his back. "Lucky you decided to stay."

"L-lucky?" He swallowed. It was a miracle.

Timoteo dropped next to him. "Now will you throw it back in the sea?" The boy's voice sounded hollow and distant. "Before more people have to die?"

Through tear-streaked vision, Wilbur gazed at the lumpy pearl cupped in his hands. Lucky? Yes. He was lucky. The pearl had saved his life. He vowed to never give it up. Not to the sea, not to anyone, not for anything. Ever.

The pearl was his good luck charm.

Chapter Eighteen

A week later, Benguet Consolidated sent another plane to retrieve their top geologist, this time a DC-3 made of metal and powered by two Pratt and Whitney Double Wasp engines. This plane had become the workhorse for the Army and the transoceanic airline industry. Wilbur bet his life it wasn't going to crash, not even with the Pearl of Allah riding in the cargo hold.

But Timoteo didn't want to get aboard. He threw such a snit that he made Tito cry. It took Liawayway's threat to leave him standing on the airfield with only the stray dogs and gulls for company to finally convince him to get on the plane.

Once inside, the boys ran up and down the carpeted aisle and tested the upholstered seats set two abreast. Each chose a window seat and cheered during the roaring takeoff, their fears quickly forgotten.

Liawayway parted the lacy window curtains and looked out at Puerto Princesa fading in the distance. Her eyes welled with tears.

Wilbur thought she might be saying a quiet goodbye. Rather than ask her what she was thinking, he leaned back in the cushy seat and folded his arms across his chest. Droning engines made him groggy.

Before last week, the time he'd spent in the jungle was always *on the clock* for the company. Everything revolved around work, whether he collected soil samples, took seismograph readings, or broke rocks. Maps were drawn. He had survey reports to write and recommendations to make. Work. Work. Work.

But the past week had been different.

With Liawayway and the boys, Palawan became a vacation

in paradise. Though the black cloud of the plane crash overshadowed everything they did, it wasn't dark enough to keep them from celebrating life. Every moment was precious, every smile, and every tear as they mourned for Bambi and the others and praised God for Wilbur's good fortune.

Losing his team made him rethink his position on not getting involved in someone else's life. It was time to commit to someone special. Someone permanent, as permanent as mortal life would allow. The past was the past, went up in the smoke of that plane crash. Liawayway and her boys were young and vibrant, filled with hurt and promise.

They needed him.

He needed them.

He had the pearl to thank for bringing them into his life.

The two days they'd spent at the falls an hour out of Puerto Princesa brought them close together. There were hundreds of streams, waterfalls, and deep pools on Palawan, formed by eons of volcanic activity and tropical rains. Dense vegetation and colorful flora filled the air with fragrances sweet enough to taste.

The gentle sway of the plane took him back...

Liawayway swam with Tito in a clear pool. A waterfall cascaded behind her. Wilbur sat on a smooth flat rock and watched her slip through the water, dive, and surface with the grace of a mermaid clad in underwear and bra. He thought of jumping in to join her, to get close to her, but decided to stay on the rock and enjoy the view.

Timoteo bounded up the narrow path beside the pool, pushed ferns aside, and sat with him on the flat rock. The knobby-kneed thirteen-year-old looked up at the forest canopy and sighed.

Wilbur let him sit there, not too close, not too far, and wondered what the boy had on his mind. They listened to the splashing waterfall. Birds chirped. Butterflies flittered about without a care in the world.

Long minutes passed.

Timoteo finally looked at Wilbur. "I miss my dad. He is dead, and now you are here."

"I'm not here to take his place." It had been five years since Etem died, a long time for a boy to be without a father—he glanced at Liawayway in the pool—and a long time for a woman to mourn her man's passing. Bogtong had tried to help her get over her grief, tried to help her get on with her life. Maricar wanted in, but she didn't want him.

Now, watching her play in the water with Tito made Wilbur believe that perhaps she was ready to let go of the past.

Timoteo scooted closer. "You like my mom?"

"Sure. And I like you too."

Tito squealed and splashed his mother.

"And Tito?"

"Of course."

"Are you going to be our new dad?"

The question jolted Wilbur. He didn't know the answer. Though he wanted to say yes, Liawayway had a say in the matter. "Would it bother you if I did?"

Timoteo looked at his toenails. "I don't like you."

"Why not?"

"You have the pearl that killed my dad."

"The pearl's done a lot for us." Wilbur watched Liawayway splash water on giggling Tito. "It's brought us together, your mother and me, you and Tito and me. I'm sorry about your father, but his death wasn't the pearl's fault."

"You forget about the malaria." Timoteo frowned. "The pearl brought malaria to our village."

"Malaria outbreaks are nothing new to the Philippines." Wilbur turned to Timoteo. "And you didn't get malaria."

"Not yet."

"If you believe malaria was the pearl's doing, then you must also believe the malaria brought me to your village, to save Pula. Now we are together. Something good came out of it."

"My father died. Nothing is good." Timoteo threw a rock into the pool. "The pearl is evil. It's just hiding the truth from you."

Wilbur pursed his lips. There was something powerful about the pearl, but not evil. It didn't feel evil. It felt more spiritual and uplifting.

"It's not hiding anything, Timoteo. The pearl is just a pearl."

"You're wrong." He jumped into the pool and joined his

mother and brother in a game of water tag. Wilbur watched them play. Compassion filled his chest. He could care about them, get involved in their lives. Make things better...for them and himself.

All day he and his newfound family soaked in the clear and sunny air of a mountainside haven, ate bananas and coconuts and wild berries, and swam in crystal clear water. By late afternoon, they decided to spend the night. He fashioned a lean-to for Liawayway using bamboo and palm leaves. He added a few flowers for decoration.

The boys insisted on building their own shelters on the other side of the pool.

He intended to sleep on the flat rock...until later that night...when Liawayway called him to join her.

He left his shirt on the rock and lay down with her on the thick mat of soft palms. "Are you cold?" It was ninety degrees with ninety percent humidity. He just didn't know what else to say.

Moonbeams filtered down through the jungle canopy, dappling her face with soft light. Wriggling close to him, she whispered in his ear. "How does it feel to be a hero?"

His heartbeat stuttered. "I haven't done anything heroic."

"You saved us." She nuzzled his neck.

Goosebumps skittered down his arm. Her hair smelled clean and fresh from her swim in the pool. He inhaled her cinnamon fragrance, the nectar of a Wild Palawan Cinnamon flower, which she had dabbed on her body here and there. The effect drew him in like a moth to a streetlamp. He concentrated on something else. "Timoteo told me—"

"Shhh." She touched a finger to his lips. "You will wake the boys." Her wraparound dress fell open. She drew him into her arms.

He trembled, felt the heat of her olive-skinned breasts against his bare chest. Hard nipples like hot pokers. His mouth watered at the thought of kissing them. "You sure?"

"I am not sure of many things. The future. Not for me, my sons, my tribe, my God." She shuddered. "The Japanese may take everything. But I am sure that I like you, Wilbur Cobb." Her eyes glistened in the moonlight.

"I'm an American."

"Nobody is perfect." She giggled.

"The boys," he whispered. "I don't think Timoteo wants me and you...you know...to be together."

"My sons like you very much." She breathed into his ear.

The message was clear. She was ready to move on with her life. A part of him rejoiced. Another part worried. For all he knew, that slimy Maricar could be out there somewhere watching them right now.

"I like your boys too."

"And me? You like me?"

Since the first time he laid eyes on her. But she didn't need to know that. Besides, she had another suitor. "What about Maricar?"

"He would kill to be where you are."

"That's what I'm afraid of."

"He is a boy in a man's body. You are afraid of him?"

"I'm afraid of you."

"I have seen the way you look at me. Your eyes wander up and down and are filled with curiosity."

She'd been paying more attention to him than he'd realized. He felt rattled at being caught gawking. "I'm sorry. I didn't mean to—"

"Etem used to look at me that way. You remind me. You make me feel beautiful again."

"You *are* beautiful."

"And so are you, Wilbur Cobb."

He'd never thought of himself as beautiful, more rugged and rough around the edges, but he liked the way she saw him. Still, if they were going to go further with this relationship, he wanted it to matter. "What are you going to do in Manila?"

"Find a place to live. Get a job."

"You can stay with me."

"We don't want to be a burden."

He didn't see her as a burden, or the boys. Besides, where would they go? Most of Manila was squalor. She'd never held a job. How would she find one now? There'd be more opportunity for her in the states. Maybe that's what this was all about. "Do you want me to take you to America?"

"No."

That surprised him. Most native women made it a fulltime occupation to rope an American into taking them home. "What's wrong with going to America?"

"The Philippines is my home, Wilbur. I won't leave it like you left San Francisco."

That stung. He swallowed and pressed on. "There's more opportunity in America."

"More money?"

"For starters."

"I don't care about money. I never had much. What would I do with more? Besides, look at the beauty around us. A simple life we have here, where a man is valued not by his money but by what's in his heart."

"So you want me to live with you here."

"In the Philippines. Luzon or Palawan. It doesn't matter." She touched his cheek. "But promise me one thing."

"What's that?"

"You'll never be a pearl diver."

That was easy. He already owned the largest pearl in the world. "I promise."

Her lips moved close to his, parted. Her hot breath on his mouth lit a fire in his heart. He kissed her with a hunger he'd left in San Francisco—

The plane hit a bump of air, jarring him awake. Last week's memories evaporated into the joyous squeals of children. Tito and Timoteo were bouncing in their window seats. "Look at the city. Look at the city."

"Manila already?" Wilbur sat upright, blinking.

Liawayway inhaled. "I didn't know it was so big."

"Boys. Put on your seat belts." Outside the window stretched Manila Bay and civilization. It felt good to be back, though he would have to leave again soon.

"Look at all the buildings." Timoteo beamed ear to ear.

Tito pressed is face to the glass. "Where will we live?"

"We are staying with Wilbur." Liawayway looked at him and smiled. "I don't know where."

"An apartment for Benguet employees. It'll be a little cramped with the four of us, but you'll be comfortable. You'll be safe. We'll find something bigger when I get back."

"Back?" Liawayway's eyes turned stormy. "You are going somewhere?"

"California."

"But we have just arrived." She slumped in her seat and looked at her fingernails.

"I travel a lot with my job." She'd really be steamed if she knew it was the pearl that was taking him away from her.

The descending plane banked right, leveled out.

"Look, Mamma." Tito poked his finger at the glass. "Are we going to live in that building down there?"

"Maybe." She looked out the window over his shoulder. "It's a big city."

"I'll get a job." Tito's face tightened with determination.

Timoteo swatted the top of Tito's head. "You're too little."

Tito rubbed his crown. "Mamma."

"Boys. Be nice."

The plane turned on final approach to the airport. A company car would meet him at the terminal. He'd get Liawayway and the boys settled into company housing and then pack for California. A three-day island hop to Beverly Hills, one day to get the pearl appraised, and three days to get back. He'd be gone a week. They'd be fine. He was sure of it.

Still, there was one thing he couldn't be sure about.

The Japanese.

Chapter Nineteen

Beverly Hills, California, October 1939

In the city of the rich and famous, excess was a common commodity. Businesses along El Camino and Rodeo Drive thrived. Having weathered the Great Depression, retail sales had topped twenty million dollars. And the real estate market was booming: clothing stores, fine hotels and, of course, movie stars' mansions. Surrounded by all this wealth and prosperity, Wilbur Cobb sat in the back seat of a '39 Packard taxi on his way to meet with Gary Kaufman to have the pearl appraised.

Wilbur managed a suit and tie for this occasion, but he missed his comfortable jungle fatigues. Folding his arms on the Rosewood box in his lap, he appreciated how the car rode smooth as scotch on the paved city streets. The Packard's cool conditioned air impressed him, the first such innovation in automotive history.

The cab turned right onto Santa Monica Boulevard. On his left, Beverly Gardens stretched as far as he could see. The *Electric Fountain* on Wilshire jetted water into the air, a symbol of the city's fertility and abundance. He couldn't imagine living this ritzy lifestyle.

But it was worth a shot.

On his right, wide sidewalks, towering palm trees, and opulent storefronts basked under a soft California sun. The marquee for Kaufman Jewelers appeared:

Jewels and Dreams, the Bigger the Better.

Wilbur patted the box and wondered how much the Pearl of Allah was worth, not that he'd sell it, he just wanted to know the value of the Panglima's gift.

The cab stopped at the curb. "That'll be seventy-five cents, pal."

Wilbur handed him a buck, and with the box tucked under his arm, shoved open the door and climbed out. As the car sped off, he hooked a finger under his collar. The tie was choking the life out of him.

At the front door to Kaufman's, Wilbur's reflection in the glass beamed back his image: a total stranger, dressed like a businessman instead of an adventurer, but this interlude in his life was necessary, revisiting the son of his father's best friend. Wilbur had only vague recollections of the jeweler, but it was his father who'd talked of big game hunting in Africa and the diamond trade, exciting stuff for a ten-year-old boy with dreams of adventure.

He pulled on the chrome door handle and stepped inside.

A bell signaled his entrance to a store empty of patrons. The air smelled of ammonia, probably from the cleaner used on all the glass display cases set about like a giant glistening maze. The air resonated with the sounds of ticking and chiming. On the back wall hung clocks of every imaginable size and shape.

"I'll be right with you," a man's voice called out from the backroom.

"No hurry." Wilbur scanned a rich assortment of rings and watches perfectly arranged in the brightly lit cases. Gold and diamonds sparkled. An entire case shimmered with pearl necklaces and earrings displayed on folded blue silk. Tiny things—

"Wilbur Cobb."

He looked up. A man, twenty years his senior approached, wiping his hands on an apron. Narrow jeweler's glasses rode low on the bridge of his nose. If Wilbur had passed him on the street, he wouldn't have recognized him. "Gary?"

A boy appeared behind him, maybe five or six years old. He wore a small apron and carried an armful of common riverbed rocks.

"It's been a long time." Kaufman offered a robust handshake.

Wilbur tipped his head to the boy. "And who's this little tyke?"

"My son Paul." Kaufman moved to the door, flipped over

the closed sign, and turned the deadbolt latch. "He'll be running this business before long."

"I believe it." Like father, like son, like grandson. "What are you going to do with all those rocks, young fella?"

"They're not rocks." His voice sounded squeaky as a dog's chew toy. "They're diamonds and emeralds and pearls."

"Of course they are." Cute kid.

Kaufman nudged Paul toward the backroom. "Run along, now. Mr. Cobb and I have business to discuss."

As the boy walked away, Kaufman leaned against a case of jewels and eyed the box under Wilbur's arm. "Is that it?"

"The Pearl of Allah. Yes. Did you get the shell?"

"It arrived this morning. Largest Tridacna specimen I've ever seen."

"The Dyak chief gave it to me, along with the pearl."

"Generous little bugger, huh?"

"Nothing compared to saving his son's life."

"Let's have a look, shall we?"

Setting the box on the glass countertop, Wilbur wondered if Kaufman would feel the same spiritual uplifting he'd felt when he first saw the pearl. He opened the box and stepped back to observe the jeweler's reaction.

Brows arched, Kaufman stood upright, walked two steps to the box and looked down into it. He said nothing, just stared.

Wilbur detected surprise—or perhaps awe in the jeweler's expression.

Kaufman removed his glasses, grasped the pearl, and lifted it from the box. Holding it with both hands, he raised it to the ceiling lights, its pearly sheen radiating like the rising sun. Eyes wide with wonder, he slowly turned it over, inspected every fold, every lump, every line. One revolution, then two.

Nothing said.

He could have been a priest reading a Bible verse and pondering its depths.

"Well?"

As if laying a newborn child in its crib, the jeweler returned the pearl to the box and looked up with wonder in his eyes. "I've seen this pearl before."

He couldn't have seen the pearl. "It's been in the

Philippines since 1934."

Gary blinked. "No. No. This pearl goes back twenty five hundred years."

"Impossible." What kind of scam was Kaufman trying to pull?

"I'm sure of it." His face blanched. "I'll show you." The jeweler rushed to the backroom.

Suspicion grew in Wilbur's head. The clocks ticked and chimed. Something wasn't right. He should've never shown Kaufman the pearl. In ten steps he could make the door. One twist of the deadbolt, he'd be outside. Close the box. Grab it and go. Go, damn it. Go. But his feet wouldn't move as if knee-deep in quicksand. He'd traveled a long way to get the jeweler's expert opinion. Left behind a new love. A new family. Only a fool would turn tail and run now.

Kaufman returned with a faded brown book. He set it on the glass countertop. Flipping yellowed pages, he found one and tapped it with his finger.

"Look."

Wilbur stepped up to the book. He saw an image of his pearl, Chinese characters, and a squiggly mark. "What the h-hell book is this?" he choked out.

"Chinese Legend and Lore," Gary whispered. "Your pearl is this pearl." He tapped the page. "The Pearl of Lao-Tzu."

"La who?"

Kaufman shut the book and shifted his attention to the pearl in the box, speaking without looking at Wilbur. "He founded Taoism in 600 BC China. According to the legend, he carved a small amulet of the faces of The Three Friends, himself, Confucius and Buddha. He put it in an oyster to coat it with nacre, but sometime afterwards he left, I don't know why, and the pearl remained. Over the centuries his Taoist followers transplanted the growing pearl into consecutively larger mollusks."

"Not my pearl." Wilbur was certain it wasn't his pearl.

The jeweler looked up. "It was lost at sea in 1745."

"This can't be the same pearl."

"The Tek Song was en route to the Philippines. It sunk in the Sulu Sea somewhere off the coast of Palawan. Eighteen hundred people on board. No survivors. It was the Southern Hemisphere's Titanic." Kaufman peered into the box. "This big bugger was on board."

Wilbur wished his heart would stop pounding so hard. He re-opened the book and thumbed fragile pages in search of the picture. He had to see it again—study it more closely.

"They shipped it in a giant clam."

"Two hundred years ago? Come on. Giant clams don't live that long."

"Don't be so sure, Wilbur. Islanders tell of Tridacnas living in their lagoons for generations."

"I don't believe it."

"They even give them names." Kaufman spoke over Wilbur's shoulder. "Nalani. Kainoa. Akoni."

Wilbur found the picture. It didn't look exactly like the Pearl of Allah, kind of droopy, like his, okay, but thinner. There was nothing to compare its size with, no hand or ruler. It could have been small as a pea, for all he knew. Kaufman had jumped to conclusions. "Look. It's not the same."

"The drawing is over two hundred years old. Wouldn't you expect the pearl to change since then?"

That made sense. Damn it.

Chinese characters lined the left edge of the old picture.

"What do these mean?"

"Sold to the highest bidder. It's a shipping order."

Wilbur refused to believe the pearl once belonged to the Chinese. "It was found on May 7, 1934. I was there. I know. A diver died for this pearl."

"Died?"

"Drowned."

Then it's true."

"What's true?"

"The curse."

"Curse?" Timoteo would like to talk to this guy. "You believe in that malarkey?"

"Read the caption."

"The pearl of Lao-Tzu was meant to be a talisman of peace, longevity, and profound wisdom for all Taoists—"

"Longevity." Kaufman stopped him. "The giant clam lived

a long time."

"Bullshit." He read on. "—*and never exchanged for money or power...lest men be damned.*"

"Qianlong sold the pearl to a governor in the Philippines. Eighteen hundred people died en route. Sounds like a curse to me."

Wilbur blinked. Etem died. Malaria wiped out half the Dyak tribe. And the plane crashed, killed Bambi...the pilot...the team. Coincidence? Had to be. "Curses are not scientifically possible."

"Everything doesn't have to be explained. Did Moses part the Red Sea? Did Jesus walk on water? Have a little faith."

"I'm a geologist, Gary. I need facts." He scanned the text, looking for anything that would discount Kaufman's contention that the Pearl of Allah was the pearl of Chinese legend. *Sold to the highest bidder.* "Why would the Taoists sell their sacred pearl?"

"They probably didn't have a say in the matter." Kaufman looked down at the pearl in the box. "Emperors were powerful enough to take whatever they wanted."

Of all the rotten things to have happen, his pearl belonged to someone else. That could create a problem. "What if they want it back?"

"Who?"

"The Taoists." Wilbur jerked loose his tie. "If it's their pearl...they'll want it back."

"It might be worth a lot of dough to them."

Wilbur blinked. He wasn't going to sell his good luck charm, not even to the people it belonged to. And according to this curse, selling it could jinx him good.

But why had it brought him luck? Because he didn't purchase the pearl? It was given to him freely...as a gift. Etem died trying to take the pearl from the clam...by force. The Panglima selfishly claimed it for his own, and his villagers suffered and died of malaria. Pula nearly died, and would have if the Panglima had not promised God to give up the pearl in exchange for his son's life.

Wilbur shut the book. His heart slammed around in his chest. Timoteo was right. This pearl was the pearl of death. It was a time bomb waiting for Wilbur to succumb to temptation. The apple on the apple tree waiting for the snake.

"I've got to go...get out of here." He closed the box, his hands shaking.

"Not so fast, Wilbur." Kaufman grabbed the box. "Don't you want to know how much the bugger's worth?"

Wilbur grabbed the box too. "That's all right." He tugged on the box to get it from Kaufman.

He tugged back. "I'll give you fifty grand."

Wilbur choked. Fifty grand? Tempting, but the Panglima had told him that owning the pearl was worth more than money. "It's not for sale."

"A hundred thousand dollars," the jeweler pushed. "Cash."

Wilbur's suit began to feel claustrophobic. "No-no thanks." He tried to yank the box from Kaufman's grip. Kaufman: the snake, tempting him to bite the apple.

"It's a lot of money, Wilbur." He jerked back on the box. "I'd take it if I were you."

How could he? The pearl had given him Liawayway and the boys. It had saved him from the plane crash. "It's my good luck charm."

"A fourteen-pound pearl? Get a rabbit's foot or a horseshoe like everybody else. You can buy a lot of good luck with a hundred grand."

Wilbur was tiring of this tug of war. "Take your meat hooks off my pearl."

"One hundred fifty."

Sweat dripped down Wilbur's neck. He had to be nuts to turn down that kind of money. "Forget it."

"You won't get a better offer."

"I don't want a better offer." Wilbur shoved Kaufman backward and yanked the box from his hands. "I'm leaving." He started for the door, drawing a bead on the deadbolt lock. "I'll let myself out."

Kaufman grabbed Wilbur's arm, spun him around. "Let's talk about this." *This* came out a hiss. "I want that pearl," said the snake in Kaufman's voice.

Wilbur stared into the jeweler's piercing eyes, seeing a dark side of Gary Kaufman, as if the pearl's affect on him manifested evil and greed. "Let go of my arm before I do something we'll both regret."

Kaufman's grip loosened. "All right. Two hundred grand." His voice sounded squeaky like his son's. "It's all I have."

"No." Wilbur jerked free. He was insane turning down two hundred thousand dollars. "Our fathers were best friends. I came to you for an appraisal, as a friend. I didn't come for your money...or a fight, but don't push your luck. Now let me leave."

Kaufman stood firm, all puffy-chested, then exhaled and stepped back. "Okay. You won't sell the pearl. Okay. Fine. Then rent it."

"It's not an apartment." He started toward the door.

"Have you heard of Ripley's Believe It or Not?"

That snagged him, sure as a snare trap would snag a warthog. He'd heard of Robert Ripley, in Manila where the internationally syndicated cartoon series *Believe It or Not* appeared in the local newspapers. "You know Ripley?"

"The bugger's got a new Odditorium museum opening in New York."

It had been a few years since Wilbur heard that word. Odditorium. The first Odditorium opened at the Chicago World's Fair in 1933. It attracted two million people, curious to see the unique and bizarre on display. His pearl would fit right in.

"They'll pay a lot of dough to exhibit a specimen like yours."

Wilbur wondered how big a cut Kaufman wanted for the referral, but quickly shook off his curiosity. It wasn't going to happen anyway. "I have to get back to Manila." He continued toward the door.

Kaufman followed him. "You wouldn't have to sell your pearl. Show it to people and tell the story about how you got it."

Wilbur clutched the box to his ribs. The snake had offered him the perfect opportunity to fulfill a dream: to go on tour, tell his tale of adventure. He turned to face Kaufman. "You can get me into Ripley's?"

"Next month. I'm showing an emerald there...for the grand opening on Broadway. With your pearl, the show will be a huge success." His voice dripped excitement. "The Guinness Book of

World Records will be there. You could get in the book."

"The Book." What a great way to market his speaking tour, to cement his reputation as a world-class adventurer. "Next month?"

"People will line up for blocks. I can see it now." He made a picture frame with his fingers and thumbs. "Wilbur Cobb and the Pearl of Allah."

"The greatest story ever told," Wilbur chimed in. "The Philippine jungles. A Dyak tribe. The Panglima and his dying son."

"That's right."

"And a Palawan princess..." The air leaked out of him. Liawayway was waiting in Manila. And he had a job with Benguet. "I've got to go back to my job—"

"You don't need that job. Quit the bugger."

"But there's a woman waiting for me—"

"Oh no. Don't tell me, Wilbur, you'd blow the big time for a nip of Flip ass?"

Wilbur clenched a fist, showed it to Kaufman. "Watch your mouth, Gary."

"Don't blow your wig over her, Wilbur."

"She has two boys. They mean a lot to me."

Kaufman held up a hand in surrender. "Then go back to the Philippines." If a snake could grin, he did. "But wait until after the show. When you're a rich man. Then bring your little natives to the United States. Buy 'em a mansion in Beverly Hills."

Images of a lavish home, ritzy furnishings, and fancy cars tempted him to accept the offer. But what was in it for Kaufman? "How much is this going to cost me?"

"We'll split fifty-fifty."

"It's my pearl. Eighty-twenty."

"Sixty-forty. What do you say, Wilbur?"

He had to decide, the Philippines or the money, Liawayway or the pearl. This was an opportunity of a lifetime. And best of all: he wouldn't have to sell the pearl.

Take the money.

Take the fame.

But could he give up Liawayway? The boys? The Philippines? For the pearl. For the money. For the fame. Why should he have to give up anything? Just put everything on hold. For a little while. But not for a lousy sixty percent. He looked at Kaufman. "Seventy-thirty or I'm walking out."

"Deal." He held out his hands, palms up. "Now I'll put that big bugger in my safe."

"Oh, no you don't." Wilbur clutched the box. "The pearl stays with me."

"And risk it getting stolen?"

"It traveled halfway around the world with me just fine."

"You're not in the jungle anymore, Wilbur. This is the land of opportunity. For burglars, crooks, and thieves. Don't take a chance on being mugged and losing our bonanza."

Kaufman made a good argument for securing the pearl. Hopefully not too good. Wilbur handed over the box, slowly, as if it were his only child. "You better not jack me around."

"Relax." He studied the box.

"I don't trust you."

"That's too bad. I'm the one who's going to make you rich."

Okay. Maybe he'd judged Kaufman too harshly. This pearl business was more overwhelming than he had imagined. He couldn't relax entirely. He could proceed with caution.

The first thing he wanted to do was call Liawayway with the good news. She'd be excited that the pearl her late husband had found would be on display in New York City. And proud.

He glanced at his watch. 4:50 pm. It was 7:50 tomorrow morning in Manila. Liawayway would be getting the boys off to school. "I need to use your phone."

"It's in back."

He followed Kaufman to the backroom.

The jeweler moved to a wall safe the size of a bank vault and worked the combination. Wilbur looked for the phone. Across the room sat a workbench where young Paul had perched himself on a tall stool. Scattered before him under a cone of light lay small tools and riverbed rocks, one of which he stroked with a fine brush, prepping himself for his future profession.

With a clunk, the safe door unlocked.

Wilbur spotted a cluttered desk and the phone. To get to it he had to step around the giant clamshell he'd shipped to

Kaufman earlier. It lay nestled in a bed of shredded paper on the floor, spread open like giant butterfly wings glistening in pearly splendor. The shell would make a spectacular addition to the show.

Kaufman pulled open the heavy safe door. A light winked on inside, setting off an explosion of glitter from a fortune in jewels.

Wilbur picked up the phone and dialed.

The relay operator came on. "What number, please?"

Kaufman placed the box on a high shelf.

"Benguet 773, Luzon."

It took a few moments to find an open line on the twelve-channel oceanic cable routed through Wake, to Guam and on to the corporate office in Manila. The delay gave Wilbur's excitement time to bloom.

Liawayway was going to be happy to hear from him.

"Benguet Consolidated. Where may I connect your call?"

"Room 517." He pictured her with Timoteo and Tito sitting around their small kitchen table, eating eggs and toast and chatting in Tagalog.

The phone rang, an eerie echo over the long distance line.

"Hoy?"

"Liawayway, can you hear me?"

A couple seconds passed before her reply came back. "You don't have to shout. Why are you calling? We are fine."

"I'm going to New York City."

A pause. "You are not coming home?"

"Yes...in a month or two."

"You promised to return in a week. What am I to do, get a job? Maybe I should waitress in a bar. You might stop in for a scotch so that I can see you sometime."

Ouch. That was unexpected. "I'm going to show the pearl at a museum. How do you like that?"

"I would like for you to keep your word and come home."

"But I'm going to make a lot of money."

"I already told you, I do not care about money."

"Well, I do. I'll call you from New York every day."

"Again, our lives are torn because of that stupid pearl."

Click.

"Liawayway?"

The relay operator came on. "Shall I try to get the call back?"

It felt like a bomb had gone off in his face. He'd better give her time to calm down. "No thanks."

He hung up the receiver. His stomach felt heavy as a chunk of iron ore. This trip to New York might cost him more than thirty percent. He could lose his new family.

The safe door slammed shut with a bang.

Chapter Twenty

Mount Luofu, China

In the Hall of the Three Pristine Ones, Moy Linshin sat cross-legged on the floor and faced an altar of seven burning candles. Share Lew Shī paced behind him, the master's sandals a mere whisper across the smooth slate. Vanilla incense sweetened the air. Bare stone-mortared walls and wood ceiling symbolized simplicity, the sublime realm of Lao-Tzu. And like the great sage, Linshin strove for stillness but found peace elusive in his young, broken heart.

He had worked the last two years trying to clean the uncleanable, wash from his mind the horrific deaths of his māma and bàba, the terrible fate of his sister, captured by the Japanese. She was probably dead by now, like his heart, that empty, aching hole in his chest that burned with the memory of lost lives, lost loves, lost innocence.

"Recite from the *Tao Te Ching,*" Share Lew said. "The book of the Way and the Law."

"The book of the Way and its Power," Linshin chanted.

"A sage has no ambitions, therefore he can never fail."

"A sage never fails." Linshin stared at the flickering candles. He had ambitions—to become a Taoist priest. To find stillness. He'd spent his first months at Wong Lung Kwan scrubbing floors and washrooms, gardening, and shoveling snow. And when he wasn't working, he was studying: math, science, literature and the way of the Tao. Like a sage, he would not fail.

"If a sage never fails," Share Lew went on, "then he always succeeds. One who always succeeds is all-powerful."

Linshin felt far from all-powerful. Every night he battled

bad dreams, sweated and vomited, wishing for the sun to rise and another day of work to wipe the gruesome images from his mind, his parent's blood-drenched faces, their heads impaled on spikes, Rea screaming as the Japanese soldiers dragged her away. He'd never know the life of a normal twelve-year-old boy. Only work and sweat and study. But he had a roof over his head and food in his belly and Share Lew to thank.

"Ambition is not only vain but counterproductive."

"If I don't strive for something and I do nothing, how will I succeed at anything?"

Share Lew glided to the altar of seven candles. "You must follow the flow of nature and not pit yourself against the universe. The natural order has purpose." He pinched out a candle flame. "Be spontaneous. The Tao is in the present."

"The present is painful."

"The past was painful." Another candle pinched out. "The present is not. A sage lets go of *this* and chooses *that*. Let go of your past and choose peace."

"I did."

A doubtful glance from Share Lew. "The screams of a boy's nightmares have not gone unheard within these stone walls. Your nightmares, Linshin. Let go."

Embarrassment heated the back of Linshin's neck. He rose to his feet and smoothed his white robe. "Easy for you to choose this or that. They are not your nightmares."

"Your tongue is sharp for one so young."

"I'm sorry, my master." He bowed in a show of submission, not regret.

"Stand before the Tao, there is no beginning." Share Lew pinched out another flame. "Follow it, there is no end." The last candle darkened, he took up his walking stick. "Only the present matters. Make the most of it."

"How?"

Share Lew turned away. "Come with me."

Linshin followed him down the hall, wondering if he was worthy of living such a sterile existence.

Outside, he looked over the Eastern River and the green fields in the Valley of Sunrise. Below him lay a flower garden with stone walkways all leading to a Lotus Pond. Fat goldfish swam in the clear water. He felt privileged to live on Mount Luofu, seemingly isolated from the world and far from the war.

Share Lew continued down the steps and across the garden. For an old man, he moved swiftly, heading toward a temple that rose behind a row of rearing yellow dragons with bulging eyes.

Linshin stopped. The Ancient Temple of the Yellow Dragon was off limits, yet Share Lew waved him to come forward.

Scrunching up his neck, he scooted between the menacing sentinels, swallowed dryly, and glanced up at the temple walls covered with overlapping yellow tiles, like scales. Honeybees buzzed flowers skirting the walkway to a door guarded by more yellow dragon statues.

Long snouts. Sharp teeth. Fierce eyes.

As he passed through the dark doorway into cool, refreshing air, a flutter of birds escaped. Palms sweating, he closed the gap to Share Lew, smelled rotten eggs and heard the echo of trickling water.

A fountain stood in the center of the dim space. Four carved giant clams held up a wide basin made of polished stone. Water burbled up from its center and trickled over the rim.

Share Lew led him to the fountain and made a palm cup with both hands pressed together. "Drink."

Linshin realized the rotten-egg smell came from the water. Repulsive this close. "It stinks."

"This spring-fed well of Wong Lung Kwan will give you strength and longevity." Share Lew slipped his hands in the water, cupped a handful to his lips and sipped noisily.

"Why am I allowed in here where no one else is?"

"That I say you are allowed makes it so." He drank again.

Linshin followed his lead. Dipped his fingers. Then his hands. Cupped icy water. Hesitated. He was about to drink where few had ever drunk. "Master, why me?"

"Let go of the past and move in the present."

"Is there no straight answer in you?"

The master stared into his cupped hands and spoke softly. "I want you to find stillness."

"I cannot forget what I saw, forget what I lost."

"Then I have already failed."

The Pearl of Death

"You cannot fail."

"My success or failure is in your hands."

Linshin felt the weight of that burden. He inhaled a quick breath and drew from the well. In spite of the smell, the water tasted bland. Yet refreshing. He drank heartily.

His heart began to race.

His skin tingled.

He dipped his hands, faster, drawing water to his mouth.

Guzzling. Dipping. Guzzling.

Sensations coursed through his body: Heat. Energy. Power. He felt bigger, faster, stronger, like the temple dragons.

Like the sage who never failed.

Like the great master, Lao-Tzu.

Linshin wasn't twelve anymore. He was a grown man. A great sage. He was all-powerful...

Chapter Twenty-One

New York City, November 1939

Dread walked with Wilbur Cobb into *Ripley's Believe It or Not* Odditorium where the Pearl of Allah was on display. Camera bulbs flashed. People cheered and applauded his entrance to the exhibition hall. He gritted his teeth and forced a smile as he waved to the crowd who had come to hear him speak. His dream of a lifetime finally realized, he feared this venture might cost him his life on a technicality. He hadn't sold the pearl, but he was still using it to make money.

His booth sat against a wall draped with two Navajo rugs similar to the ones on the floors of the Panglima's residence.

The giant clam rested on two stands situated to display the shells fully opened, butterfly-wing style.

In front of the stands, a poster read *LARGEST PEARL IN THE WORLD* across the top. Below that, Wilbur had pasted four photographs, one of the pearl and a twelve-inch ruler, one of the Dyak chief and his family, and two of the giant clam, one with closed shells and one splayed open with Wilbur posing behind it.

The centerpiece of the display was a slowly rotating pedestal with the Pearl of Allah set on top, eye level so visitors could get a good 360-degree view.

Wilbur took his seat on a stool by the spread clamshells. As much as he hated wearing a suit, on this snowy Friday night he wore a black coat and tie. This discomfort compounded his first-show-jitters.

Armed guards flanked the booth. He spoke to the crowd seated in folding chairs in front of him. Fifty or more folks had come to see this evening's show and hear the tale of his great adventure, exceeding his expectations.

The Pearl of Death

"In conclusion, my friends, I defy the richest men in the world to show me a similar pearl." He quoted the Panglima.

"How much will you sell it for?" someone shouted.

"Please excuse my blunt words, but the satisfaction of owning the largest pearl in the world is worth more than mere money." The Panglima's words again. "It's not for sale."

"Is it really cursed?" a woman shouted.

"As I told you, my young friend in the Philippines believes it is cursed." Wilbur didn't want anyone to know he believed it too. "But it has been my good luck charm. Thank you everyone for coming."

Applause filled the room. His first-show-jitters subsided. He moved to the front of his booth where Gary Kaufman stood clapping. Beside him, a fat man in his forties also applauded. He wore a long brown coat and cowboy hat. His handlebar mustache looked stiff as barbwire.

"Wilbur Cobb." Kaufman shook Wilbur's hand. "I'd like you to meet Ralph Zimmerman."

"A pleasure, sir." Wilbur offered his hand before he noticed the greedy glint in the fat man's eyes.

Zimmerman delivered a rattling handshake. "I've been looking forward to meeting you, Mr. Cobb." His voice boomed like a controlled explosion.

Kaufman stepped back. "He's a Colorado businessman."

"The Restaurant and Bar Association," Zimmerman belted out.

"And a rich bugger."

Blood thumped in Wilbur's neck. Looked as if Kaufman had called in a moneyman to help him buy the pearl.

"What can I do for you, Mr. Zimmerman? An autograph, perhaps? A photo?"

"Mr. Cobb, it is I who would like to do something for you."

Here it comes. "And what would that be, sir?"

"I'm prepared to make you an offer."

No surprise there. "I'm afraid you wasted your time coming here, Mr. Zimmerman. Seems Gary Kaufman has misled you. The pearl is not for sale."

Kaufman couldn't keep his mouth shut. "He's going to

sweeten the pot, shall we say, up the ante. Don't be a bugger about this—"

"I don't care—"

"A-hum!" Zimmerman cleared his throat. "Look, Mr. Cobb—"

"No! You look." Wilbur jabbed a stiff index finger into the fat Coloradoan's pot. "I'm not selling. Not now. Not ever. You got that?"

Zimmerman wheezed. "Then what? You gonna go back to the Philippines, keep your pearl in a shoebox, all to yourself?"

"Screw you." Wilbur turned to leave.

Kaufman stepped in front of him. "Hear the man out."

"Screw you, too."

"Mister Cobb," Zimmerman boomed. "We wish to buy shares in your pearl, like a stock investment. Museums will pay to display the pearl, in Chicago, Denver, LA. Maybe even London and Paris. You won't have to lift a finger, except to count all the greenbacks pourin' in."

Kaufman jumped in, "And you won't have to work at Benguet anymore," as if that alone would cinch the deal. "No more digging up rocks in the jungles. You'll live in luxury, buy your little native girlfriend anything she wants."

Wilbur stared at the jeweler in disbelief. They'd put the pearl in a glass case, shine lights on it, and rake in the money. Without an adventure story to go with it, it was just a lumpy, ugly pearl. What was so hard to understand about that?

"And we'll call the pearl by its rightful name," Zimmerman went on. "The Pearl of Lao-Tzu, the lost pearl of China."

Wilbur's stomach turned inside out. "You want the whole world to know it's someone else's pearl? Are you nuts? Those Taoists will want it back. They'll come after it. They'll fight for it."

Zimmerman laughed. "Taoists are pacifists. They won't do anything."

"Besides..." Kaufman patted Wilbur's shoulder. "The buggers are too busy running from the Japanese to worry about a pearl."

"This is a big opportunity for you, Wilbur."

All they saw was the money they could make. They didn't

understand the true meaning behind the pearl, the Panglima's gift, the good luck it brought him. They placed no value on his love of the Philippines or a Palawan princess and her boys.

"Two hundred fifty thousand dollars for forty-nine percent...to Kaufman and myself."

"You keep fifty-one," Kaufman added. "It's still your pearl."

Zimmerman smiled, his beefy hand extended. "What do you say, my boy?"

Wilbur swallowed. A quarter of a million dollars? God that was a lot of money—enough to make a man sell his soul.

Temptation was a powerful force. Ask Eve.

But if Wilbur caved, he'd be attached to Zimmerman and Kaufman at the wallet for half of everything. They'd run his life forever.

"We got a deal?"

"No thanks." Wilbur turned his back to the men and started walking toward the door. His scalp felt frizzy, as if his nerves expected a blow to the back of his head. Instead, he heard Kaufman tell the businessman:

"He's a stubborn bugger."

"So he can't be bought with money." Zimmerman's voice boomed. "But every man has a weakness."

Bastards!

"What would your weakness be, Mister Cobb?"

Wilbur pushed through the museum doors and into a flurry of snow, hoping they wouldn't find out.

Terry Wright

Chapter Twenty-Two

Wong Lung Kwan

Kung fu.

Linshin's favorite lesson. He'd dressed properly for the class: a one-arm smock, long left sleeve, baggy black pants tucked in white leggings and soft-soled shoes. Share Lew Shī had promised him an introduction to sword fighting afterwards. If he did well at kung fu.

He followed his master down steep steps to the garden. Orange blossom fragrance filled the air. Other *todei*, students of Wong Lung Kwan, had gathered in ranks on the lawn by the Lotus Pond. Some older boys, some younger. All with eagerness in their eyes. Eagerness to get the rice cakes pounded out of each other.

Share Lew stood before his class. He wore a long *changpao* buttoned down the front, loose black pants, bare feet. He'd tied a black cloth belt around his waist, the knot on his right hip, the tails hanging to his knees.

"Hieee!" Share Lew's signal to begin.

Linshin dropped into the crouching tiger stance, left foot planted flat and toes pointing forward, knee bent, right foot behind him, knee locked, fists balled at his waist, shoulders back. He inhaled slowly. Forcefully. His fellow *todei* did the same, some with less conviction than others.

He mirrored the master's moves through a series of poses: the riding horse stance, the seven star, bow and arrow, mouse and monkey. His movements flowed smooth as flowing water from one position to the next and ending back at the crouching tiger.

"Again."

Two more times, the same routine.

Warm-ups completed, Share Lew motioned his students to face off. Linshin found himself paired with a bald-headed *todei* named Winkles.

Linshin swallowed hard. Why did he always draw the big kids?

"Hieee!"

Winkles winked, attacked with a right hand chop. Linshin threw a left ward-off punch. The impact stung, but Winkles left him no time to shake it off, charging in with a right straight-leg kick for the chest. Linshin blocked the boy's foot, but a left leg-soaring kick landed squarely on his right shoulder and knocked him backward.

Pain shot up the bones in his neck.

Winkles dropped, spun and delivered a whirlwind kick toward Linshin's feet. He saw it coming, jump-roped the boy's leg and landed in a riding horse stance, knees bent, fists cocked at his waist. But Winkles sprang up like a monkey and struck three quick blows, a right chop to the top of Linshin's head, jamming his teeth, a left to his neck, specking his vision, and a right roundhouse to his left temple, making him angry. He grabbed Winkles' left wrist, twisted his arm hard enough to turn him facing away, then delivered a squatting leg kick to the big boy's rear end. Sent him sprawling face-first to the ground.

Linshin glanced at Share Lew.

He nodded his approval.

Linshin smiled. A thud and everything went black.

***

A dull throbbing pain egged Linshin to consciousness. He tried to open his eyes, but his left eye felt glued shut and throbbed. Share Lew leaned over him. "I thought you were dead."

Time slipped backward. Two years ago. When the nightmares began. But this time he wasn't lying in a ditch. He was lying on grass. In the garden. The scent of orange blossoms teasing his nose. "What happened?"

"You took your eyes off your opponent."

Opponent?

Winkles' smirky face appeared next to Share Lew's. "You all right?"

Linshin remembered. Kung fu class. The bastard had sucker punched him. Anger flared in his veins, hot as dragon breath. He sat up, pointed a stiff finger at Winkles. "One day I will kill you for that."

Winkles laughed, turned, strolled off. Other *todei* joined him, slapped his back. They rollicked away like playful dogs.

"I had him beat." Linshin felt his tender left eye, the swollen socket.

"You thought only of the end of the fight. To win. But there is no end. There is only the present. That is when you failed to protect yourself. In that one single moment, you lost."

"In that one single moment he cheated."

"Even more humiliating for you, I am sure. To be beaten by a cheater."

"You have no sympathy?"

"It is my place to teach, not coddle."

Linshin would have no coddling. He climbed to his feet. The earth tipped, but he quickly found his balance. "Will that be all for today, master?"

"You are forgetting your sword fighting lesson."

"I'd probably slit my own throat."

Share Lew chuckled.

Linshin hadn't said it to be a joke.

Share Lew strode to a trunk set under an orange tree. He opened the lid and removed a sword. "This is a *dai doe*, a big blade sword." Holding it level with both hands, he presented it to Linshin.

Linshin scanned the curved blade and intricate engravings of flowers, tigers and dragons. The sword must have been worth more than Lao-Tzu's lost pearl.

"Take it."

Bowing, he took the sword, felt its weight and the power it represented. He'd seen other *todei* training with swords. Now it was his turn. Excitement warmed his stomach like hot green tea.

Share Lew stepped back. "Hold it in your right hand first. Same exercise as before. And don't cut yourself."

As he settled into the crouching tiger pose, the sword felt

The Pearl of Death

ungainly at first, until he found its balance.

"Hieee!"

To Linshin's amazement, as he moved smoothly between stances, the sword always pointed forward and remained clear of his left arm.

"Again."

The monkey stance. He felt strong and powerful, gritted his teeth, and swung the sword with a roundhouse swipe. He imagined cutting off Winkles' head. It flipped in the air, spraying blood and thumped on the ground. He shoved a spike up the severed throat. Planted it in the garden.

Māma. Bàba. Winkles. All in a row.

The riding-horse pose. With a quick foot shuffle and a hard forward thrust, he gouged out Winkles' winking eye. It bounced in the grass. He smiled. The class attacked him. Crouching tiger. Slashed the sword up and down. Side to side. One head hit the ground. Then two. A chest plunge. A scream. Take this. Take that! Swipe. Plunge. Swipe. Slash.

"Stop!"

Linshin staggered, looked at the sword, expected to see blood dripping from its lethal edge. A glint of sunshine caught his eye. Made him squint. Confused...

"You think this is a game?"

"I was only—"

"Kung fu is a way of life. It takes discipline. Hard work. There is no place for childish foolery."

"I'm sorry, my master." Linshin bowed, his cheeks aflame with embarrassment.

"You will keep that sword with you day and night, in one hand or the other, and you will not put it down, not even to sleep."

"I said I was sorry, Master."

Share Lew turned away and stormed off down the path through the garden, his walking stick stabbing the slate tiles with a heart-thumping *whack, whack, whack.*

Linshin blinked. He had never seen the master get angry. Never thought it possible. The master was so displeased with his favorite student, he'd lost his stillness.

A roiling anger brewed in Linshin's belly. Self-loathing

anger. The Japanese should have killed him and spared Share Lew the anguish of knowing such an unworthy *todei*.

His eye socket throbbed. The Tao had saved him for something important. Certainly it was not for this humiliation.

He stalked off in the opposite direction Share Lew had gone. The sword felt heavy, now a burden more than a treasure. He wanted to drop it on the ground and run to the granite gateway of Wong Lung Kwan to disappear into the mountains. Never to be seen again. Like the great sage Lao-Tzu.

Tears distorted his view of the garden.

He stopped at the Lotus Pond, sat on a stone to think. Sunshine gleamed off the water, and the ripples made by rising goldfish expanded into sparkling rings. A stone tortoise poked its head above the surface, and nine porcelain cranes waded in the shadows, all symbols of longevity. Why would anyone want to live a long life this cruel?

Inhaling the cool breeze, he set the sword across his knees and savored the sweet fragrance of red and white lotus flowers floating on broad leaves. Goldfish swam so close to the edge he could touch them. The tranquil scene should have helped him to find stillness.

To stay in the present.

To stop thinking.

He wished he could ask his māma and bàba what he should do. They would say he should stay here. Get an education. Make something of the life he'd been spared. And as always, thoughts of his parents bled into horrid images engraved in his mind, their heads on spikes, eyes wide open, flies infesting the lips that had once kissed him goodnight.

Wuwei. Do nothing. His eye pounded. The way of the Tao. Don't fight the universe. But he was angry with himself and the Japanese and Share Lew.

Raising the sword, he angled it to the sun. Light glinted off the polished steel blade. "What have you saved me for?"

A gurgle in the water caused him to look down in time to see a goldfish rise to the surface, its yellow lips slurping air as if mocking him.

Linshin clenched his jaw and swung the sword down across the fish's back. Clear water turned blood red. The fish thrashed water so loud everyone would hear its death throes.

Shock blurred his vision. He couldn't believe what he'd done. The killing was spontaneous, in the present, the Tao. What was the matter with him?

Nearly cut in half, the fish floated on its side, its tail flicking its last feeble, lifeless convulsions.

His eye socket convulsed too. Something was wrong in his head, like Winkles had done more damage than blacken an eye. Linshin clenched the sword in his fist. It was the Tao. It caused him to lash out, at the fish instead of himself.

The fish—he couldn't let the fish be found.

Leaning over the water, he used his sword to retrieve the carcass. His hand shook, causing him to drop the fish twice. He almost dropped the sword. As he raised the dead fish from the water, its round eyes stared at him accusingly. The cut across its back, through its spine, was clean and straight, like the cut that severed Bàba's head from his neck.

Linshin's throat filled with the sharp sting of bile. Fear, guilt and revulsion overwhelmed him. He tossed the fish carcass into the bushes and fled the garden.

Chapter Twenty-Three

Wilbur Cobb stood in front of another audience seated in folding chairs for the Tuesday night show. As usual, taking center stage, the pearl glistened from its rotating pedestal. Armed guards flanked the booth.

Fatigue weighed heavy on his eyelids. He was about to finish his hundred-umpteenth rendition of the pearl's story, the way he'd saved Pula, the grateful Panglima's gift, and Liawayway, his Palawan princess waiting in Manila for his return. At the beginning of his contract with Ripley's, he thought he'd never tire of telling the story, but his great adventure was already getting old.

"And that's how the Pearl of Allah came into my possession. Any questions?"

"Wilbur Cobb," a man called out and stood. He held a pad and pencil. "Robert Baker, New York Times. I understand you're taking the pearl out of the Odditorium."

"Yes. After Christmas."

"Where will you be showing it next?"

"Tell your readers that this is the only show. In a month, their opportunity to see the Pearl of Allah will be gone. That should pack 'em in."

"Is it true your pearl belongs to the Chinese?"

Wilbur felt snake-bit. Damn Kaufman and Zimmerman. They must've leaked that morsel to the press. Create an international incident. Make so much trouble for him he'd be happy to sell the pearl. The bastards would stoop so low...well, he wasn't going to let them get away with it. "That's just a rumor, sir, started by some jello-belly investor out of Colorado."

"But Mister Cobb, there's some pretty convincing evidence that this pearl..." he wagged his pencil at the pedestal, "is actually the Pearl of Lao-Tzu."

"All fabricated, I assure you, sir." Wilbur smiled at the reporter, but his insides churned with dread that this news might travel around the world and land on the wrong ears. Like Chinese ears. "Anyone else?"

"Mister Cobb." A blonde woman waved a black-gloved hand. "Does that mean you'll be going back to the Philippines?"

The thought of escaping New York City and seeing Liawayway again sent sparks of excitement popping in his stomach. "Yes, ma'am, as fast as I can paddle."

A chuckle from the crowd.

"Then may I ask, would your Palawan princess have anything to do with that decision?"

"Of course. And don't forget I have a job with Benguet. I've only taken a short leave of absence. Anyone else?"

Happy to see no hands, "I'll stay a few minutes for autographs, and please, feel free to come up and take a close look at the pearl. The guards don't bite. Thank you for coming."

The audience applauded and rose from their chairs with a clatter. Wilbur rubbed his forehead, wishing for a scotch and a good night's sleep.

A kid wearing a Yankees baseball cap rushed up and offered his Ripley's brochure. "Can you sign it for me?"

"Sure." Wilbur scribbled his name, instantly converting a worthless brochure into a treasure. "There you are, son."

He looked up to greet the next person in line, the blonde doll, tall and slender. Pip all the way, she wore a fur coat and a feather-trimmed hat. His gaze attached itself to her partially unbuttoned blouse where a pearl string necklace bridged deep cleavage. She smiled with the grace of royalty, a high-society broad, but walked up to him with a showgirl sway to her hips.

His heartbeat tripped up. He felt suddenly energized.

She extended a black-gloved hand, palm down. "I enjoyed your presentation, Mr. Cobb."

He took her hand, inhaled the scent of lilacs. "Thank you, Miss...?"

"Elaine," she breathed with a slight pucker on her red-painted lips. "Elaine Meyers."

"My pleasure." He held her hand a moment longer than he

should have and gazed into blue eyes so deep he thought he would drown. More than a casual attraction beamed back.

"I'll be needing this later." She glanced at her hand.

"Oh." He let her go, chuckled like a nervous schoolboy and hoped the awkward moment would bleed away quickly. "Do you have something for me to autograph?"

"I don't think so."

"Your brochure, perhaps...a ticket?"

"Yes, sure...please. My ticket, of course." She dug it out of her coat pocket. "That'll be fine."

To the lovely Elaine Meyers, he signed. *Wilbur Cobb and the Pearl of Allah 1939.* "There you go."

A man approached, clean-cut, suit coat and hat, handed him a brochure. Absentmindedly, Wilbur autographed it, his attention still riveted on the bedazzling Elaine Meyers.

What a beautiful face, perfect white skin, with a little mole below her mouth, close enough to her lip to be a distraction. If this were San Francisco ten years ago, he'd be climbing her tree, like Tarzan for Jane.

He gave the man back his brochure. "Tell all your friends to come see my pearl."

"Amazing." The man walked off.

Elaine didn't seem in a hurry to leave.

"Is there anything else I can do for you, Miss Meyers?"

"I'd like to buy you a drink." She shifted her weight to one high heel, put a sexy smile on those perfect lips. "You're a scotch drinker, right?"

Alarm bells rang in his brain. "Maybe."

"You go out after every show, to the bar on the corner."

Had she been spying on him? "I don't recall seeing you there."

"No, not me. Not in that dive. I know a better place." She inhaled, thrusting those voluptuous mounds at him with a come-hither tilt. "I thought you might like some company for a change."

A worm of apprehension wriggled in his stomach. Someone must've put her up to meeting him. Probably Zimmerman. "My mother told me to never accept scotch from a stranger."

"You're an interesting man, Wilbur Cobb."

"Am I?"

"I'd like to get to know you better," she whispered.

"I bet."

"We wouldn't be strangers any longer."

She wanted to get her hands on his pearl. Why else would she proposition him? He should stay as far away from her...then again...she probably knew Zimmerman's angle, his plan. Playing along could put Wilbur one jump ahead of him, prepared to derail any attempt to get the pearl. "Sure, why not? And what would you be drinking, Miss Meyers?"

"J and B Rare." She fanned her face with gloved fingers. "Is there any better scotch?"

"Expensive." Another coincidence? Scotch drinking buddies were the best of buddies. Like him and Bambi... "I'm glad you're buying."

"My pleasure, Mister Cobb."

He looked over the thinning crowd, thought how easily he could slip out. "You can call me Wilbur."

"Only if you'll call me Elaine."

"Sure...Elaine." They were already on a first-name basis, a good start for drinking buddies—or a hooker and a john.

"The club isn't far." Her eyes gleamed with obvious anticipation. Too obvious. "On 21st street. We can take a cab."

Yeah, she had it all figured out. He wondered how long it would take her to work the pearl or Zimmerman into the conversation. "One drink." He grabbed his bushman hat from the booth. "Then I've got to call the Philippines."

She hooked her arm under his elbow. "Good. You can tell me all about your Palawan princess."

"Really?" He guided her toward the door. "Women don't usually want to hear about the other woman."

"I'm intrigued by a man who would travel halfway around the world for love."

"Are you one of those romance writers?"

She served up a sultry laugh. "No, silly."

Her delight was contagious, and he was laughing by the time they made it to the street.

But he remained guarded, just the same.

"Taxi."

***

Piano music plinked through the cocktail lounge, dimly lit in the flickering glow of candlelight. It was one of those bars where the pretty people hung out, survivors of prohibition who told war stories of underground speakeasies and illegal roulette wheels. On the walls, photos depicted gangsters with their Tommy guns cradled like babies. Here and there hung pictures of Federal agents busting up wooden barrels that spilled liquor and beer into the gutters. Over the bar, Bonnie and Clyde's splayed out bodies and bullet-riddled car looked down on dark wood furnishings painstakingly cleaned and polished, as if splendor alone elevated the drinking social class above the rest of the common drunks.

Elaine led him to a booth with slick leather seats and fine white linen. A candle flame in a glass orb waved *welcome, Wilbur*. She slid in first. He sat across from her...where he could look into her eyes for any sign of treachery.

She giggled. "Can you believe that cab driver?"

"His English was terrible." Wilbur loosened his tie, giving pause to how accustomed he'd become to dressing slick.

"Cap-e-tan el Sharod." She laughed. "Was he from India?"

"Pakistan." Wilbur pointed to the middle of his forehead. "No third eye."

A petite waitress appeared. She wore a tuxedo complete with black bow tie. Fake gold cufflinks gave her the glitz. "What can I get for you?"

"Two double scotches." Elaine said it with ease, as if she'd ordered drinks for men many times. "On the rocks."

Looking around, he decided he didn't like the joint, felt out of place in spite of his newfound wealth. He missed the bar on the corner, the dive where he could drink with real drinkers who didn't give a damn about him or his money. Here he expected to see Zimmerman lurking in the shadows.

He looked back at Elaine in time to watch her remove her black gloves. Elegant pale fingers slowly revealed polished red fingernails. Smiling, she slipped her coat off her round shoulders revealing skin so white he wondered if her body ever saw the sun. He wondered if he would ever see her body...

"One drink." He'd said it more to remind himself than her.

"Come on, Wilbur. Loosen up a little."

"I have to call the Philippines."

"Must cost you a fortune."

"Two minutes a day. Benguet pays. I call her at school. During her lunch break. She's taking a business course at the University of Manila. Midnight here is noon there, tomorrow."

Elaine winked. "That gives us two hours."

He'd be bombed in two hours. "One drink and I'm done."

"Party pooper."

The way she curled her lower lip, she looked innocent, or maybe spoiled...or worse, she was acting. He wished he could oblige her. Get sloppy drunk and the world be damned, San Francisco style, but he couldn't trust her. He had to expose her for who she really was: Zimmerman's sexpot puppet.

Drinks came in short glasses, over ice, his favorite way to savor scotch, every cool sip warm going down.

She dropped a sawbuck for the waitress. Ten dollars. Big spender. Obviously the Great Depression hadn't reached her lofty perch on the social ladder. Or Zimmerman had bankrolled her big time.

"Run a tab," she whispered to the waitress.

"Yes, ma'am."

He tipped his glass to Elaine's. "Thanks."

"Anytime." She took a drink.

Sipping scotch, he welcomed the smooth burn in his throat and wondered why Elaine had requested a tab when they were only having one round. Keeping a tight rein on this woman might be more difficult than he'd first expected.

Her tongue slid across her upper lip glistening with scotch. "So tell me about your princess, Wilbur."

Swallowing, he looked down into his glass of amber gold, thought about Liawayway, felt a pang of guilt. He shouldn't be coveting Elaine's sexy nuances and bodily attributes. Six months ago he would've jumped at the chance to explore her every curve and crevice. But not now. Not anymore. Not with Liawayway in his life. Besides, what would he do with a well-off, classy dame like Elaine? What would she want with a rock hound...other than his pearl?

He stared into his drink, waiting for her to make an offer. She appeared wealthy enough to afford the pearl. Maybe she was a free agent, not working for Zimmerman but in the hunt for herself.

"Wilbur, I asked you about Liawayway."

"Yes, of course. Liawayway." His thoughts wandered back to Palawan and that day in the jungle—at the waterfall, after he was almost killed in a plane crash. "I miss her. I'm going back. I promised."

"Do you love her?"

"She makes me think. To her, love is simple, a bond of trust."

"But do you love her?"

"She deserves a better life."

"You don't look like the rescuing type, Wilbur."

"Oh? You can tell by looking? What is it, something in my eyes, the way I look at you when I'm thinking of another woman?"

"You don't love her."

He glanced at his glass. "Love is complicated, but a promise is a promise."

"Of course." She tossed back her scotch, a criminal act. Scotch was to be sipped, every drop savored reverently. "Another round," she called out to the waitress and held up two fingers.

"What are you doing?"

"Drinking alone." She pointed to his nearly full glass.

"I told you—"

"Yeah, yeah. You have to call Liawayway."

"You're jealous."

"No. I'm not jealous," she snipped.

"Yeah. You're jealous."

"You make me wish I had a man like you. Most men are dogs. They'll hump anything that moves. Bow wow. But you're not like that. You're loyal as they come."

What did she know? He'd never been loyal to anyone. In his younger days, he'd laid more than his share of loose women. Zimmerman may have found Wilbur's weakness; yeah, he was a dog; but he wasn't going to admit that to Elaine. "Guess I'm just a one-woman man."

She looked him up and down with a scotch-induced gaze. "But don't you ever feel that she's so far away...that for one night, another woman could sleep with you...and that would be all right?"

Let's see, a roll in the hay in exchange for the pearl? "No."

Her lower lip twitched like she might cry any second.

He swirled scotch and ice in his glass. When it came to women, *no* wasn't a word in his vocabulary. If only she knew how much he wanted to kiss her, taste the scotch on her tongue, and bury his face between those luscious breasts.

Old habits died hard.

The waitress set down another double in front of Elaine. And another in front of him.

"Elaine? I said one—"

"Drink up. That's what we came here for, right, to get to know each other?" She gulped down a mouthful of scotch. "Or are you violating some unspoken vow to your Palawan princess by just talking to me."

He took a fiery gulp of scotch, hoping to quench the fact that he agreed with her in principle. "Try to understand." He reached across the table, took her hand, felt the warmth of her soft skin on his fingertips. "I've got a weakness for pretty women."

She leaned forward, her cheeks turning rosy. "You think I'm beautiful?" A flutter of eyelashes.

"Gorgeous." Beating back the urge to kiss her, he wasn't going to fall into her trap. Still, he had to play along, get her to talk about the pearl and find out what Zimmerman was planning. "When I look into your eyes, the Philippines is a million miles away."

She glanced down, stared at the table. "Like Pearl Harbor is for me."

"Pearl Harbor?" Not the pearl he'd expected from her.

"Michael. He's on the battleship Arizona."

"Boyfriend?"

"Kind of."

How did Michael fit in with Zimmerman?

"Michael writes me sometimes...when he's lonely. I think he likes the idea of having a girl back home, but we're not that close...not like you and Liawayway."

"Don't compare your love life to mine."

With a manicured finger, she stirred the ice cubes in her scotch. "Michael doesn't miss me. Not like you miss her." She licked scotch from her lovely finger. "I guess I am jealous."

"I guessed first." He threw down another burning gulp of scotch. The dame put on a good show, but why had she brought up her lousy love life if she was trying to seduce him out of his pearl?

Her lower lip quivered and her eyes shined with tears. "Michael is a million miles away too."

So that was it. She was battling the loneliness of a long distance love affair. Being alone tormented her. Waiting tormented her. This had nothing to do with Zimmerman. It had nothing to do with the pearl. It had everything to do with a lonely woman reaching out to a lonely man.

"Wilbur?" she whispered. "What is it?"

"We have the same problem. We deal with it the same way." He raised his glass in evidence. "Scotch."

Slowly, she removed her feather hat, dropped it on the table, and pulled the pin out of her hair. Soft golden locks tumbled over her shoulders. "Maybe we can get through this together."

Like San Francisco all over again. Dames and games. He downed the last of his first drink and half the second. His cheeks felt hot and numb. Desire overpowered caution. He slid out of the booth, moved around to sit next to her.

She watched him with wanting eyes.

He put his arm around her, inhaled the scent of her lilac perfume.

She nestled in close. "Every night I worry that he'll never come home." She nuzzled her cheek into his shoulder. "That we'll never have a chance to discover what our love might have been. The scotch helps me sleep."

"I know."

She took his hand, played with his fingers. "I want to fold myself into your arms, Wilbur, kiss you like mad before I'm too drunk to give a damn."

He felt like a heel for thinking she was in cahoots with Zimmerman. "Come on. I'll take you home."

She looked up. "Are you sure?"

"It's cold out there." He downed his scotch as if it were lowly beer. Now that he was sure she wasn't after his pearl, his defenses dropped faster than ice cubes into a cocktail glass. "Where do you live?"

"My flat is just around the corner."

A warm bed with a hot woman, two lonely adults in the big city, what harm could it do? The scotch was doing his thinking for him. He knew it. He didn't care.

He helped her to her feet and into her coat. Setting the feather hat crooked on her head, he gave it a pat. "Let's go."

Arm-in-arm they walked outside.

Christmas lights twinkled all down the avenue. A light snow fell. His breath vapors entwined with hers as he hugged her close to stave off the cold.

It was almost midnight by the time she unlocked the door to her flat.

He swallowed dryly and stepped inside. The Philippines was a million miles away. His head swam in alcohol. He leaned against the doorframe and fought off the wooz.

A dim ceiling bulb illuminated the room: brown couch, wood table, ratty-edged throw rug. No crystal chandeliers? No spiral staircase? What the...?

She started clawing off his coat. His bushman hat hit the floor. Slick as an old whore, she popped his shirt buttons, kissed his neck, his face.

Let the games begin.

He ripped open her blouse. Buttons flew. A black lacy bra whispered *Hello Wilbur*. His drunken fingers attacked the straps. It took a yank and a pull to get the clasp off. Bra cups floated to the floor like spring rose petals. Busty flesh bobbed before his eyes.

He could hardly breathe.

The scotch kicked into high gear, spinning the room. She shoved him onto his back. On a squeaky mattress. Shirt splayed open. She pulled off his shoes, her curvy silhouette backlit by the bulb in the front room. She leaned over him, fumbling with his belt buckle.

Old habits died hard.

Most men are dogs. You're not like that...

By morning she'd think he *was* a dog. Like all the other men. He had to stop her. Please stop.

His hand slid down to his buckle. She must've thought he was going to undo the belt himself because she let go and started kissing his belly, up to a tickly nipple and then to the hollow of his throat.

No. Don't stop! That tongue. Oh God. And she smelled so good.

Most men will hump anything that moves.

She felt so soft, those lips that he'd longed for now pressed to his, warm and wet and wanting.

I'm intrigued by a man who'd travel halfway around the world for love.

He'd travel halfway around the world for Elaine.

She was wrong about him.

He *was* a dog.

She moaned in his ear. Her beautiful breasts pressed against his bare chest. Michael had one hell of a sexy woman waiting for him...

Wilbur felt dog kicked. What was he doing?

Stop!

A shot of adrenaline cleared his head. He twisted around and turned her over on her back. Leaning on his elbow, he watched the frantic rise and fall of her breasts. She was the most beautiful woman he'd ever been naked with, but still, a switch inside him had turned off.

"What is it?" She breathed. "Why did you stop?"

"I can't."

"Because of her?"

"I'm sorry."

"Wilbur, why? Is she warmer than me? Is she more beautiful?" She arched her back.

His eyes slid from her neck toward her toes, over every curve and the smallest patch of pubic hair he'd ever seen.

"Stop it!" He sat up on the bed, turned his back to her.

"We'll ruin everything. The time I spent with her. It'll be meaningless."

"She doesn't have to know."

"But *I* will know. It's not right...not while Liawayway's waiting for me...not while you're waiting for Michael."

The scotch was to blame. He'd drunk it too fast. He knew better.

Stupid! Stupid! Stupid!

Elaine sat up next to him, pulled a sheet up to her neck. "I'm sorry, Wilbur."

He groaned. "I have to go."

"Meet me for lunch. You'll feel better then. Okay?"

Any other woman would have kicked his ass to Kansas for stopping in the middle of hay rolling, especially because of '*the other woman.*' Insulting. And humiliating. But not Elaine. Why not?

"My treat," she chirped.

"I don't know."

In the muted bedroom light, he buttoned his shirt. She wrapped herself in a robe and left the room. He tied his shoes. It would be past one a.m. before he got back to his hotel. Liawayway's break would be over. She'd be back in class, probably furious that he didn't call—or worried that something bad had happened to him.

Well something bad did happen.

Something really bad.

Bad! Bad! Bad!

Elaine met him at the front door, handed him his coat and bushman hat. "You okay, Wilbur?"

"I feel like a dog."

"Bow wow. I'll meet you at noon, the Madison, right?"

"So you know where I'm staying, huh."

"A little birdie told me."

Her revelations ceased to surprise him. "It's a nice hotel." Not like this dump. The drab décor didn't fit the ritzy Elaine Meyers. Didn't make sense, the way she dressed versus the way she lived. Suspicion crept back into his brain. She and Zimmerman. In cahoots. Had the evening been a sham?

"Lunch then?"

"Sure." Wilbur had to accept her invitation. He needed to know if she was genuinely attracted to him, or if her affections were staged for Zimmerman's benefit. He'd stay sober and get the truth out of her, once and for all.

She kissed his cheek and let him out.

Trudging toward his hotel, alone in the bitter cold, he tried to come up with a reason why he didn't call Liawayway, a reason she would believe.

The phone lines were down?

He got mugged and landed in the hospital?

He almost got laid?

Bow wow.

Chapter Twenty-Four

Morning brought pain. Wilbur slogged across the Madison Hotel lobby. His head hurt from the bottle of scotch he'd polished off after returning to his room. The more he couldn't sleep, the more he drank, the more he drank, the more he couldn't sleep, a typical night in the Big Apple. Now he had to meet Elaine and find out if last night was just a charade.

God he was such a dope. Flash a little money. Flash a little skin, and he fell for her. To say he had fidelity issues would be an understatement.

He took the stairs down to the arched hotel doorway, stepped outside, and inhaled icy air. The sky hung low and gloomy. He missed Palawan. Life was easier there. Even the hangovers seemed less brutal.

On the corner, a paperboy cried, "Read all about it. The Pearl of Allah."

Folks gathered around, snatching up copies of the New York Times.

Panic spurred him toward the crowd. Why was his pearl in the news? Had it been stolen from Ripley's? He pushed his way up to the paperboy. "Let me see one."

"Five cents, mister, you can see it all you want."

Wilbur dug a nickel from his pocket.

The headline made his hung-over head pound. *PEARL OF ALLAH IS LOST CHINESE TALISMAN.*

Associated Press Release. Robert Baker.

The reporter from last night. Wilbur had told him the rumor wasn't true. He ran the story anyway. Damn.

He jammed the paper under his arm and stepped inside the café where Elaine stood at the métier de stand. She wore a plain green coat over pants and a blouse with a ruffled white collar, her hair pulled back into a ponytail. He couldn't get over how different she looked from last night. The transformation unsettled his already woozy stomach.

"Are you all right?" She put her hand on his arm.

"Look at this twaddle." He handed her the paper.

She glanced at the headlines, showed marginal interest. "Front page. Way to go, Wilbur. Free publicity."

"Kaufman and Zimmerman are trying to make it look like I'm not the pearl's rightful owner."

"I don't think anyone really cares."

"The Chinese care."

A hostess stepped up. "Your table is ready."

Wilbur took the paper, gave it to a fellow standing in line, and followed Elaine into the restaurant.

The café was abuzz with patrons, lowly office clerks and sales associates, the working class of uptown New York. Brown tablecloths. Paper napkins. Ketchup and mustard bottles displayed on every table. Short water glasses. Nothing classy here. The clank of silverware mingled with the aroma of roast beef, biscuits and strong coffee.

Seated, he looked over the menu. He wasn't hungry, but he had to eat something.

"I'll have the French dip." Elaine set down her menu. "And you?"

"I'm more of a club man, with bacon and fried potatoes."

"I can't eat that much grease."

A voice boomed behind him. "Well, I'll be damned, if it ain't Wilbur Cobb."

Wilbur turned in his chair, swiveling his head so fast a dizzy spell walloped him. Zimmerman stood there, fat and pompous, all decked out in his long brown coat and cowboy hat. He stuck out like a palm tree in a flower garden. "Isn't this joint a little low class for the likes of you?"

"Best roast beef in town." He smiled at Elaine. "Miss Meyers, nice to see you."

"Mr. Zimmerman." Elaine scowled.

Wilbur's head felt gonged. He'd been right all along. Last night was a damn setup. He shot out of his chair. His brain reeled from standing too fast. "What the hell's going on here?"

"Just bein' neighborly." Zimmerman grinned.

"You hire a damn hooker to do your dirty work?"

Zimmerman puffed up like a prized bull. "Hold your horses there, partner."

"You think she can make me sell you my pearl?"

"Wilbur, please—" Elaine squeaked out.

"And you." He pointed an accusing finger at her. "What are you doing in bed with this snake?"

Elaine shrunk back in her chair. "He's a regular at Dino's, he and Kaufman. I see them almost every day."

"Dino's? What's that? Some kind of whore house?"

"I'm not a hooker."

Zimmerman laughed a big jelly-belly laugh. "Dino's is a restaurant, you dope."

"I'm a waitress." Elaine said it like the words hurt her throat.

"A waitress?"

"Is there something wrong with that?"

"But last night..." Okay. That explained her flat. No glitz. No glamour. But the clothes she wore. The money she flashed. She couldn't have put on that lavish show without financial help.

Zimmerman tipped his hat. "Ma'am." He grinned at Wilbur. "You better get some sleep. You don't look so good."

White spots flickered in his peripheral vision. "Get the hell out of here."

"It's a free country." Laughing, Zimmerman waddled away.

Wilbur felt as if he would pass out any second. "I hate that guy."

"Please, Wilbur." She indicated the chair he'd so quickly vacated. "Sit down. Let me explain."

"Forget it." He whirled around to leave, stagger-stepped, held on to the chair back as if it were the edge of a tall cliff. The adrenaline buzz was raising hell with his hangover. "I know what's going on."

She leaned forward, offered her hand. "Listen to me."

His head felt like a coconut, all fuzzy on the outside and sloshy in the middle. He gritted his teeth and sat in the chair.

"Okay. You've got one minute."

A waiter showed up. "Is something wrong?"

Ignoring the question, Elaine ordered coffee for two. "And I'll have the French Dip."

"I'm not hungry." He'd only barf it up anyway.

Coffee poured, Elaine lifted her cup. "Last night, you could have had your way with me, Wilbur." She sipped coffee. "Most men would have, without a second thought."

"I'm a saint." Wilbur's coffee was so damn hot he couldn't sip it much less guzzle it down like he wanted.

"But deep down, you don't love Liawayway. You know it. I know it."

"Last night was not a test of love. It was a con game."

"You're an honorable man, Wilbur. I admire you for that."

"Bull. Zimmerman and Kaufman are after my pearl, and you're helping them get it."

"They don't want you to go back to the Philippines." She set down her coffee cup. "I was supposed to give you a reason to stay, for love, for sex, it didn't matter, as long as you didn't take the pearl out of the show."

"Christ."

"Look. I'm sorry I agreed to help them."

"How much did they pay you?"

"Enough. But I'm no hooker."

"Sure you're not." He sounded condescending and meant it. "You got me into bed for the money."

"Money matters to me, Wilbur."

"Gold digger."

"A girl's got to eat."

"The whole night was a lie." He tried to stand, but his coconut felt like it was going to crack. A desperate sip of coffee scalded his upper lip.

"I wanted you to like me enough to stick around. But I ended up liking you instead. You're the kind of man I want in my life."

"What a crock."

"I had you in my bed and you stopped because of a promise you made to a native girl. That's loyalty, Wilbur, like it or not, an admirable trait."

"I'm a dog."

"But you made me laugh...and you made me cry. We ended up in bed. If that makes me a whore, then I'm a whore for you."

"And Michael? Another lie?"

"I opened up to you because you listened to me. Michael never did."

The waiter came by, topped off her coffee, and moved to the next table.

Elaine sighed. "Why can't we find someone to love closer to home?"

Wilbur stared into his cup. Liawayway was home. He was the one who was gone. Because of the pearl, which was evidently more important to him than being with her. No wonder he fell into bed with Elaine. At least she came clean in the end.

"Don't hate me, Wilbur."

He didn't hate her. Last night was his fault. Too much scotch too fast. Not enough love in his heart for Liawayway. Things got out of control. But he'd learned something, came clean with himself in the end, as well.

"I wish you'd stay, give us a chance."

He shook his head. "A promise is a promise. I'm leaving next month." He got to his wobbly feet. "Until then, you stay away from me."

Chapter Twenty-Five

Mount Loufu, China

G ray clouds clung to the mountain slope, swirled through high trees, and rolled across the stony path that jagged toward the summit. Moy Linshin welcomed the burn in his legs from the steep climb. He inhaled the moist breeze, smelled the coming rain, and felt a chill on the crown of his newly shaved head. With each step, the *dia doe* sword sheathed on his waist slapped his white robe. At the end of this path, in the Temple of Immortality, he would face the first test of his kung fu training.

Climbing behind him, Master Share Lew wore his green ceremonial robe and carried a pot of smoking poppy seeds, which he swung back and forth and chanted verses of the *Tao Te Ching*. "From above it is not bright. From below it is not dark."

Linshin joined him. "Form of the formless. Image of the imageless." Master Lew had not said what test awaited him at the top but to be prepared for anything. "Without form there is no desire. Without desire there is tranquility."

"Know the ancient teachings," Master Lew went on. "It is the essence of the Tao. Understand nature. Master circumstance. Follow the Way to your destiny."

"There is no beginning. There is no end."

"Only the present matters."

Linshin recited the words, but he wasn't sold on that verse.

"Stillness is the way of nature."

Linshin slipped on loose rocks, sent them tumbling downhill with a clatter. He would've fallen too if not for Share Lew's quick hands that saved him from a spill down the mountainside.

The Pearl of Death

"Death is stillness, boy, but not the stillness we seek."

Master Lew had not missed a step, his old legs agile and strong due to the well water of Wong Lung Kwan, which Linshin had been allowed to drink daily. And he had eaten the herbs of longevity not available to the other *todie*. The master had said Lao-Tzu attained immortality by drinking the water and eating the herbs. Now he was with nature and the universe that never ends. Perhaps Linshin would live forever too, alongside the great Master among the stars.

The path curved left and jogged up steeply through a thick stand of pine trees. Sharp needles scraped his unprotected head. He didn't duck to avoid them, just plodded on, his jaw clenched tight. Taoist tradition made this climb a requirement for his first test at the Temple of Immortality. A test he would not fail.

"Do nothing. Accomplish everything," Master Lew recited.

Wuwei. The Tao abided in non-action, yet nothing was left undone. Linshin pondered this concept, but still he couldn't grasp its true meaning. Food didn't simply appear on the table. Studies weren't miraculously completed. Kung fu wasn't mastered without a few lumps and bruises.

A temple came into view, made of stone on the mountaintop. Stone steps led up to an entrance flanked by tall pillars and rearing dragons, the sun and the moon carved in the gable above their fierce heads.

Linshin stopped. Inhaled a nervous breath. Smelled opium smoke wafting up from behind him. "The Temple of Immortality?"

"The order and power of nature is more enduring than the power of state. Dragons can be slain. Nations fall. The Tao is eternal."

"No beginning. No end."

"You go in first, but be careful."

Linshin felt dizzy from the opium smoke. Carefree in a strange way, not afraid of what he would face inside. He began the climb up the steps.

Be prepared for anything.

He poised his hand over the grip of his *dia doe* and trudged upward.

The heavy sky loosed a torrential downpour. The

mountaintop came alive with the sound of rain spatter on the rocks, trees flinching and bows bending. Quickly drenched, Linshin plodded up slippery steps, his bamboo sandals slogging through rivulets of water rushing downhill. Cold rain stung his bare head. The smell of wet earth rose to his nostrils, reminded him of the Lotus Pond in the garden and a dead fish cut in half. He swallowed the memory and climbed faster.

At the top, he dashed between the dragons and into the Temple of Immortality. Wall-mounted torches gave the interior an eerie, flickering glow.

The patter of rain seemed far off, overpowered by the dripping of water on a smooth concrete floor. An altar stood in the center of the room, made of rock carved clamshells encircling an odd shaped stone suspended by chains anchored to heavy log rafters.

He recognized the shape of the stone.

The Pearl of Lao-Tzu.

A marble shrine to a lost heirloom.

"Moy Linshin," an echoing voice called out. "You would enter the Temple of Immortality with a weapon?"

With one smooth stroke, Linshin unsheathed the sword. "Show yourself."

"Lay your weapon on the floor." The voice came from behind him.

Linshin pivoted around, sword ready. He saw no one. "I will not."

Be prepared for anything.

"You won't need it here." This time the voice came from his right.

He swiveled around, on guard. "I will be the judge of that."

"The one who screams in the night does not dictate the rules."

"What do you want from me?"

"Obedience." The voice came from his left. "You are a tree without roots, easily felled in the wind."

Linshin coiled into the crouching tiger stance, sword cocked and ready to strike at anything that moved. "You be the wind and try your luck."

"You have excelled in kung fu, the best *todie* here, but

your emotions make you weak."

"Because I do not accept your insult?"

From behind him now. "Because you swim upstream, fight the current. You are out of balance and harmony with the Tao."

Linshin spun around. The voice materialized into a man standing so close he could have been breathing down Linshin's neck. He wore a conical straw hat and green robe, stood seven feet tall with the bones of a stork and the posture of a pine tree. A silver beard grew long to mid-chest.

In the split second it took Linshin to realize he'd been ambushed, the sword was snatched from his hand and tossed across the floor.

"Windy enough for you now?"

Linshin stepped back, aghast. This turn of events sucked the air from his lungs. He recognized the man before him, Ghuan Yee Shī, The Spirited One. A single strike of his fist meant certain death.

"Master." He bowed.

"As you see, I am not defenseless...defenseless as a fish."

A bolt of hot panic seared up Linshin's spine. Master Yee knew about the fish. Linshin shrunk. He would hide in his skin if he could. "It was an accident."

"It was not."

"It was just a fish."

"A life lost is a life lost."

"Master Lew made me angry."

"Violence is not an answer. It is an end. Like the wind is to a tree without roots."

"But you teach me to fight."

"We teach self control. Restraint. *Wuwie* will grow your roots deep. Concentrate on the inner self. Then you will achieve your purpose."

Master Lew's voice echoed across the temple. "Linshin, the Tao saved you for a reason."

"But I don't know what it is."

"When the time is right, the Tao will show you." Water dripped from Share Lew's robe to the floor. The opium pot smoldered relentlessly. "I see you have lost your sword."

Linshin's cheeks heated with embarrassment.

Share Lew retrieved the sword, examined it, first one side of the blade then the other. "No worse for wear."

"Was that the test?" Linshin looked at Yee. "I failed?"

"Your roots will grow deeper if you learn not to fight at all."

"I should run? Like the night my parents died? I didn't fight then, and look what I am left with. Nightmares."

"You are only twelve. Give yourself time."

They didn't understand. "I want to fight."

A voice from behind him. "Me too."

Winkles!

Linshin spun around, fists up, expecting a sucker punch.

Winkles pulled a newspaper from under his rain-soaked robe and handed it to Share Lew. "See page three, Master." Then he sprang into the monkey stance.

Master Yee shouted, "Don't fight him, Linshin."

Linshin bent his knees, the riding horse stance, fists balled at his waist. Of course he was going to fight him, but he wished he had his sword. He'd slice the sixteen-year-old lug into wok meat.

Share Lew opened the newspaper, shuffled pages.

Winkles charged in with a forward thrusting punch to the face. A quick turn of his body, Linshin dodged the fist, drawing Winkles in close and leaving his side unprotected. Linshin delivered a right roundhouse to Winkles' jaw, knocking him backward.

"You should never have sucker-punched me."

"I am shaking scared, you rice worm." Winkles popped up into the crane stance, one knee up, hands and fingers raised and outstretched. He screeched like a bird and hopped forward, his kicking foot leading the attack.

Linshin threw a ward-off chop, but Winkles did a quick shuffle, switched kicking legs and delivered a side foot to Linshin's stomach. It could have been a gut-masher had he not whirled around and banged Winkles with an elbow chop to the back of his head. That tipped him forward, made him drop his kicking leg and expose his chest to Linshin's up-thrusting knee.

Gasping for air, Winkles shuffled back.

Master Yee again: "You both have enough yet?"

This time Linshin didn't take his eyes off his opponent. Winkles lunged forward and instead of punching or kicking, he stomped on Linshin's left foot, pinning it to the floor. He couldn't move back. Panic flashed in his brain as Winkles cross-stepped inside with a right elbow lead to the left temple, a bright flash of light, followed by a right hand chop to his left thigh, a Charlie-horse that would leave a bruise, and a left belly-caving hook to his solar plexus.

Linshin buckled and hit the concrete floor.

"Yeah!" Winkles clenched his fists and walked a circle around Linshin.

Angry heat surged through his body. He fought for breath and hoped a miracle would lift him to his feet so he could finish Winkles for good.

Master Yee kneeled to him. "What have you learned, Moy Linshin?"

He coughed. "How to lose." It hurt to inhale.

"The only way to win is not to fight."

Share Lew glided up with the newspaper held out to Yee. "Look at this."

Yee's eyes focused on the print. "From the China News Agency."

"Then it must be true."

Yee stood. "In New York City?"

Linshin struggled to sit up. "What is it?"

"We have found the Pearl of Lao-Tzu."

Chapter Twenty-Six

New York City

Wilbur tugged on his starched shirt collar, trying to escape the itch. Seemed New York folks didn't have anything better to do than explore Ripley's Believe It Or Not Odditorium on Christmas Eve. His hope for a quick exit crumbled in the crush of an exhibition hall filled with pearl oglers.

Standing room only.

He scanned the crowd for Elaine. Again, she was nowhere to be seen. She'd stayed away, just as he'd told her to do. Tomorrow he'd ship out for the Philippines. It would be the end for them, sad in a way; he missed her more than he thought possible.

Zimmerman shouldered his way through the crowd. Big man. Big cowboy hat. Big coat. "Wilbur Cobb."

Wilbur groaned. The greedy Colorado businessman took all the fun out of being rich and famous.

Ignoring him, Wilbur sat on the stool behind the giant clamshell, its pearly luster blinding under the hot, bright lights.

Zimmerman pulled a cigar from his mouth. "See me after the show."

"The answer's still no."

Kaufman appeared out of nowhere, like a cockroach in a dark kitchen. "We've got a better deal for you."

"I'm going back to Manila." His dream of a world tour had been poisoned by greed: Zimmerman and Kaufman both obsessed with possessing shares in his pearl. "Don't try to change my mind."

The ceiling lights dimmed.

The Pearl of Death

"Ladies and gentlemen," an announcer said. "Welcome to the final New York showing of the Pearl of Allah."

Applause.

"The largest pearl in the world."

Applause.

"Thank you for coming." Wilbur stood. "You're probably wondering why I would choose to remove such a magnificent specimen from your midst."

A murmur from the crowd.

"When I tell you the story, you will understand."

***

Never before had Moy Linshin seen such a temple, the wide expanse, tall ceiling, indoor streetlights and colored glass windows. The temple teemed with Americans wearing strange hats. Strange coats. Hundreds of Americans, their voices echoing. Some milled about. Others stood in lines. Many more sat on high-back benches of polished wood all crammed together.

All waiting.

All worshipping in the temple of the trains.

Linshin wanted to hide in his skin. The way he was dressed in Taoist robes and bamboo sandals, he felt like a Panda among Grizzlies, earning odd stares from those he passed by as he walked through the temple with Share Lew and Master Yee.

He adjusted the canvas bag strap on his shoulder. Being the youngest, his job was to carry the clothes and his *dai doe* sword, which Share Lew had told him to never be without. The hilt, protruding from the bag, kept poking him in the shoulder blade, and the soles of his feet still tingled from the vibrating railcar they'd just exited.

"Grand Central Terminal," Master Yee said in English first, then Chinese. He had been to America many times. "The largest train station in the world."

Share Lew, walking stick in hand, stepped in behind Master Yee. "You know the way to this Ripley's place?"

"No." Yee negotiated the throng and found a doorway to the outside. "But I know who does."

Linshin followed his mentors out into the cold, giant city.

Terry Wright

Odd how Americans huddled on the corner, singing joyful tunes.

"Carolers," Yee explained. "Christmas religion."

Men gathered around a burning barrel and took turns venturing to the sidewalk, accosting passersby. Beggars. In America as in China, some things were the same.

The beggars sneered at Linshin but did not approach. Perhaps the exposed hilt of his sword was enough to ward them off.

Motorcars chugged along the street, exhaling smoky exhaust. Horns honked. Master Yee hailed a passing carriage all decked out in colorful lights for the tourists. The horse clopped to the curb, whinnied and shook snow from its long white mane.

"Ripley's," Yee said.

The driver nodded.

Linshin let the older men board first. Three weeks they had traveled from China, by boat, by plane, train, and now this horse-drawn carriage with cushy seats and blankets for warmth. They had finally arrived in New York City to reclaim the pearl of their old sage, Lao-Tzu.

They would not leave without their sacred heirloom.

***

Tonight's applause swam in Wilbur's head, intoxicating as the finest scotch. Though he had long tired of his great adventure story, he relished the crowd's response to its telling.

He stepped down from his stool behind the spread-open clamshells. Two brutish guards stood cross-armed, one on each side of the pearl's rotating pedestal.

A line formed to greet him. Still no Elaine. Kaufman and Zimmerman stood off to the side, vultures, smiling at folks who had spent a week's pay to attend the show. If Zimmerman had his way, he would move the pearl to Chicago and San Francisco, London and Paris, booking yearlong contracts in every museum and gallery along the way. Six months ago, Wilbur would have jumped at the opportunity, the money and the prestige of being a world-renowned adventurer. Before he met Liawayway. Now, nothing could replace what he'd left behind in the Philippines.

He sighed. *Who am I trying to kid?* Elaine could. If she was playing the 'absence makes the heart grow fonder' angle on him, it was working. Any inkling that she didn't like him got but a glancing thought.

She liked him.

Signing tickets, brochures and Bibles, Wilbur fought to restrain his conflicted feelings. Stay professional. Be courteous. This would be over soon. His bags were packed. The plane ticket in his suit coat pocket held the promise of liberation. And no more Elaine temptations.

The next man in line stepped up. "So you are convinced of the curse?"

"I'm not taking any chances." Wilbur signed the man's brochure.

"A shame it won't be on display anymore."

"Yeah." Wilbur handed the man his signed brochure. "A shame." He lied.

There was no shame in being cautious. Every time Zimmerman and Kaufman came up with a better offer, Wilbur found it more difficult to turn them down.

Next in line stood two pretty girls dressed alike, flower bonnets, long coats, white shoes. Twins. Their mom was a knockout. She handed him three tickets. "A wonderful story, Mister Cobb."

"Shouldn't your girls be in bed, waiting for Santa?"

"This is our Christmas wish," one girl sang.

"Can we hold the pearl?" the other chirped.

Wilbur chuckled. How absurd...then again...

He glanced at Zimmerman and Kaufman. Like hyenas stalking a kill, they paced the booth, waiting for their next opportunity to tempt him with some high-as-the-moon deal, so obsessed they didn't seem to have heard the girls' request.

The mom reached out, touched Wilbur's arm. "It would mean so much to them."

"Of course." He stepped to the pedestal and grabbed the pearl from its rotating perch. After all, it was his pearl. He could let someone hold it if he wanted.

Kaufman and Zimmerman stopped pacing. The armed guards stiffened.

"Relax, boys."

He placed the heavy pearl in one girl's open hands. "Don't

drop it."

A collective gasp blew through the crowd.

The girls took turns holding the pearl and stroking its shiny surface. Wilbur held his breath, every nerve on full alert to jump in should young, excited fingers lose their grip.

Folks pressed forward as if seeing these girls with the pearl was a historical event unfolding.

With one eye on the pearl, he signed their three tickets. "Here you go."

"It's so nice of you to give them their Christmas wish," the mom said.

He didn't feel like Santa, but he did feel warm inside for sharing his pearl with them. "I'll take it back now, girls."

All smiles, they gave it up and squealed with joy.

"Merry Christmas." Wilbur tucked the pearl into the crook of his arm.

"I want to hold it too," someone shouted.

"Me too."

Zimmerman and Kaufman moved in close like his personal bodyguards.

"I'll pay a hundred bucks to hold it," a man said.

"One-fifty," someone yelled.

"See what you started?" Zimmerman hissed.

Kaufman addressed the crowd. "Everyone calm down."

"Get back in line," Zimmerman ordered.

The armed guards flanked Wilbur.

"Two hundred bucks," someone else countered.

Kaufman waved his arms. "Everybody get back."

Fear shadowed Zimmerman's face. His eyes narrowed. His hand slid under his coat.

Wilbur cringed. The son-of-a-bitch had a gun.

A fight broke out. Felt hats and fists flew. Scuffling. Shoving. Cursing.

Someone screamed.

Whistles blew. Uniformed police rushed in, beat cops drawn from the street by the ruckus. They started separating the combatants.

Wilbur stood stunned as social order crumbled before him.

In all the commotion, three robe-wearing Chinese slipped

up to the booth, two old guys, one with a long pointy beard, and one younger man, bald as a Robin egg and carrying a shoulder bag with a sword hilt clearly visible.

A shot of adrenaline jolted Wilbur's chest. Not because his fans were Chinese, but because of the intent, reverent glean in their eyes as they stared at the pearl he was holding.

The guards held out their beefy arms and stopped anyone from getting closer.

Zimmerman caught sight of the Chinese. A sneer curled his upper lip.

Wilbur felt as if he was sitting on a powder keg, the fuse lit and the sparks racing toward him. He held the pearl tighter.

Police brandished their nightsticks and started clubbing the brawlers. "Everyone clear the area," came over a bullhorn.

"Mister Cobb." The Chinaman with the pointy beard called out over the guard's extended arm. "We have traveled from China to speak with you." His English was pretty good. Kind of nasally.

"Get them out of here," Zimmerman ordered the guards.

The guards started forward, pressing the Chinamen backward.

"It's about the pearl," the elder said.

The police worked their way through the thinning crowd toward the booth, blowing whistles and shoving people back. Wilbur thought to let the cops throw the Chinese out, as well. Then again, this could be a good time to solidify his claim to the pearl.

"Wait," he told the guards. "Let them speak."

Zimmerman bulled forward. "Are you out of your mind?" To the guards: "You heard the coppers. Everyone out."

"It's Wilbur's show," one guard said and lowered his arm.

The Chinamen bowed to the guard and glided up to Wilbur. "We are most thankful."

Zimmerman pressed in close. "Make it fast." Kaufman stood behind him, his face a sheet of white.

Wilbur elbowed Zimmerman's barrel stomach. "Back off." To the Chinaman: "What do you want?"

"My name is Ghuan Yee." He bowed. "With me, my traveling companions Share Lew Shī and his student Moy

Linshin." The old man and teen bowed. "We are from the Taoist temple of Wong Lung Kwan."

Wilbur ping-ponged between panic and calm. Surely they wouldn't expect him to hand over the pearl. "What can I do for you?"

"We thought we'd never live to see our lost Pearl of Lao-Tzu." The old Chinaman's bloodshot eyes focused on the pearl nestled in the crook of Wilbur's right arm.

"You are mistaken, my friend. This is the Pearl of Allah, from the Philippines."

"You heard him," Zimmerman spat. "Now get out of here."

Kaufman chimed in, "We should negotiate with the buggers."

Wilbur shoved Kaufman back. "Shut up. It's not your pearl."

"It is our pearl." The Chinaman glared at Wilbur. "A wise man would return it to its rightful owners."

"A Dyak chief gave it to me. It's mine."

"The pearl is a gift from our great sage. It cannot be bought or sold. Only by giving the pearl back can you escape the curse of Lao-Tzu."

Zimmerman pulled a gun. "Only by getting the fuck out of here can you escape the curse of Colt 45." He pointed the barrel at the Chinaman's head.

Wilbur stepped back, coddling the pearl. Zimmerman was bluffing. He had to be.

The Chinaman stared at Zimmerman.

Zimmerman stared at the Chinaman.

His companions stood fast, fists clenched. Wilbur hoped the young one didn't pull his sword. The fourteen-pound pearl seemed to weigh a ton. "Put the gun away, cowboy."

Zimmerman clamped his teeth together and hissed, "I'm not fucking around here."

Shouting and cursing, the coppers cleared the chaos from Ripley's exhibition hall.

"With all due respect..." Wilbur bowed to the Chinaman. "I'm not selling the pearl to anyone. And I'm not giving it to you."

"You are a foolish man." Yee stood tall in the face of

Zimmerman's gun. "We will seek a peaceful resolution in the courts."

"You'll go back to China in a pine box," Zimmerman snarled out.

"Maybe." The Chinaman turned, and the others followed.

Zimmerman put away the gun. "Damn Chinks."

"This is your fault." Wilbur pointed at Zimmerman and swept his finger to Kaufman. "You guys had to leak news to the press, tell the world about the legend of Lao-Tzu's pearl."

Zimmerman said to Kaufman, "Follow them."

Kaufman lit out after the Chinese.

"You leave those people alone, you hear me?"

Zimmerman got out a cigar. "We want that pearl." He struck a match. "Three million dollars." Blew smoke. "Take it and go back to your precious Philippines."

"You don't have that kind of money."

"We have investors. You're our only problem."

"It's my pearl, damn it."

"Not for long." He removed a check from his pocket. Folded. "Take it."

Juggling the pearl, Wilbur took the check, unfolded it.

Three Million Dollars and no cents.

A swirl of anxiety sucked the breath out of him. Three million dollars. In hand. He'd be set for life. But the Chinaman had confirmed the curse. If Wilbur took the money, he'd surely die.

Zimmerman held out his beefy hands, greedy palms up. "Give it to me."

Wilbur tore the check in half. "It's not for sale." He tore it again and again and again and dropped the pieces to the floor like so much confetti.

Zimmerman swelled up. "You think we're going to let you walk out of here with our investment? How stupid are you?"

"It's not your investment." Wilbur wished he'd given the pearl to the Chinaman. "Guards!"

The two guards turned to him. "What's the problem?"

"Get him out of here." Wilbur pointed to Zimmerman.

"Yes, sir."

"And be careful. He's got a gun."

"You gonna pull anything funny, buster?" one guard asked, his hand on his holstered pistol.

"This isn't over, Wilbur."

"Yes it is."

The guards escorted Zimmerman to the front door.

Wilbur started shaking. Three million dollars lay shredded at his feet. A sick feeling stirred in his stomach.

But he was free.

He held the pearl like a football and headed for the back exit.

As he neared the door it opened.

Elaine walked in. She wore a fur-collared long coat with cuffs in the sleeves and matching fur cap over blond hair that flowed to her shoulders. Her eyes were puffy red like she'd been crying. "Wilbur."

He caught his breath and remembered her naked beauty. Her hot kisses. Either she couldn't stay away from him, or her arrival was another set up. "What are you doing here?"

"I came to say goodbye."

He wanted to hold her and kiss her, but he stepped around her instead. "Goodbye."

She grabbed his arm and stopped him. "Your plane doesn't leave until morning."

"I just turned down a three million dollar offer. They've only got one option left. Kill me. I've got to get moving."

"Come with me. I know a place where you'll be safe."

"How do I know you're not their backup plan?" He yanked his arm free of her grip. "They pay you to slit my throat while I'm sleeping?"

She threw her arms around his neck. "How can you say that, Wilbur? I'd never do anything to hurt you."

He pushed her away. "Save it for Michael."

"Give them the damn pearl. It's not worth your life."

"So I'm right. They're going to kill me."

"I overheard them at the diner. They're not going to let you get on that plane."

His mouth dried up.

"I'm your only hope, Wilbur."

"You just don't want me to leave New York."

The Pearl of Death

"I don't want you to die."

"What am I supposed to do?"

"Trust me."

***

Sprinting, Wilbur followed Elaine through an obstacle course of trashcans, litter, and sleeping hobos in the alley behind Ripley's. The air stunk of urine and garbage. He had with him his pearl, the clothes on his back, and for now, his life.

"I need to get my bags," Wilbur puffed, winded from his brush with three million dollars and the brief run. "My hotel is the other direction."

"That's the first place they'll look for you."

Zimmerman was probably on his way there now. How long would it take him to set up an ambush? Two seconds?

At the end of the block, Elaine ran to a black Packard parked at the curb. "Get in." She jumped behind the wheel.

Wilbur climbed into the passenger seat, closed the door. Her lilac perfume again teased his senses.

The engine started. Gears ground. A police car sped by, headed toward Ripley's.

She popped the clutch, and the car lurched into the street, banged over cable car tracks. Struck him odd how she didn't seem to have a knack for driving. "Your car?"

"My brother-in-law let me borrow it." She shifted gears, a metal grinding affair.

"Nice of him."

"He would've driven me himself, but it's Christmas Eve, and he has kids, you know."

"I didn't."

"I was afraid I'd miss you."

Sure she was. Or maybe she wasn't. He couldn't tell. Hell, he couldn't sort out his own feelings for her, hot and cold. "Elaine, your showing up like this doesn't sit well with me."

"You've got Liawayway, I've accepted that." She took a tire-squealing right turn.

Wilbur braced himself, left hand on the dashboard, right hand on the pearl. He recalled the spiritual, uplifting sensations he used to get when he held the pearl. Now he got the feeling of cold dread and doom.

"But that pearl is going to be the death of you." Elaine took a fast left. "That's what I'm having a hard time accepting."

"I'll be all right."

"Wherever you go with the pearl, trouble's going to follow."

He couldn't argue with her on that point.

"That Filipino boy you talked about. Timoteo? He has the right idea. Throw it back into the sea. Give it back to the Chinese. Get rid of it."

"I can't." The pearl meant more to him than money. More than good luck. It was a gift given from the heart. Too valuable to toss out or give away.

The car roared down Fordham Road, past Howard Johnson's and into the Bronx.

She pulled up in front of a dark row house. Christmas lights blinked in windows. A streetlamp bathed the block in a soft glow. She set the brake and shut off the engine. "Wilbur, listen."

"Where are we?"

"My sister's place." She turned in the seat to face him, elbow propped on the steering wheel, fur coat open just enough to show her knees. "No matter how this turns out, I want you to know...I haven't been able to get you off my mind. I don't want us to be over."

"We never got started."

She scooted closer and spread her knees a little. "You know that's not true."

His eyes were drawn to the shadowy place above her knees, his imagination inching its way under her coat and up those white thighs...

"My biggest fear, bigger than the other woman, Liawayway, bigger than the pearl's curse, bigger than Zimmerman and Kaufman's obsessions, is the fear that I'll never see you again."

If he truly loved Liawayway, he'd open the door, jump out and run. But the old dog in Wilbur surfaced with a rush of hot adrenaline. He threw his left arm around Elaine's neck, pulled her in and kissed her with lips hungry for her love.

Chapter Twenty-Seven

The night air's icy hand gripped Linshin's bald head. The sword handle protruding from his shoulder bag kept poking his armpit. If Share Lew and Ghuan Yee would stop walking long enough, he'd pull a shirt from the bag and wrap it round his freezing ears. Better yet, they should go someplace warm. Maybe that grand central train temple.

"I'm cold."

"Chinatown is not far." Yee seemed immune to the cold. "I have friends there."

Share Lew kept up the pace, the click of his walking stick echoing off tall buildings on either side of the street.

Linshin glanced behind him. Colorful strings of lights swayed above the sidewalk. And sounds echoed in the night, a chugging engine. A barking dog. The deserted street made his skin jumpy. Even the beggars had disappeared into the shadows.

Steam rose from grates in the street. A movement caught his eye, a figure sprinting from shadow to shadow. Now two figures crossed the street. Hurrying. His pulse began to race.

He ran to catch up to Share Lew. "How much farther?"

"Five blocks. Enjoy the stillness."

He glanced back, saw nothing.

Yee led them across the street, past dark alleys and boarded up buildings. Linshin looked back again, expected to see the figures behind them.

Nothing.

The sensation of doom felt familiar, like when they were sneaking past Japanese patrols in China. Yee knew the underground routes well, from Mount Luofu to Guangdong Harbor, got them out of China safely. He also appeared to know this city, too, and seemed to have no fear of the Americans.

Two figures stepped from an alley to the sidewalk about ten feet in front of them, silhouetted by streetlamps on the corner. Steam rising from a street grate made them look ghostly. Linshin felt a chill.

The bigger man wore a long coat and big hat, had his hands behind his back. The thinner man next to him had his hands in his coat pockets.

Yee stopped. "We have no money." He said it in Chinese, then in English.

Linshin's heart banged against his ribs. He'd seen these men before. At Ripley's. He balled his fists, ready to spring into the crouching tiger stance.

"Howdy, fellas," the big man said, standing tall but keeping his distance. "I believe we have some unfinished business."

"What'd he say?" Linshin asked Yee.

Yee shushed him and spoke to the man, "Our business is with Mister Cobb."

"Your business is with me." The big man stepped forward.

"Do not come any closer." Master Yee crouched into the kung fu tiger stance, a perfectly balanced killing machine.

Share Lew dropped to the riding horse stance and whipped his walking stick around into a two-hand hold. With it he could ward off many attackers at a time.

Linshin felt a sting of fear in his throat. He'd rather face Winkles than these Americans in the dark.

The big man laughed, swiveled out a gun he'd been hiding behind his back and fired at Share Lew.

He dropped his walking stick, teetered on his feet and collapsed. His throat made a gurgling sound as the gunshot echoed away like rolling thunder.

Linshin clenched his jaw, resisted the urge to run to his *shī* and kept his eyes on the gunman. It would take three steps forward before Linshin could get close enough to strike a blow. By that time, he too would be shot.

Master Yee must've realized the futility of an attack. Why else would he have pivoted around and placed his body between the gun and Linshin? "Run."

The thin man pulled a gun from his pocket and put a bullet

in Yee's back. "How do you like that, ya bugger?"

"No," Linshin cried out.

Yee staggered, back arched, and fell forward into Linshin's arms. His old eyes were wide and filled with pain.

"Master."

"Run," he wheezed out.

"Master." Linshin laid him on the sidewalk, gently as he could, and in one smooth motion drew the sword from his shoulder bag. With a swish, he swung the blade in a cross-body stance. Which man would he kill first?

"The only way to win..." Yee coughed, "is not to fight."

The big man straightened his gun arm.

"Run, Linshin, run."

The gun fired.

His training kicked in. He turned his left shoulder toward the big man, making himself a smaller target, and bent backward, leaning away from his body center.

The bullet zipped past his chest.

A spinning back flip landed him six feet farther from the gun as it fired again. He swung the sword up, deflecting the bullet with a sharp slap of metal on metal and a reverberating zing. Diving and rolling, he got to his feet and ran. A zigzagging target would be harder to hit.

A brick wall stretched from the alley to the next street corner. If he could make it that far, he could get away.

Bullets spat brick dust in his eyes. Gunshots echoed.

Again he was running for his life, unable to fight to save the ones he loved.

Share Lew was right. If he had fought the Japanese soldiers that night, he would have been killed. What could fists do against guns? He now understood the Way of the Tao. Flow with the mighty river.

Live to fight again.

***

Before the last gunshot echo faded, the Chinese kid had ducked around the corner. "Fuck." Zimmerman lowered his gun and inhaled the aroma of burnt gunpowder.

"Fast little bugger." Kaufman pocketed his piece. "I'm not

running after him."

"He'll turn up." Zimmerman paced to the Chinaman lying on the sidewalk. The old man wheezed. Pooling blood steamed in the cold night air. "Well, Mr. Yee, this doesn't appear to be your lucky night."

The Chinaman moaned.

"How many of you slant eyes know about our pearl?"

"The others...are not...your problem."

Zimmerman kicked him in the chest. "How many?"

"The boy." A cough. "You have unleashed the dragon...the Tao has shown him...his purpose."

"What are you babbling about?"

"He will kill you."

"I wish him luck." Zimmerman shot the old man point-blank in the eye, staining his white beard with a spray of red.

Kaufman looked around. "We better get moving before somebody comes."

"Yeah." Zimmerman stuck the gun back under his coat, felt the heated barrel through his shirt. "Wilbur's probably made it to his hotel by now."

***

Linshin ran down the street and ducked under a concrete stoop. Steps led down to a door below ground level. He hoped no one inside would hear his frantic breathing.

Perhaps the Americans would charge around the corner and run past his hiding spot. He would ambush them from behind. Cut out their foul hearts.

Streetlights cast eerie shadows down the block. Sirens wailed in the distance. The gunmen did not show themselves.

A shot cracked through the night. The murderers were still doing their murderous business. Ghuan Yee and Share Lew were going to meet their ancestors. It was the Way of the Tao.

But it was no longer Linshin's way. *Wuwei* would not serve him if he were to get his revenge. This time he would not only fight, he would take the fight to the enemy, cleverly, like a tiger in tall grass. Stalk his prey. Attack. He'd do the last thing they'd expect him to do. Go back to where he'd left them.

He tied the sword around his waist with the robe cord and

climbed from his hiding place. A bright light shined on him. It came from a vehicle creeping down the street. He kept moving back toward the murder scene. Any delay, he might not find the killers.

A voice shouted in English. "Stop." He wished Yee were here to tell him what the word meant.

The car tires screeched. Men wearing uniforms and caps piled out. He'd seen men like these before. At Ripley's.

"Halt!"

He broke into a run. Down an alley, pausing only long enough to test a door. Locked. Next door. Locked.

The uniformed men entered the alley, three silhouettes running. Shouting.

He had to keep moving. The dim light supplied many shadows for cover. Above, metal ladders and stairs climbed the brick walls. Odd how they were built just out of reach.

But if he could fly...

He ran full speed, leaped onto a trash barrel and jumped to a ladder, catching the low rung, which promptly rattled to the ground, jarring his teeth.

Stupid Americans. What good was this contraption?

"Stop."

Scrambling up the ladder, he made it to the metal stairs, which zigzagged up toward the roof. Laundry hung from ropes stretched from one landing to another. He snatched pants and a shirt as he scrambled past. First chance he got, he'd change into American clothes to better blend in.

The noisy ascent attracted the attention of flashlight beams that swept stairs on either side of him. As the light came close, he ducked behind hanging laundry. As the light moved off, he continued his climb.

On the roof, he sprinted to the other side of the building and peered over the edge. He was ten stories up, but even from this height he saw Ghuan Yee and Share Lew sprawled on the sidewalk below. The sight dug holes in his empty heart.

And half a block away the killers strolled off as if what they had done was nothing.

Hot anger burned in Linshin's chest. This would be their last night breathing.

Chapter Twenty-Eight

The Packard's windows fogged up; the kissing inside the car was steamy hot. Lips pressed together with such force that teeth bumped and tongues played patty-cake.

A rap on the window.

Wilbur couldn't stop, couldn't tear himself from Elaine's embrace to see who was out there.

A louder rap.

"Don't stop," Elaine breathed.

Pounding on the glass. "Get out of my car, damn it."

"When are we ever going to catch a break?" She sat up. "Okay, Eric. We'll be there in a minute."

"It's Christmas, for Christ's sake," Eric shouted.

"You still taking him to Jersey like you promised?"

"If I can get any sleep. The kids will be up early."

"Then go back to bed."

Wilbur straightened his tie. "What's this about Jersey?"

***

Zimmerman bounded up the steps to the Madison Hotel lobby. The place looked deserted, but in the bar, drunks gathered around the piano and belted out Christmas carols. He pointed Kaufman toward the reception desk. "See if Wilbur has checked out."

Standing to the side, Zimmerman waited. He hoped the clerk would say Wilbur was in his room. If so, they'd go upstairs, bust in, shoot him and take the pearl. The clerk would identify Kaufman as the man who went up. Not Zimmerman.

Slurred lyrics to Jingle Bells grated on his nerves.

Kaufman came back. "He's not here, but he hasn't checked out."

"He's probably at Elaine's getting a goodbye piece of tail."

"If you want to check her place, I'll wait here in case he comes in."

"You see him. You kill him. And get that pearl."

"No problem."

***

Kaufman watched Zimmerman rush out. Killing Wilbur wasn't part of the original plan. Nor was killing the Chinese, but if it weren't for bullets, they'd have gotten their asses kicked.

A quick assessment of the situation went through his mind like an inventory of his jewelry store. The gig at Ripley's was over. The pearl was gone. Wilbur was the rightful owner. And Kaufman wasn't about to kill the son of his best friend.

It was time to go back to California. Back to his son, Paul, his wife and his business selling rings, watches, and exotic clocks. He'd had enough of New York and the giant pearl.

He walked out of the Madison Hotel, inhaled Christmas Eve air. It was good to be alive.

A face came out of nowhere. The Chinese kid who got away. A flash of steel, then a slicing pain in his throat. A gurgly, drowning gasp. Then nothing.

***

A stalking tiger, that was Moy Linshin. He'd sliced the man's throat as easy as he'd sliced the Lotus Pond fish. And like the fish, the man convulsed in the throes of death, eyes wide open, not accusing eyes but deserving eyes.

Blood gushed from the splayed open wound.

Linshin held up the bloody sword. Energy flowed through him. He was all-powerful. This was the purpose for which the Tao had spared him from the Japanese. To hunt the men who stole the Pearl of Lao-Tzu and return it to the temple.

The Tao favored him for this work, having cleared the streets of people and given him the opportunity to strike without being seen. Now only one person stirred, the big man with the big hat walking away, down the block, under the streetlamps, unaware of the stalking tiger.

***

Without all the kissing and hugging going on, Wilbur's body heat bled off. Fog on the inside of the windows turned to frost. "I said, what about Jersey?"

Elaine leaned over him, opened the glove box and extracted an envelope. "Your new plane ticket to San Francisco." She held it out to him. "From Jersey via Chicago."

"And all the while Zimmerman thinks I'm leaving out of New York. You're a very smart woman."

He took the envelope, but she didn't let go. "Wilbur, I may never see you again, but at least I'll know you're safe."

"How much did this cost you?"

"It's not important."

"You're a waitress, for God's sake. Fur coat. Plane ticket. This stuff doesn't come cheap."

"Zimmerman thinks he can buy anyone. Makes him stupid."

"So you conned the con man?"

"Money matters to me, Wilbur."

"But if you don't deliver me, he'll come back for his money's worth, my guess a pound of flesh for every dollar."

"When you're gone, he'll go back to Colorado. Don't worry about me."

He pulled her close again. "You saved my life."

"What's a girl got to do to get her reward?"

More kissing and hugging.

***

The hallway leading to Elaine's apartment smelled like cat piss. Zimmerman approached the door quietly, listened for any sound inside.

Nothing.

He reared back and kicked open the door. Wood splintered. The door slammed against the wall. So what if he made a lot of noise. These New Yorkers wouldn't lift a finger to help a neighbor.

Inside, he swept through the two-room apartment. Checked the bathroom. The kitchenette. Under the bed in case they were hiding. Son of a bitch. Where were they? She took him somewhere. But where? Maybe to a friend's. Family?

He yanked out a top dresser drawer and tossed the contents on the bed. Panties. Bras. Socks. No address book. No notes. The next drawer came out. And the next. Nothing.

The front room bookshelves went down next. Then the kitchen drawers. Everything landed on the floor. Still nothing. Didn't this heifer have a social life?

He opened the closet door, found a shelf piled with boxes. Shoes and more shoes. Old letters.

A photo album.

He thumbed the pages. Every picture was marked with names and dates. How nice. She had a sister, Billie. But where?

Back to perusing the box of old letters. He found a return address from a Mrs. Billie Jenkins. In the Bronx.

A warm flush swept through him.

"Gotcha."

***

"Get out of my car." Eric again, pounding on his Packard.

Elaine rolled down the window. "We're still talking."

Wilbur's lips felt numb. He hadn't done this much talking since San Francisco.

"When are you coming inside?"

"In a minute."

"You said that an hour ago." He stormed across the front lawn to the house.

She rolled up the window. "Now where were we? Oh yes." She nibbled on his earlobe. "We don't want to stop right now, do we?"

He nuzzled her neck. "Do you?"

She gasped. "Not if you don't."

"I never want to stop, Elaine." There. He said it, and he hadn't been drinking. "I never want to stop kissing you."

"Never?"

A nerve inside his heart sparkled. His brain interpreted it as love. He wanted to tell her he'd give up everything for her, Liawayway, the boys, the Philippines, Benguet, if only she'd run away with him. It didn't matter where. It didn't matter how, just go and never look back.

"Wilbur?"

"I..." The words stuck in his throat.

"What is it?"

He didn't have the courage to tell her. To change his life. Hers. And Liawayway's—

She kissed him hard.

God how he wanted to tell her he loved her.

Crash.

The passenger side window shattered in a spray of glass shards.

Elaine screamed.

Wilbur shielded her with his body, even as hot adrenaline walloped his chest. "What the hell?" Eric wanted them out of his car, all right, but bad enough to break out his own window? Was he nuts?

A gun appeared in the jagged opening, a gun with a silencer on the barrel, a gun that meant business. Wilbur's first instinct was to get as far away from the gun as possible, but there was nowhere to go. The saliva in his mouth evaporated.

Zimmerman's fat face appeared next. He looked like a crazy person, all scrunched up in the eyes, teeth bared, and his head tilting back and forth. "Where's the damn pearl, Wilbur?"

He'd put it behind the seat, on the floor, safely out of the way of their necking. "Have you lost your mind? Get that gun out of here."

"Give me the pearl."

Wilbur had to think fast. Once Zimmerman got the pearl, he'd shoot him for sure. "I left it at Ripley's."

"You lying fuck. You left the clamshell but took the pearl." He tipped his head toward the row house. "It's in the house, isn't it? That's right." He grinned. "I'm going to go in there and get it, but when I come out there won't be any witnesses left alive."

"No." Elaine folded her hands, begging. "The children, please." She turned to Wilbur, her voice laced with panic. "Give it to him."

"Elaine, he's bluffing—"

"It's on the floor," she squealed. "Behind the seat. Take it and leave us alone."

"Elaine." Wilbur couldn't believe she'd given up the pearl so easily.

Zimmerman cackled. "That's my girl."

"I'm not your girl."

"Get out of the car." Zimmerman backed away from the broken window and opened the door. "Real easy like."

Wilbur swiped glass from the seat and slid out. Elaine followed him. Zimmerman held the gun on them both. "Okay, lover boy. Get the pearl."

"Get it yourself."

"You think I have cow shit for brains? I'm not turning my back on you."

He was right. First thing Wilbur would have done was hit him from behind, bash his head into the door, and kick him in the jewels.

Zimmerman waved the gun. "Get it now."

"No."

Zimmerman swiveled the gun barrel to Elaine. "I'll blow that kisser right off her face."

So it came down to attempted murder on top of armed robbery. Was there no crime Zimmerman wouldn't commit?

Wilbur opened the back door and retrieved the pearl from the floor. That feeling came back strong as ever, a spiritual kind of relief that it was over. But in the end, the bad guys won.

Holding the pearl with both hands, he kicked the door shut and faced Zimmerman's gun. "Once you take this, the curse is on you."

"Shut the fuck up and hand it over."

Wilbur glanced at Elaine standing next to him. Lines of defeat creased her beautiful face and tightened those lips he'd kissed so many times. Those lips he'd give up Liawayway to kiss forever. Those lips that had just betrayed him. What was he thinking? Zimmerman had found his weakness. The bastard.

"I'm sorry," she whispered.

"You're a traitor." Wilbur set the pearl in Zimmerman's outstretched open hand not knowing what hurt worse, losing the pearl or Elaine's fall from grace.

Zimmerman's eyes locked on the prize. In the glow of the streetlight, the pearl radiated a shiny sheen. "Finally." He laughed. "It's mine." He looked up at Wilbur. "Too bad it's the end of the trail for you, partner." He straightened his gun arm.

"Hieeee!" A sword blade came out of nowhere and sliced off Zimmerman's hand. The gun went one way, the hand another.

Zimmerman screeched, dropped the pearl in the grass and grabbed the stub of his arm. Blood squirted out, spattering Wilbur and Elaine.

She screamed.

Wilbur didn't have time to blink. A gangly form leaped in with some kind of flying martial arts kick to Zimmerman's chest. The cowboy hat flew off his head and he hit the ground hard.

The assailant jumped on the fat man's belly, raised a sword with both hands and plunged it into his chest. Zimmerman wailed in agony. The attacker yanked out the blade. Bloody air spurted from the open wound.

Fear drove Wilbur to the dropped gun. Fear that he and Elaine were next. He dove, grabbed the gun, and came up on both knees just as the killer faced him. It was the bald Chinese kid from Ripley's, barefoot, wearing jeans and a t-shirt a few sizes too large. His eyes were wild as a monkey boar's.

He swung the bloody sword up. "Hieeee!"

Charged.

Wilbur fired the gun twice. The silencer made a *fhitt fhitt* sound.

The kid kept coming.

Fhitt. Fhitt.

A bloodstain blossomed dead center in the T. Still the kid managed to swing the sword. If not for his legs buckling underneath him, the blade would've found its mark in Wilbur's skull. The kid fell in the grass, landed face-to-face with the pearl, his eyes wide open in a lifeless stare.

Wilbur swept the gun side to side, expecting an attack from the two old men who were traveling with the kid.

Nothing.

Elaine stooped to the boy, touched his neck. "You killed him."

"He was going to kill us."

She rushed to Zimmerman. "He's bleeding to death." She

The Pearl of Death

slipped off her fur cap and pressed it to the burbling wound. "Get Eric out here."

Wilbur ran to the house and banged on the door. The porch light came on. Eric opened the door. Shock raked his face. Wilbur must've been a sight standing there spattered with blood and holding a gun. "We need a doctor."

"Billie," he shouted over his shoulder. "Call an ambulance." He followed Wilbur back out to the curb. "What the hell happened?"

Elaine kept pressure on the bleeding chest. "Your belt, Wilbur. Make a tourniquet for his arm."

He set the gun in the grass, whipped off his belt, and wrapped it round the bleeding arm as tight as he could. The spurt slowed to a dribble.

Zimmerman moaned.

Elaine's hands were soaked in blood. "What are we going to tell the police?"

"It was self defense."

"He was just a kid, Wilbur."

"He had a sword."

"You were pointing a gun at him."

A chilling revelation hit Wilbur like a low punch. What if the cops thought he'd overreacted? What if they charged him with murder? Or manslaughter? There'd be a trial. It could take months if not years. They'd confiscate his pearl as evidence. He'd be locked up... "I've got to catch that plane."

She picked up the gun. "I'll tell the cops I shot him."

"You'd take the heat for me?"

"I'm not a traitor." She held the gun butt in her bloody hand. "But I wasn't going to give Zimmerman a reason to go in the house." She smeared blood on the trigger with her finger and dropped the gun next to her then went back to pressing on Zimmerman's chest.

Hot and cold. He could despise her one minute and love her the next. Dames and games. He was losing this one.

Billie ran up dressed in a nightgown and slippers. "They're coming." She looked over the carnage on her front lawn. "Who are these guys?"

Eric hugged her shoulder. "They were after Wilbur's

~183~

pearl."

She pointed to the pearl lying in the grass next to the Chinese boy's blanched face. "Get that damn thing out of here before someone else gets killed."

Elaine squeezed blood from the fur cap pressed to Zimmerman's chest. "Eric, drive Wilbur to the hotel. Clean him up and get him to the Jersey airport."

"Now?"

"Better early than never."

"What about Christmas? The kids?"

Sirens screamed in the distance.

"We're running out of time."

Wilbur picked up the dropped pearl. "I'm sorry about all this."

"Just go."

Eric climbed in his car. "What happened to my window?"

Wilbur jumped in. "Just go!"

The engine rumbled to life, and the car tore away from the curb. Wilbur looked back at Elaine, bent over Zimmerman, trying to save the man who would've killed them both.

Sorrow crept over him, a dark shadow on a dark Christmas Eve. Elaine's taste lingered on his tongue. Her lilac perfume wafted in his memory. He held the pearl in his lap and wondered how long she'd be locked up in the joint.

Chapter Twenty-Nine

Manila, The Philippines, January 31, 1940

W ilbur braced for the touchdown.
The Martin M-130 flying boat, commonly known as the China Clipper, landed on Manila Bay. Outside his window, an impressive spray of seawater shot up. Buoys that marked the landing zone bobbed and thrashed in the chop. Waves pounded the plane's hull. Passengers applauded the pilot. Wilbur applauded himself for finally making it home.

On shore, the Manila Hotel came into view, towering six stories above a waving sea of palm trees. His heartbeat quickened as he scanned the Pan Am dock, a hundred yards away, hoping to spot Liawayway.

He wondered if she'd seen the plane land, pictured her brown eyes aglow with wonder at his thunderous arrival. She'd sounded cold on the phone, when he told her he was coming back, as if she didn't believe him. He couldn't blame her for being pessimistic. Or angry at all the delays. She wasn't one for reining in her words, so he expected another tongue-lashing.

Slicing through the chop, the flying boat roared toward shore, its four propellers stripping water off the bay and churning it into a turbulent mist. He cinched his tie and buttoned the sleeves of his white silk shirt. He wanted to look sharp for Liawayway, show her that his time away was well spent. Wearing patent leather shoes instead of jungle boots, a felt fedora instead of a bushman hat, and cologne instead of mosquito repellent, he hoped to make a good impression.

The clipper coasted up to the dock. As workmen manned the mooring ropes, a stewardess hurried down the rocking aisle to the door. It opened with a clank, flooding the cabin with hot, humid air.

Wilbur's suit coat and tie wouldn't stay on long in this swelter. He hauled his duffle bag out from under the seat. He'd brought a change of fatigues, his boots, and the Pearl of Allah, rescued from the greedy bastards who would commit murder to possess it.

Passengers sprung to their feet. Wilbur took his time, let the stampede deplane, and then stepped down a shaky plank to the guano-splattered dock. A tropical breeze carried an oily smell. The sun beat down so bright he could hardly see.

"Wilbur." His name rang out from the distance.

"Liawayway?" He slipped on his sunglasses and searched the colorfully dressed crowd gathered on shore. Fellow passengers hugged greeters, shook hands and wandered off. Spectators pressed closer to get a better view of the China Clipper.

"Liawayway? Where are you?"

"Over here."

He saw her standing in the shade of a palm tree, the breeze playing in her shiny black hair. It had grown longer. The hem of her flower-print dress fluttered, and a white-sandaled foot tapped the ground. She folded her arms under her breasts. A frown creased her brow.

Exactly the reception he expected.

He hurried toward her, toting his duffle bag, wishing she were running toward him with open arms. Not that he deserved a romantic greeting. His love for her had been tested and found lacking.

"My hero has finally come home." Her eyes were like sharp black daggers. "One week you promised. Then one month. And now three have passed. What is the matter with you?"

"It couldn't be helped." Benguet held him up three weeks at HQ in Honolulu. Paperwork. God he didn't want to argue with her. He took off his felt hat. "Where are the boys?"

"In school where I should be."

"How's typing class?"

She looked away.

Setting down the duffle bag, he wished she wouldn't act so cold to him. "Thanks for coming to meet me here. Do I get a hug?"

"For what?"

"Come on—"

"You hurt me...and the boys. Why is the pearl more important than us?"

"It's not." She'd never understand. There was no point in trying to explain everything that had happened. "I'm home now. That's what's important."

She turned to him, glaring. "Look at you...your fancy clothes. You are a different man."

"No, I'm not."

"The pearl has changed you...made you rich and attractive to those American girls."

It wouldn't do her any good to push the issue. He was a dog. Dogs don't kiss and tell. "I came back to you, Liawayway."

Her eyes softened. "Yes you did. I see."

He blinked. Elaine Meyers almost kept him from coming back. He refused to feel guilty about what had happened between them. Dogs don't feel guilty. They move on. And he didn't want to worry her over what happened to Zimmerman and the Chinese kid. "We're together again. Isn't that good?"

"Until the next time you run off with the pearl."

"There won't be a next time." It was best to keep the pearl out of sight for a long time. "I promise."

"You are sure?"

"As long as you want me, I'll stay."

The hard lines on her face softened, slow as melting butter until she threw her arms around his neck and smothered him with kisses. That was more like it. And a big hug.

Looking over her shoulder, he saw a man standing close by, leaning against a palm tree. Watching.

Wilbur had to look twice. White shirt. Black pants. Unruly mop of black hair.

A hot bolt of anger sizzled through Wilbur's stomach. Maricar!

"What's he doing here?"

"The Panglima sent him to keep an eye on me. Maricar cares enough to hang around, make sure I am safe."

"From now on I'll make sure you're safe. He'd better stay

out of my way."

A formation of P-40 fighters roared overhead. Wilbur looked up. A powerful chill swept through him.

Liawayway followed his gaze and hugged her arms. "The Americans prepare for war."

No matter what course their lives took now, the Japanese could ruin everything.

He set his hat on and picked up his duffle bag. With Liawayway firmly in the crook of his arm, he headed into Manila to face an uncertain future.

Chapter Thirty

December 8, 1941

Just before 4:00 AM, Wilbur awoke to frantic pounding on his apartment door.

"Wilbur Cobb!"

"Yes, yes." He stumbled out of bed. "I'm coming."

Liawayway sat up in alarm. "What is it?"

"Better be damned important this early in the morning." He stepped into his slippers. Annoyance gnawed at his stomach.

More pounding.

"It will wake the boys. They have school today."

"All right." Wilbur shuffled to the door and swung it open.

A Benguet company courier stood in the hallway dressed like a marching band drummer. "Mister Cobb?"

"You have any idea what time it is?"

He removed his cap. "I have an urgent teletype for you, sir...from headquarters."

Through sleep-blurred eyes he read the message:

Japanese attacked US Naval Base, Pearl Harbor, Hawaii. Benguet suspending all South Pacific operations. Employees ordered to evacuate at once.

"Pearl Harbor?" Wilbur's chest took a jolt of dread. "Evacuate?"

"I have a car waiting for you downstairs."

How thoughtful... "Give me a minute to get everyone up."

"No. Just you, sir."

Wilbur felt gut-punched. "I'm not going anywhere without my family."

"Personnel will arrange their transportation. You must come with me now."

Liawayway stepped up next to Wilbur, slid her arm around his waist. "What's wrong?"

"The Japanese attacked us in Hawaii. Benguet is getting out of the Philippines. They want me to leave right away."

"Where will you go?"

Wilbur glared at the courier. "Where *am* I going?"

"Headquarters."

"Honolulu?" How much sense did that make? "The Japs hit Hawaii and we're going to Hawaii?"

The courier consulted his wristwatch. "My orders are to get you to the plane in forty minutes. You'll have to hurry, sir."

Liawayway looked stunned, her brown eyes ringed in white. "What are we going to do?"

There was no question in Wilbur's mind. "Wake the boys." Who was the courier to make his family stay behind? He was just a messenger. A driver. He had no clout with the company. "Start packing. You're going with me."

"They can't go with you," the courier insisted. "There's another plane coming. It just takes time."

"Then I'll wait. We'll all go on that plane. Together."

"You'll be fired."

"I'll quit first."

Liawayway hugged his waist. "Don't be foolish and throw away your job. It is a good job and you love it. Go with him."

"I can't leave you. The Japanese might—"

"How quickly you forget why we came to Manila." Her voice sounded soft. "The Americans will protect the city. We will be all right. Besides, the boys have school today."

"School?" Why did she have to be so damn stubborn?

"I will help you pack." She headed toward the bedroom.

Timoteo rushed up, scarecrow tall and thin in white boxers, his black pillow of hair all ratty from sleep. Tears streamed down his cheeks. "It's the pearl." Sobs wracked his chest. "You should have thrown it back in the sea." He ran to his room, shouting, "I hate you."

That cut a slice from Wilbur's heart. Seemed like only yesterday the boy had stood on the Panglima's path, bike tipped at his feet, shouting the same words. After all these years he hadn't stopped blaming the pearl for everything that went wrong in his life. Wilbur started down the hall to talk to the boy, but Liawayway stopped him.

"You must help me." She led him to the bedroom. His duffle bag lay on the bed, spread open, and his clothes from the dresser and closet were laid out beside it. The pearl was there too, in its wooden box, next to his razor and soap.

Despair drilled a hole in his gut. The thing he'd feared most was happening.

War.

Chapter Thirty-One

New Years Eve 1942, Manila

From his fifth-floor apartment window, Timoteo watched Japanese bombers roar over the city and strike Nichols Field and the naval base at Cavite, the horizon set ablaze with black smoky fires. Bombs hit the city and shook the ground. The explosions sent chills of terror through his body.

Wilbur Cobb had said the Americans would protect them. He and Tito and Mamma were safe. But as the rattle of gunfire on the streets below became louder and more frequent, the man on the radio sounded frightened, told everyone to stay indoors.

Timoteo hugged his brother and his mother who sat on the couch and rotated the phone finger wheel again.

"There was supposed to be a plane," she told the man at Benguet. "The courier promised us...three weeks ago."

"The Japs shot it down over the Pacific."

"But there must be another plane—"

"Look, lady, the airport is closed. The Japanese cut off communications to Hawaii, and Manila Bay has been mined. There is fighting all around us."

"What about the Americans? Can they get us out?"

"We're all trapped here. Just stay where you are. When things settle down, the company will send another plane."

The phone went dead. She dialed again, got a busy signal, screamed and threw the phone, then sobbed into her hands. "We're never going to get out of here."

Tito whined. "I'm hungry, Mamma."

"I know." She pulled him into her lap and rocked him.

Timoteo rubbed her shoulder. The cupboards were empty. He was hungry too but chose not to worry her.

The Pearl of Death

An explosion rattled the walls. The lights flickered out. Air-raid sirens wailed again.

Timoteo shook with fright. Clutching his mother and Tito all night, he slept very little, the sounds of battle ever present.

Day dawned. He untangled himself from their arms and went to the bathroom. When he returned, his mother was fumbling through her change purse, sobbing.

"You must go to the market." She held out a handful of pesos. "Buy all the food you can with this." She put coins in Timoteo's hand and closed his fingers around the money. "We must fend for ourselves."

Tito started to cry.

Feigning bravery, Timoteo put on his sandals and a red sleeveless shirt. At the door, he stopped and looked back at the remnants of his family. His father was dead. Wilbur Cobb was gone. Now it would be his job to protect his mother and little brother. "I'll get the food." He rushed downstairs to the street.

Muggy air swarmed with mosquitoes and the frantic cries of people running every which way. Bumping and pushing through the panicked crowd, he reached the market, but it was empty of shoppers, and the shelves were bare. Trash lay strewn all over the floors: crushed fruit, torn-open boxes, busted glass. He glanced at the money in his hand and feared that it was now worthless. Not finding food made his stomach feel emptier.

Behind him, people stormed through the streets, breaking shop windows and stealing everything they could grab. A sign made of white cloth with black painted letters hung from electrical wires that crossed above the jam-packed street. OPEN CITY. He didn't understand what that meant.

Horns honked. Canopy trucks and sedans bullied their way through the crowd. A caritella horse bolted, threw the carriage on its side and spilled the riders. Filipinos cursed each other. The chaos seemed like the end of civilization.

In a barbershop window, a withered Christmas tree twinkled. A group of men on the sidewalk huddled around a radio. "Listen, everyone," a man shouted. "The Americans have left the city."

Timoteo squeezed in closer, heard static and a squeaky voice: "Before General MacArthur and President Quezon left, they declared Manila an open city in hopes the Japanese won't bomb it to ruins."

"Open city?" Timoteo asked the man. "What does that mean?"

"It means the Americans have abandoned us...left us to face the Japanese alone."

Swallowing, Timoteo remembered when Wilbur Cobb had said the Americans would protect the city.

He was wrong.

"It will save lives," another man added. "Save the city."

"Like Nanking? Japanese soldiers murdered thousands of Chinese men, women, and children, cut off their heads like chickens to market. They'll do the same to us."

The other man stood, taking the radio. "I'm getting out of here."

"Where will you go?" another man asked.

"I'll find a Filipino army division. They're heading for Bataan to make a stand against the Japanese."

"You will fight?"

"I'd rather die with a rifle in my hand than be butchered here in the street like a chicken."

"Maybe they will have food on Bataan. I'm going with you."

As the men hurried down the street, Timoteo stood there clutching worthless money and wondering if survival meant he too would have to fight the Japanese. But how could he? He'd never fired a rifle, never even held one. Would the army train him? How could they? He was only fifteen.

Thoughts of serving in the army melted away in the heat and dust of the open city. He had to protect Tito and Mamma. They needed to eat. He was the man of the family now. They were his responsibility. It was a daunting task, but familiar, since his father died in the jaws of a giant clam. He'd stolen noodles before, and fruit from the market on Palawan, when they had no money and food was abundant. Now he had money but there was no food. Perhaps he could find some farther away.

He started running down the block, unsure of which way to go. Taking a less traveled street, he kept moving from one corner to the next. Broken glass crunched under his sandals. Sweat dripped from his face. Hope turned to despair, as all he found were looted and burning stores and people running in panic.

The Japanese were coming.

He had to find food somewhere. A house down the street, a very nice house with carved pillars and high windows, caught his attention. Surely the rich people there would have food. Running to the front door, he was surprised to see it wide open so he slipped inside.

The house was a mess, nice furniture turned upside down and smashed. "Is anyone here?"

He heard weeping.

"Do you need help?" he called out, knowing he couldn't do much.

A young girl with fierce eyes showed herself from around a wall. She held a broom like a club. "Go away."

"I won't hurt you." He stepped toward her, over strewn books and papers. "I'm looking for food."

She reared back with the broom. "Get out."

"I have money." He showed her the pesos in his hand. "I'll gladly give it to you for bread or eggs...anything."

"They took the food with them," she cried. "And left us to die."

He hoped she wouldn't strike him with the broom. "Who?"

"The High Commissioner, Sayre."

He held the girl's glare. She was probably nine years old, a servant of the wealthy government officials who ran away from the Japanese. "What will you do now?"

"I don't know." She bawled.

"Do you know where I can find food for my mother and little brother?"

"Go away."

Her fiery glare shifted, shot past him, caused him to turn. Men stood in the doorway. They came in and started rummaging through the debris. Looters.

"There's no food here," he told them.

"Shut up, kid."

"Get out of my house," the girl screamed at them.

One of the looters pointed at her. "The Japanese will take everything. We aim to get it first. And a little girl like you...the soldiers will pass around, fuck you many times before they bayonet you to death. I would run if I were you."

A deafening bang knocked Timoteo across the room and over a chair. He landed on his back, his head ringing. His eyes could hardly see through the swirling dust and smoke. Sunlight beamed in from a place that had once been the wall. He lifted his head. Blood ran from his nose. A severed arm lay beside his leg, twitching. Terror raked his spine. He checked his hands, cupped one over his bleeding nose. The other was a fist still clutching pesos. The severed arm belonged to a looter.

Timoteo's heart beat so hard it hurt. But he was alive. He'd survived a Japanese bomb. But why did they bomb the house? It was an open city.

He looked around for the girl. She'd been standing by the wall—the wall that was now gone.

Gaining his feet, he staggered through the ruins, his lungs choking on dust, his nose dripping blood. A sharp pain in his foot told him his sandals had flown off, but he kept moving. "Little girl?"

No answer.

"Little girl. Can you hear me?"

A looter moaned.

Timoteo threw down the worthless pesos and started pushing away debris from where he'd last seen her standing. He found a broken broom—and then a small hand sticking out, blue and bloody. He froze.

The looter who'd warned her to run from the Japanese, his forehead bleeding, jumped into the rubble, throwing boards and digging with his bare hands. "Don't just stand there, boy."

Timoteo dropped to his knees and took the little girl's hand. It didn't respond to his touch. She was dead. And even though he'd grown tall and strong in the years since his father died, he felt helpless and small once again.

Another explosion thundered from somewhere down the street.

Every muscle in Timoteo's body tightened.

"Goddamned Japanese." The looter kept digging.

Holding the hand and wishing the fingers would move, he feared his mother and Tito weren't any safer in their apartment than this girl was in her home. The realization felt heavy on his chest. "I have to get back to my family."

"Go ahead, kid. The war is over for this little girl."

War? He let go of the limp hand, wiped his bloody nose. For the longest time he thought the Pearl of Allah was the worst thing in the world. Now he knew different. War was worse, and he was stuck in the middle of battle.

He ran out to the street. Dust rolled away from a crumbled building where the last bomb had exploded. The air smelled like rust. As he ran, the tropical sun beat down on him. Broken glass cut his bare feet. But he had to get back to Mamma and Tito before the Japanese found them and killed them too.

Terry Wright

Chapter Thirty-Two

Honolulu, Hawaii, January 1, 1942

Wilbur Cobb plopped into an upholstered chair at the conference table, threw down his bushman hat and sunk his face in his hands. He wore jungle fatigues and combat boots. At a moment's notice, he was ready to head back to the Philippines. His bags were packed; they were always packed and waiting in the hotel room, on the bed, just in case he got the call.

Just say the word. Tell me I'm going back.

Executives and clerks filed in. The late afternoon meeting came to order.

The Chief Operations Officer of Benguet's South Pacific holdings stood in front of the committee, his tie perfectly tied, his suit perfectly pressed. "Since those dirty Japs took Wake and Guam, our communications with the Philippines have been cut."

Transoceanic cables supplied telephone and Teletype links across the Pacific, hop-scotching from island-to-island. The Japanese destroyed the local garrisons and dynamited the communication terminals. Wilbur had tried to call Liawayway a thousand times but couldn't get through.

"Our boys are taking a beating," the COO added. "General MacArthur has pulled back to Corregidor. American and Filipino troops are digging in on the Bataan peninsula, hoping reinforcements will arrive before the Japs break through their lines. The strategy will buy some time until our forces can mount a counter invasion to retake the Philippines."

"When?" Wilbur's heart raced. "When will we attack?"

"Japan crippled the Pacific Fleet so we couldn't strike back." The COO leaned on the table. "We have nothing to fight

~198~

them with."

Heart heavy with despair, Wilbur couldn't imagine the huge task ahead. "It'll take years to rebuild the fleet. I can't wait that long."

"There's nothing we can do until the war is over. For now, Benguet is out of business in the South Pacific."

Wilbur shot out of his chair, slammed a fist on the table. "Business? Goddamn the business. I've got family back there...people I love."

"You're not the only one who left someone behind," the COO shouted back.

"The company was supposed to get them out."

"The damn Japs keep shooting down our planes. We're not risking any more pilots."

"Give me a plane. I'll fly the damn thing."

"Take your seat, Cobb. I'll not have any more outbursts."

"Go to hell." Wilbur grabbed his hat off the table and stormed out, slamming the door behind him. In the opulent marble hallway of corporate headquarters, he pounded his fists on the wall. There wasn't anything he could do about the Japs, the war, or the fate that awaited Manila. He couldn't save Liawayway and her boys. But there was one thing he could do— get stinkin' drunk.

Throat burning for scotch, Wilbur shoved through the rotating doors and stormed down the sidewalk, dodging pedestrians and grimacing against the shrill bustle of traffic, MP's whistles, and the cry of newspaper hawkers: "Japs take Manila!"

"The sons of bitches." Muggy air made his shirt stick to his skin. He headed straight for an old haunt, the Zanzabar.

Two blocks down, he came to the marquee advertising the finest liquor and women in Hawaii. Big band music greeted him at the door. A Glenn Miller recording of Sunrise Serenade blared from the public address system. Colorful strobes flashed around the barroom, and spotlights swept the floor in radiant jubilation. Couples boogied on the dance floor.

The after-work crowd gathered in groups and talked of war while Polynesian waitresses scurried about with trays of drinks. Feeling underdressed and overanxious, he made his way to a welcoming U-shaped bar.

"What'll it be, Mac?" The bartender leaned his beefy paws on the bar top. In his younger days he could have been a Sumo wrestler.

"Scotch." Wilbur sat down. "Make it a double."

Two beautiful women strode by, giggling. They wore bright dresses with low necklines, showed lots of cleavage and tan thighs. Working girls. He hoped they wouldn't bother him. He had some serious drinking to do.

"That'll be forty five cents, Mac."

Wilbur felt dizzy. He wiped sweat from his forehead. The walls closed in around him. His heart beat hard against his ribs.

"You all right, Mac?"

Feeling faint, Wilbur tossed two quarters on the bar. "Keep the change." He stared into the glass of amber liquor shimmering before him. It beckoned him to partake of its sweet nectar and let it put him out of his misery.

The goddamned Japs.

Lifting the glass, he examined its promised release. His throat tightened in anticipation. He felt like he was about to fall off a tall building.

Pardon me, boy, is that the Chattanooga Choo Choo, crooned from the speakers. Glenn Miller again, all happy and jumpy.

"Jesus Christ." The glass trembled in his sweating hand.

"What's wrong, Mac?"

"Can a man drink in peace?"

"What?"

"Too many distractions in here...how can I concentrate on my drinking?"

The bartender snatched up the quarters from the bar. "We all have our private hells."

"I gotta get out of here." He threw down the scotch in one gulp and slammed the glass on the bar, earning a disapproving glare from the barkeep.

"Don't do anything stupid, Mac."

"Stupid...yeah." Wilbur swallowed the burn in his throat. "That's what I did. I left them in Manila...goddamn that was stupid." He stormed toward the door.

The Pearl of Death

Stupid! Stupid! Stupid!

Outside, sunset streaked the Pacific sky with radiant lines of orange and pink. He began to feel the amber glow rise inside him, as if he were being healed. Everything seemed to move in slow motion, the air thick as molasses, each step he took another step closer to alcohol heaven. But the feeling wouldn't last. He set out in search of a more suitable place to drink. The darker, the dirtier, the smellier, the better. If he never heard another child laugh again, never heard another woman sigh, it would be all right with him.

He came to another bar, poked his head inside, saw billiards, a jukebox, sailors and whores. They were having fun, and he wanted no part of it. Farther down, he came to the Irish Rose, a dark and smoky place, narrow as a phone booth with only a murmur of conversation—and no music. He walked in. Not a single face turned toward him, not a goddamn soul cared who he was or why he was there. He felt invisible.

He felt saved.

"Scotch," he told the bartender, a little guy with unkempt hair and choppy teeth. "The cheap stuff."

Choosing a corner booth, he tossed his bushman hat on the table and sank into a spring-worn seat. Odors of vomit and crap wafted from the open john door behind him. The mad dash of a cockroach across the floor made him feel more at home.

The bartender moseyed over and set a smudged glass on the table. He had spidery fingers with crescents of grime under his nails. "Twenty cents, mister." He poured a drink.

Anticipation sang in Wilbur's stomach. He slipped the man a five-spot and gave the bottle an obvious glance.

The bartender set the bottle down and walked off.

It was the perfect bar.

Wilbur downed the glass of scotch. Wiping his mouth with the back of his hand, he thought about how it was wrong to guzzle sippin' whiskey, even this rotgut. But now wasn't the time to savor the finer things in life. It was time to indulge—dive in, lap it up as if his life would end tomorrow.

He poured another glass of sunshine, drank it down, and wheezed. The other drinkers mutated into shadowy figures, their voices deep and distant. He hadn't eaten since breakfast and easily slipped into whiskey's gentle embrace. The Irish Rose began to feel soothing as sleep.

He went numb. Each drink slid down smoother than the last, one after the other. His mind drifted through a lush jungle, touched the fronds and the flowers, and inhaled the scent of cinnamon. A waterfall cascaded through long black hair and splashed off erect nipples. Olive skin and sweet smiles. The flutter of butterfly wings. A moan so soft in his ear. He was with her again, touching her, feeling her, kissing her—

"Hey!"

Touching her, feeling her—

"Faggot!"

Touching her—

"I'm talkin' to you, shithead!"

He blinked. Liawayway? She was gone. He felt suddenly alone. Cold. How could this have happened? Through liquored up eyes, he looked around at the same dark and smoky bar, smelled the sharp odor of scotch and vomit. A redheaded sailor bent over him, stubbly face and groggy eyes. "You're in our booth, faggot."

"Huh?"

Behind him stood several other sailors, ghostly white, leering at him as if he were the enemy. The bastards had a lot of nerve interrupting his stupor. "What the hell...?"

The redheaded asshole grabbed Wilbur's shirt, yanked him off the seat. "You're dead, motherfucker."

Wilbur grabbed his scotch bottle. The room spun. His back hit the floor. The sailor landed on top of him, his knee on Wilbur's stomach, fist reared back. Wilbur swung the bottle, hit the sailor's skull, breaking off the bottleneck. The bastard keeled over. Wilbur lashed out at him with the jagged glass. "I'll cut your fuckin' throat."

Someone grabbed his arm, wrenched the weapon from his hand.

He took a wicked kick to the ribs.

A dull, throbbing pain tore through his chest.

Fight or flight. Kill or be killed. This wasn't the way he'd planned on spending his drinking time. Damn Navy pukes. He kicked out his right foot, caught a sailor's kneecap and heard a crack, a scream. Fists flew at him like battering rams. Brilliant stars and spots flashed in his brain. He couldn't get up. He couldn't get off the floor. He couldn't get away. The bastards were on him like a pack of wild dogs. They were killing him. It was a bad dream, a drunken nightmare.

Whistles shrieked. MPs.

A chair came at his face.

The lights went out.

Chapter Thirty-Three

Manila, January 2, 1942

Timoteo struggled to make it home, his bare feet cut and bleeding. The sky was filled with ash and the filth and stink of war.

Bullets cracked overhead, tore into a wall, and spit concrete in his hair. He ducked around the corner of a blown-out storefront. Panting hard, he pressed his face against the wall. "Allah, please let Mamma and Tito be safe."

A bomb exploded down the street; the concussion hammered his eardrums. His throat ached with a dusty, choking thirst. Now he wished he hadn't wandered so far from home in search of food. His injured feet burned like the sun-baked sands of Palawan. How could he go any farther without shoes?

Amidst the rattle of war and the stench of gunpowder, the rumble of a tank approached from down the block. He wanted to run, but his feet couldn't stand another shard of glass or wooden splinter. Stooping low, he duck-waddled to the nearest wall, sat on his haunches and hugged his knees, watched the tank rumble into view. It was big and ugly and rattling loud, made the ground shake. A frightening death machine.

He felt a chill, even under the hot, glaring sun. The cannon swung back and forth as if looking for a target. Japanese soldiers followed the tank, crouching behind it for protection from unarmed civilians. He trembled, fearing they'd see him, shoot him, and cut off his head.

The Japanese turned down the next street and moved away.

Timoteo steeled himself against the pain in his feet, stood and limped away.

Around the next corner, a burning car belched black smoke

and stunk of oil. Beside it, a dead horse lay in the street, and a dead Filipino wearing sandals, sandals he no longer needed.

Timoteo crawled to the corpse, and with trembling fingers, removed the man's sandals. "Praise be to Allah," he whispered and put them on his own tortured feet. A sickness stirred in his stomach. The Japanese had reduced him to a scavenger of the dead.

Walking quicker now, he made his way through the smoke and debris to the street where he lived. Trucks and tanks idled nearby while Japanese soldiers rounded up Filipinos at bayonet-point and made them stand in line at a checkpoint table. A seated soldier wrote on a tablet. Staying close to the palm trees, Timoteo moved behind the throng and on toward the American apartment building.

"You there," a Japanese soldier shouted in English. "Stop."

Timoteo kept moving, head down, hoping he wasn't the object of the soldier's command.

"Halt."

A rifle made a clicking sound.

He looked toward the voice and saw the cruel face of a soldier, narrow eyes glaring at a stooped old woman shuffling away.

"Lord Jesus. Lord Jesus," she cried.

A shot rang out. The woman fell. Another soldier ran up to her and thrust his bayonet into her back. Timoteo's stomach squeezed hot bile up to his throat. Swallowing, he kept moving, wishing he were invisible.

A woman screamed, made his neck hairs prickle. He looked toward his apartment doors, still twenty meters away. A Japanese soldier was dragging a woman outside. He had an arm around her waist, an arm around her throat.

Terror ripped through Timoteo's heart. Every muscle in his body turned to stone.

"Mamma?"

Her hands clawed at the soldier's arm. Her bare feet kicked the air like a wild animal. "Let me go."

"Mamma!"

Another soldier joined the first, laughing as he subdued one of her flailing arms and helped wrestle her toward the street.

More soldiers rushed over. One man grabbed his crotch, pumped his hips. They all roared with laughter.

She fought them, tried to get free.

Timoteo remembered the looters telling the little girl what the Japanese would do to her, pass her around...*Oh no. Not Mamma.* He staggered forward, started running on fear-stiff legs. He had to stop them. He had to save her.

Tito burst out the apartment door. "Leave her alone." He jumped on a Japanese soldier's back, fists whaling.

"No Tito, don't—"

The soldier tossed him to the ground.

Time slipped into slow motion. Timoteo ran, stumbling, trying to keep his battered feet under him, his ribs so tight he couldn't breathe, he couldn't scream.

The soldier ran a bayonet through Tito's chest. His small body stiffened. His legs jerked with spasms.

Timoteo's knees buckled. The ground rushed up to hit him in the chin. He tried to get up, but it was as if the earth had leached the strength from his body. Terror distorted the world around him, turned everything to black and white. The soldiers moved away from Tito as if what they had done was nothing.

Mamma screamed. "Tito!" She fought the soldiers, wriggled and kicked and screamed and screamed. "Tito!"

The soldiers surrounded her, grabbed her arms and legs.

"He is just a boy!"

They tore the dress from her body and flung it into the street.

She screamed and screamed. "Tito! Tito!" Her once beautiful face was gouged with ugly lines of terror. "Tito! Tito!"

The soldiers carried her to a truck, pushed her under the canvas cover, and climbed inside.

Timoteo tried to get up. He had to save her, but his terror-stricken muscles felt like immovable slabs of concrete.

A Filipino man broke from the checkpoint line, ran toward the truck, shouting in Tagalog to let the woman go.

Maricar!

Machine guns rattled. Blood spewed from his chest and spurted from his forehead. He collapsed into a heap.

Mamma screamed and screamed.

The Pearl of Death

Timoteo shook, stayed low to the ground, afraid to move. He too would be killed if he ran to the truck. Then who would be left to help Tito? What good would it do to fight, one boy against many armed soldiers?

The truck engine revved, drowning out his mother's screams then tore off down the street. Through clenched teeth he prayed, "Allah, why have you forsaken us?"

He crawled to his little brother, took hold of his trembling hand. Fear filled Tito's wide-open eyes. His bony chest lurched with labored breaths. Bloody air burbled out the bayonet wound.

Timoteo wished for Dr. Bogtong to arrive and stop the bleeding. "I'm here, Tito."

Tito squeezed his hand. "I couldn't...stop them."

"You should have stayed inside." Even as he said the words, Timoteo thought how brave his brother had been to defend his mother, how foolish it had turned out.

Coughing, Tito's little body shuddered.

"Look what's happening to us," Timoteo cried. "Our father is dead. Wilbur Cobb left us. Mamma is gone. We're all we have left. Don't die, Tito, please, don't die. I don't know what to do."

"I'm cold," Tito muttered.

"You're gonna be okay." You have to be okay.

Tito wheezed. Blood gushed from his mouth. His head lolled to the side.

"No, Tito, no."

Timoteo buried his face in his brother's shoulder and bawled. Wilbur Cobb was wrong about the Americans protecting the city. He was wrong about the plane coming to get them. He was wrong about the pearl. It may have brought them together, but in the end it had destroyed them, one at a time, until the family was finally gone.

Through tear-stained eyes, he looked at his little brother's wrenched face, his blood-streaked teeth and empty eyes, and felt the fire of hate flare in his belly. Hate for the Japanese. Hate for Wilbur Cobb. Hate for the pearl.

"If it's the last thing I do, Tito, I'll find that pearl and throw it back in the sea." He took in a ragged breath. "The deepest sea where it can never be found—"

"You there." Rough hands grabbed Timoteo's arms and

yanked him up. "Get in line."

"He's my brother."

The soldier barked Japanese at some men guarding the line. Two soldiers rushed over to Tito and lifted his limp body, blood dripping, and tossed him into a nearby truck along with other bodies all heaped up like so much trash.

"Let this be a lesson," the soldier shouted in English. "Never touch a Japanese soldier. It is punished by death. Now get in line."

Walking backwards, Timoteo felt numb. Never before had he been so alone. His eyes burned with tears as he watched soldiers load another body onto the truck.

Maricar's body.

Another soldier booted Timoteo toward the back of the line. Limping and overwhelmed with sorrow, he complied. He wanted to fight back, but he didn't know how, one boy against an army, a boy now standing in this line of weeping citizens, all doomed by the Americans who'd abandoned the city.

"Allah," he whispered, "show me the right way—"

Gunfire erupted from down the street. Everyone ducked, squatted, looked around, their faces white with fear. Japanese soldiers started firing back, rifles banging so loud Timoteo's ears hurt. It was an ambush, Filipinos with guns, shooting at the soldiers.

"The resistance," someone whispered.

There was shouting and screaming everywhere. In that brief instant of chaos, Timoteo realized no one was watching the line. He made a decision that would either save him or get him killed.

Run!

He took off in the direction opposite the gun battle, half sprinting, half limping. His cut feet burned, but he kept moving, again thankful for the sandals, but he'd only made it a few meters before he heard the sonic crack of a bullet zing past.

"Stop."

More gunfire.

He kept running.

If the soldiers killed him, what great loss would it be? He'd see Tito again. And Dad. What good was this life without them?

And Mamma. But a force inside kept him moving, perhaps the instinct to survive or a promise he'd made to his dead brother. Whatever it was, it drove him into a narrow passageway between two buildings. He pushed on, not daring a glance back. Bullets ricocheted off brick and mortar, spraying him with stinging dust. He burst into an open yard, ducked a clothesline, jumped a toy tractor, and heard dogs barking.

Keep going. Keep going.

Japanese shouted, but he couldn't see them. He kept running, leaped a fence, and dashed through a garden. Panic pumped his legs like an engine. His lungs hurt, but he kept running. He was young, angry, and frightened out of his mind.

An alleyway behind a warehouse led to another street, this one teeming with alerted Japanese. He stopped in the shadow of the building's brick wall and watched cars speed by. Red and yellow flags flapped from the fenders.

A Japanese patrol ran past the alley, guns drawn, swords flashing. Murderers. If only he had a gun, a big gun, a machine gun with a million bullets, he would kill them all.

He bent over, and with hands braced on his knees, gasped for air. Sweat rolled off his face. He wished for a breeze to cool him and blow away the smell of urine in his pants. When did he wet himself? He couldn't remember—

"Psstttt..."

He turned toward the sound. A shutter swung open.

"Over here," a raspy voice called.

Moving to a window of the warehouse, he couldn't calm his thundering heart. "Who is it?"

"Climb in."

At the window, he couldn't see anyone, just a dark room, bleak and unfurnished. All around him, angry Japanese chatter was closing in.

"Hurry."

Fear spurred him over the windowsill. He landed on his belly on a wooden floor. The shutters closed, dousing the room in darkness. He wondered if he'd done the right thing.

"Follow me."

The silhouette of a Filipino man took shape, moving away, down a hall. Timoteo found his feet and staggered after the shadow man, turned a corner and shuffled down a flight of squeaky stairs to a musty room. The air felt much cooler, a welcome relief. Dirt floor, cement walls, gray and despairing. A peeling painted sign read: *Montoya Feed and Seed.*

The sounds of gunfire and panic in the streets became more and more muffled. "What is this place?"

"A staging area for the Filipino reserves. We need men to fight the Japanese."

"I'm only fifteen."

"You look older. Can you shoot a gun?"

"I never had a gun."

"We have guns."

"Then I will learn."

"Don't tell him you're only fifteen."

"Who?"

They came to another room, dimly lit in the yellow glow of oil lamps and smelling of cigar smoke.

"Him."

A Filipino man dressed in army fatigues got up from a plush chair. He was smoking a cigar. Two bandoleers crisscrossed his chest. A billed blue hat embroidered with gold eagles and stars sat low on his forehead, shading his sunglasses. He looked like a general, the first general Timoteo had ever seen. He felt small in the man's presence.

The general looked him up and down and sneered. "He's too tall for a Filipino."

"I'm five feet ten," Timoteo said. "And I can run."

"He was running from the Japanese," the shadow man put in. "Good enough for me to recruit him."

Other men occupied the room, squatting along the walls. Some were similarly dressed in brown shorts and shirts. Others wore colorful street clothes like Timoteo. Fresh recruits.

"You a spy?" The general blew out cigar smoke.

"I'm from Palawan."

"A little French blood, huh? Okay. That accounts for your height. What's your name, boy?"

"Timoteo Matito. The Japanese killed my little brother and took my mother away. I don't know where. Can you help me find her?"

The general swatted Timoteo's back. "Stand up straight. Let me have a look at you." He walked around him, puffed on the cigar.

Timoteo tried not to move, felt scrutinizing eyes on him, like a prize to be won or garbage to be tossed out. Whatever the general's whim might be.

"You seem healthy enough." The general removed the cigar from his mouth. "How'd you like to kill some Japanese?"

Timoteo would like nothing better, besides sinking the pearl of death in a deep sea. "Yes sir, general."

The men sitting around laughed.

"I'm not a general, son. I'm a sergeant in the Filipino reserves. We need men like you. How'd you like to join up?"

"Do you have any food?"

"All you want."

His stomach jumped in anticipation. Eat. Get a gun. Find Mamma. Kill Japanese. Allah, in his great wisdom, had showed him the right way. "Count me in."

"That's the spirit." He turned to his men. "We're moving out tonight. Our mission is to join up with the 11th Division on its way to Bataan. General MacArthur is regrouping our forces there for the big push north to the Lingayen Gulf. We're going to drive the Nips back into the sea."

The ragtag band of fighters cheered.

Excitement flared in Timoteo's chest and mixed with the hot sting of revenge.

Someone handed him a can of cold arroz caldo, chicken and rice, and a wooden spoon. He had no idea what perils awaited him fighting the Japanese on Bataan, nor did he care.

He just ate.

Chapter Thirty-Four

Consciousness brought pain. Wilbur wished he were dead. A quick glance around told him he wasn't in the perfect bar anymore, but a small room, perhaps a hospital, but the air smelled of vomit, not medicine, and the lighting was too soft for a jail cell. *Where the hell am I?*

"God," he muttered. His mouth tasted like the bottom of a toilet. "What the hell hit me?" Lifting his head, he inspected the fatigues he was wearing, all wrinkled and splotched with blood. His blood. And he still wore his combat boots as he lay sprawled on a cot. The tangled sheet he hugged was stained with vomit. His vomit.

"Damn." He pried himself to a sitting position, rubbed his face, felt a knot on his forehead the size of Texas, and remembered how it got there, slugged by a flying chair.

Goddamn his brain hurt.

Daylight beamed through a round window in the wall. He heard a distant droning sound, like an engine, a very big engine. A ship's engine?

At the foot of the cot sat his bag, the one he'd always kept packed. He couldn't remember going back to his hotel room. And how did he get on this ship? And where was it going? The Philippines? Finally?

Adrenaline hit his bloodstream like a blowtorch. He found his feet and rushed to the porthole.

Water and waves. As far as he could see, the ocean.

His head felt faint. He steadied himself against the bulkhead. *Think, damn it, think.* Which way was the ship going? The sun was aft. He looked at his watch: 3:30. The ship was heading east, but the Philippines lay west/southwest from Hawaii—the sun should be on the bow. "Fuck!"

He was going the wrong direction.

Scrambling to the door, he yanked on the handle. Locked. What the hell? Fingers trembling, he searched for the lock release but found nothing. "What kind of ship is this?" He pounded on the door. "Hey. Is anybody out there? Hey. Open this door."

"Hold it down in there, buddy," a gruff voice responded.

"Where am I?"

"The brig."

Wilbur pressed his face to the cold steel door. "What kind of ship is this?"

"The Queen Mary if you like."

"I got beat up in a bar, for Christsake."

"Two days ago, you drunken bastard."

He couldn't believe he'd been out that long. "How did I get here?"

"MPs dragged you aboard. Your boss had enough of your bullshit."

"All I wanted was to go back to the Philippines."

The man laughed.

Wilbur didn't like the cynical tone. "So where am I going?"

"Los Angeles."

His heart seized. "I don't want to go to Los Angeles."

"Like it or not, you'll be there in five days."

Wilbur felt sick. He rushed to his duffle bag. His boss must've retrieved it from the hotel room. Did he look through his bag? Did he take the pearl?

Temples hammering, Wilbur unbuckled the bag. There it was—the box, and inside...he opened it...saw the lumpy mass...the pearl, still there.

"Thank God." He hadn't lost his good luck charm.

But good luck had let him down. He was stuck on a ship, locked in a room, and moving farther away from Liawayway every second, to the other side of the fucking world.

Chapter Thirty-Five

In the dank basement hideout, Timoteo bandaged his cut feet and pulled on a pair of rubber-soled canvas shoes. The sergeant gave him a pair of heavily starched brown shorts and a short-sleeve shirt that fit loosely on his tall and lanky frame.

"The official Philippine Army uniform." The sergeant patted Timoteo's shoulder. "Now you look like a real soldier."

Timoteo didn't feel like a soldier. The uniform offered little protection against the harsh jungle brush, and the shoes were so cheap he didn't think they'd last two weeks on the lava-rock slopes of Bataan. He must've looked an awkward sight standing at attention in the dim yellow glow of oil lamps.

The sergeant handed him a rifle but no bullets. "A Springfield from World War One," he explained, then gave him a canteen but no water, and a can of fish but no opener. Timoteo looped the canteen's thin strap over his shoulder and put the can of fish in a baggy pants pocket. The rifle he held with both hands and imagined killing Japanese. If he ever got any bullets. What good was a rifle without bullets? How could he kill Japanese? The hate in his heart grew hot, but he wasn't sure if he was man enough to kill anybody.

"Men..." The sergeant paced before his band of volunteers. "General MacArthur instructed the Philippine Army to attack the Nips, but we failed to drive them back. We will retreat to Bataan and make our stand in the mountain jungles. There is only one road in. Our mission is to establish a line of defense. We expect heavy fighting. Many of you will die."

All this talk of retreating and fighting and dying did nothing to boost Timoteo's confidence in the Filipino reserves. He longed for news of his mother, mourned his brother and father, and cursed Wilbur Cobb for leaving them in this hell.

The Pearl of Death

The pearl was more important to Wilbur than his family.

"Private Matito," the sergeant barked. "Pay attention."

The gruff voice yanked Timoteo back to the problem at hand. "But how will I learn to fight?"

"Just do as you're told." The sergeant plopped a sunhat on Timoteo's head. It felt scratchy. "And keep your head down. These skullcaps aren't made of steel."

"Allah help us," Timoteo mumbled under his breath.

"Move out."

The air seemed charged with electricity as Timoteo and his fellow fighters filed from their hideaway and into the muggy night. Stopping at a fountain in the square, the sergeant ordered them to fill their canteens, then he led them across the city, sticking to the side streets and back alleys.

A Japanese patrol passed by. Timoteo ducked low with the others, wished he had bullets, wished he knew how to put them in the rifle, wished he knew how to kill.

It wasn't long before he and his band joined up with other men in other units moving under the cover of darkness toward San Fernando. There was little said between the fighters, but Timoteo sensed a common fear.

The fear of dying.

At dawn, he hid with his men in a sugarcane field, south of Plaridel and ate American C-rations, three cans of meat and vegetables, crackers and a sugar bar for each man. Timoteo thought of the empty market shelves and thanked Allah for his gracious gift.

The sergeant gathered his volunteers around him. "It will take another night's march to reach Calumpit and the bridge over the Pampanga River. They are set to blow it at oh-six-hundred. We must get across before then."

Timoteo wondered how the sergeant knew about these things then decided they had radio contact with the other units.

"Get some rest, men. We move out at dusk."

Swatting at flies that bit his skin, Timoteo tried to get comfortable among the cane roots and foul smelling dirt fertilized with water buffalo dung and human waste. It must've been a hundred and ten degrees. He closed his eyes and thought of Mamma, wondered if she was okay. What did she eat for breakfast? She was probably worried sick about him. He wished he could tell her that he was all right, now a soldier in the war.

He awoke to shaking.

The sergeant leaned over him. "You're on guard duty." He removed a bullet from one of the ammo belts that crisscrossed his chest.

Timoteo sat up, rubbed his eyes. His clothes were soaked with sweat and stained with dung. He blinked. "What time is it?"

"Fourteen hundred hours."

"Huh?"

"Two PM. Give me your rifle."

He'd propped it against a sugarcane stalk behind him. Standing, he brushed off his shorts, retrieved the rifle, and handed it to the sergeant with both hands.

"I'm only going to show you this once." The sergeant lifted the bolt lever and slid it back. "Put the bullet into the breach like this, pointy part toward the barrel, then slide the bolt forward and lock the lever down." He raised the barrel like he was going to shoot someone. "Squeeze the trigger. Don't pull. Point and shoot."

With sweat running into his eyes, Timoteo took careful note of the procedure. If he was going to kill Japanese, he'd have to know these things.

Point and shoot. Squeeze don't pull.

"The safety is here, on the front of the trigger guard. Pull on. Push off." He moved the lever. "Leave it on until you have to shoot." He gave Timoteo the rifle with both hands. "Think you can remember that?"

Pull on. Push off.

"Thanks." Timoteo swallowed dryly. Finally he was armed. What good it would do him, he wasn't sure. Hitting what he aimed at had to be much harder.

"Take the west perimeter out there." He pointed down a row of sugarcane stalks. "Relieve the guard. Someone will take over for you in two hours."

"Okay."

"And keep your head low. You're tall enough to draw aircraft fire."

Timoteo had no idea how to do guard duty. It seemed all he

had to do was keep an eye open for Japanese coming this way. He looked at the loaded rifle with mixed feelings. On one hand, he hoped he wouldn't have to use it. On the other, he hoped he would. The uncertainty came from not knowing if he would survive a shootout with a trained soldier.

Walking between the cane stalks, he took extra care to keep from rustling the leaves. His bladder ached. After relieving the guard, he relieved himself in the sugarcane—a noisy affair that he feared would bring the Japanese army down on him.

The dusty road to Plaridel was probably fifty meters away. Clanking and rattling, enemy trucks and tanks moved in a steady stream toward Manila. It appeared to be the Japanese's main thrust, and they were succeeding unchallenged. A fifteen-year-old boy and his rifle with one bullet had no chance of stopping them, though he wished he could. He crouched in the cane field and watched the enemy plod on.

***

At dusk, Timoteo stuck close to the sergeant as they moved out, side-stepping the Japanese encampments, which were lit with fires and loud with revelry. The invaders were so sure of their victory they made no attempt to hide their positions. What they didn't realize was that they were making it easy for Timoteo and his fellow Filipinos to slip around them. Even so, the sheer number of camps made the going slow and dangerous.

It was still dark when he reached a hill overlooking the Pampanga River. Torches lit the bridge railings at Calumpit. The sergeant ordered the men to stay low. Whispers among the men carried the consensus that they were supposed to have arrived before 0600. It was already 0615. They were late. The bridge was supposed to be gone by now.

Everyone fidgeted in crouched positions. "What are we going to do?" someone asked.

"We are trying to contact General Wainwright and tell him to wait—"

A flash lit up the sky, followed by a thunderous boom. Timoteo's heart lurched in surprise. The spectacular explosion froze him in place. Balls of yellow fire rose into the air, churned and threw off burning debris that arched down to earth like a meteor shower.

The Calumpit Bridge disappeared with a roar. He wanted to cheer, but nearby rifle fire cut short his elation. The blast had alerted the enemy to their presence. Filipinos opened fire on the Japanese, now advancing through a rice paddy below the hill. Rifle flashes sparkled like fireflies in the predawn darkness.

The enemy was coming. Timoteo and the fighters were cut off from the main defense force.

"We are sitting ducks," someone said.

Timoteo clutched his rifle. His hands shook. It was time to fight or die. He clicked the safety off. "Allah, help me."

A whistling sound screeched overhead, followed by a loud boom in the distance. Another whistle, another boom. Concussions pounded the air. Below, geysers of fire erupted in the rice paddy. The screams of dying Japanese gave him an unsettling sense of pleasure.

"The 21st Artillery," the sergeant said. "They're laying down a cover barrage. We must go now. Follow me, men."

Timoteo clicked the rifle's safety on and exhaled in relief. The killing and dying would wait. He scrambled to his feet and ran with the others through the underbrush, down a rocky path to the river.

"Single file," the sergeant ordered. "Keep your rifles above your heads. The water isn't deep but very swift."

As dawn winked on the horizon, Timoteo forded the river, fighting to keep his balance in the pressing current. The water sucked the heat from his chest. A line of men stretched out in front of him and behind him too. He had no idea this many Filipinos had joined the march to Bataan.

They were going to help the Americans.

The Americans who had abandoned him in Manila.

***

By noon, Timoteo's unit caught up with the 11th Division on Route Seven south of San Fernando. A long line of trucks and civilian vehicles brought traffic to a crawl. Adding to the chaos, thousands of refugees laden with their belongings walked the roadsides. It was a solemn and desperate parade of humanity, slowly moving south toward Bataan. Timoteo wondered where they would stay and if there would be food for so many people.

He still hadn't fired the bullet in his rifle, but he'd become more accustomed to it being there and the possibility that he'd get to kill a Japanese very soon.

In the distance, heavy artillery cannons boomed.

"A hundred thousand Japanese soldiers are coming," someone close by said.

"The North Luzon Force is fighting at San Fernando," another man said. "They'll give us time to get to Bataan."

"Then they'll destroy the roads and bridges."

It seemed that all of the Philippines would be in ruins before this was over.

"That should slow them Nips down."

"But nothing will stop them."

On the morning of January 4th, the sergeant ordered the 11th Division to dig in on the right side of the ten-mile road to Bataan. With impassable swamps on his right flank and the mountains on his left, Timoteo felt exposed to the full frontal force of the approaching Japanese army.

"Hold the line or die where you are," someone shouted.

Timoteo waited in a muddy ditch with the other men, sweating and praying and smelling water buffalo dung. Artillery fire echoed in the distance, exploded nearby, and rained down rocks, dirt and sugarcane. He gritted his teeth, waiting, but didn't see any enemy soldiers. All he could do was keep his head down as shells exploded around him.

Black smoke rose from the burning cane fields. Trucks carrying ammunition and fuel erupted into giant balls of fire.

The ground shook.

Droves of Filipino civilians fled toward the trees through a hellish forest of explosions that cut short many escapes. Blood and limbs flew through the air. With fires burning all around them, the wounded cried for help that would never come.

Helplessness felt like a tank parked on Timoteo's chest. He pushed the carnage from his mind, concentrated on the rifle, the stock against his shoulder, the cold sight plate against his cheek. The enemy was coming. This was his chance to kill one Japanese with one bullet.

One Japanese for Tito.

The artillery barrage ended. Fires crackled: burning trucks, burning sugarcane. The smell of oily smoke and burned flesh filled his nostrils and soured his stomach.

His eyes watered. "Allah, give me strength."

He pushed off the safety.

Waited with his finger on the trigger.

His rifle pointed down the road...at the trees.

His hands sweating—

"Banzi!"

Timoteo's neck hairs pricked up. Japanese soldiers charged from the trees, rifles ablaze and glistening swords reared back and flashing.

Timoteo swallowed, tried to aim the rifle at the chest of a soldier running toward him. His hands shook so much he couldn't line up the shot. He couldn't be sure of a direct hit. He had only one chance.

Angry bullets zinged over his head.

He couldn't breathe.

Rifle fire banged down the Filipino line. Gunsmoke and screaming filled the air. Still, he wasn't ready to shoot. He only had one bullet. And then he would die.

A thunderous roar exploded behind him. The 11th Division tanks had moved up from the rear to engage the advancing enemy.

"Fall back behind the tanks," the sergeant shouted.

Timoteo hadn't fired his bullet. He wasn't ready to retreat. The Japanese were getting closer. Some were shot down. Some kept charging forward. There were too many to count, too many to stop.

"Move! Move! Move!" the sergeant shouted and climbed out of the ditch. A Japanese soldier ran up behind him, teeth showing, and lunged forward with his bayonet. Timoteo swiveled his rifle. He didn't have time to think of anything except point and shoot.

The rifle bang and recoil startled him, but not nearly as much as seeing blood spray from the Jap's chest as he fell at the sergeant's feet.

Shock froze Timoteo. He did it. He shot a killer of children. He looked at the rifle. He looked at the body. He looked at the blood flowing into the ditch. His life would never be the same.

"Nice shot, kid." The sergeant stepped back, his face a little pale. "I owe you one." He grabbed Timoteo's arm. "Now move out."

The tanks rattled forward and reinforcements from the 26th Cavalry Scouts charged up on horseback, guns blazing. Ducking low, Timoteo followed the sergeant through a head-banging salvo of cannon fire and rifle reports. They dove over a berm along the roadside, landed in mud and raised a cloud of black flies.

"I'm out of bullets," Timoteo shouted.

"No you're not." The sergeant removed one of his bandoleers and slung it over Timoteo's shoulder then slapped the top of his sun-hat. "That'll hold you for a while."

He didn't know what to say. The sergeant had given him his bullets. The bandoleer was heavier than a string bag full of clams, bogged him down, but the gift was beyond belief.

"Stay sharp, men."

Shaking, Timoteo loaded a bullet into the rifle and shot at the Japanese. There were so many of them, it was hard to miss. The killing became easier, but he knew that a bullet could hit him any second. If that was Allah's will, so be it. He had done what he'd set out to do—except sink the pearl in a deep, deep sea.

The gun battle raged until nightfall. Again, Timoteo and the 11th Division moved back to secure another front line for the retreating defenders, this time in Layac Junction at the mouth of the Bataan Peninsula.

The next day, he moved farther south on a road congested with troops, staff cars, trucks and buses, mule trains laden with supplies, and thousands of civilians. Dust and diesel fumes choked the air. The going was slow under a burning sun.

Behind him crept the ever-present thunder of battle. Filipino and American Army units were fighting side-by-side.

A day later, Timoteo and the remainder of his battle-weary 11th Division crossed the Layac Bridge that spanned a deep rocky canyon. He and three other Filipino fighters dug a foxhole in the hard ground. The sergeant told them to protect the only road into Bataan.

Once the North Luzon Forces crossed over, the army dynamited the bridge, sending it into the canyon with a shattering roar.

That evening, he ate C-rations in the foxhole, swatted mosquitoes and flies, smelled wet earth, and thought about his mother, her sweet cinnamon fragrance, her smile, her strong arms around him, her screams as the Japanese took her away.

He had to think of something else. The pearl. Wilbur Cobb. Palawan—anything but his mother.

A gold-toothed fighter broke the silence in the foxhole. "Private Matito, why did you join up?"

"The Japanese killed my brother."

The fighter jabbed his spoon into a can of pears. "My brothers were taken for Japanese work details, whipped like slaves. I got away, joined up."

It was a familiar story, but Timoteo felt his was more terrible. "And the soldiers took my mother somewhere, I don't know if she's dead."

"Is she pretty?"

"Yes."

"Then she is alive." The fighter made a circle with his thumb and forefinger, then put the pointing finger of his other hand into the circle and quickly moved it back and forth. "But she wishes she was dead."

"No." Timoteo jumped on him, started fist-pummeling his head. The can of pears went flying.

"She's my mother."

Another Filipino pulled Timoteo off the man. "Save it for the Nips."

"He's lying."

"They use our women for sex slaves, seventy and eighty soldiers a day. She is better off dead."

"No. Not my mother." Timoteo slumped to the dirt. His eyes welled with tears. He wanted to rescue her, at least try, but he was stuck on this sweltering peninsula, trapped by the advancing enemy.

The gold-toothed fighter picked up his spilled can of pears. "Look what you did."

The Pearl of Death

Timoteo offered up his can of pears. "Eat mine."

The fighter tossed his empty can out of the foxhole and snatched Timoteo's offering from his hand. "Crazy kid."

He looked at his rifle and felt small. "I wish I could kill more than one Jap at a time. This rifle holds only one bullet."

"Nah. Let me show you." The gold-toothed fighter set down the can and took the rifle. "There's a magazine in here." He opened the bolt, shoved one of his own bullets into the rifle, but instead of closing the bolt, he pushed a second bullet in on top of the other, shoving it in deeper. Click. Then a third. Click. "Load it like this. Five bullets." He gave the rifle back.

"Gee, thanks."

"Don't ever hit me again." The fighter went to work opening the can of pears.

Timoteo stared at his rifle as if it were brand new. Now he had five bullets to shoot five Japanese. Why hadn't the sergeant told him about this before? Then again, there'd been so little time for training.

"Move out," someone shouted.

He slung the rifle across his back, felt five times more powerful, and scrambled from the foxhole.

The dirt road wandered past rice paddies dotted with stands of palms. Being taller than the other Filipinos, Timoteo could easily see the surrounding area. In the ditches, water buffalo wallowed in mud puddles. Villagers stood somber-faced and watched the columns of men and vehicles lumber by.

The natives were fishermen and farmers, simple people. Timoteo knew the Japanese would come with their planes and their tanks and their soldiers. It would just be a matter of time before these people's lives would be forever scarred by the war.

At camp that night, the sergeant allowed small fires. He sat on his haunches with Timoteo, gave him an extra sugar bar from his C-rations. "The quartermaster has bad news for us."

The name meant nothing to Timoteo. He felt the sting of a mosquito and killed it. "What is a quartermaster?"

"He's in charge of distributing supplies, the food, ammunition, medicine."

Timoteo couldn't imagine the size of that job.

"We have supplies for six months to feed and care for forty

thousand troops, but there are almost eighty thousand American and Filipino soldiers here, plus another twenty six thousand refugees the army must feed."

Several men gathered around the fire, listened to the sergeant.

"Tomorrow we go on half rations. One cup of rice, four ounces of meat, one can of fruit."

"The American C-rations are gone?" a man asked.

The sergeant nodded. "Moved to the rear, near Mariveles, where a command post has been established. The officers there have fresh meat and fish and vegetables. There is a golf course and a nightclub. They have everything, but still they fear their supplies will run short before reinforcements arrive. So they have taken our rations."

"But we are fighting on the front lines," a Filipino shouted over the fire-pit flames. "We are risking our lives."

"We will starve," another man said.

Timoteo felt his baggy pocket for the can of fish. He would save it for as long as possible.

Chapter Thirty-Six

The Battling Bastards of Bataan

Early April, Timoteo awoke in a foxhole, sick and weak. His tall lanky frame had been reduced to skin and bones. Every time he thought to open the can of fish in his pocket, he thought that things could get worse. Things always got worse, so he left the can in his pocket.

For the past four months, he and his Bataan defenders had battled the Japanese, established front lines only to watch them melt under fierce enemy attacks.

Fall back. Dig in and fight. Fall back again.

Hundreds of his fellow fighters died daily, many times more than the Americans, but they both fought and died together under the meanest conditions on the planet. Lava-sharp jungle trails had long ago destroyed Timoteo's canvas shoes, and thorny lipa plants had torn his only uniform to rags. Shooing black flies from open sores on his arms and legs became a fulltime job, yet still he had to pick out a maggot or two. His feet were so blistered and bloodied he could hardly walk, even when wearing palm leaves he had fashioned into shoes. He lived in pain every day, every hour, every step.

And every day the sergeant kept saying, "American ships are coming with reinforcements and supplies."

But the ships never came.

Down to quarter rations, malnutrition, dysentery, and malaria felled more soldiers than the enemy's guns. Timoteo wondered if each day would be his last.

A fighter scrambled into the foxhole with a dead monkey in tow. "Breakfast," he said and pulled his bayonet.

Timoteo sat up. Fresh meat. Had to be better than the

Terry Wright

worms he ate for dinner.

"Sergeant ordered the cavalry to butcher their horses," the fighter said, slicing hairy meat from the monkey's hind leg. "Then the mules." He handed a chunk to Timoteo.

His stomach clutched from the stink, like the meat was spoiled, fresh off the bone. He closed his eyes and put the chunk in his mouth, chewed rubbery muscle, sucked out bitter fluids, and swallowed the spew.

Horse meat, mule meat, worms, anything was better than monkey meat.

"Sergeant says we'll reach the Mariveles Valley headquarters camp this afternoon." The fighter stuffed monkey in his mouth. "They got mess halls with steaks and potatoes and real eggs."

"Rumors," someone said.

"No, it's true. There's an officer's club with a bar, beer, whiskey and women."

Timoteo had no use for any of those things. He swallowed the monkey meat and pretended it was steak and potatoes. At least he still had the can of fish in his pocket. The day he opened it would be the last feast of his life.

"Move out," the sergeant shouted.

"You'll see." The fighter tossed the monkey bones in the bushes. "We'll be all right when we get there."

Timoteo hoped that was true.

With the sergeant in the lead, the column of twenty beaten and ill men reached the ridge above the Mariveles Valley. Timoteo looked out over a grassy lowland. To the north stood Mt. Natib, purple and ragged. On the south, the Mariveles Mountains and its highest volcano, Mt. Bataan, overlooked a seaport, and two and half miles offshore sat the comma-shaped island of Corregidor. It was easy to see there was nowhere left to retreat. He thought there could be nothing emptier than his stomach...until now, as all hope drained from his heart.

Single file, the line of men negotiated the steep and rocky trail down the mountain and into a valley infested with the most vicious mosquitoes Timoteo had ever encountered. The stinging little bastards flew up his nose and tunneled into his ears. He wanted to go back, face the Japanese, let them end his suffering

~226~

by death or capture. But orders were: no surrender. He didn't want to die. He was only fifteen, but he felt like an old man, a battle-hardened soldier who'd seen more violence and death than any boy should ever see.

Thanks to the pearl of death, he was sure.

By late afternoon, the ratty band of fighters staggered into headquarters camp with as much dignity as they could muster. Timoteo's heart beat with anticipation as he looked for the mess hall. He hoped to smell steaks on the grill and hear music from the officer's club. Instead, he saw a sweltering tent city and men so ill they looked like walking skeletons. Those sick with malaria and too emaciated to stand lay on stretchers parked in rows under makeshift lean-tos. A black cloud of flies buzzed around them.

The stench of open latrines soured every breath he inhaled.

Broken down and bullet-riddled trucks and busses were parked every which way. A few jeeps looked usable by the fact their hoods were closed.

By one jeep, under a tarp in the shade, a radio sat on a folding table. Officers huddled around it, their dark faces hardened by war. Timoteo eased up behind the men. This was the first radio he had seen up close. Words came through, squeaky and crackly—like magic.

"The Japanese fleet is anchored in Subic Bay," the voice said. "General King, launch an attack on their base at Olongapo immediately."

"Impossible," General King barked into the mic. "My men are sick. We don't have enough food or ammunition for such an attack."

"That's an order."

"General Wainwright, it's a two-day march over rough terrain—"

A plane screamed over the treetops. Machine guns rattled, strafing the ground. Bullets stripped trees bare of leaves and ripped into a row of tents. The officers manning the radio hit the dirt. Timoteo dove under a truck.

As the plane veered off, wounded men hollered for the medic. Circling, the plane came back. Timoteo could see it between the truck's tire and front fender, flying low, a red dot on its tail, like the Japanese trucks in Manila.

Brilliant flashes burst from its guns. Dirt spit up from the ground and drew a deadly line across the road toward the hospital, a slat-board building clearly marked with a white cross painted on the slanted roof.

A bomb dropped from the plane's belly.

Timoteo covered his head, felt the blunt punch of the explosion. The truck rocked on its springs above him.

When he looked up, the hospital walls lay splayed open, roof collapsed, the area scattered with bodies and fallen trees. Paper floated down like confetti, and the air was charged with the screams of wounded and dying men. Thin, bare-chested soldiers ran toward the destruction. Only when the buzz of the plane faded in the distance did Timoteo crawl out from under the truck. Still hugging the ground, he looked for the sergeant but didn't see him anywhere.

A second later, artillery shells whistled through the air and rained down from the sky, exploding all around and setting the jungle ablaze. One hit thirty feet from where Timoteo lay, knocked him senseless, but the shrapnel flew over him and skinned nearby trees of their branches.

He spit dust.

The sergeant called to him from a foxhole in the ditch. "Private Matito...over here."

Crawling on his belly over punishing ground, he made the foxhole and rolled in. He unslung his rifle from his back, propped it on a mound of dirt. "Are they coming?" It would be a fight to the death, he was sure. He welcomed the battle. He'd already killed so many Japanese he'd lost count.

A nearby explosion tossed dirt like rice.

"Keep your head down," the sergeant said. "The Nips scaled Mt. Natib and cut our left and right flanks."

"Will we fight 'til we die?"

A jeep sped past them, throwing dust. Two officers and a driver were aboard. They carried a flag with them, made from a stained white sheet.

"We wait."

***

The Pearl of Death

On April 9, 1942, General King surrendered 78,000 men on Bataan: 12,000 Americans and 66,000 Filipino reserves. They were too sick and undersupplied to be an effective fighting force. During the night, Timoteo helped the men destroy their weapons, munitions, and supplies, anything of use to the enemy. For the Battling Bastards of Bataan, the war was over, but their fight for survival had just begun.

As enemy soldiers approached with fixed bayonets, Timoteo glanced at the sergeant, a brave man who stood tall, shoulders back and chin jutted out as he raised his hands in surrender.

Timoteo followed his lead. Hands above his head, he stood next to the sergeant and hoped to appear as brave, even as his knees shook with fear.

The soldiers shouted commands in Japanese, a sharp, repulsive jabber, but by the way they waved their rifle barrels, Timoteo decided they wanted him and the sergeant to move across the road. There, other Filipinos were assembled, hands on their heads as they stood in line under the watchful eyes of armed guards. It looked as if the Japanese were separating the Americans from the Filipinos. But why? Weren't they equal enemies?

A soldier took the sergeant's hat and sunglasses, put them on, and did a little twirl-around dance, laughing. The sergeant just stared at him with a poisonous glare.

Another soldier frisked Timoteo, dug in his pockets, came up with the can of fish and smiled, showing crooked teeth. He chattered to a nearby soldier. They laughed, and he pocketed the can.

With his food taken, Timoteo's stomach felt emptier than ever. He wanted to fight, get it back, but to die over a can of fish seemed foolish. Instead, he ground his teeth in silent defiance.

"Why do you fight for these American GIs?" an interpreter asked the Filipino prisoners standing in the ditch. "They can never win."

Timoteo knew why. America had promised the Philippines independence by 1944. The Japanese had changed all that. They made slaves of the Filipinos and put young women to work in their brothels. And mothers. His mother. He was powerless to stop them. Seemed the Americans were powerless, too. A persistent tear escaped his eye and ran down his cheek. Of course the Filipinos would fight alongside the Americans. It was their only hope to become a free nation.

Across the road, GIs were assembled, frisked, their money, jewelry and watches taken. Men were beaten for no reason.

"You must treat us as prisoners of war under the terms of the Geneva Convention," an American officer said.

"We are not barbarians," a Japanese soldier replied and knocked the man off his feet.

Timoteo cringed.

The enemy laughed.

All afternoon, he sat with the other prisoners along the roadside ditches, all jammed together five and six rows deep, the sick, the wounded, the dying. They waited in the terrific heat as more prisoners were rounded up and subjected to the same brutality. All the while, Japanese guards threatened them with bayonets or beat them with rifle butts. There was no food, no water, no place to relieve themselves but where they sat. The flies and mosquitoes were more unbearable than the heat and stink. If there was a hell, Timoteo had found it, and for all he knew Allah had abandoned the human race.

Thousands of prisoners were soon assembled in and around Mariveles, packed along the roads and in every clearing. Men suffered and moaned as the Japanese ate and drank heartily, flaunting their victory at every turn.

By nightfall, Timoteo was herded into a barbwire stockade with other prisoners and made to spend the night in his own filth. Fighting nausea, he curled up on the ground with his fellow condemned, tried to ignore their sobs and muttered prayers.

He too sobbed for his mother and Tito, and the pearl that had brought this suffering upon them. Was there no limit to the misery it would bring to the Philippines, and perhaps the entire world?

Gritting his teeth, Timoteo swore to Allah that he'd find the pearl and throw it back into the sea.

Just let me live, he prayed.

Chapter Thirty-Seven

Dawn.

Timoteo awoke from a fitful sleep, smelled feces and vomit, and swiped at flies so thick they covered him like a furry blanket. His stomach ached with hunger, and his throat felt dry and scratchy. It took all his courage just to open his eyes. His head was propped on the back of an American soldier lying beside him.

He sat up and looked for the sergeant. Sunlight glinted off coiled barbwire surrounding the field. Bodies dangled in the wire, American and Filipinos bloodied by bayonets and bullets. How foolish to surrender and then try to escape. Still, he didn't see the sergeant and hoped that one of those bodies wasn't his.

For the first time since Timoteo joined up, he felt alone.

A commotion at the stockade gate drew his attention, Japanese shouting and boots scuffling in the dirt. Prisoners stirred and coughed. A buzzing black cloud rose above the human stockade.

The gate opened. Men stood and rushed the gate. Shots rang out. The men cowered back.

Beyond the barbwire, a table had been set up, and on it sat a huge gray pot. Prisoners got in line, and one at a time dipped a hand into the pot and came out with rice.

"Come on," he said to the GI still lying on his belly beside him. "There's food." The soldier didn't move. Timoteo shook him. "We must get in line." He rolled the man over. Lifeless eyeballs stared out of a sunken face. His open mouth and nostrils writhed with white maggots. And the smell...

Timoteo gagged. Men funneled around him, heading toward the gate, the pot, the food. He got to his feet. Pain shot up both legs. Boots. The soldier's boots, like the dead Filipino in

Manila, his sandals, the ones Timoteo scavenged from his feet...but this soldier's boots had already been taken. Despair threatened to drop Timoteo to his knees, but the thought of food overpowered self-pity. He hurried to get in line.

By the time it was his turn at the pot, there were only scrapings on the bottom, which surrendered up only a half handful of rice. He shoved the meager fare into his mouth, backed away. The rice was cold and barely cooked, like chewing on gravel. Would the Japanese bring another pot? Maybe they would let him have a proper helping.

A few more hands went into the pot before the guards knocked it over. The prisoners behind him went without. His half share was suddenly a gift from Allah.

The prisoners were assembled, four abreast, about a hundred to each group, Filipinos on the left side of the road, Americans on the right. Shouting in Japanese, the guards struck them with bamboo sticks. An interpreter ordered them to start walking.

No one moved.

"Where are we going?" an American officer asked from across the road.

"To San Fernando," the interpreter guard said.

"Sixty-five miles?" the officer shouted. "You can't make us walk all the way."

The guard drew a pistol and shot him in the leg.

Agony washed over the officer's face. Hopping on one leg, he gritted his teeth in defiance and shrieked, "I'll see you are hanged for war crimes."

Grinning, the guard shot him in the other leg.

He screamed and fell.

"Now you can crawl to San Fernando, you American dog." The guard pointed his gun at the other prisoners. "Anyone else have a complaint?"

The men were mute. Timoteo said nothing.

Americans brought a stretcher for their downed officer, and a medic applied bandages to the man's legs. Four volunteers grabbed the stretcher handles and hoisted him off the ground. The columns were again ordered to move out.

This time everyone complied.

The Pearl of Death

Timoteo started walking and wondered where the sergeant had been during the shooting. Looking around, he could easily see over everyone's heads, but there was no sign of him.

An hour later, they began the brutal climb out of the Mariveles Valley. Destroyed American tanks and trucks littered the ditches, like dead soldiers in their own right. Wrecked like the lives of everyone passing by. Blown off tires. Blown off limbs. Leaking oil. Leaking blood. What little difference their sacrifices made now.

Moving south, columns of Japanese trucks and artillery bullied the roadway. Tanks and half-tracks reduced the road to potholes and loose rock. Dust swirled in the air. Guards wore white masks over their noses and mouths. Prisoners coughed and choked but kept walking.

Barefoot and bleeding, Timoteo thought this would have been the day to open the can of fish. The war couldn't possibly get any worse than this. His throat felt so dry that every swallow produced pinpricks of pain. He prayed for a drink.

All around him, men cried out for water. Their pleas fell on unsympathetic Japanese ears, who drank openly from canteens and splashed water on their faces and necks.

The GIs carrying the officer's stretcher became exhausted and pleaded for anyone to take their places at the stretcher handles. No one volunteered.

Timoteo slowed his pace to let other prisoners pass him, and watched the GIs struggle with the stretcher. He thought about crossing the road to help, but he feared he'd be shot for breaking ranks.

The four men set down the stretcher and moved on without the officer. Abandoned on the roadside, he sat up and waved his hands. "Somebody please help me."

Haggard and beaten soldiers walked past him and looked the other way.

A guard stepped up and laughed at the officer, then rammed him through the chest with a bayonet.

The body slumped.

Americans walked past. One crossed his chest, kept walking. Timoteo's stomach churned with repulsion. He turned away from the murder and plodded on with his bedraggled countrymen. Disgust over the senseless death was soon replaced with renewed concern over the pain in his own feet. He needed boots. He needed medical attention. He needed a miracle. "Allah, why have you forsaken me?"

As the day wore on and more men fell from the march, the horrors mounted—more against the Americans than the Filipinos.

One GI, skinny-sick with malaria, crumpled to the road.

The guards stopped the march and screamed at the man. "Choudai ue! Choudai ue!" He failed to respond.

Timoteo thought they should keep walking so they wouldn't have to stand there and witness another beating, another death.

Guards yanked two Americans out of line, gave them shovels and showed them where to dig. They obeyed, and when the hole was big enough, the guard ordered them to put the sick man into the grave and fill it with dirt.

The Americans' eyes flooded with terror. They backed away from the hole, shook their heads no.

Timoteo looked around at everyone's stunned faces. Bury the man alive? They couldn't possibly mean it.

A guard drew his pistol and shot the nearest American in the head. The body dropped, then he ordered two more GIs to dig another hole.

While they dug, Timoteo and his fellow prisoners stood under the blazing sun, some fainting in the heat. Nearby prisoners held up the fallen, hoping not to attract the guards' attention.

When the second hole was dug, the guard ordered the diggers to put the dead GI into one grave and the sick GI into the other.

This time the Americans did as they were ordered.

Timoteo had to cover his ears to block out the man's screams as they buried him alive. He couldn't understand the Japanese' disrespect for life, but having seen it, he knew that to fall meant certain death.

Again the order was given to march.

A truck pulled up with a dusty squeal. Two guards ran up to Timoteo, thrust their rifles at him and shouted words he didn't understand. Their eyes were narrow slits of rage.

What had he done to provoke them?

Fighting panic, he raised his hands and kept walking with the other prisoners. The guards kept shouting at him.

He kept walking.

The other prisoners cowered back, putting distance between themselves and Timoteo. He felt culled from the herd. A guard struck him with a bamboo stick. Pain sliced across his back. He staggered forward but refused to show weakness.

Don't fall. Don't fall. Don't fall.

He kept moving. A guard hit him in the back with a rifle butt. It knocked the breath out of his lungs. The guards forced him to move into the middle of the road.

Terror shot hot adrenaline through his body.

A truck roared by, nearly hit him. Dust. Dust everywhere, swirling around. He felt naked in his ragged shorts, torn shirt, and bleeding bare feet. The Japanese had decided he was weak. They were going to kill him, but he hadn't slowed the march. He hadn't fallen. Why then—?

The guards whipped him with the bamboo sticks. Timoteo backed up, arms raised in self-defense. Each blow stung, forced him backwards, across the road to the American side. A GI grabbed his shirt and yanked him into the moving line, ending the guard's assault.

"You're tall for a Filipino," the GI said. "They must've thought you were in the wrong line."

Timoteo rubbed his arms, saw the welts but refused to cry. "What difference does it make?"

"It's hot on both sides of hell, boy. Welcome aboard."

The guard hit the GI.

He stopped talking.

Things had gone from bad to worse. Now Timoteo had to walk with the Americans, and along with them, take the brunt of the guards' abuse.

His feet stung like he was walking on knife blades, but he would not fall.

That night they were forced to lie down alongside the rocky, dirty road. The ditches reeked of human excrement.

No food. No water. No rest.

The Japanese roamed among them, poking ribs with rifle barrels and kicking stomachs. The way they laughed and chattered, it seemed that they relished the suffering they doled out. When would Timoteo be next? Had he been spared only to be executed with more brutality than the other murders he'd seen?

But he had to survive. He had to find his mother. He had to find the pearl. It seemed an impossible task. He'd have to be strong, or at least appear to be strong—no matter what.

The next morning, he rose on stiff and aching legs. He peed in his pants but held his chin high. The march began again. Limping, he concentrated on reaching the next palm grove ahead, or the next bend in the road. He needed attainable goals. Live that long. Set another goal.

Stay strong. Keep moving. Don't fall.

Two hours later, the column came upon an oasis alongside the road. Water. Thirst drove him to the ditch, but the smell stopped him from jumping in. The oasis was actually a mud wallow thick with black flies, green scum, and globs of dung. Two water buffalo lounged in the muck, chewing cud, their ears batting flies.

Five Americans were fooled. They ran to the wallow, threw themselves down, parted the scum with their hands, and lapped at the mud like kittens drinking milk.

The guards stopped the march and howled. Two prisoners returned to the ranks, wiping their lips and spitting. The guards shot the other three, left the bodies to sink in the wallow.

The march began again. Japanese convoys roared by, blowing dust. Before long, the two men who'd drunk from the wallow began vomiting green liquid. They staggered side-to-side, trying to stay on their feet. One fell to the road, curled up around his cramping guts and hacked violently.

A guard ran to him shouting as if anger alone would bring the man to his feet. "Choudai ue!"

The column kept moving.

A shot rang out behind Timoteo. He ventured a glance back. As the GI lay in the road, a Japanese truck ran over him with no more regard than for a stray dog. The second man who'd drunk from the mud wallow tumbled into the ditch. Moments later, another gunshot. The murdering had become so commonplace that Timoteo thought little for the GI and more for his own resolve to stay on his feet, which had become more difficult by the hour.

Chapter Thirty-Eight

That evening they staggered into Balanga. Their orderly columns had long ago disintegrated into a mob of sick and broken men.

The citizens of Balanga stood along the road and threw them rice balls, sugarcane, and fruit. Timoteo caught a hunk of sugarcane. He tore into it with his teeth and savored the moist, sweet center.

Gunfire erupted. Civilians scattered into the surrounding streets and fields. The Japanese chased them, firing wildly. Good people fell to the barrage. Timoteo swallowed the cane sugar and thanked Allah for their sacrifices.

Near the center of town, Timoteo and the American soldiers were herded to a warehouse and packed inside. Human excrement covered the floor, left there by a previous group of prisoners on this march of death. Feces oozed between Timoteo's blistered and bleeding toes. It felt like soothing mud, but the reality and stench of it made his stomach revolt with dry heaves. A loose bowel movement soiled his pants. His stomach hurt. The sugar cane hadn't settled well.

The doors closed. Padlocks clicked.

Left in darkness, GIs collapsed against each other. They moaned and cried and prayed. Reeking of feces and bile, the air was never meant for human lungs.

Timoteo fell on a soldier. Soldiers fell on Timoteo. Fighting to breathe, he found little comfort in being off his road-ravaged feet. He asked Allah for sleep, to be taken away in a dream of a better time, when life was carefree and loving, a time before the pearl came to Palawan. Before the Japanese invaded Manila and destroyed the family he loved. Before his life became a living hell.

The Pearl of Death

The sounds of human misery resonated in the dark: men vomiting, groaning, and crying, and the constant buzz of mosquitoes and flies. He covered his ears. Squeezed his eyes shut. Cried himself to sleep.

The next morning, men stood again, helped others to their feet. Still on the ground, the soldier Timoteo had slept on wheezed. His face was splotched with feces and bug bites. It was the same GI who had pulled him into line on the American side of the road.

"Get up. Get up," Timoteo told him.

He spoke in a weak and raspy voice. "Take my boots, young fellow."

Timoteo couldn't believe the offer. A man's boots were his salvation. "I'll be okay, sir."

"I ain't gonna...need 'em." He coughed.

"I'll help you get up."

The soldier waved off Timoteo's hand. "I'm finished, son. Take the boots, before someone else—"

Guards banged on the doors. Shouted. The padlocks rattled.

"Hurry," the soldier said.

Knowing the GI would be killed as soon as the Japanese found he hadn't risen for the march, Timoteo squatted at the man's feet and removed his boots, releasing the smell of rotted flesh. Pus oozed through ragged socks. He gagged.

The warehouse doors creaked open. Light splayed across the tin ceiling. Flies scattered. In sharp and cranky voices, the Japanese shouted orders. Prisoners began to shuffle out.

Hands trembling, Timoteo pulled the boots on his own tortured feet. The leather felt stiff but warm and moist from the American's sweat and pus. Lacing the boots quickly, he looked at the soldier to say thank you, but the empty stare of death already shown in his eyes.

Standing, Timoteo felt taller and stronger. Allah had blessed him. He wished he knew the name of the GI who had given him this great gift. So many good men had died in this war. Timoteo was sure Allah had saved him for a higher purpose.

Finding his mother, perhaps? Or the pearl?

Outside, he looked back into the warehouse. Men still lay in the muck. A detail of Filipino prisoners, who had spent the night in an outside pen, went in to retrieve the dead Americans. The Japanese made the Filipino prisoners dump the bodies in a field behind the building. Several Americans stood fast, heads bowed in prayer, until the guards beat them to get them moving.

Walking in boots proved awkward at first. He followed the soldiers to a line where three pots of boiled rice sat on a table. At another table, hot tea. Last night's horrors were quickly set aside as he ate and drank with his smelly American brothers. Food at last. A meal. But no one dared speak to each other.

When the march resumed, everyone's spirits seemed lifted. GIs sang marching songs. Sound off, 1, 2, 3, 4! But as Balanga fell behind them, the roadside became littered with dead bodies, hundreds of them lined up in long rows, Filipinos and Americans, bare feet facing the road on display for everyone to see.

A horrible dread seeped into Timoteo's full belly. Why were more prisoners dying? Was it the rice? The tea? Was it poisoned?

"Hayaku! Hayaku!" the guards shouted.

"Faster! Faster!" A Japanese interpreter echoed. "You dogs walk too slow, make us behind schedule."

Guards beat them with bamboo until they broke into a run. Men fell at more than twice the rate of prior days. The guards didn't waste bullets on them. They used swords to chop off heads. It was a sport. Who could cut off a head with a single blow? Those who hacked away at a neck until the head fell were ridiculed. The Filipinos across the road got the worst of the murdering.

Timoteo kept running. Chin up, chest out. Look strong. And pray. He thanked Allah for the American's boots. Without them he would have fallen by now...and died.

***

Ten days later, the prisoners reached San Fernando. Timoteo wondered if this was where the Japanese planned to kill them, out in the cane fields where the bodies could easily fertilize the ground like water buffalo dung.

The Pearl of Death

The boots that had once been a blessing were now a curse. His feet had swollen inside them and burned from pressure and infection. Every limping step sent sharp stabs of pain up his spine to the back of his skull. Death in the cane field would be a welcome relief.

But he wasn't that lucky. The prisoners were herded to a train station. A locomotive chugged up to a platform, black smoke belching from its stack. Three boxcars in tow radiated heat. Brakes squealed.

Timoteo swallowed dryly. *This can't be good.*

The Japanese forced them into the boxcars, perhaps a hundred men in a space meant for thirty. Shoulder-to-shoulder, chest-to-back, they were packed in so tight Timoteo could hardly breathe. Small cracks between the wallboards let in slivers of light and wisps of fresh air, but from where he stood in the center, the slight relief was a million miles away.

He didn't know how many hours he traveled with this ungodly human cargo thrashing and jerking about. Men fainted and died standing. Timoteo's feet burned, his legs ached, and his stomach lurched with dry heaves. In the press of bodies, his arms were pinned to his sides. Flies walked on his face, bit his skin. Shaking his head only made them more aggressive.

When the train stopped, the doors clattered open. Men who could move on their own got out. The dead slumped to the floor. Timoteo crawled over bodies and fell out the door to the ground, gasping. A sign above him read, Capas Station. He could have been in China for all he knew.

Is this where he would die?

"Choudai eu! Choudai eu!"

Timoteo struggled to his feet and limped into the line of Americans. Again they were ordered to march. The narrow dirt road lacked the bustle of traffic. It seemed to go on forever, the heat and dust. His head hurt and his vision blurred.

The pain in his feet became unbearable. He could hardly stand much less walk. He fell behind, walking on balls of fire, getting weaker by the second. His stomach cramped. He tried to pee in his pants but nothing came out. He had to keep moving.

Don't fall.

Sunlight dimmed. His skin felt chilled. Allah's hand was

touching his soul. The breath of God was wind in his face.

Wind?

He looked up to a sky full of dark clouds. A promise of rain. Allah, thank you, Allah.

Timoteo's feet gave out. He fell. His face hit the road so hard it jammed his teeth together.

No. Not now. Not after all I've been through.

Get up! Get up!

His body wouldn't respond.

Guards shouted, "Choudai eu! Choudai eu!"

They hovered over him like buzzards on a carcass.

"Choudai eu!"

If he didn't get up he was going to die. He'd never find Mamma. He'd never find the pearl.

He couldn't let that happen. *Get up!*

Gritting his teeth, he dragged his knees up under his chest, pushed his face off the dirt, and fell on his side. Flailing like a downed dog, he kicked and twisted trying to get upright. How pitiful he must've looked squirming in the dirt.

Get up!

"Choudai ue!" A guard whipped him with the stick.

The beating heightened his panic.

Allah, why do you punish me so?

A sense of acceptance washed over him. He was going to die. The Japanese had won.

"Mamma," he muttered. "I'm sorry."

But who would save her now? If he died... No one. He couldn't die. If he died, she'd die. He couldn't let that happen. He couldn't let the Japanese win.

Angry heat shot through his body. He forced himself off the ground, staggered about, shouting at the guards, "I'm not down, see? I'm not dead."

A guard smacked him with a stick. It didn't hurt. He staggered toward the line of Americans.

The sky cracked with thunder and released a torrent of rain.

Prisoners cheered.

Timoteo raised his face to the downpour, let the water wash over his face. Cleanse his soul. Make him whole again. Mouth agape, he lapped in the rain.

He had just been reborn.

Through the deluge he limped along, determination a flower blooming in his chest. He and the Americans slogged down the muddy road. Stacked coils of barbed wire loomed in the distance. A sign read: Welcome to Camp O'Donnell.

Below the block letters someone had scribbled: the E-L-L in hell.

Chapter Thirty-Nine

Camp O'Donnell, April, 1942:

The Japanese herded everyone together in the center of the prison compound. A relentless rain fell on the huddled men. Shivering, Timoteo sat in the mud and took stock of his new surroundings. Cones of lamppost light illuminated barbwire fences, long bamboo huts, and armed guards. The air smelled of wet earth and excrement. He prayed for a cup of rice, clean clothes, and a dry bed.

Timoteo had survived the march. Now all he had to do was wait out the war at Camp O'Donnell. Though his empty stomach hurt, the condition of his feet concerned him most. Severely swollen in his wet boots, he worried that his feet were so badly infected that they might have to be cut off.

"Major Ivy," someone called out in the dark. "It's corporal Danner, from the 515th. James Ivy. Do you hear me?"

No one answered.

"Lieutenant Olsen. It's Mecklevich. Are you here? Olsen! Answer me, damn it."

No one answered.

"Sergeant Lawrence Hardy..."

Roll call of the dead. Timoteo wondered what had happened to the sergeant. "Sergeant," he shouted. "It's Private Timoteo Matito."

No one answered.

"Thomas Breslin..."

Timoteo relieved himself in the mud.

"Private Gibbs..."

All night, the dreadful roll call went on. And on.

Come sunrise, Japanese guards forced the prisoners to their

feet. Dozens of men didn't rise. Well fed flies swarmed the still bodies. The sight had become so familiar to Timoteo, he'd become numb to the horror and felt only sorrow.

The men who rose were forced to stand in formation, American and Filipinos alike. Now Timoteo got his first glimpse of the resident prisoners gathering in the distance, skeletal men wearing rags. They emerged from the hut area, Filipinos on one side and Americans on the other, separated by a fence, which they clung to like caged monkeys.

A detail of Filipino prisoners appeared carrying poles and blankets. Wearing white masks over their noses and mouths, they followed a medic who inspected the bodies on the ground. The living were taken to a nearby building. Timoteo assumed it was the hospital and hoped he would go there too.

The dead men were laid on the blankets, the corners tied around the pole in a makeshift hammock. Two men hoisted the pole to their shoulders and carried it off. Timoteo noticed precision in their movements. And teamwork. This procedure wasn't new to them at Camp O'Donnell.

Grisly chore completed, the Japanese stalked through the formation separating Filipinos and Americans at bayonet point. This time Timoteo joined his countrymen. They were separated into squads and made to stand in the punishing sun. By now, Timoteo's clothes had dried, and his boots began to shrink around his swollen feet. Excruciating pain clawed up his legs, but he didn't dare complain.

An hour passed, then two. The sun blazed directly overhead by the time a Japanese officer addressed them from a shaded platform. Wearing a long coat with medals glistening from his chest, he looked overdressed for the heat.

"You are not prisoners of war," he shouted. "You are nothing. You will bow in the presence of a Japanese soldier. Every rank is your superior. Fail to show the proper respect..." He paused and drew his saber, and then slashed it through the air in front of him. "You will be properly punished."

Timoteo couldn't imagine bowing to these murderers.

"If you try to escape, you will be shot. But first you must dig your own grave. If you succeed in your escape, ten of your fellow prisoners will be shot. But first they must dig their own graves. The bounty on escaped prisoners is one hundred pounds of rice to any civilian who turns you in." He grinned wickedly. "Then you will dig your own grave, and then you will be shot."

Escape was out of the question. Timoteo wouldn't be responsible for the deaths of ten other men. Guilt would be the death of his soul. Besides, how far could he get on his bad feet?

"And you will not be going home soon. We are prepared to fight this war for a thousand years. You are dismissed."

A thousand years? Any hope of getting out of here alive gushed from his heart like water behind a burst dam.

Batting flies, he tried to see the good side. At least he would be fed, clothed, and doctored. Right now he would settle for a drink of water.

Guards herded the Americans off to a gate on their side of the compound, and then the Filipinos to their area. He didn't know where to go from there. Where he would sit? Where he would sleep?

A prisoner motioned him toward a group of bamboo huts. Remembering the man who'd saved him from the Japanese in Manila and hoping for the same miracle, he moved in the signaled direction, hobbling in pain but determined.

He joined a group of men gathered around a water barrel, each man taking his turn at the ladle. When Timoteo's turn came, he drank heartily but slowly, savoring the warm, stale water. He wished he could jump in the barrel and clean his body and his clothes.

A resident Filipino said, "There is rice for you once a day, around noon in the first hut." He pointed. "One cup. It is all."
Flies buzzed around his mouth. "How old are you?"

"Fifteen."

"You're just a kid. How did you get here?"

"I walked from Bataan."

"My God, boy, where are your parents?"

Timoteo hung his head. "The Japanese..." A tear threatened to give away his frailty. Steeling himself, "What does it matter now? My feet...I can hardly walk. I need a doctor."

The man looked down. "We'll have to get those boots off." He summoned two prisoners. "Get him to the infirmary."

One on each side, they lifted him off his feet, cradled his

legs, and schlepped him toward a long, narrow hut set off from the others. He imagined a Japanese doctor there with a huge saber and a gold-toothed grin, waiting to cut off Timoteo's feet.

Allah, please don't let them cripple me.

Inside the hut, sick men lay in woven palm bunks stacked four high along the walls. More floundered on the bamboo-slat floor in the aisle with barely enough room between them to step. He could hardly breathe the stifling air or stomach the stench of vomit and urine. If this was the hospital, he was going to die.

At the end of the hut, the men sat him in a rickety chair. Fighting panic, he scanned the room for a Japanese butcher, but there was only a Filipino prisoner—the medic he'd seen earlier, but no doctor.

The medic inspected Timoteo's boots, his skinned knees and the sores on his legs and arms. "This is not going to be easy." He pulled a knife, knelt on the floor, and started cutting the bootlaces.

One man gave Timoteo a stick. "Bite down on this, boy. It's going to hurt like hell."

The stick had been stripped of bark and bore many teeth impressions. He swallowed.

The medic finished removing the bootlaces.

"Where's the doctor?" Timoteo asked.

"You gonna use that stick or not?"

Shoving it between his teeth, he bit down hard. What else could he do? Be brave like the sergeant was brave.

The other man grabbed Timoteo's arms from behind.

Eyes squeezed shut and heart racing, he felt a tug and a twist on his right foot. Hot pain shot up his leg to the back of his eyeballs. He bit down hard on the stick. As the boot came off, a new stench ballooned in the air, the familiar stink of rotting flesh.

Allah, help me!

Everything went black.

Chapter Forty

Timoteo awoke on a bamboo mat lying on the floor with sick men coughing and hacking all round him. Stifling heat, belligerent flies, gorged mosquitoes, and the ever-present stink in the air told him he was still alive.

Dead men, that's what Timoteo thought they were, the prisoners of Camp O'Donnell. Some walking dead men, others not so lucky, like himself. He'd heard that this place was once a training base for the Philippine Army. Now, baking under a brutal sun, it was hell on earth.

"You're still with us." The medic knelt next to Timoteo.

"I'm thirsty."

"There's little water, one spigot on the American side. We gotta drink from a dirty stream that cuts through our section of camp. Someone will bring water soon."

"My feet are on fire."

"There's no medicine." The medic sighed. "At least you are spared from the burial details. Americans are dying at the rate of seventeen per day, but we Filipinos have it worse, two hundred fifty a day. Grave digging is a full time job at Camp O'Donnell."

Timoteo couldn't walk, much less work. Lying in the heat and stench, he looked at his feet. The medic had wrapped them in boiled cactus, which was supposed to relieve the swelling.

"Will I ever walk again?" Timoteo asked him.

"You need a real hospital."

A few weeks later, Timoteo came down with dysentery so bad all he could do was lay on the floor in his own excrement. But the chills worried him most, the uncontrollable shaking from the fever. He was constantly soaked in sweat.

All around him, dying men moaned. Some cried. There

were prayers to Allah and prayers to God, as both Muslim and Catholic Filipinos suffered together. Volunteers carried out skeletal bodies and brought in their sick replacements. With them came news of American battleships in the harbor and Red Cross convoys bringing food and medicine. Tomorrow everyone would be saved.

They just had to live through the night.

But with every new dawn, no relief came, only more misery and death. The rumors were as cruel as the fever and the chills and the horrible pain in Timoteo's guts. He kept falling in and out of consciousness.

Opening his eyes, he noticed he wasn't in the same hut he'd been in earlier. There were no bunks, the walls were made of palm leaves instead of wood slats, and there was no shortage of biting flies.

Glancing at the men lying around him on the floor, the pitiful condition the Japanese had brought upon the Filipinos stabbed his heart with spikes of anger.

"Where am I?"

"The Zero Ward," a voice said.

Timoteo didn't like the sound of that. "What is it?"

"It's where men come to die."

Timoteo shuddered, the fever shaking his bones. "I'm dying?"

"Yes."

Hot tears stung his eyes. "But I'm only fifteen."

"Sorry, son."

"I can't die. I have to find my mother."

"Drink some water." A man held a canteen to Timoteo's parched lips. Each swallow lit fires in his stomach. He vomited and soiled his pants. The voice was right. He was dying.

"Allah, help me."

His mind blinked on and off like a faulty light bulb in a cellar, briefly illuminating images from his past: his mother smiling, his brother laughing, his father limp and lifeless on the reef. Rolling waves towered over him and crashed down, sweeping him into the sea, the deep sea, deeper than any sea he'd ever swam. He was too little. He couldn't swim deep enough to save his father. A million gaping giant clams snapped at him, dared him to swim deeper.

Swim deeper. Save your father.

"I can't."

"You will stay in the boat." His father's voice...

"Dad."

"Meet the great American hero, Mister Cobb."

"Mamma, where are you?"

"With Wilbur Cobb, my son."

"Wilbur Cobb? You saved Pula. Save me now."

"I can't take your father's place."

"I hate you."

"The pearl...you were right about the pearl."

"No, Tito, no. You are too little to die."

"Mamma!"

The breaking surf roared.

"I'll be bigger someday."

Fever shook him to the bones. "I'm dying!"

It was the end of the world.

Spinning. Tumbling. Rolling.

Birds seesawed on the wind, in a pale blue sky, with puffs of white clouds. The pearl appeared in beams of sunlight, descended to the shore where Timoteo stood, his feet in the white Palawan sand, the surf lapping at his toes. Floating in front of him, the pearl opened its white oval eyelids, the eyes of Allah, his head wrapped in a turban, all shining pearly bright.

Sweat oozed from Timoteo's forehead.

The powerful, mystical pearl stared at him with steel gray eyes that didn't blink. *"I am lost,"* a deep voice said, reverberating in the sky like a brass gong. *"You are the chosen one."*

"It is the fever...I am dying."

"Return the pearl to the sea."

"How can I—"

"Return the pearl to the sea."

"The pearl," he muttered. "The sea, the sea!"

Chapter Forty-One

Timoteo came to on a canvas cot. His feet were covered with a white sheet. The whir of fans filled the air, and the sharp smell of alcohol burned his nostrils. Bright lights beamed down on him, reflecting off the white shorts he wore. He braved a peek under the sheet. Thick bandages were wrapped around his feet. For the first time in months, he felt no pain.

He was floating on clouds.

A white man gave him a shot in the arm. "For the fever," he said. "You gave us quite a scare, soldier, kept mumbling about a pearl and Allah...and the sea."

"I remember talking to the pearl."

"The fever plays cruel tricks on the mind." He set the needle on a tray beside him. "You've lost a lot of weight, but you're going to pull through."

"Allah saved me."

The doctor felt Timoteo's throat with two fingers. "Conditions were so bad here the Nips had to do something. Pressure from the Red Cross and the International community convinced them to establish a real hospital, not just another Zero Ward. They brought in food, supplies and equipment, POW doctors, and truckloads of medicine. We are already caring for 5,000 patients."

Five thousand? "That many are still alive?"

"The Americans have been moved to another camp, except for about two hundred fifty GIs. They were held back for burial detail, but thirty five thousand Filipinos are still here. Better fed, they've been busy. They burned and limed the trench latrines. Cut the tall grass where mosquitoes breed. Boiled and chlorinated the water. The death toll is down to a hundred a day."

That seemed a small victory. One death at Camp O'Donnell was too many. He looked at the doctor more closely. The tag on his white shirt read *Nelson M.D.* His sunken facial features, bony cheeks, and tired eyes bore witness to his membership in this death camp. Timoteo's stomach groaned.

"I'm hungry."

***

On August 16, 1942, Timoteo sat in a chair and struggled into a new pair of green shorts and a white t-shirt. He was so skinny he could overlap a thumb and forefinger around his thigh. Though he ate rice with fish and fruit two times a day, he was slow to gain weight. Stomach aches and loose bowels were a common ailment. But this morning presented him a new challenge.

Walking.

Dr. Nelson stretched thick socks over Timoteo's bandaged feet and gave him a pair of wooden crutches. "The infection is clearing up nicely, but the cartilage damage from beriberi is a problem."

"Beriberi?" Timoteo questioned.

"Lack of vitamin B from a diet of too much rice."

"Will I walk again?"

"With physical therapy, but don't expect to run in the Olympics."

Physical therapy meant pain, but pain was a small price to pay to walk instead of crawl.

Timoteo held his breath, and hand-over-hand, he climbed the crutches to pull himself out of his chair. The pressure on his feet caused more pain than he could bear. He sat back down.

"You can do better than that, son."

He gritted his teeth, stood again and shifted his weight from one foot to the other. The right foot was less painful.

Doctor Nelson stuck close to him, poised to catch him if he fell. "Take a step."

Light-headed, Timoteo didn't think he could continue standing much less walk anywhere. He couldn't move his ankles to set his feet flat underneath him. "I can't walk on my heels."

"Come on, now. Give it a try."

The fever's dream came back to him. *You are the chosen one.* Allah had given him a mission—to return the pearl to the sea.

"I can do this," he growled, and clumsy as a toddler's first steps, leaned on the crutches and slid his right foot forward. Pain bayoneted his legs. "The medication isn't working."

"We've reduced the dosage. Morphine is very addicting, and you need to be conscious to walk."

Right now he'd rather be unconscious. He took a couple wobbly steps. The doctor followed him as he turned and fought his way back to the chair. He couldn't sit down fast enough.

"Very good." Nelson smiled.

Panting, Timoteo grimaced. Hobbling wasn't the same as walking. "It hurts."

"Give it a month or three."

"That long?"

The medic entered wearing new boots. "Private Matito, the Japanese have pardoned another group of Filipino prisoners." He waved an official-looking paper. "You are one of them."

"He's in no condition to travel," Nelson said.

"Nips don't care. The sickest and most injured are being released first, a public service propaganda to prove to the world they are not barbarians but merciful occupiers. They just want to be rid of us."

"Well, son." Nelson tapped Timoteo's shoulder. "You're going home."

His bandaged feet throbbed under the increased thrum of his heartbeat. Where was home? The American apartment in Manila? Would Mamma be there? Or Palawan? Where would he live in the village? Would Bogtong or the Panglima take him in? Why would they? He didn't have a home...except the army. "I don't want to go," he told the medic.

"This paper will allow you safe passage—"

"To where...how? I cannot walk."

"Consider yourself lucky." The medic crossed his chest. "I'd crawl out of this hellhole if they'd let me." Then he addressed the doctor. "He must be in formation at 1600 hours...by the gate, or he will be shot."

A shudder wriggled up Timoteo's spine and coiled in his

stomach.

The medic left.

"Take the crutches," Nelson said. "This time I want you to stand and walk to the window."

The saliva in Timoteo's mouth turned to sand. The window was ten steps away. "I-I can't."

"Get on your feet, soldier. You have to walk or you will die."

Chapter Forty-Two

That afternoon, the medic and Doctor Nelson escorted Timoteo to the gate. He hobbled on crutches. Another two dozen prisoners gathered to be released. Some had missing legs and others had stubs for arms. A few wore bandages around their heads, and casts and slings. The Filipinos had taken a beating during the war and their imprisonment. Seeing them, he realized his handicap wasn't so bad. At least he hadn't lost his feet, but still, walking out of here with them would be no easy task.

"Good luck, Timoteo," Dr. Nelson said.

"Thanks for the crutches."

"Take care of those feet," the medic added.

"No matter how much it hurts, you must walk. If not, you'll be crippled for life."

"I'm grateful for knowing you and sad you must stay behind. I wish you were going home, too, sir."

"I'm needed here. Besides, this war won't last forever."

"The Japanese said they would fight a thousand years."

"General MacArthur is coming back." Dr. Nelson's tone sounded confident. "And when he does, the Nips will wish they'd never started this damn war." He moved to the other pardoned prisoners, shook hands, patted shoulders, said goodbye.

Timoteo hoped he'd live to see the day when the Philippines was a free country, but today he had bigger problems. "Where will I get medicine for my feet?"

The medic whispered in his ear. "Find the Filipino resistance. They will help you."

The barbwire gate creaked open.

"Where are they?"

"I don't know, but the guerrillas are blowing up Nip convoys, stealing their supplies, and sniping their patrols."

The thought of fighting the Japanese again appealed to Timoteo, but, "I have to find my mother."

"Good luck," the medic said.

As Timoteo struggled forward on the crutches, he felt Allah's hand on his shoulder. He followed the other freed men through the open gate. His heart strummed in joyous relief as the gate screeched closed behind him. It was seven miles to Capas Station. He had no money for a train, no money for food, no money to live. What would he do?

Farther down the road, the group of released prisoners thinned as the quicker men pressed ahead. Timoteo lagged behind. Each step was torture. His right foot carried his weight. His left foot dragged in the dirt. The crutches hurt his armpits.

Freedom tasted bittersweet. He looked back and could no longer see the barbwire enclosure. There were no guards watching him. He had survived. In a small way, he felt as though he had won the war.

Struggling another mile, he came upon a group of civilians along the roadside. "*Tuloy*," they said in Tagalog. "Please, come here. *Kumain ka na?* Have you eaten?"

"I'm not hungry." Timoteo was surprised they'd asked.

"Take some food anyway." An old woman gave him buffalo jerky and bread and a sugar cookie. "We wait here every day to help the pardoned prisoners from Camp O'Donnell."

Timoteo bit off a piece of jerky. It tasted salty and was boot-hard to chew.

A girl handed him water in a bamboo tube. "Come with us, we will hide you."

"I don't want to hide." He drank the water and returned the primitive canteen. "Do you know where I can find the guerrillas?"

They backed away shaking their heads, eyes turned down.

Touchy subject? Civilians probably protected guerrillas in the area. Questions, even from a fellow Filipino, would not be answered for fear he was a spy.

An old man asked, "Where is your family, soldier?"

He'd become numb to the story he'd told so many times.

"They're dead, except for my mother...I don't know."

"Come with us. We will keep you safe."

"I'm hoping to find my mother in Manila."

"It's dangerous," the man said. "We can't help you there."

"Do you have medicine for my feet...a doctor?"

"No. Very sorry."

"Then I'll go to Manila." He waved and moved on, chewing jerky, hoping he'd made the right decision to go it alone.

***

It was dark when he hobbled into Capas Station. A vacant platform lit by a single lamppost awaited him. He sat on a step and inspected the socks and bandages on his feet. Seven miles of dirt road had turned the socks to tatters, but the bandages looked intact. He felt thankful he'd made it this far.

Looking around, he saw the twinkle of lights from the village beyond the station. Wisps of wood smoke drifted across a nearby cane field. A dog barked.

Exhausted, he took the bread from his pocket, began eating it. He had nowhere to go for the night. Who would take him in? Patting the board planks of the platform, he figured he'd slept in worse places, finished the bread and curled up to sleep.

He was jolted awake by a bright light and the familiar sound of shouting Japanese. Still groggy, at first he thought he was at the camp then remembered he'd been released, looked up, confused. Several soldiers stood around him on the platform, their rifle barrels aimed down at him.

"*Choudai ue!*" one ordered.

In the blinding light, he couldn't see their faces but knew from their harsh tone that they meant for him to stand up or they would shoot him. The march out of Bataan had taught him that much. He held up his open hands. "I have papers," he shouted. "In my pocket."

"*Choudai ue!*"

"Don't shoot." He set his crutches upright to use them to help him stand.

A soldier kicked him in the ribs; a rifle butt hit him in the shoulder blade. Pain and terror grenaded through his body.

Rough hands grabbed him, dragged him up to stand on his bandaged feet. On wobbly legs, he hunched over, gasping. What had he done wrong? He was only sleeping. There were no signs posted: no sleeping.

The soldiers must've realized he couldn't run, because they turned their backs on him, gave each other congratulatory pats, and laughing, moved across the platform where they swiveled around and leveled their rifles on him. His heart seized.

A firing squad?

This couldn't be happening. Waving his hands, he shouted, "I am unarmed. Don't shoot."

The soldiers cocked their rifles.

Timoteo scrunched his eyes closed. *Allah, why are you letting them kill me?*

Gunshots rang out.

His knees buckled. He fell to the platform. Why were the soldiers shooting him? Was it because they'd found a weak and wounded boy sleeping on the platform? What had he done wrong? Now he wished he'd gone with the civilians he'd met on the roadside instead of heading for Manila on his own. His life was draining out of his body like water from a melon. At least he didn't suffer any pain.

The crack of rifle fire went on above him, the Japanese firing wildly, but he didn't feel bullets striking him. Why? He opened his eyes. A Japanese soldier was lying on the platform, his wide eyes staring right at him. Blood leaked across the floorboards. Another shot, another soldier toppled. Two other soldiers were kneeling, firing into the trees. The station had become a war zone, and he was trapped in the crossfire.

Timoteo crabbed to the platform's edge and dropped three feet to the ground. He landed on a Japanese soldier with a bullet hole in his forehead.

Fright sucked the air from his lungs. He pushed himself off the dead Jap, rolled over, and crawled into the weeds, hoping to hide.

The gunfire stopped. Running footfalls approached the platform. Head down, he hugged the dirt like he was in a Bataan foxhole.

A flashlight beam found him.

The Pearl of Death

"I have papers," he shouted to whoever stood over him.

"He's Filipino," the voice said.

"My name is Timoteo. I've been shot."

"Timoteo Matito?" the voice asked.

He swallowed hard. "How did you know?" Looking up, he saw dusty combat boots, the top of dirty white socks, knobby knees, dark shorts and a black shirt. Shadow hid the man's face, but he wore a hat adorned with eagles and stars.

The sergeant.

"Where you been, boy?"

"I was a prisoner." He sat up, and hands shaking, searched his shirt for bullet holes, found nothing. *Allah, thank you, most merciful one.*

The sergeant helped him up. "Where are you shot?"

"I thought I was."

"What's wrong with your feet?"

Timoteo wanted to throw his arms around the sergeant and cry like a child.

Filipinos dressed in civilian clothes jumped up to the platform, stabbed Japanese, took their weapons, and searched their pockets. They were brutal and quick, like a band of thieves...or a band of guerrillas. "You are the resistance?"

"Get this man on a stretcher," the sergeant ordered. "We gotta move out before more of them damn Nips show up."

Terry Wright

Chapter Forty-Three

The Resistance

Throughout history, the Filipinos had to fight for their land, first against the Spanish, when in 1521, Magellan claimed the islands for Spain, which got him killed by Lapu-Lapu warriors. The Spanish retaliated. Three hundred fifty years of occupation and oppression followed, a time marred by countless rebel uprisings and bitter defeats.

In 1896, the Philippine Revolution began. One by one, the Filipinos succeeded in retaking from Spain all the island territories except Luzon. It wasn't until 1898, when America declared war against Spain, that the US Navy defeated the Spanish armada in Manila Bay, freeing the country from Spanish rule. But instead of gaining their independence, the Filipinos were occupied again, this time by the United States, which resulted in the Philippine-American War and another ten years of bloodshed.

Then came hope. In 1934, the Tydings-McDuffie Act promised Philippine independence by 1946, a dream of freedom that now seemed unlikely to materialize as Japan took brutal control of the islands.

As it was back in 1521 against Magellan, the Filipinos banded together to fight the invaders. Timoteo Matito found himself in the middle of this guerrilla war, being carried on a canvas stretcher through the jungle. Palms and sharp branches raked his skin. He could barely see the men carrying his stretcher, just gloomy silhouettes, but he could hear them panting and groaning. The ride was so jerky it hurt his ribs where the Japanese soldier had kicked him. He moaned, wishing the guerillas would stop for a rest.

"Hang in there, soldier," a man bearing the stretcher huffed between breaths. "We will be there soon."

"Thanks for saving my life. I was lucky you came along when you did."

"We were there...to blow the tracks...at Capas Station." He wheezed. "We are lucky you were there...or we woulda got caught for sure...by that Nip patrol."

"I helped you?"

"Saved our hides...you did...made them Nips easy targets. They was watchin' you...didn't see us sneakin' up."

As the column of men proceeded through the jungle, Timoteo felt proud that he was able to help the resistance, though unintentionally, but he wondered how he could help them in combat—considering his damaged feet and ill health. He didn't weigh more than a twig, bone-skinny, and joints so inflamed he could hardly sleep. He needed rest. And in order to regain his strength, he feared he'd have to eat more than his share of food—if the resistance had any to spare. He thought to ask the man carrying the stretcher but decided to keep quiet. He didn't want to be a pest.

They came to a nepa hut set on stilts. The air smelled of wood smoke and rotting vegetation. As the men climbed rickety steps, the stretcher tilted at a precarious angle, but Timoteo held on. Inside, bamboo floor slats creaked.

The sergeant was already there, barely visible in the dim, candlelit room. "Set him down on the floor here, boys."

"What are we going to do with him, sir?" asked one of the fighters gathered around the stretcher. "He's pretty bad off."

"I know."

"He'll slow us down."

"He saved my life on Bataan," the sergeant said. "Take first watch and let me worry about the kid."

"Yes, sir."

"I'm not a kid," Timoteo told the sergeant. "I'm a man, a soldier."

"You're a wounded soldier now, out of the war."

"But I want to fight the Japanese."

"He's got the spirit," someone said.

"That and ten pesos won't get him a cup of coffee in

Tokyo." The sergeant struck a match, bright as a flare in the dimly lit room, and set it to a cigar. "Tell the radioman to contact HQ." He blew smoke. "We have a soldier for evacuation."

Wincing in pain, Timoteo hugged his injured side. "I don't want to be evacuated. I'm going to Manila to look for my mother."

"Listen to me." The sergeant kneeled next to the stretcher. Candlelight flickered in his dark eyes. "You are crippled...an easy mark for the Nips. Look what happened tonight. Take my advice. Get out of here, get better, and then you can come back and fight."

"I can join up with you?"

"How can I promise you that? We will get you to Australia where General MacArthur is preparing forces to retake the Philippines. Maybe you can come back with him."

"With the American general?" Timoteo felt awestruck.

"But first those feet must heal."

Of course, but still... "What about my mother?"

"She is on her own, son."

"I need to find her."

"The Nips have her...look...I don't want you to lose all hope, but you must face the fact that she is probably dead."

"Don't say that." Timoteo's heart would cry if it had tears. "You don't know—"

"She may not even be on the islands. The Nips take our women to their front lines. She could be in China, Manchuria, Okinawa, or even back in Japan, for all you know, working as a slave for the emperor in his factories or brothels."

Timoteo didn't want to hear it and covered his ears.

"Listen kid, we all have sacrificed much and lost loved ones in this war, but if you are to survive, you must realize the war is bigger than you, me, or our families. We must do things against our will. We must accept things we don't want to accept. There is no way to find your mother, no way to rescue her, so don't get yourself killed for nothing. Go to Australia, get better, come back and kill more of the bastards who took her from you."

Timoteo wanted to scream, to shut out the words, but he knew the sergeant was right. It was the only way. He took his hands off his ears. "How will I get to Australia?"

"We will put you on an American hospital ship."

"You can do that?"

"The Americans and us Filipinos are in this fight together, like the fingers of a fist. We have the same military benefits as the GIs. You have a right to be on that hospital ship. It's a law in the United States."

"I want to go there someday." *I could find Wilbur Cobb and the pearl.*

"Thousands of Filipinos go every year, to live and work and learn in their colleges. They have the best veterans' hospitals for all soldiers. I will vouch for your combat on Bataan."

"And I have this paper from Camp O'Donnell." Timoteo pointed to his pocket. "They gave it to me."

"See, you are all set." The sergeant patted Timoteo's shoulder. "Tomorrow we will take you to the ship."

***

Seven days later, in the dead of night with a bright moon overhead, Timoteo and his small band of guerrillas reached Iba, a seaside village at the foot of the Zambales Mountains. It had been a dangerous journey of dodging Japanese patrols, but he had reached the place of his debarkation from the Philippines.

They joined another band of resistance fighters who had two wounded men with them. One had a cast on his arm, the other a bandaged knee and hand. A staging area was set up in a palm grove high on the beach about fifty meters from the breaking surf. The air smelled of rotting seaweed.

"We are in radio contact with the ship," one fighter reported to the sergeant. "It is holding position a mile offshore."

Timoteo looked out to the calm sea and saw silvery waves rolling in to shore. He expected to see the silhouette of a ship against the bright, moon-bathed water, but he saw nothing. And even if a ship was out there, how were they going to get aboard? Swim?

A fighter offered him a rice cake and cup of coconut milk. While he ate, another man wrapped his bandaged feet in palm leaves. "To keep them dry," he said.

Now Timoteo was sure he'd have to swim. The radio operator, who knelt in the sand next to him, cranked a wheel on a black box and tapped on a lever. Another man held an antenna up in the air.

"What are you doing?" Timoteo asked the radioman.

"Sending a secret code."

The rhythmic tapping enthralled Timoteo. He wondered how it could mean anything. "Can I learn to do that?"

"Sure, kid." The radioman listened to a device he had cupped over an ear, and then he said, "They are ready. Move out."

The sergeant gave the signal. Two fighters appeared at a full run carrying a black raft toward the water. The stretcher rose, and Timoteo hung on tightly as his bearers lugged him across the sand, following the raft. The man with the broken arm ran alongside him. The other wounded fighter followed behind, carried by two fellow soldiers. Taking up the rear, armed men shuffled backwards, guns pointed at the trees, covering the group as they made it to the shore. Tangles of black seaweed looked like beached monsters in the moonlight.

As the raft bobbed on the surf, Timoteo dropped from the stretcher to the center plank seat. He smelled the sharp odor of rubber and felt the cool spray of seawater on his skin.

It reminded him of home.

Oars teetered from pivots on each side of him. As the two wounded men got onboard, he realized the importance of his place in the raft. He was the only man with two good arms, skinny as they were. He would be the one rowing, a job for which he felt ill suited. Looking out to sea again, he only saw moonlight glinting off ripples on the surface—but no ship.

"I don't know where to go," he said as the guerrillas shoved them off.

"Keep the moon at your back and row," the sergeant said. "The ship will find you. Goodbye, Timoteo."

He grabbed the handles, dipped the oars into churning water, and drew back, his heart pounding as he remembered the pearlers on Palawan, how they had worked the oars in unison. The raft should have been much simpler than a pearling skiff, but his inexperience quickly got him in trouble. Rising with an incoming wave, the raft turned sideways and shot back toward shore. The men with him screamed.

"Quiet," Timoteo said, fighting the oars to straighten the raft before it capsized. "You want a Japanese patrol to hear you?" The guerrillas on shore had disappeared into the palm grove.

Timoteo was on his own.

Right oar, he thought and pulled. Left oar. Both oars. More left—more right. He braced his feet under the plank seat in front of him, arched his back, and with all his strength, he got the raft headed out to sea.

Stroke.

The pressure on his feet sent stinging pain up his legs, but he had to keep rowing. Over his shoulder, he still didn't see a ship.

Stroke.

How long would he have to row? It was hard work. He hadn't gone far from the beach, glowing white in the moonlight, but already his feeble body felt as if he'd rowed for miles.

Stroke.

The sonic crack of a bullet zinged overhead.

Muzzle flashes lit up along the beach.

"Nips," the wounded man in front of Timoteo shouted.

The man behind him dropped to the bottom of the raft. "They can see us! The moon is too bright."

The bang of rifle fire reached the raft.

Hot adrenaline spilled into Timoteo's bloodstream. The raft was an easy target. As he shoved the oars in the water with panicked strokes, the wounded man sitting in front rose to his knees, putting his body between the gunfire and the rower.

"Sit down," Timoteo cried out, rowing frantically. "What are you doing?"

"You must not be shot or we won't make it to the ship."

"What ship? There is no ship."

"There will be—"

A splatter of blood hit Timoteo in the face.

The wounded man screamed. A bullet had ripped through his arm, but in spite of that, he remained on his knees, a human shield. "Keep rowing."

With a rapid slapping sound, bullets drilled the water around the raft.

Timoteo's body went into a state of controlled rage, a fury that fueled his skinny arms to perform feats of strength and endurance that defied reason.

The oars hit the smooth water hard. The raft glided seaward on a straight course.

He developed a rhythm and control over the oars that would have matched the pearlers of Palawan. There was no time to understand it now, how his father had passed on to him certain instincts about the sea, the ability to row like the ability to swim. Rowing now seemed natural, and in this state of panic, he only had to know that he could do it.

Two wounded men in the raft were counting on him to row to the ship, the ship that didn't exist. And Allah too was counting on him—or empowering him, he wasn't sure which, but under this barrage of gunfire, he doubted that it mattered.

With a dull whap, a bullet penetrated the raft hull. Air screamed from the wound.

"We're going to sink," the man behind him cried out.

"Allah, help us," Timoteo prayed.

"Don't worry," the kneeling man in front said through clenched teeth. "The raft has many air chambers. Keep rowing."

From the beach, the sound of gunfire escalated into a furious battle. At the same time, the rain of bullets ended.

"What's happening?" Timoteo asked the brave fighter shielding him.

"The guerrillas have attacked the Jap patrol."

Within seconds, the firing stopped.

"We made it."

"But where is the hospital ship?"

Suddenly the sea rose up beside the small raft, and a roll of water sent it sliding sideways. Timoteo's lungs seized as a black hulk broke the surface. A scream lodged in his throat. At first he thought a whale was attacking them, but the size of the monster was beyond anything he'd ever imagined. Streams of water poured from its gills. A pointed head lunged upward, and as he turned to see the length of the beast, he saw a fat towering fin with spines that pierced the moonlit sky.

His heart beat like a brass gong. "Allah, save us!" He tried to wrench an oar free of its pivot to use it as a weapon, as meager as it was, but when the beast's head bobbed down, he saw no eyes, no mouth, and no teeth to devour him. He'd seen pictures of this thing before and suddenly felt foolish.

"The ship," the wounded man in front shouted. "It's a submarine."

Timoteo couldn't breathe. He felt redeemed.

Sailors' silhouettes appeared on top of the ship. Some ran to man big guns on the deck. One threw down a line. The wounded fighter behind Timoteo caught it, and they were quickly dragged aboard, raft and all.

"Get these men inside," a sailor said.

Timoteo stood on his palm-wrapped feet, and ignoring the pain, he stepped out of the raft and onto the pitching submarine. Sailors deflated the damaged raft. A replacement was brought out on deck. Men loaded boxes into the new raft, supplies for the resistance, Timoteo assumed, and two Filipinos wearing black clothes shoved it into the water. They saluted the sailors before they started rowing toward the beach.

Limping across the wet deck, he was led to an open hatch where an escort helped him down a metal ladder and into the submarine. Fear was like a sand crab clawing up his spine as he clumsily negotiated a labyrinth of narrow passageways lined with pipes. He passed walls of meters and dials and ducked through thick doorways that led to more pipe-lined chambers. The air smelled of diesel fumes and dirty socks. Everything was bathed in a crimson glow.

"Are we going under water?" he asked the sailor escorting him. "Is there enough air?"

The sailor chuckled. "Tomorrow you'll be on a hospital ship to Australia. Until then, you'll bunk with the torpedoes."

Chapter Forty-Four

General Douglas MacArthur

Late November sunshine drenched the hospital grounds in Brisbane, Australia. It seemed as though the sun had followed Timoteo across the equator. Wearing blue shorts, a white t-shirt, and shoes with high tops and special arches, he walked the tree-shaded garden with only the aid of a cane. He'd learned to tolerate the pain in his feet. Weighing a hundred twenty pounds now, his strength had returned, thanks to the abundance of food and physical therapy. He was ready to go back to the Philippines and fight the Japanese.

But the doctors wouldn't release him. "Corporal Matito," they would tell him. "Your feet will never be like they were before the death march. You're no longer fit for combat."

"I'll do anything," he'd begged them. "Cook and clean, drive a truck with supplies—"

"No." They always said no. So what if he couldn't run the hundred yard dash or carry forty pounds of gear? There were other jobs he could do for the army, but they wouldn't listen.

So he walked the garden path every morning and afternoon, wondering what ever happened to Wilbur Cobb and his pearl of death. Timoteo figured he'd never get to America to look for them. The world was big and he was just a sixteen-year-old Filipino boy.

There was little to do around the hospital but read. Math. Geography. History. The nurses brought him books on radios and Morse code. He quickly became the hospital's resident expert.

"Corporal Matito," a gruff voice said from behind him.

He turned. An American officer was approaching, a big

intimidating man with broad shoulders and colorful bar metals on his chest. Silver eagles glistened from his shirt collars and his cap. "Yes, sir?"

"They told me I'd find you out here. Beautiful day, don't you think?"

"It's very hot, sir."

"May I have a word with you?"

A shudder vibrated through Timoteo's limbs. Why did an American officer of such high rank want to talk to him?

"I'm Colonel Wallace from the 1st Reconnaissance Battalion. Shall we sit in the shade?" He offered a handshake. "They tell me you're itching to get back into the action."

"It's my feet, sir."

"I know all about your feet, boy." He indicated a bench under a tree. "Have a seat in the shade. We'll talk."

"Yes, sir." Timoteo sat, propped the cane between his knees, and inhaled the sweet scent of blossoms and an undertone of sharp aftershave wafting from the colonel.

Sitting next to him on the bench, the colonel removed his cap and dabbed sweat from his forehead with a handkerchief. "I hear you're pretty good with radios."

Timoteo felt small in the colonel's presence. "I met a guerrilla fighter who had one. Since then, I learned about them...how to fix them... and read Morse code."

The colonel withdrew a pack of cigarettes from his pocket, tapped one out for himself and offered the pack to Timoteo. "Smoke?"

"Sure." He'd never held a pack of cigarettes before, much less smoked one. The pack showed a picture of General MacArthur smoking a cob pipe. *"I shall return."* There was a small map of the Philippines, too, and a camel. Timoteo wished the general hadn't abandoned the islands. He let the Japanese take over Manila. They killed Tito and kidnapped Mamma. The Americans failed to protect the city, as Wilbur Cobb had said they would.

Imitating the colonel, Timoteo tapped out a cigarette and held it between two fingers. Feeling as if he'd suddenly grown up, he returned the pack to the colonel. "Thanks."

"So you're interested in helping the guerrillas?" The

colonel struck a match, cupped it in his hands and offered it to Timoteo.

He'd seen other soldiers put a cigarette to the flame and suck in some air. When he did, smoke shot up his nose, and he broke into uncontrollable coughing.

"Are you all right?" Colonel Wallace patted Timoteo's back.

Regaining his composure, Timoteo held the cigarette as before, between two fingers, and forced himself to be tough. He was a man now. "Yes...yes...I'm okay...just caught me off guard is all."

"Fine." Colonel Wallace drew in air through the cigarette and blew out a cloud of smoke. "I saw your sergeant's letter of recommendation. He says you speak English, Spanish, and Tagalog. Is that true?"

"Si." Timoteo played with the cigarette, fearful to actually smoke it.

Just as the colonel was about to reply, a nurse and a bandaged patient ambled up the path. Timoteo noticed how the colonel remained silent until they'd walked by. Then he whispered, "We have a job for you."

"In the army?"

"General MacArthur was wondering if you'd be interested in working for him."

Trying to remain calm, Timoteo puffed weakly on the cigarette while he wrestled with Colonel Wallace's words. *MacArthur—was wondering—if Timoteo would be interested—in working for him?* The man who abandoned Manila and got Tito killed, and maybe Mamma killed? Timoteo gave the colonel a harsh glare. "Why should I work for the man who ran from the Japanese?"

"The job involves using a radio. A new kind of top secret radio."

A real job? With a new radio? For General MacArthur? "I don't know."

"He would be very grateful," the Colonel added.

"The General left us to die in Manila." Timoteo dropped the cigarette and crushed it out with his shoe.

"He didn't have enough men. He didn't have enough guns.

He had to leave to get better equipped to fight the Japanese. And he's going back to the Philippines. Question is, boy, do you want to be a part of his historic return and victory?"

Timoteo blinked. Maybe working for the General was the only way Timoteo would ever get the chance to kill more Nips. He threw his shoulders back. "When do I start?"

***

Two days later, a black Cadillac arrived at the hospital. The license plate read *USA-1*, and there was a sign with four stars across the radiator grill. Timoteo leaned on his cane at the curb and watched the car glide to a stop in front of him. The duffle bag at his heels held everything he owned. The army had given him a new uniform, long pants and a stiff-collared shirt, green with short sleeves. New socks. New boots. New underwear. He had no idea where he was going, but it had to be better than hanging around this hospital.

A rear car door opened, and Colonel Wallace stepped out. "Got everything you need?"

Timoteo swallowed, picked up his duffle bag. "I'm ready."

The driver took the bag to the trunk. Colonel Wallace invited Timoteo into the car. The seats were soft as a cloud, and he detected the distinct aroma of pipe tobacco. He'd never seen a car like this, much less ridden in one. Setting the cane aside, "Where are we going?" he asked the colonel.

"Headquarters." That was all he said during the twenty-minute ride in cool comfort.

The car stopped in front of a tall building, granite gray with high arched windows.

"This is where the general lives?" Timoteo asked, getting out of the car and back into the heat.

"It's where he works." The Colonel ushered him inside. The conditioned air felt cool on his skin. Footsteps echoed through a labyrinth of hallways until they came to an elevator. "Third floor," Colonel Wallace said to a uniformed man who stood inside.

"Yes, sir."

The ride up was quick and smooth. The door slid open. Timoteo followed the Colonel out and down the hall. Another uniformed officer fell into formation beside the Colonel.

"That him?" He tipped his head to Timoteo.

"Yes."

"God help us."

"What's wrong with him?"

"He's too tall," the man said. "He'll stick out like a potato in an apple barrel.

"Just tell the general we're here."

"Yes, sir." The man rushed ahead, ducked through an open door, and reappeared by the time Timoteo and the Colonel arrived. "He'll see you right away."

They walked through a foyer to an adjoining doorway. The Colonel rapped twice on the doorframe.

"Come in," a bass voice said.

Timoteo followed the Colonel into the general's office. It wasn't anything like he'd imagined, no rich tapestries, just bare walls in need of paint, a wood floor, and narrow windows that illuminated the room. Two cushy chairs with a small table between them faced a modest desk, glass top and a holder with two black pens. Behind the desk sat the man Timoteo had seen on the cigarette pack, same long face with drooping jowls, high forehead, and eyes hidden behind dark glasses. Clenching an unlit cob pipe between his teeth, he stood and returned the Colonel's salute.

"Timoteo Matito, sir," Colonel Wallace said.

The General looked Timoteo up and down. "This is the boy you wanted me to see?"

"Yes, sir."

Timoteo tried standing at attention like a real soldier but with a cane, he felt awkward. His feet hurt. He saluted the General.

"Relax, boy," MacArthur said. "How old are you?"

"Sixteen."

"Please, gentlemen, be seated."

Timoteo sat in the cushy chair on the left, glad to be off his feet and astounded at being called a gentleman. The colonel sat to his right.

Setting down the pipe, MacArthur moved to the front of his desk, leaned against it, legs crossed, his attention firmly rooted on Timoteo. "I've been told you're a radio man."

"I can fix them...and I know Morse code."

"Good. And I hear you want to work with the resistance."

"The guerrillas...yes."

"And you want to fight the Japanese."

"Yes, but my feet..."

"For your country?"

"Of course. Yes. And yours, sir."

MacArthur nodded. "We have an isolated facility we call Camp X, a secret place where you can get more radio training. Are you willing to go?"

A real radio school. "Yes. Then what will I do?"

"You will go to the Philippines to tell me what you see. Tell me what the Japanese are doing. Tell me how many soldiers are there. Tell me how much food they have, how many guns."

Timoteo's throat felt like sand. "Me, sir? A spy?"

"I cannot win a war for you if I don't know the enemy's strength. You will go in ahead of the 1st Reconnaissance Battalion so they will know what to expect when they arrive. They won't be ready until October, but I need that information now. You'll set up a lookout post and radio to me the planes you count and the ships in the harbor. The guerrillas will help you, and you will help America drive the Japanese from your islands."

Awestruck, Timoteo thought how proud the sergeant would be. It was an important job, a job that must be done right. But his feet... "Sir, what about my feet? I have trouble walking."

"The enemy will never suspect you are a spy." MacArthur jammed his hands in his pockets. "Don't get me wrong. We realize the danger you'll be in." He paused and glanced at the Colonel who nodded. "That if you're caught, you'll be tortured and killed. Do you understand this?"

He understood very well. The Japanese had already tried to kill him countless times: on Bataan, during the death march, in Camp O'Donnell, and at Capas station. What would be the difference? He got out of the chair and stood before the general, shoulders thrust back, proud as any American soldier ever felt. "I am ready."

Smiling, MacArthur shook Timoteo's hand. "Then you are

the boy for me," he said. "When you get back to Manila, a medal will be waiting for you."

"A medal?" Timoteo huffed. "What good is a medal? I'd rather you help me find my mother. You can keep your medal."

The General glanced at the Colonel and shrugged.

"The Japanese took her, sir."

"Oh." His face turned glum but then he smiled. "Well, then. I'll see what I can do."

"And we want to go to America, on a ship or a plane. I don't care."

The General twitched his eyebrows. "I'll see what I can do about that as well. My country thanks you, boy."

Timoteo felt hope grow in his heart. He now saw the real possibility of finding his mother and going to America to find Wilbur Cobb and the pearl.

All he had to do was survive spying on the Japanese.

The Pearl of Death

Chapter Forty-Five

Manila, March 10, 1945

Just after daybreak, the C-60 Loadstar approached Manila Airport. Wilbur looked out the window. Everywhere below, the city lay in ruins: black and crumbled buildings, skeletal trees, and roads choked with debris. Paradise had been destroyed.

In order to expel the Japanese and retake the Philippines, General MacArthur had bombed the city to rubble, the very thing he'd hoped to prevent when he had declared Manila an *open city* back in 1942. Wilbur's heart hurt at the sight of the destruction below. How many Filipinos had been killed? He hoped Liawayway and her sons weren't among the dead.

The plane touched down on a rough patch of runway that jolted the passengers, mostly Benguet Consolidated Mining personnel. He was part of an advance contingency sent in to survey the damage to company assets and jump start operations. But mining gold and ore was the last thing on Wilbur's mind. After four and a half years, he'd finally returned to the Philippines to find his family.

The plane taxied to the bomb-damaged terminal. He deplaned and inhaled the Pacific breeze, which carried the scent of stale smoke. While workers pulled luggage from the plane, he walked in circles, and looking up at the gray sky, he thanked God that he'd made it back. "I'll find her," he whispered.

The blast of a horn made him turn around. Throwing dust and scattering birds, a jeep approached at high speed, engine roaring and tires crunching dirt. The commotion caused everyone to stop working and watch. As the jeep neared, Wilbur could see the driver, a Filipino wearing a straw hat and white shirt. He looked old and thin, but not totally unrecognizable. What the hell was Bogtong doing here? Wilbur's heartbeat jumped. Perhaps he had news of Liawayway.

"It's all right," he told the alerted men. "I know him from Palawan."

They went back to work carting luggage to a bus.

"Mister Cobb," Bogtong called out as the jeep ground to a stop. "On the radio news, I heard your company was returning and hoped you would be with them."

Wilbur's heart warmed to a familiar face. Accepting an exuberant handshake, "I'm glad to see you, doc. Where is Liawayway?"

"I am trying to find her, but I have no luck."

A worker brought Wilbur's bag and set it at his feet.

"She has to be here somewhere."

"Don't get up your hopes, Mister Cobb."

His hopes were already up. If he didn't find her, he swore he'd crawl into a bottle of scotch and never come out. He hadn't taken a drink since he awoke on that ship to LA. He'd stayed sober, hoping to get passage across the Pacific. But every attempt failed. The company had claimed it was too dangerous. Ships were being sunk, and even the China Clipper had been shot down. Letters to Congress and the Navy went unanswered. Futility turned to despair, but still he resisted scotch's healing embrace.

Wilbur tossed his bag on the back seat. "Move over. I'm driving." He climbed in behind the wheel.

Bogtong settled into the passenger seat. "Where are we going?"

"Benguet's employee quarters. It's the last place I saw her." Wilbur shoved the shifter into gear and tore off across the tarmac. "Where have *you* looked?"

"The Red Cross has no record of her," Bogtong said, hanging on to the windshield with one hand and pressing down the straw hat on his head with the other. "And the hospitals...most are destroyed, the records lost. During the war, the Japanese made me work at University Hospital here in Manila. I know she wasn't there, but I cannot say for sure she wasn't a patient or a casualty at another hospital."

"There must be records somewhere."

"I have looked, found nothing of her or the boys."

"What about the village on Boligay Creek? Did you look there? Maybe she went home."

"There is no village. Burned by the Japanese."

He remembered the Panglima and his son Pula, all those natives, the women and children. "What happened to the Dyaks?"

"Missing. In the jungle. In the ground. Who knows?"

"Somebody has to know."

"Listen to me, Wilbur Cobb. We suffered through hell because of this war. Hundreds of thousands of us Filipinos are dead and missing. Too many to count. Too many to know. It is best we accept our losses and go on with our lives. Rebuild our country. Don't look behind us. We must look forward. This advice may be good advice for you, as well."

Wilbur gritted his teeth and fought back tears. He would not accept losing his family. He would not give up the search as long as the iron fist of hope gripped his heart.

He floored the accelerator. The jeep sped away from the airport and down the main road. Rubble had been cleared recently, the pavement scarred by bulldozer tracks and blade scrapes. Remains of buildings and wrecked vehicles lay in jagged berms along each side of the roadway. Power lines dangled from canted poles.

Filipinos with vacant eyes probed the rubble, looking for anything of value. The once proud people had been reduced to scavengers. *The damn Japs!*

Ahead, MPs directed traffic around a work zone where sweaty, shirtless men labored in the tropical heat, working shovels and picks and wheelbarrows and buckets.

The farther he drove, the more disoriented he became. He remembered the route from the apartments to the airport. He'd traveled it many times, but now the cityscape had changed. Landmarks were unrecognizable. He turned at a corner where the bank used to stand, but the road became a dead end.

He slammed on the brakes, stopped, and scanned the destruction. Where there once was a park, there now was a collapsed building. "This doesn't look right. I made a wrong

Terry Wright

turn."

"You know what I would like?" Bogtong asked, calm as
the breeze.

"What?"

"A Coke," he said. "There has been no Coke since the
war."

Wilbur looked at him, a small man under the straw hat. His
request was simple. A Coke. That would make him happy.
"Don't worry, doctor. Before you know it, Coke and every other
American product will return to the Philippines."

"Maybe. But the mining companies and timber cutters will
be back too. It will be the same old thing, take, take, take from
our islands."

"By this time next year the Philippines will be an
independent country. Then you'll share in the prosperity."

"More promises."

Wilbur patted Bogtong's boney knee. "The Japanese are
gone. Anything is possible. Have faith, my friend." He tromped
on the throttle. Engine roaring, the jeep spun around and sped
back to the main street.

An MP directing traffic stopped them at the intersection.

Wilbur leaned out the doorway. "Hey, Sarge. I'm looking
for Benguet's employee apartment building. I thought it was
around here somewhere."

"There's not much left of this area," the MP said. "It'll be
weeks before we get the streets open."

"Can you tell me where the bank was?"

"Manila Western?"

"Yes."

"Two blocks down."

"Thanks." Wilbur heard the MP shout, "good luck," as the
jeep sped off. "The bank wasn't far from the apartment
building... Look, right there."

A brick and mortar building stood gutted, its fire-blackened
innards clearly visible through a blast-damaged outer wall. The
toppled sign was hardly readable: *anila Weste.*

Wilbur turned on the side street, saw trees that lined the
way stripped of their branches from intense American bombing.
He drove two blocks before downed power lines blocked the

way. "We walk from here." Shutting off the engine, he noticed a crowd gather. He feared for Bogtong's jeep. It might be stolen or stripped in the few minutes they'd be gone. "On second thought, you stay here."

"Bring Liawayway and the boys back with you, Wilbur."

Charged with that encouragement, Wilbur set out across the ruins, careful to stay clear of the power lines. He imagined Liawayway waving to him from the front door as he approached the apartment building. *She's smiling. Timoteo and Tito are jumping up and down, squealing with joy. She's running to him. He's running to her.* His heart raced. His feet moved faster.

As he rushed along the debris-strewn street, the images faded. He felt a thousand eyes staring at him from the black windows of wrecked buildings: forlorn eyes, defeated eyes, hungry eyes. No one was smiling. No one was jumping with joy around here.

With every block that he passed, the conditions worsened. Everywhere he looked, he saw the true horrors of war. Bloated bodies lay scattered about. Some floated in gutters. Some were covered with palm leaves and rags. The farther he walked, the thicker the stench and the flies became. He felt as if he were walking through the valley of the shadow of death. But he did fear the evil, and God did not comfort him.

He steeled himself and kept moving forward. Get Liawayway and the boys and then get the hell out of here as fast as possible.

But when the bombed-out remains of the apartment building came into view, his throat closed up. He couldn't breathe. His heart pounded. The twelve-story building had been reduced to a pile of debris. Tunnel vision set in. He staggered, imagined the walls crashing down on Liawayway and her boys. A horrible sense of loss swept over him. They were gone.

Turning away from the ruins, he started back toward the place where Bogtong waited with the jeep. Each step was torture as he remembered Liawayway's smile and the boys' laughter. Wilbur wanted to fall to his knees and howl in despair, but his feet kept moving him forward, faster until he was at a full run, scrambling over rubble and jumping fallen trees, his eyes blurring with tears. He couldn't move fast enough. He should've never left them. It was his fault.

Stupid! Stupid! Stupid!

He tripped on loose bricks, fell to his hands and knees, but kept pumping his legs and clawing his way over a fallen wall. His fingers bled, but he didn't care. All he could think of was getting away—making it to the jeep—all the while crying out, "I'm sorry. I'm sorry."

The Pearl of Death

Chapter Forty-Six

Independence Day, July 4, 1946, Manila

Under a glaring tropical sun, Timoteo and his fellow Filipino fighters stood at parade-rest in Luneta Park. The streets around the park were crammed with people waving a million Philippine flags. Tickertape and confetti floated down from the windows of war-scarred buildings, dusting the jubilant crowd that had gathered for the upcoming Independence Day ceremonies.

Timoteo held his cane at his side as if it were a rifle and glanced down the perfectly aligned ranks of the First Reconnaissance Battalion. His newly starched fatigues and shined boots felt comfortable in spite of the heat. Even the constant pain in his feet couldn't dampen his mood. Today he would see General McArthur and hopefully get a ticket to America.

On the nearby bandstand, President Manuel Roxas spoke over the microphone, talking to the people assembled, but Timoteo didn't pay any attention to what he was saying. The only words he heard were in his memory, the words of the General when he was in Australia, when he'd agreed there be no silver medal for Timoteo.

Standing next to him, the sergeant adjusted the ammo belt across his chest as if making room for the medal he would soon receive.

Timoteo asked him, "What are you going to do without a war, Sergeant?"

"I don't have to fight to be a soldier. What about you, young man, will you continue to look for your mother?"

Timoteo's heart thumped. As hard as he'd tried, he'd failed

to find any trace of her. She was lost, as were thousands of civilians lost during the war and the retaking of the Philippines. While MacArthur's forces shelled and bombed Manila and fought block by block to uproot the Japanese, the retreating Nips murdered every civilian they came upon. One hundred thousand died in the butchery of Japan's scorched earth policy. No wonder so many victims were unaccounted for, including his mother.

"I hope she is still alive somewhere, starting a new life." Hope was a funny thing, how it left the door open when he knew it should be closed. "I will carry her memory with me always and live my life to her highest expectations, honoring her in everything I do—for her and Tito."

"Look forward, Timoteo. Don't look back."

Timoteo's life was changing again. Sadness and excitement scrimmaged inside him. He wasn't sure if he would cry or cheer. One thing was certain. "I'm going to miss you, Sergeant."

"America is not the land of milk and honey that you think it is. The Philippines needs you."

"I made a promise—"

"To your brother, I know—"

"And Allah," Timoteo added, recalling the fever's dream as he lay dying at Camp O'Donnell. "A man needs a goal, a reason to go on. There's nothing left for me here."

"I have watched you grow, Timoteo, from a boy to a man." He smiled. "I am proud of you."

"I couldn't have done it without you, sir."

"You had it in you all along."

Pride overcame his sense of sadness. He was going to miss all the men who fought with him. But in America, he would get the surgery he needed for his feet. Everyone had been talking about how America's congress had promised full veterans benefits to all Filipinos who had helped the army free the islands. Their suffering and sacrifices would be well rewarded.

Military dignitaries gathered around a microphone. General MacArthur stepped up. He wore baggy pressed pants, a stiff shirt, and a billed Army hat that looked too big for his narrow head. He looked over the crowd behind dark glasses. "People of the Philippines, I have returned."

The crowd cheered.

As the band played the Philippines' national anthem, President Manuel Roxas began raising a Philippine flag up a tall flag pole in front of the bandstand. There was no wind, and the flag hung limp in the stagnant heat, not waving gloriously as Timoteo would like to have seen. Even so, proud tears stung his eyes. As the anthem ended, the flag made it to full mast alongside the American flag. Without missing a beat, the band began playing America's national anthem, and Ambassador McNut lowered the American flag. Church bells rang throughout the city to announce the Philippines' independence.

"This is a proud day for us all," MacArthur said. "It marks the end of mastery over peoples by force alone, the end of an empire." He turned to the Filipino troops assembled below him. "America owes you a debt of gratitude that can never be repaid."

The crowd waved their little flags and cheered.

MacArthur left the microphone and walked down the bandstand steps to the rank and file. The band played a march. Timoteo tried to keep his eyes facing forward, but he couldn't resist a glance down the line.

The General stood in front of a soldier, shook his hand, pinned a medal to his shirt, and moved to the next man. Colonel Wallace and a Captain followed him, carrying a box of medals. Within moments they'd be in front of Timoteo, a thought that caused his heart to beat faster and his feet to throb.

"Good job," MacArthur said to a man down the line.

Timoteo swallowed as the General moved closer.

"Congratulations." He pinned a medal on the Sergeant's shirt.

"Thank you, sir."

"Yes, you did a fine job."

MacArthur stepped in front of Timoteo. "And how's my number one boy?"

The General had remembered Timoteo. He threw his shoulders back and teetered on the cane. "I am well, sir."

"America will never forget how you went in ahead of the strike force and set up radio and observation posts. Your work was vital to the mission. And for your dedicated service, I have your medal."

The Captain handed the General a medal to pin on

Timoteo's shirt, a shining silver bar.

Timoteo shrunk back. "You said you would send me to America and keep the shining bar."

He leaned to Timoteo's ear and whispered, "Don't muck up my ceremony. Take the medal."

"You will keep your word?"

His eyes narrowed. "Now look, boy. I only said I'd see what I can do."

"I'm not a boy. I'm a man."

"Take the damn medal."

"Tell me I can go to America. I will take it with me."

The General smiled and turned to Colonel Wallace. "Gotta love these Filipinos."

"Yes, sir."

"Put him on the next ship to San Diego."

The Pearl of Death

Chapter Forty-Seven

The Rescission Act of 1946

"We hold these truths to be self-evident, that all men are created equal, that they are endowed by their Creator with certain unalienable Rights, that among these are Life, Liberty and the pursuit of Happiness." The Declaration of Independence

It was under these principles that America was born, but somewhere along the line, the interpretation of our forefather's wishes was contrived by some to mean: *white men are created equal.*

For the Filipinos, this racial injustice wasn't their only burden. Not only were they discriminated against on every level of American society, so were they oppressed by the United States Congress. To wit: The Tydings-McDuffie Act of 1934, which on one hand outlined a ten-year plan for the Philippine's independence, and then on the other, classified Filipinos as aliens who weren't entitled to own land, vote, or serve in the US military. The Philippines became a foreign country despite the fact that the islands belonged to the United States.

The result, Filipinos lost their status as American nationals. A quota was established—no more than fifty Filipinos per year were allowed to immigrate into the United States.

As fate, luck, or history would have it, the Japanese invaded the Philippines, and America suddenly needed the Filipinos. President Franklin Delano Roosevelt revised the Selective Service Act to allow them to enlist. He encouraged them to become US citizens. They were promised all the benefits afforded to everyone else who served in the United States military, including those serving under General MacArthur in the

South Pacific and all recognized guerrilla units fighting on the islands. Of the 250,000 Filipinos who fought for the United States against the Japanese, over half died. Their sacrifice was a testament to honor, valor, and commitment second to none during World War II.

But they would never see their just recognition.

Again, enter the United States Congress and the most racially discriminating piece of legislature in history: The Rescission Act of 1946 stripped Filipino veterans of their earned entitlements, except those wounded in battle or killed. A handful of congressmen presented evidence that benefit payouts would surpass 3.2 billion dollars, an expense American taxpayers couldn't afford. Never mind the sixty-five other countries that allied with the United States and retained their veterans' benefits. Other lawmakers argued that the Philippines was now an independent country, a goal Filipino soldiers were fighting for in the first place, thus the new government should be responsible for their own veterans—though it was common knowledge there was no money in the young nation's coffers. So the Rescission Act passed and Filipino veterans fell victim to the Congressional axe.

A bleak future awaited Timoteo Matito in America.

***

Carrying wounded soldiers, the C-54 buzzed over the Pacific Ocean toward America. For as far as Timoteo could see out the window, blue water sparkled under a blazing sun. He braced a varnished cane of twisted driftwood between his knees, a parting gift from the Sergeant in remembrance of their friendship.

General MacArthur had kept his promise and, two weeks ago, put Timoteo on a ship bound for Hawaii, then finally this twelve-hour flight to California. He didn't know how, but he would find Wilbur Cobb and the Pearl of Allah.

As land appeared, his determination met reality head on. A city took form below the wing, perhaps a million times bigger than Manila. Clumps of tall buildings poked the sky. A maze of traffic-cluttered streets spread to the horizon. The plane banked right, and the pilot's voice came from the speakers. "If you look out the windows, you'll see we're flying over Los Angeles."

It was only one of hundreds of big cities in America, a country so large Timoteo couldn't picture it all in his mind. He'd seen maps and listened to American soldiers on the ship, returning from the war. Only now did he realize how huge a task he faced to find one pearl among the masses.

"We'll be landing in San Diego shortly," the pilot finished.

Murphy, the wounded man sitting in the seat next to Timoteo, stirred from his sleep. "What? Already?" He raised the cast on his arm and adjusted a green wool blanket across his chest.

Timoteo had hardly slept during the flight, unlike Murphy and many of the other wounded soldiers on their way to the VA hospital in San Diego. At one point during the night, Murphy awoke and talked about his home in a city called Philadelphia, wherever that was, and his mother and sister. Timoteo told him about his missing mother, his dead brother, and the desperate fighting on Bataan before he became a prisoner. He even showed Murphy the letter from General MacArthur:

To Whom It May Concern, it started. *By order of the Supreme Commander of the Army, this soldier, Timoteo Matito, is to be granted free and priority passage by any mode of transportation available from the Philippine Islands to the VA Medical Center in San Diego, California to have his feet examined.* It was signed: *General Douglas MacArthur.*

He'd folded the letter and tucked it into the buttoned pocket of his fatigue shirt, which bore no insignia of rank because he'd been discharged from the service. The Army had given him two changes of clothes, canvas shoes, and heavy socks that helped cushion his damaged feet. He didn't know what the VA doctors would do to repair them, and he wondered how much more pain he'd have to endure. For him, the war was not over.

Mountainous terrain slid below the plane, reminding him of Palawan, Boligay Creek, and the simple life he once knew. He could see the shoreline and the white lines of foaming waves roll in. The bay, the reef, his father, the giant clam, he remembered them too. It was hard to believe he'd turned twenty-one years old during the journey to America.

Small towns and farms drifted by, then more city sprawl reached to a harbor packed with Navy battleships and aircraft carriers. The plane descended, rolled right and left, and moments later set down on a smooth runway.

"Welcome to America," the pilot said.

GIs cheered.

Timoteo felt warm pride swell in his chest. *America at last.*

He helped Murphy get out of his seat and fold the blanket. Some wounded men were carried off and laid on stretchers. Ambulances sped away. Hobbling on his cane, Timoteo followed Murphy off the plane. The air felt moist and cooler than he'd expected. Seagulls darted about on the wind, like on Palawan, and he welcomed the familiar sight.

Men in blue coveralls unloaded duffle bags from the plane's cargo hold and set them in a line. He found the one with his nametag and stood around with Murphy and the other walking wounded wondering what to do next.

A bus pulled up and squealed to a stop. The door opened, revealing a fat-bellied man with a bushy mustache and bald head. He tromped down the steps, flung open a hatch. "Throw your bags in here, boys, and get aboard."

Falling in line behind Murphy, Timoteo tossed his bag in the compartment and proceeded toward the open door, where the fat man greeted his new passengers and conducted a headcount. "Welcome home, son," he said to Murphy.

"Thanks, but I'm still a long way from home."

"Your folks know you're here?"

"Yes, sir." Murphy bounded up the steps.

Smiling at the fat man, Timoteo limped past him, relying heavily on the cane to get to the door, but the man grabbed him by the arm and spun him around. "Where the hell do you think you're going, Flip?"

Alarm pumped through Timoteo's veins. "The VA hospital, sir."

"You're gonna have to walk. I don't allow no stinkin' Flips on my bus."

Timoteo didn't understand the word *flips*, but by the gruff tone of the man's voice, he figured *flips* wasn't a good word. "Flips, sir?"

"Filipino savages," the man growled. "Now get lost." He shoved Timoteo out of line.

"Hey," Murphy shouted down from the bus steps. "Leave him alone. He's with me."

The fat man looked up at Murphy. "Then you can walk with him, savage lover."

"It's all right," Timoteo said. He'd rather find his own way than cause a fight.

Murphy jumped off the bus, slammed the fat man against the fender, and pinned his throat with the cast arm. "Show some respect for the soldier," he growled. "Timoteo fought the Japanese with us on Bataan."

"I don't care if he fought all of Tokyo," the fat man spat, his face turning red. "He's a fucking Flip."

Soldiers crowded around. Some had scrambled off the bus to get a view of the action. A couple guys were trying to pry Murphy's cast off the fat man's windpipe.

"You're going to kill him," someone shouted.

"Anyone here know how to drive a bus?" Murphy asked, pressing harder on the man's throat. "We don't need this bigot."

The man's eyes were bugging out.

"Stop it," Timoteo shouted. "I have a letter. Let me show him the letter."

"Yeah," someone said. "The letter."

Murphy released pressure against the fat man's throat, pushed him away. "It's from General MacArthur."

Hacking, the fat man stared at Timoteo with that same hateful glare of the Japanese prison guards. "Are you people crazy...taking sides with a Flip?"

The shriek of a whistle blasted through the commotion. A sergeant MP shoved soldiers aside to get to the bus. "Break it up."

"The Flip started it," the bus driver said.

"What's your problem?" the MP demanded of Timoteo.

He pulled the letter out of his pocket. "It's from General McArthur." He held it out for the MP's inspection. "I'm going to the VA hospital."

"Sure you are." The MP didn't take the letter, just glared at him. "Are you some kind of troublemaker?"

"I was just getting on the bus," Timoteo said, "when this man pushed me out of line and called me a Flip. Here." He poked the letter at the MP. "Read it for yourself."

"I should haul you in for disturbing the peace."

"Me?" Timoteo couldn't believe it. "I didn't do anything."

"Flips are nothin' but trouble," the fat man said.

"Please read the letter," Timoteo said to the MP. "I need to go to the hospital."

Murphy bulled his way to the MP. "Let him get on the bus, sarge. I'll watch over him."

Grumbling, the MP looked back and forth between Timoteo and the bus driver. "One more complaint." He shook his finger at Timoteo. "It's the stockade for you, boy. Got that?"

"I didn't do anything."

"Never mind," Murphy said and motioned him toward the bus door. "You can't win."

On the bus, Timoteo put the letter back into his pocket and sat next to Murphy. "Thanks for sticking up for me."

"Don't worry about it."

"I don't understand what I did wrong."

"Look," Murphy said with hard brows. "It's different here, the way people treat each other, especially the races. We have names for them, not nice names."

Timoteo grimaced. "Why?"

"A lot of folks think they're better than everybody else. They're bigots. It's just the way it is."

Timoteo swallowed. The sergeant was right when he'd said that America was not the land of milk and honey. Timoteo would have to get used to being treated like he was less than everyone else.

Chapter Forty-Eight

The VA hospital, San Diego, California

The bus rumbled up to the white-brick hospital. Timoteo took the letter from General MacArthur out of his pocket and held it in his fist. Brakes squealed. The front door folded open. Braving the bus driver's glare, he hobbled with his cane past the man who hated him for being a Filipino. He didn't dare breathe for fear the air between them was poisonous. Struggling down the steps to the pavement, he inhaled, relieved he was getting away from the bigot. A new word Timoteo just learned.

The hospital towered before him, casting its shadow across green lawns and leafy trees. A million windows gleamed in the sunshine. Next to the building, a skeletal frame rose from the dirt. Men on scaffolds laid brick and mortar, digging machines growled, hammers banged, and saws buzzed. The hospital would soon be much bigger.

Murphy got off the bus and set Timoteo's duffle bag at his feet. "Good luck, soldier." He walked toward the hospital's front doors.

Watching him go, Timoteo felt proud that he'd called him a soldier. He was equal to the GI in every way, except for the way he looked. Filipino: broad nose, thick lips, big teeth. Until he'd arrived in America, he always thought he looked normal. Now he knew he looked different, and being different in America had already proven to be a problem.

Timoteo held onto his pride. He'd sacrificed a lot to help America retake the Philippines. His feet seemed a small price to pay for the honor of serving in the army.

Using the cane for support, he stooped to pick up his bag

and joined the wounded men lumbering toward the entrance doors.

Inside the cavernous building, the air was hot and muggy, as if the walls couldn't breathe. He'd expected cool conditioned air like in the General's headquarters. The antiseptic smell reminded him of the hospital in Australia, a half a world away and a lifetime ago.

A bald man wearing a gray smock met the arriving soldiers in the sweltering hallway. "This way, boys." He dabbed sweat from his brow. "We have chairs for you. In that room. A nurse will check you in." He pointed at Timoteo. "You, you there. What are you doing here?"

"My feet—"

"We don't serve your kind here."

"I have a letter..." Timoteo felt the sting of being singled out again. "From General MacArthur."

The other men moved into the room with chairs. Nurses greeted them.

"I need to check in."

"Let me see the letter." He held out his hand, palm up and motioned *come here* with his fingers.

Timoteo didn't want to give him the letter. What if he didn't give it back? "Are you a doctor?"

"Close enough for you, Flip." He snatched the letter from Timoteo's hand.

"I need that back."

"Shut up." He unfolded the letter, read a moment then looked up. "This has to be a forgery."

Timoteo didn't understand the word *forgery*, but the man's tone reminded him of the bus driver. Timoteo's palms began to sweat. "What are you saying?"

"You expect me to believe this is from MacArthur?"

Frowning, Timoteo gripped the cane, hoping to hide his growing anger. He never thought someone might doubt the General's letter. "I watched him write it."

"Sure you did."

"Give it back." Timoteo reached for the letter.

The man jerked it out of Timoteo's reach. "You can go to jail for this, boy."

"I'm not a boy."

"What's the holdup out here?" a voice barked from behind him. He pivoted on his cane. A doctor stood at the door to the room of chairs. His white smock bulged around his round belly.

"He took my letter and won't give it back," Timoteo told the doctor.

"This letter, sir," the man said, waving it above his head. "It's an obvious fake."

"General MacArthur gave it to me," Timoteo shouted.

The doctor moved to the man. "Let me see." He read the letter.

The bald man huffed. "No general is going to vouch for a Flip."

"Timoteo?" the doctor murmured. "Timoteo Matito?" He looked up, recognition sparkling in his eyes. "Yes. It's you."

Timoteo's heart lurched in surprise. He studied the doctor and realized who he was, a much healthier version of the man in the POW camp. "Dr. Nelson?"

"The last time I saw you, you were a skinny kid who could barely walk. You're looking pretty good now."

Timoteo resisted the urge to hug the doctor. "You're back from the war."

"I'm a civilian, now. Working for the VA."

"I'm glad to see you, sir."

Nelson glanced down at Timoteo's canvas shoes. "Still having trouble with those feet, huh?" His tone sounded more friendly than professional.

"They've gotten me this far, sir."

"Good, good." He took Timoteo's duffle bag. "Come on in. If MacArthur wants us to have a look at your feet, that's good enough for me." Nelson shot the bald man a piercing glare. "Get back to work, corporal."

"Yes, sir."

Looking back at the corporal, Timoteo grinned, savoring the sight of him put in his place.

Nelson handed Timoteo the letter. "I believe this belongs to you."

"Thanks." Taking it, he noticed Nelson had neatly refolded it, as if he understood its true value.

Inside the room, a nurse called out, "Dr. Nelson, could you look at this?" She stood by a wounded soldier. "It's serious."

"Have a seat over there, Timoteo." Nelson handed him the duffle bag. "One of the aides will check you in."

Feeling faint and in need of fresh air, Timoteo sat in a folding chair, set the bag on the floor at his feet, and propped the cane between his knees. He glanced around the room, sunlit from high windows. Soldiers from the bus sat in chairs along the walls. Several tables were arranged in the center of the room. There were stacks of papers, boxes marked with red crosses on white labels, and books the nurses wrote in as they moved back and forth between the wounded men and the tables. One nurse glanced at him sitting alone, and as if embarrassed for looking, quickly glanced down at her book.

Timoteo's heart jumped. An American girl had noticed him. Her hair was the color of sunshine and her skin was white as Palawan sand. But she wouldn't have anything to do with him. He'd come to get his feet fixed. He had to find Wilbur Cobb and the pearl. He didn't come here for love, but she made his chest feel warm inside.

"Ahhum."

He flinched. A Filipino girl had come up beside him. Her nurse's hat was pinned in a nest of curly black hair. She had caught him gawking at the American girl. Embarrassment heated his cheeks. He was speechless.

"*Anong pangalan mo?*" she asked. What is your name?

"T-Timoteo," he stuttered, surprised to hear Tagalog this far from the Philippines. "Timoteo Matito."

"Ako si Jenny Arguello. Do you speak English?"

"Si."

"You need to fill in this form." She offered him a paper and a pen. "Can you read and write?"

He couldn't take his eyes off her. Jenny Arguello was as beautiful as his mother, dark eyes, olive skin and full lips. An unfamiliar urge struck him. To kiss those lips. He'd never kissed a woman. Didn't know how to ask for a kiss, but for those lips he'd—

"Cat got your tongue?"

"Huh?" More embarrassment.

"Can you read and write?"

"Oh. Yes. I went to school on Palawan and in Manila before the Japanese came." He took the paper and pen, eyes riveted to those lips. The flush feeling in his face drained. What was the use? He wasn't just a Filipino in a new country; he was a crippled Filipino. She would never let him kiss her.

"You don't have to be afraid."

"I'm not afraid."

"Then what's the matter?"

"My feet hurt."

"Jenny," another nurse called.

"I'll be back in a few minutes."

He looked at the form with all its blank spaces to fill in, and then glanced up at the American nurses. They didn't look his direction, not once, but Jenny did, many times. A glance. A smile. That was all, but it was enough to give him comfort. She was there to help him, where the others didn't seem to care.

Filling out the form, in the box marked: *reason for this visit* he wrote: *Bad Feet.* Dr. Nelson would know what that meant.

Jenny came back and sat next to him. "You are finished?"

"Yes." He gave her the paper and pen, sat back in the chair. "It's hot in here."

"The air conditioning system is off during construction," she said, hands in her lap. "It's so noisy and dusty we must keep the windows closed. They're building a new wing, you know."

"Business that good?" he asked, thinking how the war had taken a heavy toll on both American and Filipino soldiers.

She shrugged.

"Taga saan ka?" he asked her in Tagalog. *Where are you from?*

"Mindoro." She sighed. "My father is a Senator. I'm here to learn nursing."

"You're not a nurse?"

"A nurse's aide—"

"You look like a nurse."

She smiled at his compliment. "A Pensionado, actually. I'm stationed here until I'm certified. Then I'm supposed to go back to the Philippines. Nurses are needed there. Where are you from?"

"The war," he replied instead of telling her about Palawan, the giant clam that killed his father, his lost mother and dead brother. "When are you going home?"

"I hope never. And you?"

"I'm staying."

"And your family, are they coming?"

He shook his head, cast his eyes to the cane propped between his knees. "They're all dead."

"I'm sorry." She put her hand on his knee.

The weight of her fingers shot electricity up to his heart. "Allah has not been kind to me."

"You're Moro Muslim?"

"Dyak."

"On Palawan. Yes. I know of the Boligay Creek village. That is where you're from?"

He looked into her dark eyes, amazed at how she'd found the answer to her own question. "Yes, how do you know?"

Her pretty face sagged. "I have heard the news."

"What news?"

"The Japanese burned the village."

"I know." The Japanese destroyed everything they touched.

"They hanged the Panglima and his son. Some villagers escaped into the jungle and lived to tell of the massacre."

Timoteo's heart hardened. A soldier in the war did not cry over the dead. If he did, he would never stop crying. But a traitorous tear stung his eye anyway.

A gray-haired nurse approached. "Dr. Nelson will see you now."

"I'll show him the way," Jenny said.

On his feet, cane in hand, he followed her down the hall to a small room. Shiny metal cabinets lined white walls, and black floor tiles surrounded a padded examination table.

Dr. Nelson was standing at a counter, busy with paperwork. "Have a seat, Timoteo." He cocked his head toward the table.

Timoteo inched up on the white paper covering that crinkled under his weight. "Should I take off my shoes?"

"Sure."

"Let me help you." Jenny took his cane and propped it

against a cabinet.

"I can do it." Timoteo wished she would leave the room. He didn't want her to see his ugly feet.

"Don't be silly." She untied the laces on his canvas shoes then gently pried them off his thick socks and set them on the floor.

"I'll take off the socks myself."

"It's no trouble, really."

"Don't." He pulled his feet out of her hands.

Looking him in the eyes, she frowned. "Why are you so stubborn?"

"That's all right, Jenny." Dr. Nelson rolled a wheeled chair to the table. "I'll do it."

"See you later, Timoteo." Jenny left the room.

He didn't like the sound of the door closing between them. She'd been nice to him.

"Let's see how well you've healed." Dr. Nelson pulled down the socks on Timoteo's dangling feet.

He watched the first sock slide off, and then the other. His stomach squeezed tight. The scarred skin resembled dried mud. His toes were bent at strange angles, and the toenails had rotted off long ago.

Nelson tested each foot's range of motion. Pain shot up Timoteo's legs. He grimaced but didn't cry out. Pain had become a way of life.

"You have the feet of a ninety-year-old man," Nelson commented. "That's one reason for your discomfort."

"Pain is the reason," Timoteo countered.

"The other is this scar tissue."

Timoteo stared at the inhuman stumps stuck to the end of his legs. "Can you fix them?"

Dr. Nelson stood, walked to the counter. "You need a few skin grafts, special shoes, physical therapy—"

"When do we start?"

Turning from the counter, the doctor looked at him with sullen eyes. "I'm sorry, son, but no matter how much success we might have, you can't be treated here."

Confusion flooded Timoteo's brain. "This is the VA hospital." He pulled the letter from his pocket, poked it at Dr.

Nelson. "General MacArthur sent me here...for my feet. He promised."

"It's not that." Nelson moved to the table, put a hand on Timoteo's shoulder. "It's the Rescission Act Congress passed."

"What do my feet care about your congress?"

"It's a law that denies benefits to Filipino veterans. Even the great General MacArthur can't overrule Congress."

"But my feet...they are ruined from fighting with the American Army. I almost died...many times."

"You could go back to the Philippines and file a veteran's claim there, but don't count on any help from your country. They can't afford to pay benefits."

"That's not fair."

"War is never fair, son."

Scowling at the doctor, Timoteo felt another slap of betrayal. "If you knew you couldn't treat me, why did you look at my feet?"

"The letter. I did what MacArthur asked. I examined your feet. Out of respect for you, and the sacrifices your people made."

"If it wasn't for us Filipinos, all the American soldiers would be dead."

"I know."

Timoteo could hardly breathe. "What am I to do now?"

"Put on your socks and shoes. Go home."

"I don't have a home."

Timoteo's plans to get well and find the pearl were dashed. He was a cripple in a cruel country with no hope of ever walking normally again. No money. No job. No home. "I was supposed to get GI benefits, like the American soldiers I fought with on Bataan, the same soldiers I marched with to Camp O'Donell. I am equal."

"The United States won't help you. No disability, no medical, no educational assistance, no job services, no financial aid...nothing. I'm sorry, Timoteo. All I can do is enter this in your medical records...in case the law is changed someday." Nelson opened the door. "Jenny."

"Yes, sir." She appeared in the doorway.

"Take him back to admissions and discharge him."

"But what about his feet?"

"Legally, we can't help him."

"The Rescission Act?" Her dark eyebrows cocked in dismay.

"At least he's able to walk." He stepped out the door. "Most Filipino veterans are in worse shape." With a parting glance to Timoteo, he added, "I hate this job," and shut the door.

Timoteo felt like he'd been run over by a tank. He sat staring at the folded letter in his hand, the worthless letter from a famous General. Temples throbbing, he crumpled up the letter and threw it on the floor. "Lies. All lies."

"Let me help you." Jenny stooped to pick up his socks and shoes.

Now he didn't care that she saw his feet. They were ugly like the Americans, warped like their empty promises, a ghastly souvenir of their lies. "Look at what they did to me," Timoteo told her, his legs straight out and feet in plain view.

"Stop complaining. I should take you upstairs to the burn ward and to the amputee wing where you will see GIs much worse off than you."

"The army gave me canvas shoes to wear in the jungle, and when they were torn and broken, they made me go barefoot because we couldn't get resupplied on Bataan. I was forced to stand in the excrement of prisoners. Maggots ate my flesh. It was more horrible than words can explain, but still I was proud to fight for America. And this is the thanks I get, to be tossed out like garbage."

"Please lower your voice," she whispered. "The MPs will come."

Choking back tears, Timoteo knew his suffering would never end—not until he found the pearl and returned it to the sea. But why had Allah made the task so difficult?

Pulling on his socks, he vowed not to let this setback stop him. Shoes on, he dropped from the table, not caring how much it hurt. He grabbed his cane and bulled his way to the door.

Jenny held it open. "Timoteo, I can help you."

"I don't need any help."

All the way down the hall, she kept pace with his wretched walk. "There is a large Filipino community here."

"Good for them."

"You'll need a place to stay."

"I'm a soldier. I will survive."

"What about a job? You need money for food. We can help you get a job."

Timoteo never had a job. Never needed one. The army had taken care of him—until now. The thought of getting a job in this country frightened him more than fighting the Japanese on Bataan. "I don't want a job."

"Don't be so stubborn. You have to eat. You'll need money to fix your feet."

Stopping short of the room with the chairs, he leaned on the cane. "What do you care? I'm not your problem."

"You need to learn the ropes."

"What are the ropes?"

"How to survive in America."

"And you're going to teach me?"

"The first thing you must do is calm down."

He didn't like her telling him what to do. "Why should I trust you, Jenny? And what kind of name is that? It's not Filipino."

"My real name is Juni, but I adopted Jenny to sound more American."

"Why?"

"The less we are associated with the Philippines, the better. Timothy would serve you well here, instead of Timoteo. Take my advice—"

"I'd rather fight the Japanese."

"At least think about it." She took his arm, guided him to the doorway. "Go inside. Sit. I will get you a sandwich and some milk."

Eating made better sense than walking out angry *and* hungry. "Okay."

Sitting in the chair by his duffle bag, which was safe thanks to Juni, he couldn't imagine what he would do next. Where would he go? How would he find Wilbur Cobb and the pearl? The huge task seemed more impossible than ever.

And he would have to find them while his feet were constantly in pain.

Chapter Forty-Nine

Chicago, 1948

"**L**adies and gentlemen," an announcer spoke over the PA system. "Direct from San Francisco, California, the Field Museum of Natural History brings you the amazing story of the lost Pearl of Lao-Tzu."

Music from the Philippines, heavy on gongs and horns, played through loud speakers on either side of the stage as black velvet curtains rose slowly, first revealing a marble pedestal and then a glass container on top, which housed the lumpy pearl. Under hot stage lights, Wilbur Cobb stood behind a podium and watched the huge gem sparkle. There were no guards, no trip wires, and no alarms this time, as there had been in New York, at Ripley's, nine years ago.

Camera bulbs flashed.

"Give a welcoming hand to Wilbur Cobb."

The anorexic applause wasn't encouraging. Wearing a suit and tie, he felt like an old man, beaten by the guilt of past mistakes. And as always, the devil in his throat begged for a relieving belt of scotch.

Through the glaring lights, he could barely see the audience. People sat in rows of folding chairs, maybe fifty had showed up for this free show.

When the music ended, "Good evening," Wilbur began, his voice as hesitant as an old woman about to cross a busy street. "You may be wondering why this exhibit isn't guarded. After all, this is the lost pearl from 600 BC China. It's worth a fortune."

A murmur rippled through the room.

"The truth is...this is not the real pearl. It's a replica, but painstakingly true in every detail."

Terry Wright

"What a sham," someone shouted. "I'm getting out of here."

Chairs scraped on the floor.

"No, wait—"

"What a waste of time."

"Hear me out," Wilbur shouted, fearing he'd lose them all. "It's the story you've come for. That's what this free show is all about. The story..."

Still people walked out, maybe half, but as long as one person remained, he would continue the show.

"Everyone sit down," a woman shouted. "Let's hear what he has to say."

He shielded his eyes from the glaring lights but couldn't see who had spoken up in his defense.

The room quieted.

"Go ahead, Mr. Cobb," she said.

"Thank you, ma'am." Wilbur gave up trying to locate her. "The real pearl is in a San Francisco bank vault where it can't do anyone any harm. This replica was prepared by the professional curators of this museum. It's made of plaster and the finely ground Mother of Pearl scraped from inside the original giant clam's shell. There are three others like it...on display in San Francisco, LA, and Denver. The shows are free, folks. I won't accept any money, not a penny, and the reason for this is a matter of life and death."

The room was so quiet he could have heard a mouse fart. His confidence ballooned, and he continued before the impact of his last words waned.

"This pearl, once known as the Pearl of Allah, is actually the cursed Pearl of Lao-Tzu."

On cue, a panel dropped down from the stage rafters.

"Here is an enlargement of the original shipping order...sold to the highest bidder, it says in Chinese, and a drawing of the pearl. This is two hundred years old, folks. You can see the same droopy features, a face, eyes, flattened nose, and look at the swirling necre on top, like a wrap of cloth or a turban."

"It's thinner," the same woman said.

"Because it grew for two hundred years, in the giant clam,

before it was found."

Did he have to explain everything to this woman?

"Scientists have examined my pearl. Based on the time it takes to produce a pearl, two centimeters diameter in six years, they have calculated that it would have taken twenty-five hundred years to achieve the size and weight of this pearl. I have their certification right here, folks." He removed the folded paper from his coat pocket and waved it at them. "And in New York City, nine years ago, a Chinese monk came to my show, confided in me that this was the Taoists' lost pearl. And he warned me of the curse."

The audience stirred, mumbled.

"What curse?" the same woman asked.

"If the pearl was ever exchanged for money or power, it would become the pearl of suffering, folks. The pearl of death."

The claim sounded so ludicrous he'd have to expound on the consequences. "I was paid to show this pearl at Ripley's. I sold my story to the American Museum of Natural History. After that, my life turned tragic. I lost my family in the Philippines. I lost my job at Benguet Consolidated. I became an alcoholic. Yes, believe me, people, this is the cursed pearl of Lao-Tzu."

A moan rose from the crowd.

"All my shows are free. And one day I'll save up enough money to return to the Philippines and throw the cursed pearl back into the sea."

"And throw away a fortune," the woman's voice said.

"I'd rather crush the pearl to dust with a sledgehammer, but that would be like smashing the Arc of the Covenant, breaking the Holy Grail, or burning the Dead Sea Scrolls."

"Donate it to the museum," a man shouted out.

"Someday people might have to pay to get into a museum. If money ever exchanged hands over this pearl, no matter how far removed, someone will die. The risk is too great."

The woman again: "You're a superstitious man, Mister Cobb."

"Have you been listening, lady? This is not make-believe. People are dead—"

"People die in war," she shot back. "It's not the pearl's fault."

His tie felt tight as a hangman's noose. He remembered when he believed the pearl wasn't the cause of his troubles. Logic and science had dictated his thinking. Legends. Myths. Curses. How ridiculous. How impossible.

"I'd sell the pearl," she said. "Take the money and run."

"Are you really that stupid?" He stepped out from under the glaring stage lights, searched the crowd for the heckler. "Where are you? Please, come up on stage and—"

A woman stood. Long blond hair flowed over her shoulders. She wore a small black hat and a mink coat. The mole close to her lower lip gave her identity away. His heart flip-flopped. "Elaine Meyers."

"We meet again, Mister Cobb."

"I'll be damned."

***

After the show, Wilbur met Elaine in the lobby near the concession stand. She hadn't changed, still statuesque as a princess in high heels. Her ankle-length coat was buttoned to her throat, and she carried a black handbag under her arm. Red lips begged to be kissed.

"Buy you a coffee?" he asked.

"I'd rather have something stronger, say scotch." Her eyelashes flitted.

Sure she would. "Two coffees," he told the concessionaire.

"Fuddy-duddy."

"I quit drinking."

"Awe." She made her lips all pouty.

He put a dime on the counter. "How are you?"

"Been better, been worse."

"I see you're still playing dress up."

"The clothes?" She laughed. "Zimmerman paid me a lot of money for saving his life."

"The cops bought your story about the Chinese kid?"

"Self defense. They believed me because he'd killed Kaufman earlier that evening."

That news caused a jolt in Wilbur's chest. "I didn't know." Seemed everyone involved with that pearl was dead. He wasn't going to be next.

An uneasy moment passed. He watched the concessionaire pour coffee, but his mind slid back nine years. To New York. To Elaine Meyers...naked. To the Packard...hot lips and heavy breathing. To the night he almost professed his love for her and almost didn't go back to Liawayway. The Chinese kid had stopped that...

"Michael died at Pearl Harbor," Elaine said. "When the Japanese attacked his..." Her breath hitched.

"I'm sorry."

She looked into his eyes. "And I'm sorry about your Palawan princess. I always wondered what happened between you and her."

"I was forced to leave her there and never saw her again."

The concessionaire set the coffee on the counter and snatched up the dime. "What? No tip?"

"You're lucky I've got a dime."

"Money problems?" Elaine asked.

"Things are tight."

"You could be a rich man, you know."

He looked at her beautiful face, stirred a scoop of sugar in his coffee. "Always the gold digger."

"I'm an opportunist."

"A rose by any other name—"

"You've got to do something with that pearl. Can't just leave it in a bank vault forever."

He moved to a small table, already wishing she hadn't shown up. His heart longed for her company, but his brain knew better. She was trouble. He pulled out a chair and offered it to her. She sat, and as she crossed her legs, her coat came open revealing a beautiful knee, which he tried to ignore, but failed at miserably.

Swallowing, he took the opposite chair, sat with his back to the window. Wind-driven sleet pelted the glass. Déjà vu hit him like a board, that cold and snowy night in New York City, the bar, the scotch, the bedroom...

Watching her pull a cigarette from her handbag, he decided to ask, "What brings you to Chicago?"

"You." She handed him a matchbook.

He struck a match and lit her cigarette, a good reason to

stare into her eyes. "I bet."

"I heard you were doing the museum circuit again."

He blew out the match and dropped it in the ashtray. "Who sent you this time?"

"Santa Claus." She grinned, leaned back in her chair, and exhaled smoke.

"I don't doubt it."

She touched her chin with a polished nail. "What are you trying to prove, Wilbur? I mean, staying broke and all."

He looked into deep blue eyes that reminded him of Palawan waters. "So I don't forget. Keeps Liawayway alive, and the boys. It's my penance for leaving them behind to die at the hands of the Japanese."

"How do you make a living?"

"I received a severance from Benguet. Invested it."

"How much?" She flicked ashes in the ashtray.

She *would* ask that question. "Enough." He sipped his coffee.

"But the pearl is money in the bank."

"It attracts the wrong kind of people." Another sip of coffee. "Believe me, I'd just as soon be rid of it."

She looked at her cigarette. "Then sell it."

"The curse, Elaine, it's my burden to bear."

She blinked, took a drag, blew smoke. "It's good to see you, Wilbur."

"You too." He couldn't believe he said it, but it felt good to be near her.

"Let's go somewhere. I know a little place."

That could lead to more trouble than the pearl. "I'll take a rain check."

"Come on." She smiled. "You don't have to make a phone call this time."

There was no reason in the world why he couldn't go with her, except he wasn't sure about getting on that cyclone ride again. "I can't."

She stood. "Tomorrow night then. I'll meet you here—"

"But Liawayway is still with me." He touched his heart.

"I can't replace her," Elaine breathed, "but I can numb the pain."

"My pain is my friend. It keeps me from going insane."

She leaned on the table, her lips so close to his he could smell the cigarette on her breath. "We could have a second chance at love, Wilbur. Don't throw this one away too."

He wanted to grab her face and smash his lips into hers.

She turned and strode through the door and into the snowy night.

Stupid! Stupid! Stupid!

How long was he going to keep screwing up his life?

He scrambled to his feet and rushed outside, hoping she hadn't already caught a cab.

Chapter Fifty

Joe's Hideout, Colorado Springs, November 23, 1975

Illuminated by the barroom glow of neon beer signs, smoke hung so thick in the air that Joe Giodano could hardly breathe. He dried a whiskey glass, stacked it with the others he'd just washed, and looked forward to last call.

His wife would be dead by then.

In the corner, a club of bikers played pool. Country music blared from the jukebox. Quiet drunks sat at the bar, staring into their drinks. Joe's Hideout wasn't the best bar in town, but it was Joe's bar. To keep the joint running, he'd spent all his savings. His wife bitched about how much it cost to cater to alcoholics and the riffraff of Colorado Springs. If he divorced her, he'd have to sell his bar to pay her half its worth. Damn community property state. Life insurance and a hit man cost him much less.

"Rum and Coke," Val said from the waitress dock. "With Bacardi."

"Comin' right up."

As Joe made the drink, he glanced around to be sure he wasn't being watched, and setting the glass on the tray, he kissed her cheek. "Three-fifty."

She paid him from a wad of bills clenched in her fist. "Are you coming over tonight?"

He shook his head. "Sorry."

She twirled around, her long black hair fanning out. He watched her walk away, the round lobes of her perfect ass winking at him from below her blue jean short-shorts. His eyes traveled down her long legs to her cowboy boots. He wanted to see her tonight, but he couldn't. He had to go home and discover his wife's body.

"Hey, barkeep." Tom Phillips strode in, shouting as if everyone were deaf. Dressed in a gray Armani suit, his black hair slicked back, he stuck out like a dog at a cat fight. The greaser elbowed his way between two patrons sitting at the bar. "Scram."

They grabbed their beers and moved to a table.

"Can a guy get a drink around here?"

Joe couldn't believe the man's arrogance. And why tonight of all nights? "What are you doin' here?"

"Are you saying I'm not welcome in this joint?" He said it loud enough to attract the attention of City Hall.

"Keep your voice down, for God's sake."

"I'll have a Seven and Seven. Make it fast."

Joe grabbed Phillips by his paisley tie. "Look here, you fuckin' prick. I warned you not to come around here."

Phillips squirmed and tried to pull away.

Joe yanked the tie knot tighter. "You got the memo now?"

"What's the matter with you?" Phillips hissed through clenched teeth.

"I don't want to be seen with you," Joe growled.

"I'm on your side, man."

"You've got my money. What kind of sick-ass game are you playin'?"

"Lighten up," Phillips choked out. "I'll explain."

Joe glanced around the barroom. Their tussle hadn't gone unnoticed. That was all he needed, people talking about what they saw unusual tonight, of all the nights for Tom to pull this stunt. Joe let go of the tie. "Sit."

"It's all right, everyone." Joe painted a smile on his pissed off face. "Just a little misunderstanding over his bar tab."

"My tab is paid up," someone said.

"Mine too."

A moment later, everyone was back to doing what they'd been doing.

Joe scowled at Phillips. "Okay, I'm listening."

He loosened his tie. "We're in this together. We need each other now."

"I don't need your bullshit."

"I'll cover your ass, you cover mine." He looked around.

"So how about that drink? Let all these nice people think we're still friends."

"I don't want any trouble from you."

"Seven-Seven. And don't expect a tip. The service around here sucks."

Pouring Seagram's over ice, Joe knew Phillips was right. They were stuck with each other. Tom owned a restaurant and bar on Fillmore Street. Last year, after a late-night poker game at his place, they'd hung out smoking cigars, drinking brandy, and bitching about their wives. Phillips had told him how he'd gotten rid of his first wife for $10,000 and then pocketed a $300,000 life insurance check.

Tom Phillips knew how to fix problems. Better yet, he knew how to get away with murder. So when the investment opportunity of a lifetime presented itself, Joe turned to Phillips to fix his problems: his wife and his lack of cash flow, both at the same time.

A quarter million dollar life insurance settlement would secure his stake in the World's Largest Pearl Company. *Thank you, Ellen.* He didn't know which thug Phillips had hired to do the killing. He didn't want to know. And he didn't care how it was done. A knife, a gun, a garrote, it was all the same to Joe, as long as the murder couldn't be traced back to him.

He set the drink in front of Phillips. "You're supposed to be in California with Barber, so why are you here?"

"I'd just be in their way."

"So now you're in my way."

"Barber is meeting with the jeweler, Paul Kaufman. His father was murdered in New York, you know the one?"

"Some Chinese kid killed him. So?"

"They're going to talk to Wilbur Cobb and convince him to sell them the pearl."

"I'm excited to be in on this," Joe said, thinking of the riches to come.

"Yeah, about that." Phillips lifted the glass. "There's a problem with the investment."

"I'll have the money...you know...as soon as the insurance company pays up."

Phillips sipped Seven-Seven. "Zimmerman's got first

dibs."

"Dibs? Are you shittin' me?" Joe's blood pressure shot up.

"Zimmerman? He'd lost a hand over that pearl." Joe leaned on the bar. "Last I heard he didn't want anything to do with it."

"Relax. He's just putting up the money to buy the pearl from Cobb. As the number of shares increase, you'll get your chance to buy in."

Anxiety wormed in Joe's gut. His so-called friends would soon have a stake in the most lucrative investment scheme of all time, and they'd left him out because he didn't have the cash on hand. He should've had his wife killed sooner.

"You screw me, Phillips, I'll kill you."

"Same thing back at ya, pal." He grinned.

Val stepped up to the waitress stand. "Are you boys going to play nice now?"

"Last call, everybody," Joe shouted. He had a date with his dead wife.

***

In a dark alley off West Arvada Street, Roberto Delgado parked the Ford Torino he'd stolen from a body shop in Pueblo. Turning off the headlights, he knew how to get away with auto theft. He also knew how to get away with murder.

This would be his second hit.

Ducking low in the seat, he trained his eyes on the house across the street. Lights glowed in the windows. A woman and three kids lived there. The woman was his target. He hoped the kids would sleep through the killing.

Delgado thought of himself as a professional hit man, a mobster, a hired gun. A movie of his life would make one hell of a blockbuster, like *The Godfather*. And he dreamed of working in Chicago someday. Now there was a city that could use his talents, the real mob: the Marcellos, the Saladinos, the Lombardos. He would be someone respected. And feared.

In Colorado Springs, he was a baker, a good baker of buns and muffins and cakes, but he thought of himself as a better hit man. Dressed in black, he could move through the shadows like the Invisible Man. His gloves ensured there'd be no fingerprints left on the window frame. And the gun in his pocket, a stolen .38

snub nose, he would melt it down in a Pueblo steel mill after the hit.

Already, the November night air chilled the windshield enough to cause his breath to fog the glass. He was about to wipe it clean when a hazy beam of headlights swept around the corner and barreled toward him. Hoping it wasn't a cop, he scrunched lower in the seat, listened to his chest pound.

The car didn't pass by the alley.

Peering over the dash, he saw the glow of red taillights in the driveway of the house he was watching. He wondered what the hell was going on and swiped a clear spot in the fogged window to get a better view.

Car doors opened. The porch light winked on. A gray haired man and woman got out of the car. The house door creaked open and threw a V of light on the front yard. Squealing children ran outside, a boy and two girls, and greeted their visitors before they'd even made it to the door. The kids wore coats over pajamas, slippers, and carried blankets and pillows.

It looked like they were headed for a sleepover at grandma's house. How nice. His client had moved the children to safety. The boy's name was John, Delgado knew. Six years old. His sisters were Beth and Susan. Beth was a knobby-kneed fourteen-year-old. Little Suzie was five. Delgado made it a point to know everything about his target, like any professional hit man. That left only the woman inside, Ellen Giodano.

The car backed out of the driveway and drove off.

The porch went dark.

He got the gun out of his pocket.

This was going to be a piece of cake.

Chapter Fifty-One

Laguna Beach, California

Wilbur sat in his favorite recliner and read the morning newspaper. The fall of Saigon dominated the headlines, and he felt trepidation for the South Vietnamese who'd collaborated with the United States during the war.

He puffed on his pipe, savoring the cherry tobacco aroma as he flipped to the TV guide section: *Gunsmoke* at eight this evening, then *Maude, Rhoda, and Medical Center.* It sounded like a good night to read the book on his desk, *Carrie,* written by some guy named Stephen King.

The doorbell rang.

"I'll get it," Elaine shouted from the kitchen.

He looked up and wondered who would be calling at this time of morning. "It's not even ten."

"Probably the paperboy." She passed by the open glass doors to his study, drying her hands on her blue and white apron. She moved with the same grace as always, her elegant stature still evident at sixty-three, every bleach-blond hair glued in place as if she'd just returned from the beauty salon.

"Shouldn't the paperboy be in school?" Wilbur tamped out his pipe.

"I don't know," she said from down the hall.

Wilbur hadn't finished his first cup of coffee, which sat cooling on the end table beside him. After folding the paper, he got up from the recliner and shuffled to the desk. If the paperboy wanted money, Elaine was going to need a check.

Locating the checkbook, he sat in the desk chair, and opened to the ledger. Three check numbers were missing, and no amounts had been entered in the columns. He gritted his teeth. Elaine spent money faster than the government could print it.

She appeared in the study doorway. "There's a man to see you. He's waiting in the foyer."

"What happened to these checks?" He waved the checkbook at her.

"He says it's important."

"Elaine?"

"Okay. I went shopping with the girls yesterday. I'll fill in the ledger later."

His wife and daughters were going to land him in the poor house. "How much did you spend this time?"

"Quit your bitchin', ya old fart."

"Is there enough left to pay the paperboy?"

"It's not the paperboy, Wilbur."

"How much, Elaine?"

"I don't remember. Neiman Marcus, Montgomery Ward, and I bought you a new pair of shoes at Penny's."

"I don't need new shoes. When are you going to stop...?" A pang in his chest silenced him. He grimaced. Damn heart. He hesitated reaching for the nitro tablets...in the desk drawer. He didn't want to alarm Elaine.

"Are you all right?"

"Yeah, yeah," he said through clenched teeth and waited for the pain to subside. "Our money isn't going to last much longer."

She frowned. "The man is still waiting for you."

"Who?"

"The man at the door." She shook her head. "I swear you're losin' it, Wilbur."

"Oh." He'd forgotten. "Who is it?"

"He looks like a detective to me, fancy suit and slicked back hair. His partner is outside on the porch."

"What do they want?"

"How should I know? You still want orange juice and oatmeal for breakfast?"

He closed the checkbook. "I want you to stop spending so much money."

"If you'd sell that damn pearl we wouldn't be in this fix."

The Pearl of Death

It was the same old argument. He didn't have the energy to go through it with her again. "I'll see what our visitors are here about."

Rising from the desk chair, he took a deep breath. The chest pain subsided. Feeling stiff in his joints, he padded down the hall, still wearing slippers. If he'd known company was coming he would have put on slacks instead of jeans, and a white shirt instead of this silver and black Raiders bathrobe.

"Mister Cobb," the man said, hand outstretched. He had wavy brown hair, wore black bellbottom slacks and a gray Continental jacket over a black collarless shirt. Diamonds and rubies glistened from rings on every finger of his offered hand. "Thank you for seeing me." His brown eyes beamed with enthusiasm.

"Don't thank me...thank the missus." Wilbur looked him up and down, but didn't accept his handshake. A glance through the screen door revealed the man standing guard on the porch, a barrel-chested Italian wearing sunglasses. He had black hair combed Afro-style and long bushy sideburns. His hands were clasped behind his back. Either his suit coat was a size too big, or he was packing a holstered pistol. Trepidation seized Wilbur's throat. He swallowed. "What can I do for you...boys?"

Retracting his offered hand, the man said, "You might remember my father, Gary Kaufman."

"Gary Kaufman? I don't know..." A jolt of painful recognition shot through his chest. "The jeweler. Gary Kaufman, yes." He looked at the young man again. "I forgot your name."

"Paul, Paul Kaufman. I own the jewelry store in Beverly Hills."

"Your dad was killed. In New York. I remember now."

"My mom took over the store. She died last year."

"I didn't know."

"Now I'm running the company. We have a proposition for you." He tipped his head toward the man on the porch.

"What kind of proposition?"

"I found my father's notes on a pearl that belongs to you."

"There's no pearl."

Paul drilled him with an I-don't-believe-you look. "You still own the pearl, Mr. Cobb. My father said you'd never sell it."

"That's right. It's not for sale." Wilbur hoped the deliberate growl in his throat would convince them he was serious. "You better go now."

Elaine strolled in with a perky smile. "Coffee for you boys?" She made an obvious glance toward the man on the porch. "Why doesn't he come in?"

"Coffee would be nice, ma'am," Paul replied. "Thank you."

"They were just leaving," Wilbur said.

"Now, Wilbur..." Elaine patted her apron. "They haven't had their coffee yet."

"Will you forget the damn coffee and go back to the kitchen." Wilbur wanted her out of harm's way in case these men wouldn't take no for an answer.

"Is everything all right?" Her voice squeaked like an old hinge.

"Of course," Paul put in. "It's just business."

"He didn't break the law, did he?"

"They're not detectives," Wilbur told her. "They're crooks."

"We're businessmen," Paul blurted out. "We want to buy the pearl."

"Oh my, that ugly old thing?" She put her hand on her heart. "What on earth for?"

"I'm not selling it." Wilbur squared his shoulders to Paul. "Now you boys better get back to Beverly Hills and leave us alone."

"You're making a big mistake, Mister Cobb."

The pang in his chest returned with a vengeance. His left arm throbbed. This time the pain was bad enough for the nitro.

"Why do you keep it locked up?" Paul pressed. "Out of sight, when the pearl could be enjoyed by millions of people?"

Wilbur winced. "I'm doing you a favor. I'm saving your life. I'm sparing the world from Lao-Tzu's curse."

"Come now, Wilbur, you certainly don't believe in that crap."

Stepping between them, Elaine said, "He's not feeling well. You should talk about this some other time."

"There's nothing more to talk about." Wilbur's chest was

pounding so hard he couldn't stand up straight. "Show him out. I have to sit down." He staggered to his study, slammed shut the glass doors, and rushed to the desk drawer for his nitro tablets.

Back in the foyer, "Forgive my husband's rudeness," Elaine said to Paul Kaufman. "Please, allow me to see you to the door."

"He's a stubborn old man."

"Tell me about it." She opened the screen door, nodded to the man standing guard. "Who's your friend?"

Stepping out on the porch, Paul said, "An investor, ma'am, Vince Barber from Colorado Springs."

"I want to buy the Pearl of Allah," Barber said, his voice eerily deep. "Perhaps you can change your husband's mind."

She couldn't see the man's eyes behind his sunglasses, but she felt his stare. Glancing back and forth at the men, she fought a chill that squiggled up her neck bones. They didn't look like detectives, after all. They looked like mobsters.

"In case he changes his mind..." Barber stepped forward and handed her a business card. "Call me."

The card read: *The World's Largest Pearl Company, Inc.*

"What's this business about?"

Barber thrust his chin up. "I represent a group of investors seeking to purchase shares in the pearl. We're willing to pay a great deal."

She swallowed. The savings account was dwindling. These men could solve her money problem. Wilbur would be furious with her for asking, but, "How much?"

"It's negotiable, of course."

"How much?"

Barber looked at Paul Kaufman with pursed lips.

Paul nodded.

Barber said, "How does a hundred-grand sound?"

She grinned. They didn't know who they were dealing with. She was around in the old days when Gary Kaufman tried to buy the pearl from Wilbur for twice that much. "What are you boys, a couple of cons? You know it's worth two hundred grand."

"All right," Barber said. "We'll pay two hundred grand."

Kaufman looked like he was going to pop. "Your investors

have that much money?"

"We'll get the rest from Zimmerman," Barber said.

Elaine shivered at the sound of Zimmerman's name. She looked at her hands and remembered the time they were young, pretty, and soaked in Zimmerman's blood. These guys had no clue that she was the one who'd saved Zimmerman's life.

"So, Mrs. Cobb, perhaps you can take our offer to Wilbur," Barber added. "You can be our go-between."

"It won't do you any good." She sighed. "For years I've tried to convince him to sell the pearl. He won't listen."

"If we don't get that pearl," Barber spat. "Our investors won't be happy with us. We'll have to give back a lot of money."

"Or go swimming with concrete shoes and our hands tied behind our backs," Kaufman pressed in a grating voice, like his throat had suddenly dried up.

"The stakes are high, Mrs. Cobb." Barber seemed more determined than afraid.

Elaine blinked. These men had taken a lot for granted, already starting up a company when they didn't own the pearl. She looked behind her for any sign of Wilbur. He was still in his study, probably chucking nitro tablets like M&Ms.

She stepped out the door and closed it behind her. "You boys have to understand something. Wilbur won't sell the pearl. He believes it'll cause more suffering, for him and for anyone who buys it."

"We're not interested in superstitions," Paul assured her. "We want the pearl."

"As long as he's alive, you won't get it. Tell that to your investors, and Zimmerman."

"We know about Wilbur's health problems," Barber put in. "His past bouts with malaria have taken their toll on his body. His heart. His liver. His kidneys. It won't be long—"

"Don't say it." She bared her teeth. Wilbur's health could fail him at any time: today, next month, next year. He was only sixty-eight. She didn't want to hear how he was dying, not from his doctors and certainly not from these mobsters standing on her porch. "He's going to be all right."

"And if not?" Barber lowered his sunglasses and glared at

her with soulless gray eyes. "What are you going to do with the pearl then?"

She felt snared by his wicked stare. Wilbur had told her what to do. There was a safety deposit box. In it, the pearl, some expense money, and instructions to fly to Palawan. She was to rent a boat and toss the pearl overboard above the reef at the mouth of Boligay Creek Bay.

He didn't have the heart to dump the pearl himself. It would be like tossing Liawayway and the boys into the ocean, the Panglima, Pula and the Dyak tribe, his memories of a job he loved and a life he lost during the war, all gone by his own hand, sent to the bottom of the reef where it all began.

No, she would have to do the deed herself. She'd be broke in the process, a kind of financial suicide. His daughters wouldn't have an inheritance. Two hundred thousand dollars would be thrown to the fishes, just because a superstitious old man couldn't let go of his past.

She looked at the card in her hand. "I'll call you when Wilbur is d...d..." She couldn't say the word.

Chapter Fifty-Two

Pacific View Memorial Park, California, July, 1980

n the sprawling cemetery that overlooked the beach at Corona Del Mar, Elaine Cobb looked out over the green lawns that sloped down from the gravesite where mourners stood over Wilbur's coffin. In bad health, he had held on for five years. Meanwhile, their savings account had drained to nothing. Living on a pittance from Social Security was torture, all because Wilbur wouldn't part with his precious pearl. Well that was about to change.

A breeze played in the trees and carried the sweet aroma of freshly cut grass. She inhaled and dabbed tears from her eyes, tears of relief mixed with tears of sadness. No one attending the funeral would know the difference. With her daughters at her side, she placed a white rose on the coffin and kissed the polished wood.

"Goodbye, Wilbur."

The girls sobbed. Jean was thirty-two and married. Diane was twenty-nine and single. She and Wilbur had raised two fine young women, and she couldn't be prouder.

"I'll miss you, Dad," Diane said.

"He lived a good life," Jean added.

"Now girls..." Elaine turned to her daughters. "He wouldn't want us to be sad."

"I can't help it," Diane cried.

The minister opened his Bible. "Ashes to ashes, dust to dust, I commend you into the house of the Lord, Wilber Cobb." He made the sign of the cross over the grave. "Amen."

"Amen," murmured through the group of mourners.

"Everything is going to be all right." Elaine embraced the

girls and squeezed her eyes shut. "He gave me two beautiful daughters. He was a wonderful husband."

"If only his heart..." Diane sobbed, "hadn't given out."

"It was broken a long time ago," Elaine whispered, thinking of his Palawan princess. "We did well to have him at all."

She opened her eyes and saw a man standing on a knoll overlooking the proceedings. Dressed in black, he looked as if he could meld right into the small crowd that came to send Wilbur off to heaven. Even from this distance she could tell the man was Paul Kaufman. Rich Paul Kaufman. For a moment, she wished she were forty years younger. She'd give him a go he'd never forget.

"Who is he?" Diane asked.

Elaine didn't realize she'd been staring uphill. "Nobody to worry about, dear."

As the minister walked away, well-wishers moved toward Elaine. She painted on her sad face, greeted folks, and every once in a while cast a glance up the hill at Kaufman. He was waiting like a vulture perched on a high branch.

As the last guests departed, Kaufman approached, his hair tied back in a ponytail and an inappropriate smile on his face. "Mrs. Cobb."

"Wait for me in the limo, girls," Elaine said, not wanting them to hear what Kaufman had to say. "I'll be there in a minute."

"What's he want, Mother?" Jean asked.

"He's an old friend of your father's."

"He looks creepy. I don't trust him."

"It's all right. Run along, now."

As the girls walked downhill toward the limo, Elaine felt a sense of duty to her daughters. Their father had left them nothing. They deserved an inheritance, and she was going to make sure they got one. Whether Wilbur would have agreed or not, she was doing the right thing.

"Paul," she said, glowering, hand outstretched. "You couldn't wait for my call?"

"Mrs. Cobb, you're looking well." He bent like a prince and pecked the back of her age-spotted hand. "I saw the obituary and funeral notice. Hope you don't mind if I pay my respects."

"You never had any respect for Wilbur. My girls are here, my friends. This is no place to discuss business."

"Listen." He glanced back and forth as if the boogieman might be watching him. "I had to see you before Barber arrives. He'll be here tomorrow. They know Wilbur died."

"They who?"

"Zimmerman and the investors."

Mobsters was more like it. "His casket's not even in the ground. What's the hurry?"

His nervous eyes fluttered. "It's complicated."

Wilbur was so close, just an arm's length away, in the casket, dead, but still she worried that he'd hear her betray him. "Let's walk."

He offered his elbow.

Such a gallant gesture for a mobster. She cast a parting glance to the casket over her shoulder. *It'll be all right, Wilbur. You're safe from the pearl now.*

Paul Kaufman spoke as he walked. "It's imperative that I purchase the pearl from you directly, before Vince Barber low-balls you again."

"He seemed like such a nice man," she said, though she doubted it. Kaufman didn't have much time to convince her to make a deal with him. The limo was fifty yards away. The girls were leaning on the front fender, watching her and the jeweler come down the hill.

"He's not to be trusted," Paul went on.

"What do you propose, Mister Kaufman?"

"Two hundred thousand dollars, certified funds, tomorrow morning, transferred to your account, before Barber gets here."

"Oh dear," she said, trying to sound dumb. "Won't that get you in trouble with your *investors*?"

"You let me worry about Barber. It's you I'm concerned about now. If Zimmerman didn't come through with a loan, Barber will offer you less. I've got the money, all of it, myself."

"Why Mister Kaufman, chivalry is not dead. Two hundred fifty thousand—"

"Two hundred fifty? Mrs. Cobb. Be realistic. We already agreed on two hundred grand."

"Perhaps I should wait to hear what Mister Barber has to offer, don't you think?" Paul may have taken over his father's jewelry business, but to Elaine, he was just a punk kid.

Thirty yards and closing on the limo. Time to tighten the screws on the punk's wallet. "His *investors* might not think kindly of you going behind their backs. Two-fifty sounds about right."

"I've only got two hundred thousand dollars, Mrs. Cobb. That's a reasonable offer for the pearl."

They were getting closer to the limo. She had a decision to make, take a sure thing with Kaufman's money, or wait for Barber to jack her around.

She grabbed Paul's suit coat sleeve, yanked him to a stop, and looked him straight in the eye. "I may be old, but I'm not stupid. I'll take the two hundred thousand bucks, in cash, nine o'clock tomorrow morning, Manufacturers Hanover Bank, or your *investors* will be fitting you with cement shoes by midnight. You got that?"

Kaufman grinned. "Will you have the pearl with you?"

Nodding, she glanced at her girls waiting at the limo. "And I don't want my daughters to know where the money came from."

"I won't say a word."

She released his arm. "Don't be late."

Chapter Fifty-Three

Manufacturers Hanover Bank

A t nine o'clock sharp, Elaine swallowed frayed nerves and watched a bank officer open the vault. She wished she'd slept better. Wilbur's voice had tormented her all night. *Don't do it, Elaine. Don't do it.*

She glanced around the lobby of plush carpet and crystal chandeliers, but Paul Kaufman was nowhere in sight. Gritting her teeth, she wondered if the jeweler had second thoughts about one-upping his investors.

"Right this way, ma'am," the officer said.

She followed him down a hallway lined with lock-boxes in the walls, where he located number 1123: Wilbur's treasure chest. She imagined him walking down this hallway, his forehead sweating, his hands trembling as he hid away his precious pearl.

"Ma'am." The bank officer had produced a key.

"Oh, yes, of course." She removed a key of her own.

He indicated the lock for her key and inserted his into an adjacent slot.

With trembling fingers, she pushed her key in and gave it a twist. A click. Sweat beaded on her forehead.

The officer turned his key. A clank. He grasped a handle on the front of the box and slid it from the wall, juggling it a bit.

"Don't drop it." She removed her key from the lock.

"It's heavier than I expected."

He led her into a windowless room with gold-framed pictures of past Presidents on the wall. A richly polished walnut table surrounded by leather chairs sat in the center of the room. The familiar scent of furniture polish floated in the air.

The Pearl of Death

"Will this be all right?" He indicated a chair.

"Thank you." Tucking her blue and white summer dress under her legs, she sat in the chair and set her handbag on the table.

As if the deposit box were a birthday cake with lighted candles, he carefully set it in front of her. "I'll be right outside."

"I'm expecting a Mr. Kaufman to arrive."

"Shall I show him right in?"

Not having seen the pearl for over forty years, she wanted to be alone with it a few minutes. "I'll tell you when it's okay."

"As you wish." He walked out and closed the door.

Heart pounding, she stared at the box. It sparkled like gold. A chrome key slot glistened under the ceiling lights.

She licked her upper lip. Electricity jumped up and down her spine, made the hair on the back of her neck tingle.

Alone with the pearl at last, she looked at the key in her hand. All she had to do was unlock the box and claim her fortune. Trembling fingers inserted the key, but she couldn't turn it. Wilbur's voice shouted in her head.

Don't do it, Elaine.

She rubbed her palms together. It was only natural that she hesitated, after years of listening to Wilbur's banter about the pearl's curse. Fear was pulling on her reins. If Wilbur was right about the curse, something terrible would happen to her... No, she hadn't believed him before. Why would she now? Still there was the guilt gnawing at her stomach. She was going against her husband's last wishes, but selling the pearl shouldn't surprise him. She'd harped on him for decades... No. Her hesitation was totally unfounded.

She twisted the key. The lid popped open. She half expected to see a beam of light shoot out, a hiss of air, or trumpets blaring. Clenching her jaw, she lifted the lid, and peered inside.

A blue velvet cloth covered the contents. It wasn't too late. She could close the lid and leave, but curiosity and her desperate financial situation pressed her onward. She unfolded the cloth. Nestled in velvet lay the Pearl of Lao-Tzu, gleaming, its iridescent luster stealing her breath. It was a magnificent sight. Lying beside the pearl, there was a brown envelope, a big brown envelope. Folded. From Wilbur... She took it out of the box.

Inside, she found a bundle of money and a note from Wilbur, handwritten:

If you are reading this, it means that I am gone. Here's enough money to get you to Palawan, directions from Puerto Princesa to Boligay Creek, instructions where to rent a boat, and a map that shows where to sink this pearl in the sea.

She removed the money, ten packs of one hundred dollar bills, rubber-banded together, she counted, ten per pack... *Ten thousand dollars!* A bolt of anger jolted her. They'd been living in poverty while the old fool had this much money stashed.

Elaine, the note went on, *do the right thing. Don't sell the pearl. It will only bring you suffering, and maybe Diane and Jean. I'm counting on you to fulfill my wishes. It's for your own good. I loved you all, Wilbur.*

"You loved us?" she growled. "You cheated us, Wilbur. But I'm going to set things right, once and for all."

Now the pearl seized her attention. Setting aside the money, she touched the lustrous, lumpy surface of Lao-Tzu's creation.

How could anything so beautiful be dangerous?

She wrapped her fingers around the pearl. As she lifted it, her previous fears evaporated. It felt solid and heavy, and its features resembled the turbaned head of a man, just as she remembered it, with distinct askew eyes, a flat nose, and droopy mouth.

Wilbur had thought the pearl was ugly.

"Beauty is in the eye of the beholder," she whispered. This beauty was going to make her rich.

As she drew the heavy pearl to her chest and cradled it like a child, its pearly essence glowed under the ceiling lights. Only twice before had she experienced such a warm feeling in her heart, when each of her daughters were born. Now she imagined gold and diamonds glittering from her fingers, her neck, and her ears. Fashion and flowers, bright city lights, and strains of classical music. "It's beautiful, Wilbur," she said, entranced by the spiritual uplifting she felt. There *was* a God. She had touched his face...

A knock came at the door. "He's here," the officer said.

His voice broke the trance. "What?" She realized her heart was beating hard.

"Paul Kaufman. Should I let him in, ma'am?"

"No...no...in a minute." God, what had just happened to her? How much time had passed?

With one hand, she fluffed the blue velvet cloth on the table, and with both hands, she set the pearl on the cloth, as gently as she would lay down a sleeping infant. She jammed the envelope and money into her handbag, took out a tissue, and dabbed sweat from her forehead. Opening her compact, she saw her flushed reflection and patted powder on her face to cover it up. Satisfied her lipstick wasn't smudged, she checked to see her teeth were clean then snapped closed the compact and put it away.

Shoulders back, she fought for composure and took a deep breath. Exhaling, she felt as ready as ever to begin her new life. "Officer?"

"Yes, ma'am," he replied from behind the door.

"Send him in."

The door clicked open.

Paul Kaufman stepped in carrying a brown satchel. He wore a tan V-necked sweater, white shirt, and a gold chain necklace. "Good morning, Mrs. Cobb."

The officer closed the door. She felt claustrophobic, trapped inside the vault with a mobster. She wanted to get this over with as quickly as possible. "Did you bring the money?"

Mute, he set the satchel on the table and fixed his gaze on the pearl. "May I?" he asked, pointing.

"The money, Mr. Kaufman."

Without removing his eyes from the pearl, he said, "I've every right to examine the merchandise before we close the deal."

He was stalling. She didn't trust him. "Show me the money first."

He stared at the pearl.

Her nerves began to unravel. She fought to keep them from crippling her resolve. "The money. I need to see the money."

His dark eyes darted to hers. "What's the rush?"

She glared at him with equal intensity. "I've got an

appointment with my manicurist. I don't want to be late."

Shifting his eyes from her to the pearl and back, he opened the satchel, removed a fat brown sack tied with a string and plopped it on the table, just out of her reach. "It's all there."

As she leaned forward to take it, he grabbed her wrist. "After I inspect the merchandise."

She clenched her fist. "Let go of me or I'll scream."

"I need to know this isn't one of Wilbur's replicas," he said, showing teeth. "If you scream, the deal is off."

"I mean it. I will—"

"And I'll tell my *investors* you tried to bilk them with a phony. See how long before your feet are fitted with concrete shoes."

She wouldn't put it past him, but she needed to be sure he wasn't about to cheat her the same way he was trying to cheat his investors. "I need to know there's money in that sack and not a bunch of cut up newspaper."

"You're as stubborn as your husband."

"I take that as a compliment."

He released her wrist, untied the sack, and dumped the money out on the table. "Ten thousand per bundle, twenty bundles." The pile of money looked bigger than the sack. "Are you satisfied now?"

It was more cash than she'd ever seen. Her heart beat faster. "The pearl is authentic," she said, forcing calm. "It's the largest pearl in the world. The Pearl of Allah, The Pearl of Lao-Tzu, call it what you like. It's yours now."

Kaufman shoved the deposit box aside, slid the velvet cloth and pearl to him. Picking it up with both hands, he tested its weight, turned it over and over, and inspected every lump, crease, and ripple.

"It's not a fake," she said.

He didn't say anything, opened his mouth, and rubbed the pearl against his upper teeth.

"What are you doing?"

"An imitation pearl feels smooth against a tooth. A real pearl feels gritty." He licked his upper teeth. "This one is gritty."

"I'm too old to play games with you, Mr. Kaufman."

He wrapped the pearl in the velvet cloth and tucked it into

his satchel. His face shined with sweat. "It's been a pleasure doing business with you, Mrs. Cobb." Tucking the satchel tight up under his arm, he quickstepped to the door. "Officer."

The door opened. He squeezed past the bank officer and was gone.

"Everything okay, Mrs. Cobb?"

"Yes...fine." Elaine started stacking the money bundles, keeping her body between the officer and the cash. "One minute."

"Whenever you're ready." He closed the door.

One by one, she stuffed the bundles into her handbag. Then two at a time. Her hands shook with excitement. There was so much money she couldn't fit it all in her handbag. She didn't want to walk out of the bank carrying a sack of cash, so she put the overflow into the deposit box.

She couldn't wait to get started on her new life. There were fashions she'd longed to wear, perfumes she'd only tested at the sales counter, and furnishings for the house that would erase the memory of Wilbur's presence. She could travel again: New York, Chicago, even Paris if she wanted.

The deposit box, too, was quickly filled. There wasn't any more money on the table. This brought her to an epiphany. The money could be easily spent. It wouldn't last forever.

She clutched the stuffed handbag to her chest. How could she make this windfall last and still live in luxury? The girls would need to get some of this money. If she kept it all to herself, they'd be suspicious of her newfound wealth.

Five thousand each, she decided. The money Wilbur had left her to go to the Philippines. That would be the girl's money to split.

She would keep the two hundred grand for herself. After forty years with Wilbur, she'd earned it.

Chapter Fifty-Four

The next day

While traffic on the California freeway sped by at seventy miles an hour, Diane Cobb's 1968 Ford Bronco rattled and banged along at a laborious fifty. Her four-wheel-drive truck was on its last leg. The fenders were rusted and the tires were bald. She didn't have the money to fix the front end, but it usually got her where she was going. Usually.

Today, she and Jean were on their way to her parents' house in Laguna Beach. Mother had unexpected news about their father's estate. Seems they'd inherited some money, after all.

Glancing at Jean riding shotgun, Diane thought her sister looked overdressed in her white slacks and a red blazer. She was a businesswoman, owned a real estate company. Jean had everything going for her, fancy home, fancy car, fancy husband. On the other hand, Diane worked for UPS, wore brown shorts, wool socks, high-top boots and liked getting her hands greasy in the garage. She'd probably die a spinster.

Wrestling the loose steering wheel, she wondered how much money Dad left them and hoped her share would be enough to buy new ball joints for her Bronco.

"We should've taken my car," Jean said, her pretty face pinched. "I hate this piece of junk."

"You always drive to Mom and Dad's, just to show off, I'm sure."

"It's Mom's house now."

"You should rough it with your little sister more often, see how the other half lives."

"Ya all livin' like the poe' folks," Jean said in her fake

Southern accent then laughed.

"Very funny."

A semi blew past. The unexpected gust of wind pushed the Bronco into the next lane. Horns honked. The steering wheel started shaking, the ball joints were that loose. Diane fought for control, thankful there wasn't a car alongside her.

She punched the gas. The engine popped and surged. Damn fuel pump was acting up again. "Come on, baby." She patted the dash. "Be good to your mamma."

"Maybe you should buy a new car," Jean said. "With your share of the inheritance."

"Dad didn't have much. What could I buy?"

"Anything's better than this junker."

Ahead, the exit ramp for Laguna Beach appeared. Diane flipped on her right turn signal. "I like my truck just fine, thank you. I could fix it myself if I had the money for parts."

Jean frowned. "Tomboy."

There wasn't anything wrong with that. She drove down the exit ramp and merged with traffic on the boulevard. She'd always been more rough-and-tumble than her prissy sister.

Accelerating, the engine hacked and coughed. A taxi swerved around her. The driver gave her a middle finger.

Diane flipped him off. "Bozo!"

Pumping the gas, she kept the Bronco moving. Maybe Jean was right. A new car might not be a bad idea, but she doubted her father had left enough money for that extravagance. Besides, Mom had to fly to the Philippines to get rid of the pearl.

A railroad track crossed the road up ahead. The drawbar was up and the warning lights were off. Diane looked up and down the tracks. No train.

"Do you think it's true about a curse on the pearl?"

"I don't know what to believe."

The Bronco hit the railroad tracks so hard the impact sent a shudder through the frame followed by a bone-chilling bang. It sounded like the left front tire blew. The jolt caused the inertia switch to trip and shut off the engine. With a jarring clunk, the Bronco lurched like a trapped animal and stopped on the tracks.

"Not now." Diane turned the key to crank the engine. Nothing. "How could the battery be dead?"

"Try it again," Jean said.

Still nothing.

"A cable must've shorted out." Trying to see humor in their predicament, Diane clawed the air with bent fingers, "It's the curse of the pearl, he, he, he," and hummed the opening bars of *The Twilight Zone*.

"You're sick. I'm getting a cab." Jean pulled on the door handle...then pulled on it again. "What's the matter with this damn thing?"

"It's got a bad latch," Diane released her seat belt. "That door always gives me trouble."

Cars went around them, honking.

She leaned over Jean's lap to open the door herself. It wouldn't budge.

The railroad crossing alarm started dinging.

She looked up, frozen at the sight of the drawbars coming down, in front of her and behind her.

Jean started yanking on the handle so hard the Bronco rocked on its bad shocks. "Open up, you piece of shit!"

"Get out my door. Come on. You can crawl over."

The warning bells kept dinging. A low rumble rose in the distance.

Fighting panic, Diane knew there was plenty of time to get out. She pulled on her door handle. The latch popped, but the door wouldn't swing open. She pushed harder, but the door kept springing back. The gap wasn't wide enough to squeeze through. Slamming her shoulder into the door, she wished they'd taken the Mercedes. She wished she'd taken better care of her Bronco.

The loud grumble of diesel locomotives bore down on the Bronco, and like the howl of a storm, the train's whistle blared.

Diane's nape hairs tried to leap out of her skin.

"Hurry!" Jean shrieked.

"Something's wrong!" Diane leaned out the window to see what was wrong. The tire wasn't flat. It was jammed against the inner fender, shoving it backward into the door. No wonder it wouldn't open. "A ball joint must've broken."

"Crawl out, crawl out," Jean shouted, pushing on Diane's legs.

The scream of train brakes tore through the air.

Panic fueled her legs and arms. Pumping and flailing, she wriggled through the open window, got her butt halfway out, but her legs were suddenly pinned.

Jean was pressing against her, trying to get the door open.

"I can't move."

"Let me out." Jean shoved on Diane's legs, seemingly unaware that her panic was impeding their escape. "Let me out."

Struggling to pull her legs free, Diane glanced up over the roof and saw the train engine roaring toward her, big as a building, the headlight bright as the sun. Her jaw clamped shut, and she clenched her fists.

Jean screamed.

Steel struck metal with a crushing bang.

Silence.

Chapter Fifty-Five

Beverly Hills

In the back room of Kaufman Jewelers, a desk fan whirred. The swirling air did little to relieve the heat or cool the sweat on Paul Kaufman's brow. He sat behind his desk, shoved the clutter of papers aside, and set down the velvet-cloaked pearl. Careful as a surgeon, he peeled back the cloth, revealing the luster of his newly acquired prize. The Pearl of Allah was about to make him a rich man.

Staring at the pearl, he felt dizzy. The elation in his stomach turned to nausea, as if he'd just eaten something rotten. Three evil faces appeared in the pearl, their eyes shifting back and forth. Demon eyes. An aura of doom enveloped him, deep down inside. He felt alone. Hot fear sizzled in his chest. The fires of hell rose up around him. Choking smoke burned his lungs. He couldn't breathe. He couldn't scream. Echoing laughter filled his mind with terror.

All the clocks on the walls started chiming.

He lurched in his chair. Heart pounding, he remembered the curse of Lao-Tzu and pushed back from the pearl. The damn thing had just scared the hell out of him. Or was he going crazy? How could he hallucinate like that? His mind must've been playing on Wilbur Cobb's fears.

Still sweating, he felt foolish but thankful his collection of clocks had broken the frightening spell. It was three o'clock. Vince Barber's plane should have landed at Orange County by now. He was probably on his way to the store. The biggest deal in the history of Kaufman Jewelers was about to go down. His dad would have been proud.

Energized by the thought of his newfound wealth, he

draped the blue velvet cloth over the pearl. He didn't want to look at it anymore for fear of reliving those visions of hell again, so he gathered up his father's notes on the desktop.

The pearl is worth millions, he'd written. He'd outlined a scheme to sell shares in the world's largest pearl. Rich people would pay a lot for those bragging rights. Kaufman wasn't interested in a long-term investment. He was going to turn the pearl quickly for a huge profit. All he had to do was put the squeeze on Vince Barber without getting killed in the process.

***

The limo cruised down Santa Monica Boulevard. Vince hated California. The place was hot and sticky and smelled like burned rubber, but he was dressed for the weather: white slacks, black short-sleeve shirt. He checked the time on his Rolex. *3:30 PM.* Kaufman had better be ready to go. They had to meet Mrs. Cobb. They were going to get their hands on Wilbur's pearl.

In the briefcase on the seat next to him, he carried a hundred grand, enough money to buy the pearl from the old widow. *More like steal it.* Sure, they'd agreed on two hundred thousand, but he figured she'd take this cash and run.

The limo parked at the curb in front of Kaufman Jewelers. The driver got out and opened the rear passenger door. "Will you be long, sir?"

"Only a moment." Vince got out, taking the briefcase with him. The muggy heat hit him like a water balloon. He smelled the unexpected aroma of fresh bread wafting from the bakery next door. Donning sunglasses, he wanted to seal this deal and fly back to Colorado Springs where the air was cooler and drier.

A sign on the door said the store was closed. He shaded his eyes from the glare on the glass and peered in. Beyond the open blinds hanging on the door, he saw rows of jewelry display cases and hundreds of clocks hanging on the walls. A light shined from the backroom doorway. The jeweler was in there somewhere. He pounded a fist on the door. "Kaufman."

"He's closed," a woman's voice said.

Barber turned to see a fat woman standing in front of the bakery next door. "Mind your own business, lady."

She huffed, "Asshole," and turned back inside.

Paul appeared at the door. His face looked chalk-white as he turned the deadbolt. The door swung open.

Vince stepped back. "Let's go. The meter is running."

"There's been a change of plans," Kaufman said, still holding the door open. Sweat bathed his neck. "Come in."

Vince gave the jeweler a slanted look. "You sick?"

"Sir?"

"You look as nervous as a school girl in a porn shop."

"There's something I need to show you." He waved him in.

Vince glanced at the limo driver leaning on the front fender and gave him the one-minute sign with his index finger.

"Yes, sir."

Then Vince wagged the same finger at Paul Kaufman. "You better not be wasting my time."

"I've got an offer you can't refuse."

Vince scowled at the reference to *The Godfather*. "I hope you're not getting in over your head."

"Just hear me out."

Inside, Kaufman locked the door and closed the blinds. Turning suddenly, he slammed Vince against a jewelry case like a cop tossing a crook on the hood of a police car. "Spread 'em."

"What's the fuckin' matter with you?"

"Got any heat on you?" He frisked Vince's shirt and pant-legs.

"I'm not packing," Vince said with his face pressed into the glass case of rings and watches. Kaufman was sick, all right, mentally deranged. A hand went up Vince's crotch and down his ass. His first instinct was to kill the prick, but he had to give him credit for not taking any chances. "You getting your rocks off, boy?"

"You're not my type." Kaufman yanked the briefcase out of Vince's hand. Any sign of nervousness was gone. Briefcase set aside, Kaufman stood him upright. "But I feel better now."

"Good for you." Vince glanced at his briefcase. "I've got the money, so what's with all the theatrics?"

He cocked his head to the backroom. "I've got something to show you."

"Mrs. Cobb? She's here?"

"Better." Kaufman shoved him toward the back doorway.

"My briefcase—"

"It's not going anywhere."

In the backroom, a lamp hung from a chain above a cluttered desk where Kaufman stopped. "Get a load of this." He lifted a blue velvet cloth, unveiling the huge pearl that glowed on the desktop. "The Pearl of Allah."

Vince couldn't take his eyes off the baroque gem. He'd seen pictures, but this, in real life, was magnificent. "How did you get it?"

"I made a deal with Mrs. Cobb."

The way Kaufman grinned, Vince figured it had to have been a one-sided deal. "I smell a monkey fuck."

Kaufman wrapped the pearl like a newborn and moved to a wall safe. "I don't want anything to do with your World's Largest Pearl Company." He opened the safe's door and placed the pearl on a shelf inside. "However, we both realize you're out of business without my pearl."

"Your pearl?" Vince wished he had brought a gun. "We were partners."

The thick safe door closed with a dull thud. He spun the dial. "Now I'm calling the shots."

Without the pearl, the company and his plans to get rich were useless. Vince had no choice but to barter with the backstabber. "What do you want?"

"Three hundred fifty thousand dollars," Kaufman said and strutted back to the desk like some cocky rooster. "Cash."

Vince's heart almost stopped. "I only have a hundred grand, in the briefcase."

Kaufman sat behind the desk. "The deal was 200K to Mrs. Cobb."

"I figured I'd lowball her."

"You see why I don't want to do business with you?"

"For Christ's sake, be reasonable. I don't have that much money."

"But you do have connections... I believe you called them *investors*."

Jabbing a finger at the jeweler, Vince seethed. "You son of a bitch. I'll kill you."

Kaufman pulled a gun. "Don't do anything stupid."

Vince looked at the gun and wished he was Superman. He'd put his finger in the barrel and dare the bastard to pull the trigger. "You really think you're going to get away with screwing me?"

"You may be a big-dick in Colorado, but you're a just a butt-pimple here in California. Do we have a deal, or would you rather I go public?"

Vince flinched. Kaufman could sell the pearl at auction. That would be a death sentence for the *World's Largest Pearl Company*. He had big plans. He was going to sell shares. He was going to make millions. To avoid a total loss he'd have to salvage something from this toilet-bobber. "I can come up with two K more, that's it, plus what's in the briefcase. Three hundred grand for the pearl, then I never want to see your dumbass again."

Kaufman rose, all puffed up. "You've got forty-eight hours." He pushed Vince through the store toward the front door, gun prodding the way, stopping only to pick up the briefcase and tuck it under his arm.

Vince weighed a quick turn and a right uppercut to Kaufman's jaw against the speed and punch of a bullet. The bullet won without even leaving the gun.

Kaufman turned the deadbolt and opened the front door. "And come alone." He shoved him outside and locked the door.

"Bastard."

Seated in the limo, Vince opened the bar and found a bottle of Jack Daniels. Each swallow went down fire-hot. As the car sped away from the curb, his guts churned with dread. He needed money, fast. The only way to get it was to borrow it from Ralph Zimmerman, the real Godfather.

***

Two days later, a chartered Learjet screamed down the runway and climbed into a crystal blue sky over Colorado Springs. Onboard, Vince Barber tried to get comfortable in a leather high-back seat. It wasn't easy. He hadn't slept, and his nerves were tingling like short-circuited wires. On the floor at his feet lay a briefcase filled with two hundred thousand dollars of Ralph Zimmerman's money. Mob money. Vince's ass was in a sling over it. If anything went wrong, he'd end up floating face down in Pueblo Reservoir.

In the opposite seat, Zimmerman's enforcer, Roberto Delgado, gazed out the oval cabin window. He wore an all-black business suit and carried a black gun in his coat pocket. Vince had seen it before they boarded. A Glock, thirteen rounds in the clip, all with Paul Kaufman's name engraved in the lead. He'd get his money, all right, but he wouldn't keep it for long, the backstabbing bastard.

As the plane leveled out, the pilot's voice came over the intercom. "Good morning, gentlemen. We've reached our cruising altitude of 37,000 feet. Expect to arrive at John Wayne Airport in approximately an hour and twenty minutes. Enjoy the flight to Orange County."

Vince tried to relax, thought about the plan. It required split-second timing. Delgado would have to be at the top of his game. And quick. Get in. Get out. But Vince worried that Delgado didn't have enough experience with only two hits to his credit—two defenseless women—that was all. How well would he handle killing a man?

"Delgado," Vince said. "One more time."

The hit man looked at him with gray eyes, his thin lips a hard line of determination. "I know what to do."

"If Kaufman has time to lock the money in his safe, we're both in big trouble with Zimmerman."

"Don't worry."

"I'm worried. That's why we're going over the plan again."

Groaning, Delgado withdrew the gun from his jacket. "I wait in front of the store..."

Chapter Fifty-Six

Delgado paid the driver. The cab sped off and the hired killer looked up and down Santa Monica Boulevard, noted heavy traffic but few pedestrians. A block away, the store marquee hung over the sidewalk:

Jewels and Dreams, the Bigger the Better.

"Sweet dreams, Kaufman."

The limo carrying Vince Barber would arrive in ten minutes.

With a casual stroll, Delgado made his way to a newspaper machine and bought a paper. Then he moved into position in front of the jewelry store, leaned against a lamppost. Happy as a girl scout counting her cookie money, he opened the paper and hid his face from the street. He'd seen it done this way in the movies. Doing it for real made his pulse race and his palms sweat. People passing by didn't know how dangerous he was, how close to a killer they had come. They were so busy in their own little worlds that they wouldn't notice him; they wouldn't connect him to events that would soon make the five o'clock news.

Right on time, a car pulled up to the curb, not ten feet away. Delgado didn't have to look over the paper to know it was the limo. Anyone else would have shut off the engine by now. He heard the doors open and close. A good hit man didn't need to see these things, only sense them. And he was the best damn hit man in the business. When this was over, the Chicago boys would know his name and personally request his services.

***

Vince got out of the limo, saw Delgado reading a newspaper and hoped he was paying attention. A woman came out of the bakery next door. A little ways down, two girls played hopscotch. "One two, buckle my shoe. Three four, close the door."

Vince loosened his tie. "Five six, kill the prick."

Briefcase in hand, he went directly to the front door of Kaufman Jewelers. This time Kaufman was waiting there, and as he unlocked the door, Vince saw Delgado's reflection in the glass, nose still in the newspaper.

Vince had to step back to allow the door to swing open. One step forward, his body could stop the door from closing. Two more steps, he was inside. "I'm not packing," he said. "You can check, but you don't have to rough me up."

Kaufman locked the deadbolt and pulled a snub-nose .38. "Set it on the counter."

A knot twisted in Vince's stomach. "You don't need a gun."

"The briefcase. Now."

Slowly, Vince set it on the display case, raised his hands. "It's all there, two hundred grand. Just put it in your safe, give me the pearl, and I'm outta here."

"Assume the position," Kaufman waved the gun.

Vince faced the counter and spread his legs.

One handed, Kaufman frisked him.

Vince felt violated. "Satisfied?"

He backed away.

"Can I put my hands down now?"

When Kaufman didn't say anything, Vince realized he'd put himself in a vulnerable position. All the jeweler had to do was shoot him, lock the money in his safe, and tell the cops he'd killed a robber. His having a damn gun wasn't in the plan. Worse, he had the means to defend himself against Delgado.

"Come on, Paul. We've known each other too long for this. I knew your father." Hands still raised, he turned around, saw Kaufman at the window looking out a chink in the blind. Did he see Delgado? Did he suspect Delgado? "What's wrong?"

"Did you come alone?"

"Just the limo driver. It's an airport service. He doesn't know anything."

Kaufman turned from the window, wagged the gun. "Get

the briefcase."

"Take it easy with the gun, will you?" The last thing Vince wanted was to get shot before his plan got off the ground. He pulled the briefcase from the counter.

Kaufman muscled him into the backroom. Vince scanned the place for anyone else, any possible ambush. The room was empty. "I just want to get back to Colorado."

With the swipe of his arm, Kaufman cleared a swath across the desk, paper flying. "Let's see the money."

"Sure." Vince opened the briefcase and dumped the cash on the desk. Two thousand loose one hundred dollar bills fell out and scattered everywhere.

The look of shock on Kaufman's face almost made Vince bust out laughing. Almost. The beauty of delivering the money this way was the amount of time it would take Kaufman to pick it all up.

"Smart ass." Paul stabbed the gun behind his waistband, shuffled through the loot as if checking for funny money. Vince knew better than to run a scam on the jeweler. Authenticity was the only way to pull off the plan.

"Congratulations," Paul said, turning to the safe. He worked the combination dial. The door opened. "Your investors have just bought the world's largest pearl."

"It wasn't supposed to go down this way, Paul. Because of you, I'm in hock up to my neck. Zimmerman doesn't want any part of this pearl, just twenty percent on the loan."

"Careful of the friends you keep." Kaufman extracted the pearl, and still wrapped in blue velvet, offered it to Vince.

Careful who you try to fuck. Vince took the pearl from the backstabber. It felt heavy and lumpy under the cloth, but just to be sure, he peeled back a corner, saw the pearl's luster and quickly covered it again.

By that time, Kaufman had already begun gathering up his money. "Good doing business with you, Vince."

He set the pearl in the briefcase and snapped the latches shut. "Yeah, I'm all choked up. Now let me out of here."

"Not until the money is in the safe and the safe is locked."

It was going to take a while to transfer it all to the safe. "Let me out first. The limo's meter is running."

"You can afford it." Already Kaufman had gathered up a handful of money. He moved to the safe and put it on a shelf.

Damn. Vince had to get that front door open. "Never mind. I'll let myself out."

"Hold your horses," Kaufman said, returning to the desk for more money.

"Fuck you." Vince headed for the front door.

"Stop."

Click!

He recognized the sound of a cocking gun, gritted his teeth but kept walking.

"Don't make me splatter your brains all over my store."

"You've got your money. I've got my pearl. Our business is finished. I'm leaving."

"You go when I say you can go."

Vince stopped at the door and turned to Kaufman. "What's the matter with you, boy? I could be halfway to the airport by now."

He looked at the gun, shook his head, and glanced over his shoulder at the pile of money on the desk. "The door stays closed until my safe is secure. It's the way I do business."

"Christ." Vince reached up, twisted the deadbolt.

"Don't." Paul rushed forward.

Vince pushed his way outside, hesitated just long enough for Delgado to brush by, then dashed to the limo.

Gunfire popped behind him.

He swung open the rear car door. Blaring heavy metal music nearly blew him backward. The driver had his face in a porn magazine.

"Move it!" Vince shouted over the noise.

Startled, the driver tossed the magazine on the floor, peeled away from the curb, and shut off the music. "Sorry, sir."

"Just get me back to the airport." Vince set the briefcase on his lap. His hands were shaking, his palms sweating. That was too close. But he was sure the driver hadn't seen or heard anything.

The limo careened around a corner and headed toward the airport. Delgado had thirty minutes to get the money and meet them at the plane.

Inside Kaufman Jewelers, bullets flew. Glass displays exploded, and shards shot through the air in a flurry of glistening shrapnel. Clocks jumped from the back wall and crashed to the floor, dinging and chiming.

Head down, Delgado ducked between two jewelry cases, popped up, and squeezed off two rounds at his target, Paul Kaufman. The bastard had a gun.

Fucking Barber didn't say nothing about no gun.

Delgado dove back down to the floor, ducking under a shower of tinkling glass. *Fucking Kaufman.* The son-of-a-bitch was going to kill him.

Crawling toward the back of the store, Delgado knew he had to outflank the jeweler, and quickly. Gunfire wouldn't go unnoticed for long. Someone was bound to call the cops. That would mean arrest and trial, the end of the greatest hit man in mob history.

A barrage of gunfire blasted the counter and sent wood splinters ripping through the air like flying razor blades.

"Shit!" Maybe this hit man business wasn't such a good idea, after all. He remembered how easily he'd killed the two women. But this target was stark-raving mad, firing away at every movement, every sound. And he had good reason to be trigger-happy. He was defending his money.

The gunfire stopped. Delgado figured his target was reloading, a revolver by the clicking sound that each bullet made as it dropped into the cylinder, six clicks, a six-shooter, probably a thirty-eight caliber. A good hit man knew his guns.

The barrage started up again. Cabinets spit out a storm of watches and rings that clunked and pinged all around him. Damn! He should have popped Kaufman when he was reloading.

Heart hammering, Delgado fought to remain calm. He kept his head down and counted the shots. After six, silence again.

This would be the time to jump him, but Delgado noticed a nice Rolex lying on the floor by his knee. He picked it up, slipped it on over his black glove, and savored the feel of gold against his wrist. Then he saw a ring, big diamond, thick band. That went into his pocket. He was rich—

The shooting started again.

The Pearl of Death

Two shots knocked a mannequin bust off the counter, breaking a necklace and flinging pearls through the air like hailstones. Two more shots blew holes in the case next to him. Obviously, Kaufman had no idea where he was hiding. Another shot tore through a display case of earrings. His last shot hit a cabinet two rows away. Then silence.

Kaufman was reloading. His head would be down. It was time to show him how a real hit man worked. He picked up a watch with a shattered face and stood, gun outstretched in one hand, sweeping left and right. The target wasn't in sight, as he'd expected. He tossed the watch into the far corner. It bounced off a counter and banged against the wall.

Kaufman bobbed up. He fired into the corner.

Delgado squeezed the trigger.

There was nothing like the sound of a bullet tearing into flesh. Made a sort of *thwap!* sound. Blood sprayed from Kaufman's chest. He crashed into a display case and keeled over.

Delgado started toward his downed target. The fire of adrenaline raged in his bloodstream, which now wracked his gun hand with tremors. The tart odor of gun smoke scented the air.

A warm sensation of pride glowed inside him. Glass and jewels crunched under his boots. He stopped and looked around at the destroyed glass cases, bullet-riddled walls, and debris-strewn floor. It was probably the messiest hit in mob history. If word got out about this, his reputation would be ruined. No respectful mobster would ever hire a sloppy hit man.

"Goddamn you, Vince Barber," he growled. Vince knew Kaufman had a gun. It was a trap. But why?

Phillips and Giodano...they were in bed with Barber. That was it. They wanted their hit man out of the way. After all, he was the only witness to their murder-for-hire conspiracies. If he'd gotten killed in this gun battle, there'd be no way he'd ever implicate them in their wives' murders.

"Your scheme didn't work, you fucking bastards."

But he wasn't home free yet. Every cop in the city was probably on their way here right now. The heat of fear burned in his chest, hot as any lead bullet that Kaufman could've slugged him with.

He rushed to the front door and peered out through a chink

in the blinds. Traffic slogged by and pedestrians walked along, all oblivious to the carnage in the jewelry store. Then he noticed the deadbolt. Unlocked. He pushed on the door handle. The door creaked open. Anyone could have walked in.

"Goddamnit!" He locked the door and ran into the backroom. There he saw the open safe and a pile of money on the desk. His heart started racing.

It was his job to kill Kaufman, get the money, and give it back to Barber. But Barber had double-crossed him, tried to get him killed. For that he would pay, big time.

Delgado looked at the pile of money, more money than he'd ever seen in his life. *Fuck Barber. Fuck Zimmerman.* "Fuck them all," he sang as he gathered up the loot. He'd take the money and run—to Mexico, Puerto Rico, or anyplace that ended in 'o'. He could hide out there until things cooled off. In the meantime, Zimmerman would send Barber to the bottom of Pueblo Reservoir wearing a new pair of concrete boots.

Piece of cake.

***

Thirty minutes passed, then forty. Vince paced the tarmac alongside the chartered Learjet. Idling engines whined. He could taste jet fumes in the air. Under the hot glare of California sunshine, his eyes probed the busy Orange County Airport for any sign of Delgado.

He was late. He was supposed to bring Zimmerman's money. It was on the desk. Vince had prevented Kaufman from locking the money in the safe. He'd executed his part of the plan perfectly. The hit man must've fucked up.

The pilot appeared at the cabin door, checked his watch. "We have to go, sir."

"We go when I say, captain."

Looking across the tarmac, the pilot said, "It doesn't work that way, sir. I have a flight plan to follow. Air Traffic Control has given us a slot to Colorado Springs. If I miss it, I'll have to file another flight plan. Besides, we're burning fuel for no good reason. Don't get me in trouble with my boss. Okay?"

"Damn!"

Vince wished he could order Delgado to appear. Hashing

over the last few moments at Kaufman Jewelers didn't make him any more optimistic.

Guns were blazing.

Delgado may have been killed. That realization felt like a knife in the back.

Worse, he might have been wounded. Right now, the cops could have him downtown. He could be singing like the proverbial canary. A posse might be on their way to the airport, to stop the jet from leaving, to arrest the co-conspirators.

The knife blade twisted and plunged deeper, as if the devil himself had a grip on the handle.

Whatever the case may be, by now, the jewelry store was probably swarming with police. It wouldn't do him any good to go back there. If Delgado had made it out, he'd have been here by now. Zimmerman's money was gone. Jesus! How was he going to explain that to the Godfather?

"All right, captain." Vince stepped aboard, as a man would climb the gallows. "Let's get the hell out of here."

Chapter Fifty-Seven

Colorado Springs

Joe Giodano felt on top of the world. He stood in the maternity ward of Penrose Health Center, holding a brand new baby girl in his arms. "Carolina Giodano," he whispered to her. "For you there will be great things in your life."

"She's beautiful." Val's hair hung in tangles, but her eyes beamed as she lay back in the upraised bed. "I told you so."

"Yes. She'll grow to be as beautiful as her mother."

After years of sneaking around to see each other, and with Ellen out of the way, he and Val were finally able to get married.

Poor Ellen. She'd wanted it all, a divorce, the kids, and his money, but she ended up just another murder victim in the cold case files of the Colorado Springs police department.

"Dad?" His son John stood in the doorway, Ellen's son. "The nurse said we could come in."

"Of course, come on." His kids had been waiting in the outer room. "Where are your sisters?"

"We're here." Beth and Suzie skipped in and gathered around him on tiptoes to see the new baby.

"Now don't scare her," Val said.

John sat in a chair by his stepmom. "How are you feeling?" He was quite the gentleman. Since Ellen died, the kids needed a mother in their lives and Val had given up serving drunks and stepped in with open arms.

Carolina was a bonus.

"Mr. Giodano," a nurse said from the doorway. "There's a man in the lobby to see you. Says he's the child's godfather."

Val shot Joe a narrow-eyed glare. "We haven't decided on godparents yet. Did you go behind my back?"

The Pearl of Death

"It's some kind of mistake," he said, not wanting to upset her. "I don't know what he's talking about...godfather." Hoping it wasn't the real Godfather, Ralph Zimmerman, Joe placed Carolina in his wife's waiting arms. "I'll be right back."

His daughters cuddled around her. "Do we get to see her eat?"

"Not now, girls."

John popped out of his chair. "Can I go with you, Dad?"

In case it was Zimmerman downstairs, Joe didn't want his son in danger. "Watch over the family 'til I get back."

"I'm only eleven."

"So don't drive them anywhere."

Val winked. "Hurry, dear."

Downstairs in the lobby, Joe stepped off the elevator and flinched when he saw Vince Barber charging toward him.

"Joe." Barber's armpits were circles of perspiration. "We gotta talk."

"Not now, Vince, for Christ's sake, we've just had a new daughter."

"Congratulations." He spat out the word sarcastically.

"I'm not in the mood for your bullshit. You're not her godfather."

"So I lied. Get over it." Barber grabbed Joe's arm and nearly dragged him down the hall. "This is important."

From the tone of his panic-stricken voice, Joe knew this wouldn't be an invitation to a weekend barbeque.

Barber pushed open a side door. He was acting skittish, looking all around. Joe followed him out to the garden where people lounged around soaking up sunshine. "Too crowded," Barber grumped and moved to a dumpster behind the kitchen.

The stench of rotting garbage turned Joe's stomach upside-down. "What the hell is going on, Vince?"

Barber kept his voice low. "I'm in trouble."

"Your wife got the credit card again?"

"This is serious."

Flies buzzed all around.

"I lost his money, damn it!" Barber put a hand on his forehead, looked like he would faint.

"Whose money?" Joe pressed.

"Zimmerman's. He made me a loan at twenty percent. I figured I'd have it back to him within a week."

"How much money?"

"Two hundred K..."

Joe whistled. "Are you nuts?"

"That goddamned Delgado, it's his fault."

"You lost two hundred thousand dollars...of the Godfather's money?"

Barber bit a knuckle. His eyes bugged out as if the heat and stress were going to make his face explode.

But his problem was way above Joe's pay-grade. He didn't want anything to do with the Don. One screw up, somebody died. "Don't expect me to bail you out."

"I've got the pearl." His eyes shifted back and forth as if he feared someone would hear him. "A hundred percent of it."

"Really?" *The World's Largest Pearl Company was suddenly a one-man show?* "What happened to Kaufman? I thought he was in for half."

"He got half of nothin'," Barber snarled. "The bastard tried to cheat me."

Joe held up his hands. "I don't want to know what happened." He turned from the stink of garbage and his so-called friend. "I've got a new baby." He started walking away. "And a family, money in the bank. Don't try to drag me into your mess."

"Zimmerman is going to kill me, Joe."

Joe kept walking. It wouldn't be the first time the Don took out someone for a bad debt. And if Barber was on Zimmerman's hit list, it wouldn't be wise for anyone to associate with him.

Fly with crows—expect to get shot at.

Barber ran after him, grabbed his arm, spun him around. "It's Delgado. He took the money. I put out the word to our West Coast boys. Nobody's seen him. It's Phillips who got me into this jam, recommending that amateur to Zimmerman."

Joe scoffed. "Last I heard Zimmerman wouldn't have anything to do with that pearl. He blames it for the loss of his hand. How did he get involved with you?"

"He made me a loan and wants his money back."

"I'm not lending you the money."

"Not a loan. I'll sell you half of the pearl. Fifty percent of the company for two hundred grand."

"You made your bed." Joe yanked his arm free of Barber's grasp. "Now sleep in it." He walked away, eager to get back to his precious Carolina.

"The pearl's been appraised for three point five million dollars," Barber shouted behind Joe. "You can have half. That's over one and a half million dollars profit in your pocket, right out the gate."

Joe stopped cold. *Profit?*

"You get in on the deal, just like you wanted, and I get Zimmerman off my back. Win-win, Joe. Don't let him kill me over this."

Without turning around, Joe thought the numbers through. He still had two hundred thousand dollars from Ellen's life insurance. It could easily be invested in the pearl. What a wonderful birthday gift for Carolina, the largest pearl in the world.

"What do you say?" Barber choked out.

Joe faced him. The one-time champion boxer was now stooped and sweating. He looked broken. Was this the price he'd paid for the pearl? His dignity? "I'll get the money."

"Thanks, man. You just saved my life."

"My new daughter is waiting for me." He turned his back on him. "Don't call me. I'll call you."

"Sure, sure, whatever you say, Joe."

As he rushed into the hospital, he savored the moment. He'd just purchased half of *The World's Largest Pearl Company*. Instead of being left out of the deal, he was now a major investor. And to top it off, Barber was on his knees.

What could go wrong with that?

Chapter Fifty-Eight

Laguna Beach, California:

Sitting in the back seat of a taxi, Timoteo Matito inhaled cool ocean air that rushed in through the open window. Laguna Beach came into view. It was a quaint town of white cottages framed by manicured lawns. Tropical gardens bloomed with clusters of brilliant flowers. Palm-tree-lined streets gave the city an air of wealth and leisure, a lifestyle he hadn't found for himself in America.

The taxi rambled down South Coast Highway. He held his crutches in his lap and imagined the life Wilbur Cobb had lived here, so near to San Francisco yet so far away he might as well have been on Jupiter. But finally, after three decades of searching all over the country, Timoteo felt closer to the pearl than ever before.

He'd read the obituary. Wilbur Cobb was dead. Immediately, Timoteo caught a plane to Orange County Airport. It was a ten-mile drive to the house. "How much farther?" he asked the driver.

"We are almost there, señor."

"Don't take the scenic route." Timoteo knew how to jack up a cab fare. He'd driven one for years. It was a hard way to make a living but the only job he could manage with his crippled feet.

He dug an aspirin bottle from his pocket, shook out four tablets, and swallowed them without water.

The US government had promised to take care of him after the war, but they'd reneged. Now his feet were beyond repair. The cartilage was totally destroyed. Bone grated against bone. There was no elasticity left in the scar tissue. His toes were curled under. He'd gone from using a cane to these crutches, and eventually he'd end up in a wheelchair.

Thanks for nothing, Uncle Sam.

On his right, a morning mist swirled up the bluffs, nearly obscuring the sandy beach. He remembered the white sands of Palawan when he could run in the surf and swim in the bay. The decades had numbed the pain of losing his mother and Tito, but the promise he'd made to his little brother remained a large part of his life. Find the pearl.

But every attempt to locate Wilbur Cobb had met with failure, until now.

The cab turned left on Seaview, and after traveling a few blocks, it negotiated steep streets and switchbacks up the estate-dotted hillside until it came to a development of ranch homes near the top. From up here he saw a billowy fog bank lying on the ocean like a soft white blanket under the bright sun. Wilbur had a spectacular view of the ocean that separated him from his past.

The cab stopped in front of an ugly lime-green house, the paint flaking from the window trim and the eves.

"This is the place, señor."

Looking at the home of Wilbur Cobb, Timoteo's heart slammed against his ribs like the violent banging of a windblown shutter. The lawn was overgrown and brown, the garden flowers wilted, and the window shades drawn. Among all the beauty of Laguna Beach, this place was a scar on the land.

"Maybe I should wait," the driver said. "It looks like no one is living here."

That wasn't possible. Timoteo removed a copy of the report from the National Obituary Registry and read: *Wilbur Cobb is survived by his wife Elaine and two daughters, Diane and Jean.* He'd subscribed to the service, in case Wilbur died before Timoteo could find him, and he received announcements every month. "This is the address listed. It couldn't be wrong." He got out of the cab and mounted his crutches. "But wait for me...just in case."

Hobbling up the sidewalk to the porch, his hands felt sweaty, knees wobbly. Leaping grasshoppers crisscrossed his path, their wings batting with the same fury as his heart.

At the door, he inhaled a calming breath then rang the bell.

Seconds passed. Leaning on the crutches, he tried again, heard the bell chime inside. Still no one answered.

He knocked on the screen door. "Mrs. Cobb, please answer the door."

Nothing. He looked around the neglected grounds and thought the cab driver might be right. No one lived here anymore. But then again, there wouldn't be a paper on the porch or mail in the slot. He banged on the door again. "Mrs. Cobb," he shouted. "I've come a long way to see you."

A neighbor's dog started barking.

"I know about Wilbur," he shouted. "I'm sorry that he died before I could find him."

No response.

"I knew him in the Philippines."

Nothing.

"My name is Timoteo. Has he spoken of me?"

Silence.

He felt foolish. She'd probably moved out. Another dead end.

He turned to leave, heard a click, and looked back. The door creaked open just a crack. A broken and feeble voice said, "W-what do you want?"

"Mrs. Cobb?" He couldn't see her in the shadowy gap. "Please, Mrs. Cobb. I need to talk to you."

The door opened wider, revealing a haggard old woman wearing a torn robe, her gray-streaked hair in tangles and eyes so bloodshot he thought she would bleed to death. "Your mother's name," the voice rasped. "Was it...was it...Liawayway?"

The old woman's tone, the way she said his mother's name, it sounded ripe with contempt. Never before had he heard such spite, not even from those who hated Filipinos.

He swallowed. "Did Wilbur tell you about her?"

"As if I haven't suffered enough," she cried out. "Now his Palawan princess has come back to haunt me."

"I didn't mean to upset you, ma'am."

"My girls are dead, damn it. Hit by a train, their bodies torn and crushed. How much more am I supposed to suffer?"

"The pearl, Mrs. Cobb, I'm looking for the pearl."

"The curse," she shouted. "I didn't listen to Wilbur, I didn't believe him, and my girls...oh God... That pearl killed my girls...my poor sweet girls."

Timoteo feared her cries would be heard for miles around. "I need to find the pearl," he told her, trying to keep the conversation on track. "Do you have it?"

Her eyes bore into him through the screen door. "It's my fault. I didn't listen to Wilbur. He was right. I killed my girls," she screamed. "It's all my fault. It's all my fault."

Neighbors appeared on their front porches, some dressed for work, others in robes and slippers, all gawking, their expressions stern.

"The pearl, please, may I have it?"

"You're too late," the old woman shrieked. "I sold it. The pearl is gone."

It felt like a blow to his chest. His breath left him in a swirl of disappointment. He leaned on his crutches to keep his balance. He'd come so close to the pearl, and yet again it had slipped away. "Who did you sell it to?"

"I shouldn't have sold it." She screamed the words.

"Who has it now, Mrs. Cobb?"

"I burned the money, yah hear. Blood money. My daughters' blood...all of it. Two hundred thousand dollars...gone to the devil himself." She cackled. "How do ya like that?"

A neighbor shouted, "What's going on over there?"

Another yelled, "I'm callin' the cops."

That was all he needed, to be hauled off in handcuffs. A Filipino found in a rich, white neighborhood, bringing trouble. He'd be locked up for a long time. "Please, Mrs. Cobb, who did you sell it to?"

"He'll pay next," she hissed. "The pearl's going to get him, too. It's going to kill his family and tear out his heart."

"Whose heart? Please, ma'am. I have to know."

"Kaufman. Some slick jeweler in Beverly Hills. He's mixed up with the mob, but they're no match for the Pearl of Lao-Tzu. It'll kill 'em all."

Sirens wailed from somewhere down the hill.

Timoteo remembered the name Kaufman. Wilbur had talked about him before the war. A wisp of hope rose inside him.

The sirens were getting closer.

"I have to go, Mrs. Cobb. Thank you."

"And don't come back." She slammed the door.

Timoteo hobbled to the cab, pain burning his legs like hot pokers. He had to find that pearl before more people suffered and died. As he pitched his crutches on the seat and got in, he told the driver, "Beverly Hills."

Again, he dug out the aspirin bottle.

***

An hour later, the cab pulled up to the curb in front of Kaufman Jewelers. Timoteo sat up, rubbed his eyes, wondered what he was seeing. Yellow crime scene tape cordoned off the jewelry store. Sheets of plywood covered the windows. Someone had stapled a paper to the wood. From the car, he couldn't read it, but it looked official.

Was it news of the storeowner's whereabouts?

"Are you sure this is the place, senor?" the cabbie asked.

Timoteo felt the cold stab of dread, same as the time his father failed to surface with the other divers on the reef.

He got out of the cab, and hobbling on his crutches, approached the boarded storefront. He hoped to find information on the note, perhaps a forwarding address or a new phone number for customers. But instead, it was a notice from the police department about prosecuting anyone who entered this crime scene.

His mouth turned dry as Palawan sand. He contemplated breaking in, found a crack in a seam between two boards and pressed an eye to the gap. He couldn't see anything inside but darkness.

Where was Kaufman? Where was the pearl?

"Get away from there," an angry voice shouted.

He jumped back, nearly dropped his crutches. A fat woman wearing a checkered dress and white apron stood in front of the bakery next door, a squeegee in one hand, a sponge in the other, and a bucket of water at her feet. She had an extremely gruff voice for a woman.

"You deaf? Go away."

"I'm just looking—"

The Pearl of Death

"That's what they all say." She dipped her sponge into the bucket and started scrubbing the storefront window. "You all wanna see the blood, that's all."

"No, ma'am." Timoteo hobbled toward her on his crutches, wondering what she meant about blood. "I'm looking for the owner."

Like a bull, she bent over, slopped water from the bucket, and charged the glass with a fresh soapy load. "You wanna know about the robbery. How did they pull it off in broad daylight? How many were shot?"

"I didn't know about a robbery." He stood as close to her as he dared, not wanting to get splashed. Behind the soap-bubble-drenched glass, he saw a tall chocolate cake, a rack of donuts. The aroma of fresh-baked bread wafted from the open front door, lighting his appetite. He hadn't eaten all day. "Is the owner dead?"

"You knew him, did yah?"

"A friend of mine knew him."

"Paul Kaufman didn't socialize with no foreigners." She raked the squeegee across the glass, which made a squeal that raised the hairs on the back of Timoteo's neck. "You are a foreigner, right?"

"The Philippines," he said but left out the part about becoming an American citizen over thirty years ago. He didn't see any sense in telling her about his three children and five grandchildren either. But he couldn't refrain from telling her about his wife. "I married a Filipino. We met after the war...at the VA hospital."

"That's when I met my husband. We're from the old country, Hungary." She slapped more water on the window. "We were very poor. Only rich folks went into Kaufman's over there."

"Where can I find him?"

She stopped washing the window. "They hauled him off in an ambulance, last I knew." She spit as she talked. "I think he was dead, though. The police took all his stuff, as evidence, they said. Now go away. Can't you see I've got work to do?"

Timoteo moved backward, let her work, and mulled over what she'd told him. Kaufman bought the pearl and got robbed and shot. Maybe killed. Was this curse ever going to end?

He made his laborious way back to the cab, step by aching step. Another dead end. If the pearl was stolen in the robbery, it could be anywhere in the world by now. More likely, Kaufman sold it to someone, and that's why he was shot.

There was no way to know, unless he could find Kaufman, alive, which seemed unlikely. He probably wouldn't know where the pearl could be found anyway.

Timoteo would have to go back to San Francisco and wait for the pearl to show up again, somewhere when death would bring it out of hiding.

Chapter Fifty-Nine

San Francisco, January 13, 2005

"Juni, I found it." Timoteo rolled his wheelchair closer to the computer monitor and nudged his reading glasses up the bridge of his nose. It had been twenty-five years since he'd gone to Kaufman's jewelry store, twenty-five years since the pearl had reared its ugly turbaned head...this time in Colorado Springs. Two dead housewives, a convicted killer named Roberto Delgado, and the largest wrongful death suit in Colorado history, it all played out like a horror novel.

"Juni, look." His heart beat so hard he thought he was having that heart attack the doctors had been warning him about. "It's all here on the internet." His crippled feet throbbed. "Look. The pearl."

His wife appeared in the doorway to his den, which was strewn with books, magazines, and newspapers from around the country, piled high along the walls, in boxes and in bags and lying loose all about. Call it research. Call it hoarding. Call it a quest for the pearl. She called it a mess. "What is it now, another false alarm? Another wild goose chase?"

"It's an article from the Rocky Mountain News in Denver."

She looked at the computer screen, read the headline aloud: *"Pearl of Allah part of $32 million award.* Wow!"

"Vince Barber and Carolina Giodano co-own the pearl. Barber purchased it from Paul Kaufman. Remember, I told you about the boarded up store and the robbery. Says here they sold shares in the pearl...look at this... It's worth sixty million dollars... ah... rich people paid for the bragging rights that came with owning a piece of the world's largest pearl."

She huffed. "That wouldn't be us. We can't afford fake

pearls."

"They never had any intentions of selling the pearl. No wonder it's been quiet all these years."

Juni punched his shoulder. "Come on, Timoteo, you know how dumb that sounds?"

"Dumb maybe, but true." He went back to reading the online news from Colorado. "Some Federal Judge... ah... Finesilver... back in 1994... settled claims from duped investors, the most difficult case of his career, then he gave some guy named Vince Barber two thirds of the pearl, and the other third went to a bar owner by the name of Joe Giodano."

Reading all this was like Timoteo had just found a long lost part of his life, its whereabouts and activities now being slowly revealed to him, like the pearl had existed all this time in a parallel universe.

"Now twenty-five-year-old Carolina, Joe's daughter, has inherited her father's share of the pearl. He died in 1998. That's when the trouble started."

"The lawsuit?"

"Not yet. Says that Giodano had his first wife killed... let's see... another man, Phillips, introduced him to a hit-man, Delgado, he's the one who killed both their wives. The deal was, that when Giodano died, he was supposed to leave Phillips his share of the pearl, but he didn't. He willed it to his daughter instead. Carolina wouldn't give it to Phillips, so he got even, turned state's evidence, and fingered Delgado for the killings. He's serving life in prison."

"So everybody's dead or in prison. Who sued who for thirty-two million dollars?"

"Get this. Giodano's children from his first wife, Ellen, the one he had murdered, they sued his estate for the wrongful death of their mother. They're the ones who got the money... No. That's not true. It's a judgment. Says here... that in order to pay the judgment, Carolina and Vince must sell the pearl."

Timoteo's old insides quivered. He looked up at his wife. "Juni. If they sell the pearl, somebody is going to die."

"You don't know that."

"I've got to stop them."

"How?"

~360~

"Go to Colorado."

"You can't travel. You are too old."

"I can make it."

"When will you learn? You are crippled."

She didn't have to remind him. He and other Filipino veterans had banded together and lobbied Congress to reverse the Rescission Act of 1946. From time to time, a few legislators backed their cause, but every bill they introduced died in committee. Hunger strikes and demonstrations in front of the White House failed to persuade the government to admit the mistake and reinstate their veterans benefits.

Now, like Timoteo, the remaining veterans were dying off. It seemed the government was intent on holding out until every last Filipino veteran was dead, silencing their pleas for help, once and for all.

But Timoteo wasn't dead yet.

He wanted to leap from his wheelchair and run to the bedroom, pack a suitcase and head to the airport. But first he had to talk to Carolina Giodano.

Mouse in hand, he set to searching Google.

"What now?" Juni asked.

"I've got to find Carolina's phone number, or Vince Barber, either one."

"I'm going back to the kitchen."

"Bring me some iced tea."

She left the room.

White pages.com ... Colorado Springs...

"Got it," he muttered. "Carolina Giodano." He dialed the number.

"Hello?" Her voice sounded soft and innocent.

"Carolina?"

"Yes."

"You don't know me. My name is Timoteo Matito. I'm from the Philippines."

"Why are you calling me?"

"I can't find a number for Vince Barber—"

She let out an audible sigh. "Is this about the pearl?"

"Yes."

"If you want to buy it, it's for sale, you know."

"I'm calling to warn you about the curse."

"Oh brother. Not another prankster. I have to go now."

"Wait. It's a matter of—"

Click.

"Life and death," he finished, the air leaking out of his lungs. She didn't believe him. But she had to be convinced. He called her back. "Please listen to me."

"Do you want to make an offer for the pearl?"

"My father is the diver who found it. He drowned. I was only eight years old."

"Sixty million dollars, it's all yours."

"I don't want to buy the pearl. I want you to throw it back into the sea."

The silence that followed unnerved him. What could he say to make her understand? "It's cursed. If you sell it you'll die, or someone you love will die. I'm telling you the truth."

"And I'm telling you not to call back."

"Wait. Don't hang up. I'm not a prankster. Please listen. I'm willing to fly in from San Francisco to Colorado Springs to talk to you and Vince Barber."

"It's a long way to go to talk for nothing. We're not throwing it back in the sea."

"A lot of people are dead because of that pearl. I don't want that to happen to you. Hear my story before you decide."

"Okay. Why not? It's your time wasted."

"I'll call you with my itinerary."

She hung up.

Timoteo would've stood and done a jig if he could have.

Juni came in with the glass of tea. "You talked to her?"

"I'll pack while you book us a flight to Colorado Springs."

She set the tea on his desk. "I'm due at the hospital. I have patients to care for. You can't be serious."

Dr. Juni Matito had grown old with him. By now she should know he was always serious when it came to the pearl.

"Fine. I'll go by myself." He maneuvered the wheelchair around her and headed down the hardwood-floor hall. "Are you going to help me pack or not?"

"What about your tea?"

***

The Pearl of Death

Timoteo and his wheelchair were first off the plane at the Colorado Springs airport. The terminal windows rattled as a jet took off. While waiting for a porter to escort him, he sat in his wheelchair and swiped dust from his brown slacks, made sure his white tennis shoes were properly tied, and straightened the collar of his white polo shirt. He wanted to look his best for the upcoming meeting.

The porter arrived, a young black man who stood tall as a basketball player. "Are you here on business, Mr. Matito?" He pushed the wheelchair down the concourse.

"Yes, the business of fulfilling a promise." His heart panged as he anticipated finding the pearl. The problem was convincing Carolina and Vince to throw it back into the sea.

"There's someone waiting for you at baggage claim," the porter said.

That would be Carolina or Vince Barber.

"She's very pretty," he added.

He hoped Carolina was smart too, at least smart enough to see the danger she'd be in if she sold the pearl.

Baggage claim came into view. A shapely woman approached, white sweater over a yellow dress, white sandals, black hair short and curly, her brow furrowed. "Timoteo?"

"Hello, Carolina?"

"I fear you have wasted your time by coming here."

He shook her hand. "I've spent my whole life looking for that pearl."

"What a shame. I'd think you would have had better things to do with your life." She tipped the porter. "I'll take him from here."

"Good luck with your business," the porter said and walked away.

"Nice young man." Timoteo wanted to lighten up the conversation.

As she wheeled him to the luggage carousel, she asked, "What happened to your legs?"

"My feet...they were injured in the war."

"Which war? There have been so many."

He inhaled her flowery perfume. Though he couldn't place the brand, he was sure it had been in his taxi quite often. "World

War II."

"For a country that proclaims peace, we sure do a lot of fighting."

"I fought with the Americans on Bataan."

"You're not an American?"

"Yes. For sixty years." The jury was still out on whether he was proud of it or not. Sometimes it seemed like naturalization was his greatest accomplishment, sometimes his biggest embarrassment. When would the Americans learn that justice, equality, and opportunity were meant for everyone?

Including Filipinos.

He retrieved his travel bag from the carousel. As Carolina pushed his wheelchair toward the exit, he asked her, "Did you contact Vince Barber?"

"He's suspicious of you."

"I only want to talk to him, not rob him."

"Nevertheless, we'll meet him in the park where there's open space and other people around."

"Fair enough." Timoteo thought the cloak and dagger theatrics were unnecessary.

Outside, a September breeze swirled dust about. He looked up at a clear blue sky, inhaled the thin Colorado air, felt so starved for oxygen he thought he was drowning. A Mercedes pulled up, driven by an older woman.

"It's my mother," Carolina said. "Her name is Val."

"Hello, Val." He scooted from the wheelchair to the car seat by using the open back door for support. The interior smelled new, the leather smooth and soft.

Carolina put his bag in the trunk.

"Do you need some help with that?" Val indicated the wheelchair.

"I can handle it." He released the brace locks, folded the lightweight wheelchair, and pulled it into the car after him.

Carolina closed the door and got in the front passenger seat. "He's from the Philippines, Mom. He was wounded in the war."

Technically, that wasn't true; he wasn't wounded, he was injured; but he chose not to elaborate. They didn't need to know about that horrible time in his life. "Now I live in San

Francisco."

"You should like Colorado," she replied via the rearview mirror then accelerated the car away from the terminal. "Will you be staying long?"

"I don't know." He gazed out the window at a magnificent mountain rising to the sky.

"Pikes Peak," Carolina said as if she'd seen him admiring it. "You can go to the top if you like."

Mount Bataan was the last mountain he'd hiked. He had no desire to go up another one, as if he could, considering his physical condition.

The car glided off down Platte Avenue, headed west. Traffic was light.

"Where are you staying?" Carolina asked. "Which hotel?"

"The Broadmoor."

"Nice."

"Hotels.com. I got a deal."

Val turned the Mercedes off Platte Avenue and stopped in a parking lot. The sign etched in stone read *Acacia Park*. Timoteo looked around, saw children in the playground, heard their squeals of joy. The engine shut off. Carolina's door popped open.

Val said, "Barber should be here by now. I'll leave you two alone to speak with him."

"I'll call you on your cell, Mom." She opened the rear door for Timoteo. "When we're ready to go."

Timoteo pushed the wheelchair out and spread it apart until the locks snapped in place. Trying to remain dignified, he pulled himself out of the car, and pivoting on his wretched feet, plopped down into the nylon seat.

Standing behind him, Carolina waited until the Mercedes sped off before she wheeled him into the park. "So, Mr. Matito, tell me your story."

Timoteo looked at the age-spotted hands in his lap, dappled with sunlight through the trees. These hands had killed the Japanese, made love to Juni, and burped his children. His life was a long story of suffering and loss and struggle with highs and lows like everyone else's. He wasn't here to talk about himself. He was here to warn her about the pearl of death.

Terry Wright

"You can't sell the pearl," he said. "It's cursed."

"There's no such thing. It's just a pearl."

"It killed my father." Timoteo recalled that day on the reef as if it were only yesterday, the fear, the shock, the pain of losing Etem.

"I know how you must feel. I sometimes wonder...did the pearl make my father murder Ellen?" She pushed the wheelchair a little faster. "No. His greed, his selfishness, his spite for Ellen, that's what made him a murderer."

"It must've been a shock...when you found out."

"He'd paid Delgado to kill her. How do you think that made me feel? My God, I cried for months. And the money... he'd used her life insurance to buy the pearl... a gift for me... he bought it for m-me," her voice hitched, "with blood money. I'll never forgive him for that."

"I'm sorry."

"And his poor kids. He'd left the pearl to me, everything else to Val, and nothing to them. I don't blame them for suing his estate for wrongful death. They'd lost their mother."

"I lost my mother. I know how much that hurts."

"See. Was it the pearl's fault?"

"Japanese soldiers took her away."

"So there you have it."

"But everywhere the pearl goes, people suffer, people die."

"People always suffer and die." She sighed. "That's life."

Timoteo had to get through to her, somehow, that this was different.

A couple steps later, she said, "Truth is, I wish I'd never seen that damn pearl. It reminds me of my father...and that's not a good thing, believe me."

"Then let's get rid of it. Together. Let's throw it back into the sea." He imagined taking a boat ride out of San Francisco Bay, maybe ten miles and tossing it overboard.

"It's okay with me," she said then huffed. "But you're forgetting one thing."

"What?"

"Vince Barber. He's the majority partner."

"Then I'll have to convince him."

"Good luck with that."

The Pearl of Death

They arrived at a picnic area bordered by a black wrought iron fence. Trees grew from square cement planters and provided shade for metal tables and stools. At one of the tables sat an old man, gray bushy hair with matching sideburns. A plastic hose ran from his nose to an oxygen bottle on a wheeled cart at his feet. He stood as they approached.

"It's him," she whispered.

Vince Barber looked overdressed in a black suit and tie. A brown satchel rested on the table beside him.

"Over here," he said, waving.

While pushing the wheelchair across freshly cut grass, she said, "He didn't want to meet you, Timoteo. I told him about your father, how he'd died finding the pearl. That changed his mind."

"I thank you for arranging this meeting."

"He's in very bad health."

Timoteo knew all about bad health. It was a miracle he'd lived to see seventy nine.

"Vince had to fly in from Florida. After the lawsuit, he moved there. This thin Colorado air made it hard for him to breathe."

Timoteo found it hard to breathe up here, as well. His heart raced, each beat a sharp pain. He couldn't take his eyes off the satchel, wondered what it contained.

"Mr. Matito." Vince offered a handshake. "I hear you and our pearl go back a long way. You're Etem's boy, huh?"

"Yes, my father. He drowned for your pearl."

Vince sat on the metal stool facing the wheelchair. "That's rather old news, don't you think? I mean...there's no basis for any legal claim to the pearl."

"I'm not here to claim it," Timoteo said. "I'm here to make good on a promise...to my brother...and to save your life."

That made Vince's eyebrows arch. "Tell me now. How are you going to save my life, sir?"

"By giving you some advice."

"I'm listening."

Timoteo thought Vince was just being polite, respectful of an old Filipino man's age and the fact they'd both traveled from both ends of the country to meet each other. This would be a hard sell, but he delivered the pitch, "You need to throw the pearl back in the sea."

Vince scowled. "You can't be serious...throw away sixty million dollars? What are you thinking?"

Carolina sat on the stool next to him. "He says it's cursed."

"We're well aware of the legend, Mr. Matito. Fortunately, we're not superstitious. Not like Wilbur Cobb was."

"He loved my mother back then." Timoteo remembered the pool on Palawan where Wilbur had said he couldn't replace Etem. "When the war broke out, he left and never came back. I don't know what happened to him, but the pearl had something to do with it."

"The war had something to do with it," Carolina put in. "Millions of people were lost, all over the world."

"The pearl destroyed Wilbur's wife."

"Elaine Cobb," Vince said. "She always wanted the money...God rest her soul...but she got what she deserved."

"Her daughters were killed because she sold the pearl to Kaufman."

"Not at all." Vince coughed. "Those girls died because their vehicle broke down on the railroad tracks. It should have been better maintained."

Timoteo leaned forward in his wheelchair. "Then explain why Kaufman was murdered right after he bought the pearl."

"Kaufman's not dead. He tried to pull a fast one. Back in those days, you got shot for double-crossing your friends. The pearl didn't shoot him. Delgado did."

Indicating Carolina, Timoteo asked, "What about *her* father?"

"Joe Giodano didn't own the pearl until five years after his wife's murder. He had her killed to protect his assets, the bar, his bank account. It happens all the time."

Carolina said, "My dad was a murderer long before the pearl came to Colorado."

Barber glared at her. "Your father saved my life when he bought those shares."

"He bought into your scheme with blood money." She spat the words. "Insurance money. He didn't earn a nickel of it."

"I don't care where the money came from. Zimmerman

would have killed me—"

"Listen to you two arguing. Don't you see? The common denominator is the pearl. Get rid of it...before it can do you any more harm."

Vince turned to the table. "It's just a pearl." He opened the satchel and pulled out a velvet cloth, tattered with age.

Timoteo's brain got dizzy. He remembered seeing that cloth at Boligay Creek when the chief gave Wilbur Cobb the pearl. It was wrapped in velvet then, as now.

He suddenly felt afraid.

Vince set the pearl in Timoteo's lap, uncovered it. "This is the pearl you believe to be cursed. Look at it."

His mind slipped through a time warp, took him back to the fiesta. The sound of brass gongs and the aroma of cook fires and roasted pigs filled the air. He saw Tito, Mamma, Bogtong, Pula, and the Panglima. Everyone was happy—everyone except him. He was sad, so sad, even five years after his father's death. And angry. Why couldn't he accept his father's death? Why couldn't he let it go? The trauma of seeing him drown had haunted him all his life. And the fact that he was too small to help him. What could he have done differently to save his father? Nothing. So he blamed the death on the pearl.

With trembling hands he lifted the pearl from his lap, felt the heat of its lumpy surface on his palms, saw the lustrous shine of nacre in the sunlight. His father had seen it, too, just like this, five fathoms down on the reef. He'd reached inside the clam to get it. To take it. To hold it. To sell it.

How could he have been so foolish, so careless to put his life in danger for the wealth this pearl could bring him?

All at once everything became clear.

It wasn't the pearl's fault.

It wasn't the fault of an eight-year-old boy who couldn't swim deep enough to save his father.

It was his father's fault.

Not the reef, not the clam, not the pearl.

All along it had been his father's fault. Some degree of greed had compelled him to gamble his life. And he lost.

Bombs exploded in Timoteo's mind, the roar of battle, and the buzz of Zeros strafing Bataan. The war wasn't the pearl's fault either. It was the Japanese' fault, the American's fault, the German's fault: the inherent drive of mankind to wage war against each other for any reason imaginable. Man created his own hell on earth. He had no one to blame but himself for the horrors he had to endure.

Timoteo could hardly breathe. He knew now that the pearl represented beauty, the magic of nature, and the wonders of Allah. The Panglima had given it freely, as a gift that came from the bottom of his heart filled with gratitude for a man who'd saved his son's life. This was not a curse but a blessing, one Filipino to one American. The pearl became a bond between the two men, a true gift from Allah. And Wilbur Cobb had held on to that gift his entire life, refusing to let go of the memories that came with it. That was why he never sold it. He never got rid of it. He never let it get far from his sight.

Setting the pearl in his lap, he inhaled thin air, felt light-headed, as if floating above the reef.

"Mr. Matito," Carolina said. "Are you all right?"

Allah had just spoken to him. Only now did he understand. Throwing the pearl into the sea would solve nothing. Smashing it with a hammer would not change a thing. The world was as it always had been, a boiling caldron of peoples and ideals constantly clashing for supremacy. And there was no end to the carnage in sight.

"Mr. Matito?" Carolina shook his shoulder.

Tito, I'm sorry. I cannot keep my promise.

He inhaled. "I've lived a good life, but how much better could it have been if I hadn't wasted so much of it chasing a pearl?"

Vince retrieved the precious artifact from Timoteo, wrapped it in old velvet again, and slipped it back into his satchel. "Go home, Timoteo. Don't waste another minute."

He looked up at Carolina's smiling face. "I have a big mess to clean up in my office." All the papers and boxes...a testament to futility, all going in the trash. "There's no saving this world from itself."

Epilogue

For the better part of eight decades since its discovery, the world's largest pearl has been locked up in one bank vault or another, this truly miraculous work of nature hidden from human eyes. Few have known the wonder of being in its presence.

Timoteo lived another seven years, free of his obsession with the pearl of death, but forever plagued by his deformed feet. Few Filipino veterans are still living. Their fight for just and fair treatment by the US government will soon die with them.

Today, the Pearl of Allah is called by its legendary name, the Pearl of Lao-Tzu. It remains stashed in an undisclosed location. All involved have passed into history. As of this writing, there have been no viable offers to purchase the sixty-million dollar relic.

Terry Wright

The Pearl of Death

Dear Reader.

Thank you for reading my historical novel "The Pearl of Death." I was inspired to research and write this story after reading an article in the Rocky Mountain News (now defunct) about the Pearl of Allah being part of a $32 million dollar award in a wrongful death suit in Colorado. Fascinated by the article, I dug deeper and entered a world of history and myth that transfixed me. I became obsessed with developing a plotline that would encompass such a spectacular story. After a while, I discovered a huge problem. There were too many holes in the history, too many holes in the legends. Nothing tied it all together. Rather than give up, I set out to patch the holes with fictional events and characters.

The trick was to mix history, fact, legend, and fiction together in such a way as to make the lines between these elements invisible. As in all works of fiction, everything had to make sense. So for each beat of history and myth, I had to create characters that would bring these events to life and tie them together over a long timeline. I was told by New York agents and editors that this was impossible, the story would never sell, and readers wouldn't stay engaged over such a long span of time. I abandoned the project for several months, convinced it was doomed to failure.

Then I picked it up one day, my drafts, my notes, and was again inspired to tell this story. It took me two years and a million rewrites before I had accomplished the impossible. I released the e-book in 2011. As luck would have it, I was contacted by a relative of a key player in the latter part of the story. He filled me in on some valuable details of which I was unaware, and those details went into a later rewrite.

Oh, I've heard from naysayers who claim the true story is a hoax, but I've seen the pictures and read the accounts. Hopefully you don't care what's fact and fiction, that you enjoyed the adventure of the World's Largest Pearl enough to tell all your friends. An honest review on Amazon would also be helpful.

—Terry Wright

About the Author

There's nothing mundane in the writing world of **Terry Wright**. Tension, conflict and suspense propel his readers through the pages as if they were on fire. Traditionally published in Science Fiction, Supernatural, and Horror, his mastery of the action thriller has also won him International acclaim as an accomplished screenplay writer. A decades-long member of the Rocky Mountain Fiction Writers, he coordinated their annual Colorado Gold Writing Contest for six years, received their highest award for service, The Jasmine Award, and was nominated for the Writer of the Year in 2014.

Terry is a Vietnam Veteran (USAF – Red Horse - SAC), a certified pilot of single engine light aircraft, and an avid Harley Davidson enthusiast. After 36 years in business, he sold his auto repair shop and started publishing authors from around the world through his publishing companies, TWB Press and Amore Moon Publishing. When he's not writing and editing, he enjoys cross-country motorcycling, country dancing, and playing guitar with his friends. He lives in Centennial, Colorado, with his wife, Bobette, and their four dogs.

Enjoy more novels and short stories by Terry Wright

The 13th Power Quest, Book 1
The search for the secret of the universe
Science Fiction novel, technology, action, adventure
https://www.twbpress.com/the13thpowerquest

The 13th Power Journey, Book 2
Mankind's first journey across the galaxy
https://www.twbpress.com/the13thpowerjourney

The 13th Power War, Book 3
And then came man, and war, and death
https://www.twbpress.com/the13thpowerwar

The Duplication Factor
Behold the first human clone
Science Fiction novel, thriller, action, adventure
https://www.twbpress.com/theduplicationfactor

Black Jack
A Denver detective searches for his wife's killer
Crime drama novel, thriller, action, mystery
https://www.twbpress.com/blackjack

Undead in Paris (a screenplay)
Vampire wars: the old ways vs the new ways
https://www.twbpress.com/undeadinparis

Justin Graves
A dead detective makes a deal with the devil
A short story horror series
https://www.twbpress.com/justingraves

Z-motors - The Job from Hell
An unemployed master mechanic finally gets a job
Zombie short story, thriller, satire
https://www.twbpress.com/zmotors

Street Beat
A woman reporter matches wits with a serial killer
Crime drama short story, action-thriller, romance
https://www.twbpress.com/streetbeat

Return Me to Mistwillow
A dusty ghost town gets a visitor from the past
Ghost short story, Colorado history, action, thriller
https://www.twbpress.com/returnmetomistwillow

Wilderness Rampage
A motorhome vacation trip turns deadly
Action adventure short story, bad guys and a bear
https://www.twbpress.com/wildernessrampage

Find these and more at:

https://www.twbpress.com